"Nothing is wrong with vanilla," Cal said.

"Only because you've never tried Firecracker Surprise." Glory took a lick of her ice-cream cone and moaned. It was a sexy moan that had him scooting closer. "It's the perfect combo of sweet and spicy. Here, try it."

Cal prided himself on his ability to follow directions. So he leaned in until their mouths were a breath apart and whispered, "If you insist."

Then he kissed her, tugging at her lower lip with his teeth, then taking a taste of Glory's entire mouth. It was everything she'd promised and more. Sweet, spicy, and so damn surprising it could tempt even the most honorable gentleman. And Cal was tempted all right, but come hell or high water, he was going to be a gentleman tonight. Even if it killed him.

Which it might...

Sugar on Top

A Sugar, Georgia Novel

Marina Adair

FOREVER

NEW YORK   BOSTON

Copyright © 2015 by Marina Chappie
Excerpt from *A Taste of Sugar* copyright © 2015 by Marina Chappie

Forever
Hachette Book Group
1290 Avenue of the Americas
New York, NY 10104

www.HachetteBookGroup.com

Printed in the United States of America

First Edition: April 2015
10 9 8 7 6 5 4 3 2 1

OPM

Forever is an imprint of Grand Central Publishing.
The Forever name and logo are trademarks of Hachette Book Group, Inc.

The Hachette Speakers Bureau provides a wide range of authors for speaking events. To find out more, go to www.hachettespeakersbureau.com or call (866) 376-6591.

The publisher is not responsible for websites (or their content) that are not owned by the publisher.

ATTENTION CORPORATIONS AND ORGANIZATIONS:

Most Hachette Book Group books are available at quantity discounts with bulk purchase for educational, business, or sales promotional use. For information, please call or write:

Special Markets Department, Hachette Book Group
1290 Avenue of the Americas, New York, NY 10104
Telephone: 1-800-222-6747 Fax: 1-800-477-5925

To my daughter, Thuy, who always reads the last page of a story first. You remind me it isn't about the destination, it is about the journey and relationships we make along the way.

Acknowledgments

Thanks to my editor, Michele Bidelspach, and to the rest of the team at Grand Central for all of the amazing work and support. And to my agent, Jill Marsal, for being more than just an agent, but also my friend, partner, and sounding board.

As always, a very special thank you to my daughter for your giggles, snuggles, and including me in your Teen Wolf marathons, even when you drop the spoiler to end all spoilers. Finally, to my amazing husband for the endless love and support—you are my reason.

Sugar on Top

Chapter 1

Every Southern belle knows it's not so much what you do, but rather what you're wearing while doing it. And when in doubt, always apply more lipstick.

Good thing Glory Gloria Mann had never been mistaken for a belle, because there was no shade of lipstick in the South that matched grand theft auto charges while wearing ducky galoshes.

"Either get on or get out of the way," Glory said to the stubborn male standing between her and freedom.

Diablo had mammoth thighs, a trunk for a neck, and as Mr. Ferguson's contracted stud bull, horns that could tear through a steel wall. And right now those horns were pointed at Glory.

But she wasn't about to let some misinformed male with caveman tendencies and bad breath stop her from doing what was right. Even when doing what was right sucked. Even when it accompanied a brutal summer storm, interrupted the only solid sleep she had gotten in weeks, and landed her smack dab in the middle of trouble.

Even then. Because Glory could live with trouble. But regret was something she never wanted to feel again.

"I know you survived that eighteen-wheeler incident," she said, wiping at the rain streaming down her face. "And won the county stud-off, but we both know you are no match for the Peach Prowler." No one was a match for the nine-time Sugar Pull champion tractor—or its owner. Which was why getting it back to the mayor's house was imperative.

Joyriding a tractor in the middle of the night would have been considered a laughable redneck offense if that tractor wasn't the shined-up Peach Prowler—pride and joy of Sugar, Georgia.

"The only thing separating you from becoming a pair of boots is my lead foot," she said, giving Diablo the stink eye. Because the only thing separating her grandma from going to jail was Glory's ability to return the tractor before someone noticed it was missing.

Glory didn't know how the tractor ended up in her grandma's garage, or who put it there. All she did know was that while possession of another man's vehicle was a serious offense in Sugar County—possession of another man's tractor was a deadly sin. And between trying to graduate nursing school, and coming off a double shift, Glory was too damn tired to deal with the aftermath of what would appear to be her grandmother calling backwoods jihad on the mayor's mother.

Not to mention, she couldn't stand the thought of her grandmother behind bars. Jelly Lou might be a prankster, but she was Glory's entire world.

"So unless you're willing to offer up some rocky mountain oysters to the mayor to pay for my grandma's bail, I suggest you move off the road and let me pass." She revved the tractor's engine for emphasis. "You know how much he loves rocky mountain oysters."

That got his attention. In fact, Diablo made one last snort, his hot breath crystalizing in the rain, and then slowly walked off—down the middle of the highway.

Not wanting to follow him, but knowing time was of the essence since the sun would be up soon, Glory pulled her rain slicker tightly around her, dropped the tractor into first, and drove through the easement between Ferguson Family's Feed Line and Fertilizer Farm and the highway.

Even before she hit second gear, spinning the tires with enough force to cover her flannel pajama bottoms with sludge, she knew that it wasn't the easement she'd accidentally trudged through. No, Glory's good intentions had, once again, landed her in deep—

"Shut off the tractor and put your hands in the air." The command came through the speaker attached to the top of the sheriff's car, which was right next to the flashing red and blue lights.

Squinting against the rain, Glory stared in panic at the speed trap up ahead. A floodlight clicked on, blinding her and causing her foot to slip off the clutch. The engine sputtered to a stop.

Determined to see this through, Glory cranked the engine and spun the tires, kicking up loose gravel and a few cow pies. She hadn't come all this way, spending thirty minutes on the muddy back roads in the middle of the night to right someone else's wrong, just to get caught now.

"Come on now, Ms. Hattie. Step on off that tractor so we can all get out of the rain."

Ms. Hattie?

Ms. Hattie was the town busybody and one of Glory's

grandma's oldest and dearest friends. Which explained how the Prowler ended up in her grandma's garage.

The roadblock of wet and irritated officers obviously had no idea who was driving the tractor. If they had, Glory was certain that their boss would have her butt tossed in jail before she could say, "Morning, Sheriff."

Plus she was pretty sure the smug-looking guy in the department-issued hat, weighing in at two hundred pounds of bad attitude, *was* Sheriff Jackson Duncan.

"Look, I promise my grandma won't press charges." *Yup. Sheriff Duncan.* The entitled drawl was a dead giveaway. And if he thought Ms. Kitty wouldn't press charges, he was insane. "Heck, Ms. Hattie, as long as the Prowler is back in the bay before she wakes up, she doesn't even have to know it went missing and we can all go home and back to our respective business."

"Do I have your word on that, Sheriff?" The second Glory opened her mouth, Jackson realized Hattie McGraw wasn't behind the wheel because he went from leaning against the grill of his cruiser to reaching for his gun. She also knew that only ten feet and some plywood separated her from a mug shot—a mug shot that was not going to happen. She had enough mascara under her eyes to pass for a linebacker and enough emotion built up that, after one too many double shifts slinging beer and a lifetime of double standards, getting arrested would fill out her already unflattering résumé.

Jackson silently made his way toward the tractor, boots clacking against the slick concrete, cuffs jangling in his hand. Knowing nothing good could come from that, she rested her hand on the gear shift and asked, "I'm guessing by the pissy look on your face that your generous offer is no longer on the table."

"Sorry to say, but you'd guess right," he said, not sorry at all.

Jackson Duncan had been sheriff of Sugar County for the past four years, and he'd hated Glory for at least twice that amount of time. He was uptight, by the book, and still blamed her for his older brother leaving town. Not that he had ever bothered to listen to her side of the story. No one really had. But everyone knew that he would love nothing more than to parade Glory around town in cuffs and prove that she was a menace to Sugar's properly polite society.

"Even if I told you that I wasn't stealing Ms. Kitty's tractor? That I was trying to return it?"

"Even then. Possession is nine-tenths of the law."

And wasn't that just great, because in this county possession might constitute only nine-tenths, but being the girl who cost Sugar High their beloved football coach *and* the state championships all in the same year surely made up the other one-tenth. Which meant the odds of her getting out of this mess with a friendly warning were a big fat zero.

There was no way she was letting him take her in. Not dressed in flannel and fertilizer. And sure as hell not when she had a Pediatric Health Theory midterm in six hours. It had taken her the better part of a decade, juggling part-time classes and full-time bar tending, to get to where she was, and she wasn't about to let one mistake screw up everything. Not again.

"Sorry then, Sheriff."

Grabbing the edges of her rain slicker, she flipped it up to cover her face and gunned it. The tractor roared as she threw it in second. The gear kicked in, causing the Prowler to pick up in volume and speed—surprising speed for a machine that looked like a giant peach and was built when she'd been in preschool.

"Aw, hell," Jackson said, racing back to the cruiser. "Let 'em go, boys."

The deputies scattered to the side of the road and two metal strips with spikes rolled across the slick asphalt, covering both the north- and the southbound lanes.

Heading straight for the road, she vowed that she would drive right through that speed trap, over the metal spikes and all, if she had to. Her grandma was counting on her, and the entry to the Prowler's parking bay was only a few yards past the sheriff's patrol car. She could slip in, park the vehicle, and hightail it out of there.

Glory dropped the tractor into third and rain pelted her face. She burst through the wood-slatted fence, cow pies and feed kicking up angrily in her wake, and skidded on to the Brett McGraw Highway. Jackson had his spikes, but according to the flyers hanging around town, the Prowler had all-terrain mud tires and a steel-reinforced undercarriage.

She hit fourth gear right as the Prowler's wheels cruised over the first set of shredders—tires unscathed, the shredder looking puny and weak as it kicked out behind them. The image made Glory grin and she sank the gearshift even lower. Only before she reached that second strip, Jackson stepped in front of the tractor.

"Dang it, Jackson," she screamed over the roar of the tractor's engine. "Move your overentitled, stubborn ass out of my way or I'll run it down!"

"And miss busting yours for grand theft auto and assaulting a police officer?" he yelled back, smiling as though he'd just won box seats at the Georgia Dome. "No, ma'am."

Glory looked from side to side, weighing her options. Had she been thinking with her head instead of her heart, she would be warm and snug in her bed, not facing jail time in little more than a pink slicker and ducky galoshes. Instead she was trying to solve a feud that had been brewing since Glory turned seventeen and made the biggest mistake of her life.

Before Glory could react, she crossed the second trap and the back two tires exploded simultaneously. The tractor jerked forward and she didn't know what was thumping louder, her heart or the deflated tires struggling to roll over the blacktop.

The Prowler decelerated and slowly crawled toward Jackson, who stepped out of the way right as the tractor made its final stop—giving the cruiser a big smacker to the front bumper. The Prowler wasn't going that fast but the thing must have been made of steel because a loud crunch broke through the night's air, followed by an awful sizzle and finally steam, which drifted up from under the hood and into the inky sky.

"I guess I can add destruction of city property to the charges," Jackson said with a smile.

"Damnit, Jackson." Glory picked up a stray cow pie, which had landed in the back of the tractor during her off-roading excursion, and threw it on the ground. It shattered, splattering right up his department-issued boots and onto his pant legs. "I'm just trying to return it."

"And I'm just doing my job," he said as he approached the vehicle and hoisted his smug self up. "Now, do you need me to read you your rights? Or would you like to say them with me?"

And right then Glory understood that no matter how hard she tried to atone for her past, she was never going to be free of it.

Glory had never been arrested before, just as she'd never had to spend the night in jail, so she wasn't sure of the exact protocol, but she knew bullshit when she heard it. And Deputy Gunther's excuses were starting to smell worse than her manure-crusted pants.

"I bet if you called over to the Sugar Country Club, they'd tell you Judge Holden is somewhere between the third and fourth hole," Glory said, pinning Deputy Gunther with a glare.

"The sheriff's on it, Miss Glory," the deputy said, shuffling nervously from foot to foot. He was built like a bull, only with puppy-dog eyes, a gentle smile, and a soft center. Glory had always liked him. He was one of the few football players who hadn't made her time at Sugar High miserable.

"So you said. Three hours ago." When he silently lowered his eyes to the floor, she added, "Come on, Gunther, I'm freezing and tired and you and I both know that the sheriff is just trying to mess with me."

His ploy was working. She was about two minutes from tears. The ugly kind.

She'd been arrested, booked, and locked in a concrete square. She hadn't eaten since her second break yesterday, hadn't slept in over forty-eight hours, and her midterm, which she'd busted her butt studying for, had started over an hour ago—meaning the only way she was going to pass that class in time to apply to be the community outreach manager at Sugar Medical Center was to ace her final.

Gunther looked from the empty front office back to her, and the tips of his ears went pink. "I guess I could let you have another call. Just one, though. And you have to use this."

He dug through his pocket, handed her his cell, and Glory felt her heart tighten painfully.

"And call who?" she mumbled softly. Not that it mattered. It was already too late.

Gunther's eyes darted to the floor again.

They both knew that the sheriff wanted to milk the situation, just as they both knew that neither Glory nor her grandma could afford whatever obscene bail he'd convince the judge to set.

Her best friend, Brett, could afford it, and he'd pay it in a heartbeat, which was why in her moment of desperation she decided to call him.

Too bad she remembered *after* she'd left a voice message that he was in California and that she'd promised herself never to put him in a position to choose between his best friends again. She was trying to keep her distance, give Brett and his new wife, Joie, the space they deserved as newlyweds.

Last year Brett had added Sex-Stud YouTube Sensation to his impressive credentials, a title that nearly cost him his career as a professional golfer. The last thing he needed was more people whispering. And anytime Glory so much as smiled at a man, people whispered.

"That's all right, Gunther." Glory tightened her arms around her bent legs and dropped her head to her knees. Her body ached to be back at home, in her own bed, with the covers pulled securely over her head—fast asleep.

"Can I at least get you a blanket? Maybe some hot coffee?"

"That'd be nice."

"All right, then. Sit tight."

An aching sadness tore through her chest and Glory didn't answer—couldn't—afraid of what might come out. She felt her tears coming closer to the surface and the last thing she needed was a public pity party. But she was locked in a cell, facing a possible *F* on a test she was more than ready for. Her only crime being—she was too damn nice.

"I didn't steal the stupid tractor," she whispered to herself.

"I know you didn't, Miss Glory."

She slowly lifted her head, startled to see Gunther still standing there. And damn it if the tears didn't spill.

"Ah, don't cry." Gunther fumbled for his handkerchief. "The sheriff's not a bad guy. He, well, some people don't know how to let go."

Ain't that the truth?

Glory made her way to the cell door, took the offered hankie—a difficult task since Sheriff A-hole had insisted on keeping her cuffed—and wiped her eyes.

"Thanks. It's just been a really shitty night."

With a solemn nod, he made his way toward the end of the corridor—toward freedom. Only he stopped in the doorway and turned back to face her.

"For the record, I never believed what everyone said about you and Coach. I was even planning on asking you to Homecoming, but you transferred schools."

"I decided to homeschool," she corrected.

Actually, she'd made such a mess of her life that she'd quit. Not her education, just the school part.

Gunther shrugged. "Yeah, well, I would have still asked you."

"I would have gone." Glory cleared her throat. "To Homecoming. If you had asked, I would've gone with you." She gave her sincerest smile. "Your wife is a lucky lady."

With a sheepish nod, he was gone, disappearing around the corner, the security door shutting with a resounding thud behind him. And Glory was alone. Really alone. Something she'd had thirty years to master, but never quite gotten the hang of.

She paced in front of the bars, feeling a little cagey

and a lot scared. She had just been cuffed, fingerprinted, photographed, and processed, for God's sake. Glory Gloria Mann was a criminal with a record.

At least she and her mama had something in common now. Not that she planned on seeing her mama anytime soon. If Julie-Marie Mann hadn't bothered to come see her daughter when she'd been suspended from her senior year in high school for "inappropriate relations" with an older man, she didn't think a grand theft auto charge would do it either.

No matter how hard her life got, and senior year had been hell, her mama had never shown up. Not even to stand by her daughter's side when she was wrongly accused of having sex with a faculty member—when in reality all they'd ever done was kiss. She hadn't shown up when Glory had been bullied or teased or chose not to walk the stage with her classmates even though she graduated with honors. Nope, not once in the entire time that Glory's life was falling apart did her mama even call to see if she was all right.

A sniffle escaped as she walked back to the lone steel bunk at the far side of the cell and plopped down, the mattress expelling enough dust bunnies to give her acute asthma. Exhausted, she leaned against the concrete wall and closed her eyes, but her entire body shook as a cold chill seeped through her thin tank top and right into her soul.

She had just given up hope of Gunther finding that blanket when the heavy metal door unlocked, startling Glory to semi-alert and bringing her to her feet. With a gracious smile, she walked to the front of the cell—and stopped short.

The door swung open and in walked Sheriff Duncan. He strode down the corridor, a ring of keys in hand, a gun strapped to his hip, and a smile so smug it made her heart die a little.

She'd learned senior year that if she wanted to live peacefully in Sugar, and God, she wanted a semblance of peace more than anything, then avoiding people with the last name *Duncan* was crucial—especially ones with *Sheriff* in their title. It was scandalous when Coach Damon Duncan, hometown hero and Sugar's favorite football coach, lost his job for being involved with an underage student. That the offense happened at the Duncan Plantation during the Miss Peach Pageant, with a girl from the wrong side of the tracks, made it downright blasphemy.

That he tossed her aside and never once defended her had been heart shattering.

Glory had wanted to graduate like everyone else, wear a cap and gown, and make her grandmother proud, especially since Jelly Lou had sacrificed so much to see that Glory got a good education and had choices in life. But the thought of walking across that stage, having her classmates shout cruel or embarrassing things in front of the one person who believed in her, was too much, so she quit. She let the Duncans and the bullies take away something that she was proud of.

She glanced down at the cuffs cutting into her wrists and sighed. If she didn't get out of here soon, she'd miss another chance to prove that she was more than her past. She only had a month left before she'd graduate nursing school and fulfill her dream of working as a registered nurse. And to do that she needed to get out of there and call her professor.

But that wasn't what inspired her sudden urge to make a noose out of shoestrings and be done with it. No, what made her chest lodge itself painfully in her throat was that Jackson wasn't alone. He'd brought friends. Two of them to be exact. Deputy Gunther and—she swallowed.

Oh, God! It couldn't be him.

And when she said *him*, she specifically meant Cal McGraw.

Glory's heart pounded against her chest, so hard and fast she was afraid she might just pass out. As far as everyone else knew, her connection to Cal was nothing more than his being her best friend's older brother. Which was sadly true. But to Glory, Cal was so much more. Always had been. Not that he knew—or even if he did, that it would change things. She'd long ago given up hope that he would see in her what she saw in him.

Forever.

Panic welled up and she mentally struggled to keep it together as his intense blue eyes locked with hers. She wasn't sure if it was a low blood sugar thing, since she hadn't eaten in nearly twenty hours, or if the huge lump in her stomach had slowly expanded its way to her throat, cutting off her air supply. But Glory knew that if this was karma, it packed one hell of a punch.

One look at the six-foot-plus wall of sexy contractor for hire encased in butt-hugging denim and high-octane testosterone making his way toward her cell and Glory knew that her day, which was already smothered in cow patties, was about to turn into a gigantic pile of 100 percent, grade-A shit.

And no amount of lipstick could cover that.

Chapter 2

~

Looks like you made bail." Jackson sniffed the air and grimaced.

Brett owed Cal big time. When his kid brother had called earlier that morning, asking him to post bail, Cal had no idea how it would screw with his day.

Glory was the last woman he wanted to see. She was a walking wet-dream, and Cal wasn't interested in going there—ever. At least that's what his head said. His dick on the other hand gave up listening the second he saw her in a thin tank top that showed off every womanly curve she possessed. Which was why he'd always kept his distance.

A hard thing to do when Gunther was huddling protectively at the cell door, making Cal wonder just how badly Glory had been treated. Jackson was all but smiling and Glory looked as though she was one smart-mouthed comment shy of bursting into tears. Something he figured she'd done earlier, since she was sporting two faint tear tracks down her pale cheeks.

It was obvious from the way she was doing her best to ignore him that she wanted him there about as much as he did. Brett had his loyalties, but so did Cal. Another reason he should head out. He'd posted her bail, she was alive, and—

What else did Brett expect him to do?

But instead of excusing himself, he stood there, staring and wondering (a) if she was wearing a bra, (b) if so, what color it was, and (c) how the hell a woman who looked like she'd been bathing in manure could still look so damn good.

God, he needed help.

"What the sheriff was trying to say is that you're free to go, Miss Glory," Gunther corrected with a glower.

"Why don't you go make sure the paperwork is all filed properly, Deputy?" Jackson said.

"Seeing as how you forgot to mention that your daddy called, I figured I'd come in and tell her the good news myself," Gunther said to Jackson, before turning to face Glory and lowering his voice. "Mayor Duncan is dropping all charges. And I hope that you will accept our apology for the delay in telling you. I know that last night was pretty awful."

Apparently not as awful as his statement, because Glory didn't move. Those big mossy eyes of hers zeroed in on Gunther, wide and expectant, waiting—for what, Cal didn't know. From the way the deputy stood silently shifting his weight, he was equally confused. Jackson just looked pissed.

"So, that means you're free," Jackson grumbled, turning the key. "For today anyway."

The cell door slid open and the clanging of metal echoed in the silent corridor, but Glory didn't move.

"How long?" she whispered, and that small catch in her voice did something to Cal's chest that had him sweating. She cleared her throat, threw her shoulders back, narrowed her gaze on Jackson, and tried again. "How long ago did he call to have me released?"

"About three hours ago," Jackson said.

"Three hours?" Glory tucked her arms under her chest and glared.

The movement pushed her breasts slightly up, answering questions A and B—no, and he was fucking toast—and proving what Cal had long suspected but diligently ignored: Glory Gloria Mann had one spectacular body. She had legs to her neck, a surplus of curves, and enough sex appeal to make Cal forget why he stayed away from women like her.

Not that he was interested—because women like Glory were tempting and tantalizing and a whole lot of trouble.

The kind of trouble that's bound to disappoint, Cal warned himself even as his eyes slipped over the length of her—incarcerated, coated in sludge, but damn near the most incredible woman he'd ever seen.

He forced his gaze away from her chest, and when they settled on her face, he called himself a hundred kinds of bastard. Because the way her lips trembled, she was in desperate need of a champion in her corner.

Not your problem, buddy.

Cal had enough problems of his own without adding another woman to the equation, especially a woman who came with more baggage than he did, and who was a walking talking reminder of the kind of heartache that came with chasing wild. So he shoved his hands in his pockets and stomped down every protective instinct that gnawed at his gut.

Nope, his days of playing the shining knight to a beautiful lady were long over.

"The mayor figured that stealing his tractor was a prank gone bad, but then he found this in the parking bay. Right next to an empty bottle of moonshine." Gunther approached the open door and held out his hand. Resting in his palm was a single red poker chip with THE FAIRCHILD POKERS engraved in gold.

Cal looked at the ceiling and groaned.

"I've never known you to be a big gambler, Miss Glory."

Gunther also knew what everyone in that cell now knew. Cal's Grandma Hattie and her Bible-toting poker cronies had stolen Ms. Kitty's tractor. Not Glory. She was just trying to put the Prowler back before things got out of hand. But why hadn't she just told the truth? They could have avoided this entire effed-up situation.

She strode out of the cell and, stopping in front of Jackson, held out her cuffed hands. "Take them off. Now."

"Your sentencing is next Monday at nine," Jackson said, slipping the keys into the hole. He paused. "So don't think about taking a vacation between now and then."

"Sentencing?" Those gorgeous eyes went wide with confusion. "I thought Mayor Duncan dropped the charges."

"He did." Jackson smiled, a little too smug for Cal's liking. "Against my advice. But there are still the resisting arrest and assaulting an officer charges to be dealt with."

"Assaulting an officer?" Cal laughed. He couldn't help it.

Glory was all of five-seven and a buck twenty to Jackson's towering six-plus feet. With her dark hair pulled up into a ponytail and those flannel pajama bottoms, which were fuzzy and pink and kind of adorable, she looked more like a co-ed than a criminal. And the only thing her sleepy state and vulnerable eyes dealt Cal was a kick to the gut.

"You can't be serious," he heard himself say. "There is no way you're claiming that. And why the hell is she still cuffed?"

"Can. And am. What part of assaulting me and my men did you miss?" Jackson sounded betrayed. "And since I'm not easily swayed by a pretty face and neither is Judge Holden, I think these charges will hold."

"For Christ's sake, JD, just uncuff her so we can go." Jackson shot Cal a look, serious as hell, and he knew just how Brett had felt all these years being stuck in the middle of this feud. "Look, I don't know about you all, but I have more important things to do than stand around arguing about a silly tractor that she may or may not have stolen."

"Right," Glory clipped off. His comment only seemed to make her more upset.

Jackson released her hands, and as Cal watched Glory rub at her reddened wrists, a slow anger began to twist in his gut.

"I believe that Judge Holden will be swayed by the truth." Glory picked the chip out of Gunther's hand and settled on holding it when she realized she had no pockets. "And I happen to be an excellent poker player. So thank you for returning this."

And with that she strode toward the exit, her backside every bit as tantalizing as her front. But what had him doing a double take was the lengths she'd clearly go through to protect her grandmother. That kind of loyalty was as surprising as it was sexy.

"Hold up, are you admitting to stealing my grandma's tractor?" Jackson said, hot on her trail.

"I'm not admitting to anything," Glory shot over her shoulder, her tone dripping with smart-ass. But Cal noticed that her hands were trembling as she pushed open the metal door—and it wasn't just from the cold. "Does it even matter? What is a grand theft auto compared to assaulting an officer, right?"

"May or may not have stolen, my ass," Glory mumbled as she yanked open yet another door. She stomped past the

break room, past three glaring deputies, and—ignoring the steady drizzle—across the parking lot, not stopping until she reached the steel gate enclosing the Sheriff Department's new parking area.

At eight feet high, with cross bars too small for a baby coon to squeeze through, the only way out was up. Glory stood on her tiptoes and reached to grip the top of the fence—crap!—make that twelve feet.

The light drizzle turned more end-of-summer storm, and she looked back at the closed door and swore. She had no phone, no way home, and no jacket.

Even worse, Glory thought, resting her head against the bars and letting out a stifled sniffle when she looked down and saw that her ducky galoshes were ruined, Jackson's little stunt had cost her the chance to graduate nursing school summa cum laude. He probably even cost her her dream job.

Charlotte Holden, head of family medicine at Sugar Medical Center, had taken a chance on Glory, putting her recommendation behind Glory's proposal, which, if approved by the hospital board, would make her the community outreach manager for the soon-to-be-built Fairchild Pediatric Center. The position would be working directly under Charlotte, whom Glory admired and respected, and working with kids—which was what Glory wanted to spend her life doing. And although she was pretty sure that her current situation counted as an "excusable absence" for missing her exam, it wasn't as if she could call her professor and say, "Sorry I missed the second most important test of my life but I was incarcerated for grand theft auto and, oh, I might have accidentally assaulted an officer of the law with a peach-colored tractor."

Feeling helpless and out of options—no way was she going back inside to ask for a ride—Glory kicked the gate.

Still not satisfied, she hauled back her left boot and
kicked the metal bars as hard as she could. The gate didn't
even rattle, but managed to split the rubber, right up the
duck's face and over the big toe.

"Stupid piece of shit!" she yelled as loud as she could,
kicking it again.

A low masculine whistle made her stop mid-kick. "Assaulting an officer and now an innocent fence? I never took
you for such a rebel. Especially not in rubber ducky boots.
Those come in steel toe?"

Glory spun around, ready to show him just how painful
her ducky boots could be, when she stopped. One look at Cal
and everything inside her went still and she felt like she was
going to crumble right there.

Cal leaned back against the side of the sheriff's cruiser,
one arm resting leisurely on the roof of the car, the other
hung loosely from his belt loop, looking big and safe and
badass. He wore a McGRAW'S CONSTRUCTION cap, a really
warm-looking jacket, and that sexy grin which always managed to make her stomach do these silly little flips. The man
looked so at home in his own skin it ticked her off even
more.

"Apparently, it *may or may not* have pissed me off,"
Glory said, proud her voice gave off that unaffected tone
she'd mastered over the years.

Cal's smile died at her comment. His boots clicked on
the pavement and he walked forward, not stopping until he
was standing so close she could smell the rain on his skin. "I
know you didn't steal Ms. Kitty's tractor. Never thought you
did, not for a second."

Glory felt her chest tighten and all she wanted was to do
was lean forward and disappear into his big, strong arms,
just for a minute to know what it was like to have someone

to lean on. But she wasn't sure if he'd hold her back and, she realized with a wrinkled nose and a sinking heart, that if she could smell every ounce of yummy-macho-male on him, then he could smell Mr. Ferguson's cows on her.

She stepped back and to the side, making him turn so he was standing upwind.

"Maybe you could have voiced that opinion a few minutes ago, while Jackson was twisting the rope for my public lynching."

Cal let out a tired sigh. "I was just trying to diffuse the situation, remind everyone that this was all over some stupid tractor so we could get out of there."

"Really?" she said in a tone that translated into *bullshit*. "Because it seemed to me that you were reminding everyone there you are a bros-before-hoes kind of guy," Glory said, hating that her throat caught on the last few words.

She wasn't an idiot. She knew what everyone in town thought: that she had slept with an off-limits man—just like her mama. But the truth was, Glory and Damon had never made it past second base. Not that *that* made what she'd done any less wrong. He'd still been a teacher at her school, a judge in the pageant she was entered in, but he'd made Glory feel something that she'd never felt before— wanted.

Not in a sexual way; she'd never had a problem with that. She'd been fending off boys since she grew boobs in the sixth grade. But Damon had sought her out, taken an interest in her life and her dreams, told her how smart she was. Made her believe, for the first time in her life, that maybe she deserved what everyone else had.

As an adult looking back, Glory could see that he had taken advantage of a confused and lost girl. But at the time he'd made her feel as though she mattered, as though she wasn't just her mama's cast-off, as though she wasn't a complete waste of space.

"Does it hurt?" Cal asked, reaching out to touch her wrists.

Shocked that he would try to touch her, since he'd clearly gone out of his way to avoid being near her over the years, she stepped back right before his fingers made contact. Not your fault, Glory reminded herself, since she couldn't remember the last time Cal initiated a conversation that extended beyond what kind of draft he preferred, let alone physical connection.

Irritation curled at his lips and he reached up to fiddle with the bill of his cap, cupping it in his palm and pulling it farther down on his head. The movement tugged his shirt up, giving her an unobstructed view of his flat stomach disappearing behind his button fly.

Oh my...

She jerked her gaze up and off his more than impressive package, hoping it was raining too hard for him to notice her ogling. "It's fine."

Cal pushed up the bill of his hat, his intense blue eyes flickered with amusement, and—*crap!* He'd noticed. "You sure, Boots? Because you're looking a little flushed there."

"Allergic reaction. Close proximity to assholes for extended periods of time tends to have that effect on me."

"So you're saying a ride to the hospital with me would only add to your discomfort."

It would, but not in the way he was implying.

"I don't need to go to the hospital, and—" She took in a deep breath and added, "You're not an asshole, Cal."

"That seemed painful for you to say."

Swallowing a big bite of humble pie, she looked him in the eye. "No, I mean it. I was so ticked I forgot to thank you for coming down and bailing me out. I know you probably did it because Brett forced you to, but I appreciate it all the same. And you don't have to worry about me leaving town and costing you..."

She looked up in question.

"Five grand."

Glory gasped. "Five grand?"

There was no way she was leaving town, because there was no way she could afford to pay him back if she did. Then all of her earlier anger vanished, leaving behind a deep sense of gratitude. If he hadn't posted bail, she'd be calling Sugar County Jail her home until the sentencing. And based on how that went, maybe even longer.

"Judge Holden's a fair guy. You don't need to worry, JD was just trying to scare you," Cal said softly.

Glory looked at the shattered lights of the cruiser, the accordion hood, and she wasn't so sure.

"I'm not thinking of skipping town, if that's what you mean," she said. "But if it makes you feel any better, you can hold the keys to my car. It isn't worth five grand, but that way you know I can't leave."

"I don't need your keys, Glory. I don't think you're a flight risk," Cal said and the belief she heard in his voice made speaking hard.

"Okay, then. Thanks." She gave a silly little flap of the hand that she hoped came off like a wave and walked backward. Right into the gate.

Glory turned around and dropped her head to stare at her ruined boots. And just when she thought it couldn't get any worse, she felt a warm jacket slide over her shoulders. She opened her mouth to tell him that she was covered in shit and she would ruin his soft and fuzzy and incredible-smelling jacket, but instead a sob came out. Followed by another one and a mortifying snort. Until finally her entire body was shaking.

Large hands settled on her hips and slowly turned her until she was nestled in the most glorious chest she'd ever felt. Wanting to grab on, but terrified of looking as desperate as she felt, Glory dug her fingers into the edges of the jacket, pulling it closed. She rested her cheek over his heart and tried to calm her breathing to match his steady beat.

And somewhere between his arms coming around her and feeling his lips press against the top of her head, Glory wondered if she would ever figure out how to become the kind of woman that good men, men like Cal, saw forever in.

Chapter 3

He was screwed. One simple contact and he knew that touching her had been an incredibly bad move, because his entire body registered just how amazing she felt in his arms. Soft and fragile and holding on to him so damn tight, as though he alone could make everything better. A dangerous position for a guy who'd spent his entire life playing hero, only to be benched, one by one, over the years by the people he loved.

Cal's parents died when he was a sophomore in college, and even though his grandma moved in and took over running the house, Cal took it upon himself to make sure his brothers grew up to become the kind of men their dad would have raised. Instead of finishing college with his buddies, he gave up an engineering scholarship to Georgia State and took a job swinging hammers for a local construction company, keeping him in Sugar.

Only Brett and Jace left rubber tracks at the county line when they each turned eighteen, Brett chasing a golf career and Jace chasing freedom. Cal's wife, Tawny, was the next to flee, and lately Payton, his daughter, had been wavering between needing him and needing space, and he knew it was just a matter of time before she took him out of the game altogether. Which was the only reason to explain his current situation.

He'd gone in for the shoulder pat, the kind he gave his daughter when she was disappointed, the "hey kiddo, you'll get 'em next inning" squeeze. Then Glory's body crumbled on contact and instinct took over, taking it from touching to holding to an "I'll fix everything, baby" hug. Before he knew it, the sound of her sniffles slid through his heart and the way her soft body pressed against his packed one hell of a protective punch.

"You okay?" Cal asked, thankful when she wiped her face on his shirt and took a teensy step back.

"Yeah, um, sorry about all of that. Long day, harder night, and..." She paused, nibbling at her full lower lip, and— *sonofabitch*—he wanted to kiss her. "I guess it's been a hard everything."

He could attest to that.

"Then let's get you home." He placed a hand at the small of her back.

"Thanks, but I'll just call Jelly Lou." Face averted, feet stuck to the wet concrete, and he knew she wasn't going to give in—easily. Which was too bad for her, because the way she kept eyeing the clouds and Maple Street meant she was considering walking, not calling her grandma. And he was a gentleman, so that wasn't going to happen. He'd get her home and then go back to ignoring her. "I appreciate you paying my bail, though."

"Yeah?" He laughed. "Because I heard what you said, but the tone was more of a screw off."

When she looked up to argue, he raised a challenging brow, and she cracked a smile. A small one, but it was enough to show off those little dimples of hers.

Man, she had a pretty smile. Even prettier lips. He dropped his gaze, and remembering that she was wearing a thin tank and no bra—and that it was raining—he grabbed the edges of his coat and zipped her up tight. Better.

"Now," he said, giving a casual shrug, not feeling the least bit casual. "We going to hop that fence or go through the station? Normally I'd be up for either, but since we have an audience"—Cal's eyes darted across the street to take in the two women standing at the top of the marble steps in front of town hall, staring their fill—"I suggest we head out the front door like law-abiding citizens."

He said it to lighten the mood, but Glory didn't laugh. In fact, her face sank and she took a little step back, right into him. Because standing across Maple Street, wearing a prim attitude and a stick-up-her-ass smile, was Darleen Vander, current vice president of the Sugar Peaches, Sugar's honored and most distinguished ladies society—and the woman who had made Glory's life miserable.

To her right, digging through her enormous purse, for what Cal could only assume was a phone or a camera, was Darleen's second in command, Summer Sheen. All they needed was one shot of Glory making her big escape and it would be all over town by lunch.

Eyes still glued to the growing crowd across the street—two more pairs of cardigans and pearls had joined the gawkers—Glory asked, "Were there a lot of people out and around town when you came in?"

Cal moved to stand in front of her, back to Darleen and blocking her shot. "Not too many people because of the rain."

Glory looked up and squinted as water streaked down her face, blinking as though just remembering that it was coming down pretty steady. He took off his cap, placed it on her head, and ignoring how good she looked in his clothes, pulled up the collar to shield her even more. "Why don't you duck under that overhang by the station door and I'll go get my truck. Gunther can open the gate and you can climb in."

Standing on her tiptoes, she peered over his shoulder at Darleen and he saw her weighing her decision. But instead of heading back to the station, she shrugged and started climbing the fence.

"Whoa now, hang on there a second." Call gripped her by the waist and, after prying her sticky little fingers off the metal, set her back on the concrete, water gushing out of her torn rubber boots.

"What?" she said, heading back for the fence. He wrapped an arm around her middle before she could get very far.

"They're going to talk no matter what," she said. "Plus, it's the first Monday of the month."

"Meaning?"

"Meaning that it is the official Sugar Peaches meeting day and in about two minutes that little angora flock over there will become an annoying herd. Especially since they are picking the committees for the Miss Peach Pageant to-day."

As a horny young teen, Cal had loved that pageant. As a parent of a girl old enough to enter, he was determined to have it outlawed. Especially when he came across the stack of ads with pictures of dresses in her room—not a single dress age-appropriate.

"Yeah, well, I'm more interested in you breaking your

neck and me having to haul your stubborn ass to the hospital," he said, tightening his arms when she seemed set on squirming away.

Taking out his cell, he dialed the sheriff's department. When Gunther answered, Cal asked him to open the gate.

A second later a loud beeping echoed across the lot, followed by the sound of jangling metal. By the time it opened, the steps were filled with the clicking of pearls and judgment. It appeared Glory was right—every Sugar Peach from the beginning of time until last election was lined up and looking their way.

"I guess they have already assembled a jury of my peers," Glory joked with a tight strain in her voice.

"My truck is just down the street. It'll only take me a minute."

She looked at the pack of Peaches and faltered. From the depths of the courthouse emerged a bulldog of a woman dressed in mourning black and clutching one of those little basket purses and a good ten-plus years of indignation tightly to her chest.

"No way." Glory shoved Cal aside. "And miss all the fun?"

Before Cal could stop her, Glory stepped out onto the curb and hollered across the street, "Morning, Ms. Kitty. It's a lovely day, wouldn't you agree?" With a big-ass wave and a parting smile, she made her way down the cobblestoned sidewalk toward his truck.

Ms. Kitty stood under a flapping SUGAR COUNTY: WHERE THE PEOPLE ARE AS SWEET AS THE PEACHES banner, lips peeled back and teeth bared, a pink hat capping her silver bob. She didn't return the wave.

Over the next two blocks every person who happened to be downtown came out of their respective storefronts to witness Glory's walk of shame. Cal wouldn't know if he'd call what happened fun, but after several polite nods and a few sunny "mornings" for every person she passed, Cal was damn impressed. Glory walked head high, smile on that pretty face, acting for all the world as though she wasn't strutting down Maple Street in her shit-stained pajamas, her boot slushing with every step. Or facing a sentencing in seven days.

He caught up to her quickly as she had to take two steps for his every one and placed a hand on her back, ushering her toward the passenger side of his truck. Unlocking the door, he reached around and helped her inside but she paused, her eyes locked on the big cow-sized dent marring the back of his truck. Then she took in the flecks of peach and gold paint covering the tailgate and grinned.

Yet another issue he had to deal with and he was pretty sure that his grandmother and her "Pokers" were behind it.

"You getting in or are you walking?" he warned, holding the door open.

Pressing her lips in a firm line, which didn't hide her amused grin, she hopped in. After enjoying the view of her backside encased in shrink-wrapped flannel, he slid around the car and started the engine. Cranking the heater to full, he pointed the vents at the waterlogged woman shivering beside him.

Truck in Drive, Cal made a U-turn and drove past the cluster of society women who were waiting for their final glimpse of Sugar's Most Wanted.

Glory didn't hide under the ball cap or duck down as the women all watched his truck blow past, but she did swallow hard a few times, her eyes glued out the front windshield. When they were clear, she slipped out of his coat and huddled around the vent, rubbing her hands back and forth.

"There's some coffee in that thermos." He pointed his chin to the lunch pail at her feet. "You're welcome to it."

"You sure?" She was eyeing it like if he said no, she'd die of frostbite.

"It's all yours. I can fill it up when I get to the work site."

She picked up the thermos, her hands a little unsteady as she undid the top and moaned at the bittersweet scent filling up the cab of the truck. She eyed him over the steam rising from the cup. "Hazelnut and vanilla? Surprised the guys at the site don't make you turn in your man-card."

Cal ignored her. Partly because he didn't care what she thought—one sip and she'd know it was a damn fine cup of coffee. But mostly he kept his mouth shut because his men had taken to calling him Princess ever since his daughter, Payton, had turned him on to lattes.

Glory took a tentative sip and then a big swallow. "God, this is good."

"I would offer you my lunch, but seeing as Payton made it, it comes with a warning." He slid her a sidelong glance. "Eat at your own risk."

"It can't be that bad." Suppressing a grin, he watched Glory bend over and take out the wrapped breakfast cake. She poked it a few times, took a tentative sniff, a bite, then made a gagging noise and put it back.

"Care to change your answer?"

"No," she said, taking another hearty sip, most likely to wash down the cake.

"Because that would mean admitting I was right?"

She gave a cute little shrug and went back to gulping down his coffee. When her fingers were no longer purple and her chattering teeth had quieted to white noise, he heard himself ask, "So want to talk about what happened last night?"

So much for his idea to get in and get out and *not* get involved.

"Nope."

"You sure?" Not that *he* wanted to talk about it, but her hands were still trembling slightly and those dark bruises under her eyes advertised more than just a lack of sleep. She looked chewed up and spit out and talking was what women did in these situations. Correction, talking was what women did. Period.

She gave him a long look. "You want to talk about that big-ass peach-colored dent in your truck?"

"Fair enough," he said, a little shocked, and went back to staring out the windshield in utter silence.

After a few more blocks of listening to the wipers squeak across the glass, he became twitchy. Watching the clapboard-siding storefronts fly by without so much as a word from her made him worried. Maybe she was more upset than she was letting on.

Telling himself that he was just being neighborly, Cal came to the Brett McGraw Highway, and even though both ways were clear, the truck crawled to a stop, and resting his arms on the back of the bench, he looked over, letting her know that he was in no rush—that if she needed to talk it out, *he* was her guy.

"Glory," he gently nudged like he would when trying to pry something out of Payton, only Glory just looked at him—for a long time.

"Oh," she finally said, her hand coming up to flutter in front of her mouth.

Yup, Cal thought, settling in for the duration, *here it comes*. The rain and lack of building inspector meant that his day was blown to hell, so he made sure his body was relaxed and giving off the "you take all the time you need" vibe.

"Right, um, I just assumed," she faded off, looking a little lost. And how could he blame her, she'd had a pretty rough night. "Well, I live about a mile west. Right off Old Mill Road."

She pointed and then went back to staring out the window.

Cal blinked. Then choked a little before pointing the car west. That had never happened before. The women in his life lived to fill the silence. They couldn't help themselves. In fact, Cal hadn't had a quiet meal in over fifteen years. *Not Glory, though*, he thought as he pulled onto the highway. She seemed content to just stare out the window and watch raindrops slide off glass.

"How come you never moved into town?" he asked as the highway stretched into a half-kept road on the outskirts.

She gave a small shrug and said, "Jelly Lou refuses to leave her house," as though that answered everything.

He knew her grandmother was her only family and that Jelly Lou needed help from time to time since she was in a wheelchair, but he couldn't help but wonder if Glory ever got lonely living all the way out here. Then he wondered how she spent her free time, and about the point where he began wondering if she had anyone special to spend that free time with, Cal said, "How about some music?"

He flipped the knob before she could answer, which was fine with him. He was done talking and wondering.

A sugary voice with more pop than twang filled the car and poured out of the speakers. Immediately he shut it off. Too fast to cover Glory's soft snort.

"Taylor Swift?"

"It's a first-day-of-school thing." He shrugged, feeling stupid.

"That's right. School starts Wednesday. Is Payton excited?" Her eyes grew soft and she flashed him a smile so sweet he forgot how to talk. Which was a problem because Glory wasn't talking either. Nope. She was sitting quietly, patiently waiting for him to answer.

"It's all she's been talking about." Just not to him. Lately his baby girl had taken to locking herself up in her bedroom, talking on the phone to who knows, about hair and shopping and that damn Miss Peach Pageant.

Cal felt himself scowl.

"Good," she sighed, looking relieved. "She was nervous about starting sophomore year because she has all of those AP classes. She was *really* worried about getting Mrs. Fry for biology but I told her that she was a great teacher and if she did the work she'd be fine."

Payton was nervous about her school? Why had she told Glory? And more important, why *hadn't* she come to him?

Cal must have looked confused because she added, "Your grandma sometimes brings her to Quilting Night at the Fabric Farm, and since Payton and I are the only two born after the Second World War, we talk."

"You quilt?" he asked as he eased on to Old Mill Road, his tires kicking up water. "You don't look like a quilter."

"What is that even supposed to mean?" she asked, the offense clear in her voice. "What does a quilter look like?"

"I don't know." But when he took in the sexy woman next to him who loved bartending and beer, he had a hard time picturing her sewing on a loose button, let alone making something as domestic as a quilt. St. Polly's Girl she was, Holly Homemaker not so much.

"Well, I can assure you that I'm a damn good quilter. Almost as good as Hattie. She started teaching me after, well . . . I started quilting senior year." *After I got chased out of school* wasn't said but it hung between them nonetheless.

He'd heard enough stories from Brett to know that her senior year had been rough. He'd had no idea just how bad until one day Cal was driving home from a remodel across town and came across Glory walking down the highway heading home. She was cornered by a truck full of football players offering her twenty bucks for a BJ.

Cal chased off the guys and, after she'd promised him that she was okay, drove her home, wondering how her grandma continued to let her go to that school. The next day she unenrolled.

"I'm right there." Glory pointed out the window. "The one with the big lemon tree on the porch."

Cal pulled off on the gravel road, coming to a stop in front of her house. If the lemon tree landmark was accurate, Glory lived in the apartment above a detached garage that sat kitty-corner from her grandma's farmhouse. He squinted through the windshield, noticing a small herb garden on the apartment's porch and a couple of potted peonies lining the steps. It was small but welcoming.

The truck idled but neither moved. After a long moment Cal said, "If you called Jackson and explained what really happened to the tractor, I bet he'd drop the assault charges."

"And tell him what?" she asked quietly, looking him right in the eye. And man, something deep inside of him tightened. "That *your* grandma took the company truck for a joyride on a suspended license and stole Ms. Kitty's tractor with *my* grandma?"

Right, there was that. "It would get you off the hook."

"That's not the way I'd want to be exonerated. Plus, Ms. Kitty would just use it against my grandma somehow..." Glory swallowed hard and looked out the window. "Jelly Lou isn't doing well. She's back in physical therapy to help with her leg pains. I don't want to add to her stress. Not until I know what's going on."

Everything inside Cal wanted to call Jackson, tell him to stop being a little bitch and let this all drop. But he knew that his buddy would only back down if someone confronted him with the truth. And he had a sick feeling that someone was going to have to be him.

"Jackson and I go way back. I could call him and discreetly—"

"Jackson and I go way back, too. So we both know that it won't help, so please don't." Glory turned to face him, her hand resting gently on his arm, and damn it if he didn't feel heat slide straight through to his core. "We don't know who all was there or why they stole it. Plus, we both know Jackson's just flexing his muscles. It's nothing I can't handle."

Cal ran a hand down his face. He should have felt relief that he didn't have to get involved any more than he already was—only he was too busy feeling angry. He knew Jackson would drop the charges because, even though he hated Glory, in the end he was a good guy and a great sheriff. Just like he knew that Glory could handle Jackson if it came to that. Hell, she'd been doing it most of her life. Didn't mean she should have to, though.

"I'll be fine, Cal. I promise."

Cal let out a breath and gave a tight nod. "All right. But if you need anything..."

She was silent for a long moment, studying his face as though searching for the words. Or maybe she was waiting for him to finish. Only he faded off because he wasn't sure what he was offering anymore. Something about the way she always seemed to stand alone got to him—and not much got to Cal.

"Thanks. For everything," she finally said and tried for

a smile, but it faltered under the strain of the night so she bit her lip to keep it in place. Her eyes were shinier than he'd like, and the way the delicate column of her throat worked overtime, he wanted to pull her into his arms again. She looked like she had all those years ago, vulnerable and scared and staring up at him as though he'd just made her fucking world. And damn it if that didn't do something to his chest.

"No big deal."

"To me it is. If you hadn't come ... I don't know..." She broke off and shook her head. Rubbing out one of the million creases in her pajama bottoms, she looked up at him through her lashes, then opened her mouth. But when nothing came out, she gave a self-conscious smile that made him want to—

What?

He didn't know. And staring at that mouth was stupid because he started making a list of exactly what he'd like to do to those lips. But looking into those gorgeous eyes proved even more dangerous, so he dropped his gaze to her hands, which had somehow gotten tangled with his, and he felt his pulse pick up.

Son of a bitch. He wanted to kiss her. He wanted to kiss Glory Gloria Mann. Which made not one ounce of sense, because she was definitely *not* his type. Okay, with her killer body, full mouth, and exotic eyes, she was every man's type. But what got him was that smile. It was sweet and sad and so damn determined, it broke his heart—and it pulled him in. Every time. And Cal couldn't afford to be pulled in. He was a single dad, trying his best to be everything his daughter deserved. There wasn't room in his life for a smile like that.

"Cal," she whispered, and he realized his eyes were back on her lips.

"Yeah?" He threaded his free hand through her hair. It was silky and a little damp and felt amazing.

"I bake, too," she said.

He blinked. Twice. "What?"

"I bake," she repeated. Her breath was warm on his lips, and she smelled of vanilla and hazelnut and all things delectable. "I bake and I quilt and I like to garden. And thanks for saving me..." She leaned up and gently pressed her warm lips to his cheek and whispered a broken, "Again."

She reached for the door, but before she could open it, Cal leaned forward. "Glory—"

She turned back to face him and whatever the hell he'd been about to say died because her mouth was right there, aligned perfectly with his. All he had to do was lean forward a smidge, and—

Sweet baby Jesus, her lips parted on a breath and he watched the pulse in the base of her neck quicken. She knew exactly what he was thinking, indecision playing out in those expressive eyes, and his heart literally tripped.

He should leave. Leave her and this stupid idea and—

Her eyes dropped to his mouth.

That was all the welcome he needed. He cupped her face and kissed her. He kept it gentle, brushing her upper lip and finally delivering little nibbles to that lush, plump lower one that had been driving him crazy for years. Her mouth was soft and warm and so damn sweet a jolt of heat shot straight through him, warming up the car and making him want to strip off his clothes—then hers.

He pulled back, his hand was gripping the back of her neck. When her lashes finally lifted, her eyes were dazed and hungry and he knew he had to get out of there.

With one last brush of their lips, he whispered, "Thank you." Her eyes narrowed in confusion. Welcome to it, he thought, since she'd been screwing with his brain all morning. "For taking the time to talk with Payton. About school."

"I like talking to her, she's a great kid," she whispered, then looked him dead in the eye and, as if knowing exactly what he needed right then, said, "And you're a great dad."

He gave a single nod, not as confident as he'd have liked. "I have my moments. But lately I feel like it's more misses than hits with her," he said, surprised at his admission, even more surprised that he wanted to keep talking. To her. It was wild—talking to Glory about his life felt easy.

"You love her, that's all that matters," she said with so much confidence he had to check himself. She had been covered in cow shit, falsely arrested, and yet she refused to give in to the unfairness of it all, instead offering him sweet words in a moment when he really needed them. "Most girls dream about having a dad like you."

Her voice cracked on the last few words, reminding him that growing up, she was one of those girls.

With a shaky smile, Cal watched her scurry out of the car and up the steps, his hat planted firmly on her head and his eyes planted firmly on the sway of her ass. His phone started buzzing, but Cal ignored it, ignored the fact that she was already inside and that he was sitting there idling in her driveway like an idiot.

What he couldn't ignore was that a night with her would be the worst decision he could make since Tawny—or that out of all the women in this goddamned state, he had to feel that undeniable, sexual pull with this one.

Chapter 4

To keep her mind off Cal, Glory took a shower. A hot one. But when all the not thinking about Cal turned into thinking about Cal's mouth—on hers—she switched to a cold one. It didn't help.

Who knew Cal could kiss like that? That he could kiss *her* like that? Besides their lips and his hand gently cupping her face, he hadn't really touched her at all, and yet she felt him everywhere. Still could.

She let out a breath and grabbed the meatloaf and a crock-pot of low-sodium chili she'd made for her grandma to get her through the next few nights while Glory worked the closing shift at the Saddle Rack. Wrapping her raincoat over her new flannel PJs, she darted down the stairs and into the small farmhouse she grew up in.

Jelly Lou sat in her wheelchair watching the limbs of the peach trees droop with rain. She wore teal sweats, matching fuzzy slippers, and pink lipstick.

Glory kicked the door shut and low grunting was the only

warning she got before a soft nose and scaly head disappeared beneath her pajama leg.

Part dinosaur, part honey badger, and wearing more body armor than a gladiator, Road Kill, her grandmother's armadillo, was so excited by the smell of the chili that he was trying to climb her leg to get it and leaving little claw marks all down Glory's shins.

"Down," Glory said, giving her leg a little shake.

Fingers between her teeth, Jelly Lou let go a whistle that had Road Kill peeking out from the fabric and scurrying over to his master, his weapon of a tail smacking everything he passed.

"We thought you'd come right over to tell us how your test went," Jelly Lou said, picking up Road Kill and placing him in her lap. He curled up, but his eyes stayed locked on the crockpot. "Then we saw Cal McGraw's truck in the drive and figured you needed some time to pull yourself together."

Glory shrugged out of her raincoat. "He was just being neighborly."

Jelly Lou raised an amused brow. "Is that why your face is all flushed?"

Since Cal was a topic she was determined *not* to obsess about, Glory went into the kitchen and straight to the coffeemaker, not slowing down until she poured herself a big steaming mug.

A warm calmness washed over her as she breathed in the familiar scent of freshly baked cornbread and lavender soap. So many times over the years, Glory had come home from school to find her grandma at the counter cooking up dinner, a bowl of potatoes waiting to be peeled or peas to be shucked. Jelly Lou believed that family was about caring, standing together—side by side through even the toughest times.

There had been a lot of tough times in Glory's life and Jelly Lou had never faltered in her support. She had given Glory stability, affection, a safe place to be a part of—and so much love.

Glory took her first sip of her coffee when Jelly Lou and Road Kill rolled in. Not wanting her to bring up the midterm again, or God forbid Cal, Glory gave her a kiss on the cheek and asked, "Did you reschedule your physical therapy appointment?"

"Who says I missed it," Jelly Lou asked causally, stroking Road Kill's head, and Glory pierced her with a knowing look—which was met with an innocent shrug, so Glory waited.

A good and long time.

With a huff, Jelly Lou caved. "I called his receptionist this morning and she said Dr. Moore is booked out for two weeks. Then she had the nerve to say she was charging me, even though he didn't help me none. How can someone charge for doing nothing?"

"Easy. He got to sit around wondering why he rushed to work at eight o'clock on a Monday when his eight o'clock was a no-show. And since you didn't call in advance to cancel and you don't have a good excuse for missing it, he gets to charge you for his wasting his time."

"I had a good excuse."

"Breaking into Ms. Kitty's barn and stealing her tractor?"

Jelly Lou said not a word, just grabbed some napkins and spoons, and rolled over to set the table.

With a sigh, Glory served up two bowls of chili, topped them generously with shredded cheese, and set them on the table. She set a cob of corn on a napkin and placed it on Road Kill's chair—which he vacuumed up the second his feet made contact with the cushion. "I'll stop by Dr.

Moore's office tomorrow and see if he can squeeze you in this week."

Jelly Lou clasped her hands together. "Such a good granddaughter. How did I get so lucky?"

"We can discuss *that* after you explain exactly what you were thinking stealing Ms. Kitty's tractor."

Her request was greeted with more silence, broken only by the occasional slurp, clanking of metal on porcelain, and Road Kill's grunting.

She had to remind herself that she was a lucky girl. She had an amazing grandmother. Sweet, patient, loving—and stubborn as hell. Good thing Glory had spent a lifetime waiting for answers to questions she didn't know how to ask, so if Jelly Lou thought she could outlast her, she was greatly misinformed.

Glory lifted her spoon and dug in. Except for Jelly Lou asking for a second helping, they finished their chili in silence. Then as though Glory hadn't been waiting fifteen minutes for an answer, Jelly Lou leaned over and, with a warm smile, patted Glory's hand. "Now, tell me about that test."

She dabbed her lips with a napkin and went for honest. Well, as honest as she wanted to get with a woman who wore her guilt like lipstick. Heavy enough to be detected from outer space. "I missed the test because I was returning the Prowler."

"Oh, Glo." She clutched Glory's hand to her chest and held it there. "What on earth were you thinking?"

"That I didn't want my grandma incarcerated for stealing the mayor's tractor."

"The mayor doesn't care; he knows his mama is petty. Plus, Jackson wouldn't have arrested us." Glory snorted. "And we weren't stealing it. We were gathering evidence. Kitty is a cheat and the whole town knows it. They're all just too scared to speak up. That's the only way she could win nine Sugar Pull champions in a row."

"Maybe she's just got the better tractor and driver," Glory said, but even *she* didn't believe her argument.

Jelly Lou was the proud owner of the only ten-time Sugar Pull champion in the history of the event, the Pitter. The woman knew what it took to win, as it had taken her and her husband, Ned, over fifteen years of racing to accumulate that many titles. So if Jelly Lou was claiming foul play, then Ms. Kitty was cheating the system—and most likely bribing the officials to look the other way.

Not that Glory was surprised. Sneaking and scheming to win, even when harmful to others, was Ms. Kitty's MO.

"Please don't tell me this is because of what happened with Damon." When her grandmother stared at the floor, tension knotted painfully in Glory's chest. "Because I'm over it. Really. I am."

There, that sounded convincing.

"A good Southern woman always forgives, but only a stupid one forgets. And I won't forget what her family did to you. Ever." Jelly Lou's words were strong and laced with a protectiveness that made swallowing difficult. "But, the good Lord knows, I have forgiven them."

Glory raised a brow and Jelly Lou cracked a weary smile. "Okay, the good Lord also knows that I have to reforgive them every Sunday and on all religious holidays. But this is about something else I've been meaning to talk to you about."

The last time her grandmother had used those words, it was when Glory had come home to find her mom had decided to move to Florida. Without Glory.

She didn't know which hurt worse. That her mother had

admitted Glory wasn't Billy Mann's before skipping town with someone else's husband. Or that after hearing, Billy took off, too, leaving Glory behind. All she knew for sure was that her daddy wasn't Billy Mann—and Glory was all alone.

Jelly Lou fixed that, though. She had taken a heartbroken Glory into her home and explained that Glory was hers, forever. No matter what.

Which was why, no matter what this town threw at her, Glory wasn't leaving as long as Jelly Lou was breathing.

She scooted closer and took both of Jelly's Lou's frail hands into her own. "You can tell me anything."

Jelly Lou gave two squeezes, then smiled, big and bold. "Good. Because I'm entering the Sugar Pull. Hattie, Dottie, and MeMaw have signed on to be my pit crew. Etta Jayne's the pit boss. We call ourselves the Pit Crew Mafia."

An overwhelming sense of panic blew through Glory at the thought of her grandma racing again. "Is that safe? You haven't raced since Billy was in high school." Since she'd taken a debilitating fall off a ladder during harvest and broken her back. That had been thirty-five years and three wheelchairs ago.

"Then I'm long overdue to defend my title," she explained.

"Against men half your age?"

"The first time I raced, I was sixteen and steamrolled over men twice my age. Still managed to win with a one point six second lead. I can do it again."

"A lot's changed since then." Like automatic transitions, disc breaks, and YouTube. Now every redneck who owned a computer knew how to make a turbo injector with dental floss, tinfoil, and a nine-volt battery.

"Which is a shame because the Sugar Pull used to be

about celebrating this town and the men and woman whose backs it was built on. Your Granddaddy Mann was one of the first farmers to plant sugar peaches, and his daddy was one of the first peach farmers in this whole area. So when I see Ms. Kitty importing drivers from NASCAR and flashing around her high-priced fuel pumps, it goes against everything the Harvest Fest is about."

In Georgia, harvest season brought out hundreds of thousands of peach-loving visitors and their spending bucks. In Sugar, harvest season brought about the annual Harvest Fest—a weekend-long festival to celebrate the fruit that was the heart of their community—peaches. It was a time for friends and family to gather, and for the community to pull together and pay tribute to those who had come before. It was also where Jelly Lou met and fell in love with Ned Mann.

"Have you tried talking to Peg?"

"She wanted proof before she took it to the Harvest Council." Peg Brass was the current harvest commissioner, and therefore the final word on all things peach related—including the Miss Peach Pageant and the Sugar Pull. "We had the proof but you took it back before Peg could get a look under Kitty's hood."

"Which is the only reason you and the blue-haired brigade aren't sitting in Judge Holden's courtroom." Or worse, jail.

"Pit Crew Mafia," Jelly Lou corrected, then went serious. "That Kitty isn't throwing a stink, is she? Using her power and influence to make trouble?"

"You stole a decorated town treasure." Glory thought of Jackson and her night in jail and shivered. "So, sure, she called the sheriff and reported the tractor stolen. You would have done the same."

"Stolen?" she mumbled. "What a crock. Go get me my best dress. I don't want to be looking all down and out when the sheriff arrives to take my statement."

Glory cleared her throat. "He isn't coming."

"Probably because he knows that his grandma's a cheat and making a big deal about this would look bad on his family." Glory remained silent and she saw the understanding dawn on the older woman's face. "He isn't coming because I wasn't driving the tractor, you were." Glory looked out the window. "Oh, Glo, I'm so sorry. I won't forgive myself if this causes you any trouble."

"It won't," she said softly, while reminding herself that Judge Holden was a fair man. Cal had told her so.

"Well, if it does, you be sure and let me know so I can invite Little Jackie over for dinner and set him straight. You weren't a part of this and I don't want anyone saying differently."

She was already a part of this, from the second she started up that tractor. And having *Little Jackie* over for dinner wasn't going to solve anything. Neither was telling Jelly Lou the entire story, so she settled on the highlights.

"There was a little misunderstanding, but Jackson made sure the Prowler got home safely and then he"—*cuffed, booked, and left me in a cold cell all night*—"gave me a lift to the station and Cal dove me home." She stretched her neck side to side because she didn't like lying; it gave her a headache. "Nothing I can't handle, but you have to promise me no more antics. This feud between you and Kitty needs to end."

"As soon as Kitty fesses up to being a liar and a cheat." Her voice was so melodic she sounded as though she was giving one of her famous Sunday school lessons. Only the moral of this story was an eye for an eye.

"Grams," Glory said softly, looking at the photo that hung above the sink showing a very young Jelly Lou sitting atop the Pitter while kissing her Ned. "I know how important the Sugar Pull is to you, and what that tractor means. If Ms. Kitty wins, then the Prowler will be tied with Grandpa's tractor for most wins on record. But I don't think Grandpa would have wanted you to steal her tractor. Or that he'd be comfortable with you racing. I bet Dr. Moore wouldn't be thrilled either."

"Why do you think I've been going to PT? To get ready." Jelly Lou narrowed her eyes. "And I'm doing it because I promised Ned I would."

Oh boy. Jelly Lou might be the only woman in history crazy enough to petition that Road Kill should be a certified therapy companion so he could eat in restaurants, and she had been known, on occasion, to play forgetful when caught pushing her '67 Camaro over eighty in a sixty zone, but she was as sharp as her quilting needle. Downright poky if riled. And sure, Glory had been working a lot lately, and with the condensed summer school schedule, she hadn't been around as much as she'd like. But had she been too busy that she overlooked that her grandma's mental state was slipping?

"Don't look at me like that," Jelly Lou chided. "I haven't gone and lost my mind. Although I do admit that from time to time I talk to Ned. And sometimes, when I really need him, it feels as though he's right there holding my hand and talking back."

"Me, too." Glory had never met Ned. He'd passed before she was born, but she'd heard enough to know that she would have loved him. And Jelly Lou swore that he would have loved Glory right back. Most days Glory believed her.

She thought of returning the tractor and smiled because today happened to be one of those days. Then again, Jelly

Lou also swore that she was just going to play poker with the girls last night.

"When I lost use of my legs, it was like I'd lost all my usefulness. I couldn't cook or do simple housework, or stroll down Maple Street with Ned on my arm. I couldn't even help him in the orchard and he always had a problem telling which ones were ready for picking." She gazed out the window to the orchard, which was now leased to a tenant farmer. "One day he came in and tossed his hat on the table, the straw one hanging above the fireplace, and said, "Lou-Lu, picking peaches without your harping is about as exciting as whoopee with the lights off." Then he picked me up right out of my chair and carried me outside. And there, sitting in the barn, looking as new as the day I got her, was the Pitter."

Glory sighed and felt it from her heart straight down to her toes. And like every other time she'd heard this story, she found herself wondering what it would feel like to be loved like that. To be so ingrained in someone's heart that you need the other person to live.

"Secretive old coot." Jelly shook her head, a crop of silver curls bouncing as she chuckled. "Your granddaddy spent every spare minute that year rebuilding the Pitter in secret, from the brakes up. New engine, new seat with a special harness, even crafted hand-powered paddles for the accelerator and brakes. He said that I didn't need legs to drive the tractor, but he needed his wife to tell him which peaches were ready for picking."

Jelly Lou's face went soft, the way it always did when she talked about Ned. "Took me two years until I could operate it by myself, another three until I felt free again, but I worked that land right next to my husband every day from then on. Then a few years in, Ned said we were ready and he signed us up for the Sugar Pull. I was going to drive and he was going to be my pit boss. It was all he talked about but he passed before the next harvest."

Road Kill, feeling Jelly Lou's stress, hopped down and started grunting while brushing up against her feet.

"So you never got to compete?" Glory asked, wondering why she'd never heard this part of the story.

"I tried but I just couldn't. Not so soon after losing him. For nearly three decades that man loved and cherished and believed in me. I wasn't ready to let him go, and somehow entering his tractor would have been like saying my final good-bye." Glory handed her grandmother a napkin to dry her eyes. With one final dab, she gave a good blow and straightened her shoulders. "So I'm racing in this year's Sugar Pull. Win or lose, doesn't matter, it's time I live up to my end of the deal and take the Pitter for her final lap. And when I do, I just want to make sure that everyone is playing by the same rules."

Glory didn't have the heart to point out that Jelly Lou and her new pit crew had broken several rules last night—one really big one that carried really big consequences. Federally enforced consequences, which could get her suspended from competing. Instead she pulled her grandmother in for a hug and said, "How can I help?"

Tuesday afternoon, Glory was midway through her rounds at Sugar Medical Center, searching for a bulb syringe in Exam Room 7, when she happened to look out the window and— *holy hotness*—her heart stopped working. Right there in her chest.

The storm had finally blown through Sugar, leaving behind clear skies, green grass, and temperatures hot enough to melt the clothes right off a man's body. Something she hoped would happen because there were enough heat-slicked biceps and glistening tool belts on display that, even in an air-conditioned hospital, Glory could feel the heat.

With one last excited fist bump to the sternum, her heart gave pause as everything in her body went on standby and Glory knew that she wasn't over yesterday's encounter with Sugar's Sexiest Bachelor.

Or that kiss.

No matter how many times she told herself to knock it off, to act professional and get back to work, she couldn't help but stare. One look out the window and her mouth went dry—the exact opposite of what was going on below the equator.

Because there, three stories down and—if she stood on her tippy toes and pressed her face to the glass—directly to her right, where the foundation for the new pediatric center was prepped to be poured, walking the perimeter in a pair of worn jeans, an impressive tool belt, and a T-shirt that clung to his chest with the day's humidity, was the sexy general contractor on the job and that work-honed body of his. The one that tended to have men flexing and women straining for a better view.

Women like me, she thought as she nudged a footstool out from under the exam table and shoved it flush against the back wall to watch as, in one fluid motion, Cal hopped up in the bed of his truck and opened a big metal toolbox, where he proceeded to bend over—way over—so he could dig out, well, she didn't really know. Didn't care. All she knew was that the best ass in nine counties was practically begging her to look her fill.

And look she did—until the glass started fogging up. He kept digging so she kept staring, amazed at just how well he filled out a pair of jeans.

"This is ridiculous," she said to herself, pressing even

closer to the window when he rested his hands on the toolbox to dig deeper, causing his biceps to bulge a little and the
hem of his shirt to rise a lot. The sheer amount of exposed
muscle was enough to make her hyperventilate.

"It was *one* kiss." And she had better things to do. Such
as locating the bulb syringe so Angela, the pediatric nurse
Glory was shadowing, could complete the retrieval of Lego
Luke Skywalker and, Glory was pretty sure, his trusty pal
R2-D2 out of Cole Andrew's left nostril. The result of a
schoolyard dare gone bad.

Not to mention she had to find Charlotte Holden. And
soon. Glory needed to explain to the doctor why she missed
her midterm before word spread about the arrest. Finding
out how the Great Tractor Heist of Sugar County would
impact her future at the hospital should have been at the
forefront of her thoughts. Only Cal took that moment to
glance behind him—and directly up at her window.

He paused.

She panicked.

Even though his ball cap was pulled low on his head,
shadowing most of his face, she could still feel those intense
blue eyes when they zeroed in on her. Buns of steel still
to her, he nodded in greeting and, *oh boy*, smiled. Actually
it was more of a grin, which implied smugness. And the
only reason he'd be smug was if he knew she'd been caught
ogling the goods.

Which she totally had, but would rather die than let him
know.

You got this, she told herself, proud that she managed a
serene smile. At least she hoped it came off as serene. Hard
to tell when her lungs had stopped functioning properly.

All she needed to do was give a causal, *Oh, hey there*
wave, and he'd turn his head back around, bury it in his tool-

box, and it would be business as usual. Then she could slink
off. It was what they did. What they'd spent the past fifteen years mastering. She'd ogle, he'd catch her, she'd play
it cool, and he'd go back to ignoring her.

Rinse and repeat.

Her hand rose and fell. She gave it a solid 9.2 on the cool
and unaffected scale. It was short, to the point, and not a single finger broke away from the pack to flit in his direction.
Good start.

He returned the gesture with a set of double-barreled
dimples and perfectly white teeth, but there was no business
as usual. Instead he didn't break eye contact, didn't ignore
her, just stood there, flashing her his sugar-shaker, amusement clear on his face. Then he craned his neck even more
and looked at his butt and then back to her.

Oh God.

Straightening, he turned to face her and lifted a single
finger then twirled it around in the universal gesture for, *I
showed you mine, now show me yours.*

She shook her head and his hands went to his hips. She
mimicked his stance. So he reached into his pocket, pulled
something out, and—

Her phone vibrated. It was Cal. She considered ignoring
it, but what would that accomplish since he was watching
her, waiting for her to answer?

"I'm working," she said by way of greeting.

"I can see that." She wondered what else he could see, such
as the way his voice rumbled over her skin and had her nipples
waving their big welcome flag. She crossed her arms.

He smiled.

"If you're calling to make sure I didn't skip town, your
bail is safe."

He walked to the end of his tailgate and studied her

through the glass for a moment. "I was calling to see if you were okay after yesterday."

"Yeah," she said but suddenly she wasn't sure what okay even meant. Ever since that kiss she'd felt...off somehow. And she wondered if he was feeling the same. "I mean, it was just a kiss."

He shifted slightly and cupped the bill of his hat. "I was talking about being arrested, but we can talk about the kiss," he said almost in horror, the pitch of his voice making her cringe. "If you want."

Did she want? Hell, yes she did. Was she going to admit that to him? Not when he sounded like he'd rather talk about the birthing process. "Nothing to talk about."

"You sure?"

"Yup."

"Good." He sounded a little too relieved for her liking. "Because Payton is my number one focus. And my life, my family, my career..." He sounded weary just talking about it. "I'm not in a position to start up anything right now."

She wasn't sure if he meant that he wasn't in the market or if it was more of a buyer's remorse kind of issue. Either way, she let the unexpected wave of disappointment roll right off her and then gave an unaffected chuckle. "It was a long night, I was tired, and then there was the rain. It was bound to happen."

She could see the easygoing amusement creep back into his stance. "Rain, huh? And here I thought you'd just been chilled from the cold."

She opened her mouth to tell him he'd been pretty damn affected by their kiss, too, when someone cleared their throat behind her.

Hand on her chest, Glory turned to find Peg Brass leaning heavily against the door frame. Her lavender dress was wilted, her purse hung from her clutched hand, and her usually sharp tongue seemed subdued by her loud panting. In fact, it was as though the door frame was the only thing keeping the owner of Peg's Brass Peaches, the largest peach plantation in the county, from kissing the floor. Which was odd since the woman was the fastest peach packer in the sixty-five and over division.

"I have to go." She disconnected and made her way toward the older woman's side.

"Hey there, Mrs. Brass." Gently she took the woman's wrist, checking her pulse. It was erratic and her skin was clammy to the touch. "What seems to be the problem?"

"The problem is I can't breathe, my hand's gone numb, I'm pretty sure I'm dying, and you're too busy playing Who's Your Doctor with Hattie's oldest grandson to do your job," she said between gasps.

"Does it hurt anywhere else?" Glory asked and steered Peg toward the exam table.

"I'm squeezing my chest. Where do you think it hurts?" the woman barked but her lips trembled. Peg was built like a horse, tall, sturdy, and bucked at any sign of weakness. She was also one of Jelly Lou's childhood friends and her weathered skin was a little too pale for Glory's liking. "Just my luck, I have a heart attack in a hospital and the only person around to help is still testing to get her license."

Ignoring this, Glory squeezed Peg's left hand. "Can you feel that or is there any numbness or tingling in your left arm?"

"What the hell?" Peg flinched. "I got the arthritis. What kind of medical expert smashes a patient's hand when they got the arthritis? Especially when I already done said it's my chest. It's giving me the palpations, squeezing the breath right out of me. Fix that."

"Let's check your heart rate." Glory unsnapped her oxygen tester off her lanyard and slipped it on Peg's pointer finger. Although her heart rate was elevated, the oxygen level in her blood seemed to indicate there wasn't any blockage to the heart.

"When did the symptoms start?"

"Yesterday," Peg said, and Glory felt herself relax. If this was a heart attack, and it had started yesterday, then Mrs. Brass wouldn't be breathing much less talking. "After the Sugar Peaches' meeting I was feeling dizzy. Then I went to the market and the palpitations started up."

"Did you call Dr. Holden?"

"Why would I? The woman's an idiot. Gave me these little pills to fix my cholesterol problem. A year later my cholesterol's even worse."

As one of the top family practitioners in the state, Dr. Holden was far from an idiot. But preaching preventative medicine in a town where gravy, country fried, battered, and à la mode made up the four food groups had its limits.

"Plus, I had a new *Wheel of Fortune* on the recorder," Peg said as though that explained away everything. "And that Pat Sajak was wearing a blue tie." The more the older woman talked about her game show, the slower her heart rate became and the steadier her breathing sounded. "He always looks good in blue."

"I want to try something. Can you close your eyes for me and think about something that relaxes you?"

"Why? You think I'm dying?" And just like that her heart rate increased.

"No. I want to rule out a heart attack, since I am pretty sure you're having a minor panic attack."

"Minor? This ain't minor. Plus, I lived through three husbands, I don't do panic."

"Uh-huh," she said, smiling. "Now close your eyes and try to relax."

Peg closed her eyes, and after a few minutes, her breathing returned to normal as well as her heart rate. The woman was even smiling. "Where are you?"

"Fishing. Watching the water and enjoying the absence of arguing," Peg said in the same tone she used when retelling how she scared small children every Halloween. But Glory had never been scared of Peg. She'd always felt sorry for her, living that far out of town all alone.

"How does your chest feel now?"

"Better. Much better." She opened her eyes; they were dazed and sleepy. "So I'm not dying?"

"No, I think you're suffering from panic attacks, which can seem a lot like having a heart attack," Glory explained, proud of her quick assessment. "Have you been under a lot of stress lately?"

"It's that damned Harvest Fest," Peg said and—*whoa*— the mere mention of the annual festival sent Peg's heart rate bordering on dangerous and her breathing became jerky. "I tried to retire from the Harvest Council last year, and the year before that, but every time I do, Ms. Kitty and that Hattie McGraw start flapping their gums and scare off anyone thinking about running. No council means no festival."

Which would mean a lot of lost income for the people of Sugar.

Between the Miss Peach Pageant and the tractor pull, the festival usually generated enough money to float the town's economy until the next harvest. That it was hosted by the Harvest Council, a board constructed of the ever so entitled Sugar Peaches and other social-climbing ladies of peach country, meant finding a willing participant to take over as committee chair would be impossible.

Glory was the least involved woman in town with regard to the harvest—peaches gave her hives—but even she knew how much time, patience, and referee skills it took to organize the town's biggest event. Peg was the only person in Sugar who had brass peaches big enough to put themselves in the middle of one of the longest-standing feuds in Sugar. And since she'd been doing it for over two decades, the woman deserved a break.

"You know what I think you need," Glory asked.

"One of those fighting cages to lock Kitty and Hattie in?"

"Nope. You need to go fishing."

Confident that the situation was not life threatening, Glory helped Mrs. Brass get comfortable on the exam table and left her with the latest edition of the *Saltwater Sportsman* and a promise that the doctor would be in momentarily. Grabbing the bulb syringe, she hurried back to Exam Room 9 and little Cole Andrew's obstructed left nostril.

Twenty minutes and a successful retrieval later, Cole was on his way home with his Lego toys safely stored in a plastic bag and an "Unencumbered Sniffer Is a Happy Sniffer" pamphlet in his backpack, and Glory made her way to the break room. She grabbed her snack from the fridge and was about to take a seat when she noticed the big, pink box of doughnuts on the counter. Convincing herself that it would be empty by now, she took a long detour on her way to the table and—

Damn it!

She looked at her yogurt parfait, healthy and sensible, then at the maple doughnut with pink sprinkles looking ever so lonely in the near empty box. Glory leaned down and took a big sniff, closing her eyes as the sweet scent drifted past, then remembered the old-fashioned doughnut she'd inhaled *before* her shift and the fact that she'd hadn't run since last week, and plopped down at a table with her yogurt.

"Nasal obstruction and Mrs. Brass all before noon?" Mouthful of yogurt and granola, Glory looked up to find the woman she'd spent her morning avoiding. "I would have gone for something stronger."

"Dr. Holden." Glory forced an innocent smile.

Poised, sophisticated, and with a grace that rivaled Princess Kate's, Dr. Charlotte Holden was the epitome of Southern belle. Her blond hair was pulled up into a complicated up-do as always, but her cool as a cucumber exterior was replaced with amusement. "Your Ken doll frequented my Barbie's dream house in the third grade; I think that puts us on a first-name basis."

Glory laughed. "Even back then you made me call you Dr. Holden."

"Yes, well I'm not so uptight anymore," Charlotte said with a smile and took a seat—and the last doughnut. Charlotte and Glory hadn't run in the same circles as teens, but they'd played some as kids and that small connection had grown since Glory started at the hospital. "So what was it this time? One of his matchbox cars or a Tater Tot?"

"R2-D2 and Luke Skywalker," Glory said, eyeing the doughnut while she swallowed her nutritious snack. "I guess someone at school told him he had bats in the cave so he thought Luke Skywalker and his light saber could help. He took one look at the syringe and sneezed, the droids were liberated, problem solved."

"Until next week," Charlotte said, breaking off a chunk of doughnut and popping it in her mouth, moaning in ecstasy as she licked icing off her fingers. Glory ate a huge spoonful of her yogurt and moaned just as loud.

"Now, you want to tell me why I signed a prescription

for fishing?" Charlotte lifted a brow and in a teasing tone whispered, "I don't remember them teaching that in medical school."

"A little unorthodox, I know, but Mrs. Brass needs a little R&R and I figured the only way she'd get some was by doctor's orders."

"You figured right. I have been after her to slow down for years, but she is too stubborn to listen." Charlotte broke off a piece of doughnut and offered it up. Glory admitted defeat and, caving like a cheap suitcase, snatched the iced goodness. "And here I thought you'd been avoiding me on account of yesterday's arrest."

The doughnut hit Glory's stomach with a thud. "You know?"

"Honey, this is Sugar. News about your tussle with the Duncan family reached town before you even got off the tractor." Charlotte's expression went giddy as she leaned in and waggled a manicured brow. "Having a McGraw post bail, now that took it from teatime gossip to *the* topic on every lady's agenda. It even had an honorable mention at Sugar Peach's meeting."

And wasn't that just great. Glory knew it wouldn't take long for people to start talking—especially since it involved her and the Duncan family. She'd just hadn't anticipated Cal would have gotten caught up in the gossip.

"I was going to find you on my lunch break, so I could explain," Glory began.

"Explain what?" Charlotte waved a dismissive hand. "That you threw cow pies at Jackson's car and bruised his ever so delicate man-feelings?"

"Actually, I threw one at him," Glory admitted, smiling when Charlotte laughed but quickly sobered when she remembered just how serious Jackson had been about pressing assault charges. "I think I screwed up this time. And I'm afraid of what the hospital's board will think when they hear."

She was more afraid of what they would do, which made what she was about say next so hard.

Charlotte had not only approved Glory's proposal to head up a new teen volunteer program for the pediatric center, but believed in her idea so much she'd given it the Holden stamp of approval with the board—which went a long way since her family founded the hospital. Ever since then, chatting over doughnuts and coffee in the break room had become a habit, and as of late it had become the best part of Glory's day. Charlotte was quickly becoming her biggest cheerleader and, more important, a good friend. And Glory didn't want to mess that up.

"I would understand if you wanted to pull your support from my proposal and back one of the other candidates," she said honestly, even though the words burned her throat coming out.

Charlotte's face softened. "You have worked so hard on creating this program. I thought it was what you wanted."

More than anything.

Outside of Brett, Glory didn't have many friends after the scandal. Homeschooling only made her feel more secluded and alone. So when her grandmother's doctor mentioned that the hospital was in desperate need of a junior aide to help with the long-term patients, Glory applied. It was better than the alternative—sitting at home all day. Plus, it gave her the chance to show a different side of herself, the kind that people could be proud of.

Later she learned there was no such program, just an astute doctor who saw Glory's need to belong. Dr. Blair changed Glory's world because what started out as a way to earn a few extra bucks a week ended up becoming the thing that changed her life.

"It is," she admitted. "But I missed yesterday's midterm, which means I'll have to ace my final if I have any chance of passing. The board is already skeptical about a nursing student heading up an internal program." Especially since the other three candidates were already hospital employees with stellar résumés and experience under their belts. "When they hear about the Great Tractor Heist, it will give them one more reason to go with a more experienced candidate."

"Glory," Charlotte said, her Southern lilt thick with emotion, "I believe in your idea. Not only is it the best use of the grant money, it is the perfect solution for this hospital and this community. But I agreed to put my name on the proposal because I believe that *you* are the perfect person to head the program." Charlotte rested her hand on Glory's. "You're driven, amazing with kids, and have a huge heart. More importantly, you understand how powerful this kind of program can be for the patients as well as the volunteers. This hospital would be lucky to have you, not the other way around."

Glory swallowed, uncertain what to do with the praise. Those words coming from someone as accomplished as Charlotte were humbling.

"So, if you still want this, and I think that you do, then all that matters is if you ace that final and make sure your proposal is ready for presenting at the end of the month."

"It will be." She would make sure of it. "But—"

Charlotte squeezed her hand. "Let me worry about the board and don't give Jackson a second thought. He's a good guy, Glory, he'll come around. You'll see."

Glory wasn't so sure. She'd been waiting for that good guy everyone spewed on and on about to show himself for over a decade with no luck. "And if he doesn't? Because he's so pissed that he can't get me on tractor theft he's threatening assault charges."

"Assault charges?" Charlotte's tone was one of humorous disbelief, but her expression confirmed Glory's biggest fears. If Jackson got his way, Glory would lose everything she'd worked for. Because even with a Holden stamp of approval, there was no way any medical board would hire someone who had an assault charge on their police record. Let alone put them in charge of minors.

"Then let's make sure it doesn't come to that."

Chapter 5

⌒

The next morning, Cal stared at the blueprints. Strategizing the build for the new pediatric ward at Sugar Medical Center was a safer alternative than demanding to know what the hell his teenaged daughter was thinking. Because the strips of flimsy fabric and lace held together by spaghetti straps and suction that Payton was sporting as "back to school" wear were enough to make him consider homeschooling.

She was already going elsewhere for advice. He didn't want to give her more of a reason to shut him out. So he hung his head as Payton fussed over his breakfast, recalculating the dimensions for the foundation. For the third time that morning.

"Thank you, baby," Cal said when Payton set down a cup of coffee, a decent attempt at a breakfast cake, and the most pathetic-looking omelet he'd ever seen. But the girl was trying to cook and Cal appreciated the effort. Without hesitation, he dug in, prayed for a miracle, and took a bite—freezing mid-chew.

"Well?" Payton asked, pulling her blond hair over one shoulder and twirling it into a single spiral. Cal resumed chewing—and chewing—while she sagged into the chair across from him. "Oh God, it's awful, isn't it?"

"No, baby, it isn't awful," he assured her, willing the brick-like chunk of cake down his throat and a smile to his lips. Awful was being too generous, but his little girl had been working herself up in the kitchen since last week, trying to perfect this breakfast cake, and she had finally hit critical mass. Payton was primed for a good pout.

Once upon a time, that had meant a cute puckered lip and a few sniffles. Nowadays, it was more a devastated, end-of-the-world explosion with a ninety-percent chance of major tears. Being a single dad to a teenage daughter meant he'd gotten used to tears. Didn't mean he had to like them, though.

"Yes, it is," she whispered, sagging ever more and breaking his heart a little. "Everyone is going to laugh."

Cal swiveled his body sideways and popped out his left leg, making a daddy-sized knee-chair. He gave his thigh a pat. "Come here."

When she didn't roll her eyes or scoff, and instead plopped down and wrapped her arms around his waist, Cal felt his world go right. Fashion magazines, hormones, and hair products couldn't hide the fact that this was his little girl. Although when he pulled her to him in a bear hug and buried her head under his chin, he registered that she didn't fit like she used to. She was growing again. The long arms and legs to her neck were all McGraw. The other parts—the curvy parts that he didn't like to acknowledge—those were all his ex-wife's doing.

"Now, you want to tell me what's going on, since I am pretty sure this has nothing to do with a breakfast cake?"

Payton took a dramatic breath and snuggled closer, resting her cheek against his chest. "Saturday is the Cleats and Pleats Pep-Luck." She leaned back, flashing those baby blues his way. "Get it? Potluck meets pep rally?"

"I remember." Cal already knew he wasn't going to like this story. *Cleats* and *pep rally* were each a single degree of separation from his least favorite word—*boys*—and the way Payton was smiling, big and broad and not reaching her eyes, he knew that she had been excited about going and somehow his ex-wife had ruined it.

"The football team has been pulling double days all summer, so to pump them up for the scrimmage, the cheer team always hosts a breakfast after their 6 a.m. practice. I was signed up to bring Mom's rise-and-shine cake, you know the one with the cinnamon and peaches that you used to say was magical?"

Cal nodded. He knew the one. And he knew where this was going.

"Well, Mom called Friday. I guess she can't come this weekend 'cuz she's going to Cabo with Randal." Payton sniffled and Cal wanted to throttle his ex. And good old Randy. "She e-mailed me the recipe but I think it's missing something because no matter how many times I make it—"

She gave the cake a hopeless glance and shrugged.

"Did you try calling her?" Cal already knew the answer and felt like kicking himself for asking when his daughter's eyes went misty. As usual, her mom was probably too busy with the new hubby to answer.

"No, and she also told Kendra's mom that she'd head up the griddle. And I'm going to be the only girl there without a m—mom and the older girls are going to think that I'm not pulling my weight." And just like that the sniffles took a sad turn.

"Hey, no tears." He wiped the corners of her eyes with his thumb. "We're McGraws. We've got this. You and me."

Her face lit up with hope. "You know how to make the rise-and-shine cake magical, like Mom's?"

"No." He used to think that just about every damn thing about Tawny was magical, but just like her breakfast cake, Cal never figured out the right ingredients. "But we can figure it out. Plus, I'm killer on the griddle."

Okay, he was killer on the BBQ but they were pretty much the same thing, right?

"I thought you were going fishing with Uncle Jace this weekend."

"Are you kidding, and miss the chance to hang with my favorite girl?" Payton came first. Always. Jace would understand. "Plus, your uncle snores and isn't nearly as cute as you are."

A small smile tugged at his daughter's lips. That was more like it. "You'd have to wear pajamas. All the moms are."

"Do my Sponge Bob boxers count?" He tugged a lock of her hair.

"Gross." She giggled, shoving playfully at his chest. "Although I bet Kendra's mom wouldn't mind. She was hoping you'd take Mom's place on Saturday. She's working the bacon station."

Shit. Kendra's mom was tall, stacked, and the kind of blonde that came from a bottle. She was also twice divorced and extremely interested, something she'd made painfully clear the last few times Cal had dropped Kendra off. Not that Cal was. Cal wasn't interested in anything more than two adults enjoying a few hours of fun. And one-nighters with mothers of his daughter's friends was a bad daddy move.

Not that kissing Glory yesterday had been a good move.

It had been downright stupid, because for the first time since Cal's ex-wife had walked out on him, there was interest on both sides. And a whole hell of a lot of chemistry.

"Yeah, well, I'm going to have the prettiest girl in all of Sugar on my arm." He leaned forward and pressed a kiss to Payton's forehead.

"Oh, and one more thing, no glaring at the boys." Cal felt his jaw clench. Payton must have noticed, too, because she leveled him an icy glare. "We are supposed to be feeding them for the big scrimmage and no one is going to come over if you're giving them *the look*."

"What look?"

"The one you're wearing right now that says, 'If anyone so much as looks twice at my baby, I will straighten them out like a piece of wire.'"

Cal was pretty sure his look was more of an "eyes on your own package or lose it" kind of look. In any case, *that* look was the only thing keeping boys from swarming his front porch with flowers and empty promises.

Payton reached up and mushed her fingers into his forehead, pulling and massaging until she ironed out the furrow of his frown. Her other hand tugged Cal's lips up into a smile. "That's how you have to look. Promise? For me?"

"You're killing me." Cal looked up at the ceiling. "But yes, I promise to *try*, if you promise to go upstairs and find the other half of your outfit so we can head out. Don't want to be late for the first day of school."

"I'm not wearing this to school," Payton said, offering up a sweet smile. "I was just trying it on."

Thank God.

"For Miss Peach nomination day next week," she said as though *that* were going to happen. "Varsity girls have to wear our cheer gear to school on the first day."

He liked the sound of that. Not the cheer part, or the varsity part for that matter, but the uniform part. Ever since Payton hung up her State's Champion softball mitt for a set of red and blue pom-poms, Cal's life had gone from manageable single-dad status to full-on panic researching all-girl schools. But her uniform was swishy sweatpants, a T-shirt with the school mascot on it—a giant sheep—and a matching jacket. He should know; she'd pretty much lived in it all summer, telling anyone who would listen how she was the only underclassman on the varsity cheer team.

Payton slid her arms around his neck and gave him a peck on the cheek. "You know, show school spirit."

"Uh-huh." What he knew was that his little angel was buttering him up. For what, he wasn't sure, but he had a feeling that it was going to cost him a few more gray hairs. And maybe an early-onset heart condition.

"It's supposed to get people excited for the scrimmage Saturday." She smiled, her pearly whites making his rise-and-shine cake even harder to digest. "Speaking of Saturday. After the scrimmage a few of the—"

"No." His tone left zero room for discussion.

When it came to his daughter, Cal had always been a yes man. Part of it was him trying to make up for his poor choice in spouse, but Payton made giving in easy. She was sweet, smart, and one bat of those baby blues always did him in. Until she started growing—

Cal grimaced.

"But I haven't even asked you anything," she said, her lower lip sticking out in a well-practiced pout. Another trait she'd inherited from her mother.

When had his baby become a bombshell? And why couldn't she take after his side of the family? Instead of coming out like his homely great-aunts with bucked teeth and built like ranchers, Payton looked just like his ex-wife—too damn pretty for her own good. At least she got the McGraw sense of direction. And up until last summer it was that sense that had kept her on the straight and narrow and away from boys, although he was pretty sure that the estrogen would somehow screw with that, too.

"Does it involve a boy?"

"He's really sweet and—"

"No, Payton. We've talked about this." He pinned her with his dad-knows-best glare.

"God." She stood up, flinging her hands. "All of my friends have boyfriends. I'm going to die the only girl at Sugar High who's never been kissed."

Fine with him. Cal forked off another bite of coffee cake and smiled. As far as he was concerned, if he got through the next three years without Payton bringing home some punk-ass kid whose scholarly interest was what lay beneath Payton's cheer skirt, he'd be a happy man.

"No dating until you can drive," he reminded her. It was something he'd agreed to when she'd been twelve and he'd caught her batting those lashes at the punk who worked the pump at the gas station. Payton got a free candy bar out of the deal, and the kid got an up-close and personal introduction to Mr. Smith & Wesson.

At the time, sixteen had seemed so far away. Not anymore, which meant he had eighteen months to convince the state of Georgia to change their driving-age laws.

"It's at Padre Point, and before you say anything, the whole cheer team is going. So, it isn't just like me and the football team or anything."

Cal had been a football player. Done the Cleats and Pleats Pep-Luck. Gone to Padre Point. He had even invited the cheerleaders. "No. No. No. And no."

"I know what you're thinking and you're wrong. Not all guys are interested in, well..." Her cheeks flushed slightly and her eyes darted away. "Well, you know."

Yeah, he did know. And the fact that she blushed while avoiding the word *sex* told Cal that she hadn't gone there. Whoever this kid was could live. For today anyway.

"You're right, baby." He stood and pulled her into his arms. God, when had she gotten so tall?

"I am?" she whispered in that sugary Southern drawl of hers while looking at him as though he had all the answers and Cal felt like a fucking superhero. His ex-wife might have put him through hell, but Payton was worth every heartache. Just looking at her made his world right.

"Yes, you are." He tucked a blond curl behind her ear. "They're interested in sex *and* sports. Every single one of them. In that order."

"God, Dad!" She shoved at his chest, but he didn't move.

"Look," he said, tightening his arms and smiling down at her. "It's just that I don't trust football players."

She didn't smile back. In fact, she looked as though she just might cry. "Yeah? Well, I trust *me*. And I thought you did, too."

Cal looked up at the ceiling—it was easier than looking at her hurt expression.

"I do trust you, Payton." And he did. But he also knew how persuasive an older, smooth-talking jock could be. And his Payton was so trusting and sensitive—he was just trying to protect her from guys like him. "How about you finish getting dressed? If we get out of here in the next few minutes, we'll still have time to stop by the Gravy Train."

"I don't need you to tell me that you believe in me when you obviously don't. And you know what? I don't need a ride. I'll walk." And with that, she stormed out of the kitchen.

Cal watched her stomp up the stairs, heard a few dramatic sniffles echo down the hall, finally the slam of her bedroom door—and something in his chest constricted.

I don't need a ride!

Sometimes she caught a ride with one of her friends or her Uncle Brett. And sometimes she walked.

But today was the first day of school. Cal always drove Payton on her first day of school. It was their thing. They would blast some Taylor Swift, he would sing at the top of his lungs, she would pretend to be all embarrassed, then they'd suck down an extra-large, double-shot hot cocoa from the Gravy Train, polish it off with a burping contest, and all before he saw her off to class.

"Five minutes," he hollered while doing some stomping and pouting of his own. Right over to the sink, where he slammed his plate down and rinsed it off before jamming it in the dishwasher. When Payton slammed her door again, for added emphasis, Cal dropped his head and took in a deep breath.

"And I'm driving you to school," he mumbled to no one in particular, but it made him feel better.

"It's just the hormones," a weathered and understanding voice came from behind.

Cal turned and saw his grandmother. Dressed in a lime green track suit with matching ball cap, Hattie McGraw stood in the doorway, dangling his truck keys, her gray halo shaking with every nervous tap of her orthopedic shoe.

She walked over to rest a pudgy hand on his arm, giving him a little pat. "Why don't you let me take her to school?"

"Thanks, Grandma. But this is our thing. Not to mention—" He snatched the keys out of her meaty little hands, but not before delivering a kiss to her puckered brow, to soften the blow. Last thing he needed was another pissed-off female. "You can't drive."

"Sure, I can. Just did as a matter of fact." She snatched the keys back and stuck them in her pocket, then went about making his lunch. "And before you go hemming on, my reflexes are just fine."

"Not according to Jackson, who last I heard tore up your license."

"Man's a moron."

Cal ran a hand over his face. "You drove through the side of Kiss My Glass Tow and Tires." Thankfully the owner, Lavender Spencer, was a family friend and didn't press charges—or sue for damages.

"Actually, I was aiming for Kitty Duncan and her cart full of enough high-performance air filters to power the entire NASCAR fleet. Seeing as how I made that turn on a whim and smashed her cart while missing *her* entirely is a testament to just how good my reflexes are. Damn fine eyesight, too, if that was what you were going after next."

Cal took a seat. In ten minutes his entire day had turned to shit. He had a hormonal daughter, five separate construction permits to file at three separate county offices, and a crew on the clock that couldn't start running plumbing and electrical for the hospital's new pediatrics ward until he got the inspector to sign off on the footings.

And if that wasn't enough, now his grandma was justifying nearly taking out the mayor's mother because of a damn tractor pull. Although the feud between Jelly Lou Mann and Kitty Duncan was legendary in Sugar County, it had been pretty quiet for the past few years—the two women agreeing to coexist in the same town without bloodshed. But if there was one woman who could rile everything back up again, it was his grandma.

Oh, she wouldn't do it on purpose. She would go into it with the intent of protecting her friend. But Hattie's best intentions usually ended with him negotiating her bail. And he'd already bailed one woman out of jail this week; he was hoping to avoid the sheriff's station for a while.

"Nothing's illegal about buying car parts."

Her eyes went hard. "It is if you're soupin' up a tractor for the Sugar Pull. Which I know that cheat of a woman, Kitty Duncan, is doing. It goes against every bylaw of the competition, and because her son is the mayor and her grandson the sheriff, she would have gotten away with it, too."

"So you want to talk about what you did the other night?" Cal asked. He'd put off talking to her about the stolen tractor and big-ass dent in his truck until he'd calmed down.

"Me? It's that woman." Hattie snapped open her lunch pail. "She cheats every year and every year she wins, then she rubs it in Jelly Lou's face. Well, this year, if she wants the Prowler to be the lead tractor for the Peach Day Parade, then she's going to have to win that spot, and win it fair! And that means no high-octane fuel."

Cal pinched the bridge of his nose. He couldn't put this off any longer. Hattie was a danger to Sugar's residents, not to mention his peace of mind. She belonged behind a wheel about as much as he did cooking up pancakes at a mommy-daughter potluck. "We need to talk about your driving."

"No. We don't." She stopped mid-slice into last night's leftovers, shoving a chunk of Payton's cake in his lunch pail instead of that tri-tip sandwich she was ready to make. Snapping the lid shut with force, she leveled him with a practiced glare. "And I don't want to talk about the dent on the back of your truck either."

His phone buzzed and a photo of Brett giving the camera the finger appeared on his phone. The way his luck was going, it would wind up being his sister-in-law, Joie, with another blind date for him. A date who would be prim, proper, perfect wife material—and boring as hell.

"Fine. But just know that until we talk, you aren't going anywhere."

"You can't ground me," Hattie harrumphed, dangling his keys.

"Watch me." Cal shot up and, after wrestling his grandma for the keys and taking a few cheap shots to the ribs, he finally managed to snag them away and make his way to the front room.

His phone vibrated again. He sat on the couch, rested his head against the back, and answered, "McGraw."

"Morning." His kid brother's greeting came through the phone, low and muffled. The rasp in his voice told Cal that he'd either just woken up or was still half asleep.

"How's California?" he asked, wondering why Brett was up so early the day after his golf tournament, and thanking God that it wasn't Joie.

"Smoggy, crowded, and beer comes in a damn mug. What kind of man drinks beer from a mug?"

Cal smiled. "So, I take it you're still pissed that you ended up somewhere other than first?"

"Nah. It's just a charity event," Brett said with casualness that Cal knew was bullshit. He could almost hear him force out a shrug. "The new children's ward will still get their money."

Cal had to smile. Even though his kid brother drove him crazy, it was good to hear his voice. Good to talk with another guy. Because guys didn't include the words *feelings*, *hair*, or *dating*—ever. Plus it might help alleviate the permanent twitch forming behind his right eye.

"Nice double bogie on the eighteenth. I really thought

you had it in the bag. Too bad about that kid." Cal grinned. "What is he, fifteen?"

"Nineteen."

"Right, nineteen. He really came out of nowhere and kicked your ass."

"One stroke!" Brett said and—yup, definitely pissed. Brett lowered his voice and Cal could hear him press the phone closer to his mouth. "The little prick won by one stroke and he's pissing himself like he just won the Masters."

"Where are you?" Cal asked because it sounded like Brett was standing in the middle of an echo chamber mumbling into his armpit.

A moment passed. "The john."

"You're calling me from the bathroom?" This would be good. Brett had a knack of getting himself into stupid situations, which used to drive Cal nuts, but right now Cal could use a good laugh. "Crazy night, huh?"

And Cal could almost imagine it. A bunch of buddies, throwing back beer—from mugs apparently—watching highlights from the tournament, ribbing each other until Brett passed out, only to wake up locked in some poor guy's bathroom.

"Crazy doesn't even begin to describe it," Brett said and Cal crossed one ankle over the other and found himself relaxing and settling in. "I'm hiding in the hotel bathroom, sitting in the fucking tub because"—his voice dropped two levels—"I don't want to wake up Joie."

Cal felt his smile fall. "Joie?"

"Yeah, she flew out yesterday to watch the tournament. She was up all night icing her swollen feet from standing all day, poor thing. Can't even wear those sexy little heels of hers anymore," Brett said as though it was a national travesty.

Brett McGraw had more championship titles and bunny-buckles notched in his career belt than any other golfer in the history of the PGA. Then he met Josephina Harrington, socialite turned Sugar's hospitality specialist, and Brett traded in his playboy swagger for a prissy pooch and domestic goddess. Yeah, his life was as pathetic as Cal's.

"Then last night the back aches started again. I swear—" Brett sighed—*sighed*. "We're supposed to head out this morning for the Napa Valley, for our babymoon," he added like Cal knew what the hell a babymoon was. "But between the bloating and the morning sickness—"

Cal hung up. He couldn't do it. He just couldn't listen to one more womanly problem. It wasn't that he didn't like women. He loved women. He was just surrounded by them all the damn time. Hell, couldn't even remember the last time he'd thrown back a cold one in silence or watched a ballgame without someone asking him what a first down was or if cottage cheese caused cellulite.

His phone rang. Three rings and a calming breath later, he said, "Yup."

"Sorry, the phone must have cut out."

"Must have," Cal lied. "Look, I've got to get going. School starts today and we're finally pouring the concrete in the footings at the hospital."

"I'll make it quick then," Brett said, giving a big pause that wasn't quick at all. "I got a favor to ask."

"Your last favor ended up with me spending five grand," Cal said, thinking back to the way Glory's lips had felt against his. "The one before that landed me on a blind date with a dental hygienist."

"She was sweet."

"She spent the entire night looking at my teeth. I flossed obsessively for the next month."

Now that his sister-in-law had found love, she was determined to find Cal the perfect woman, not understanding that those two words didn't belong in the same sentence as far as he was concerned. Not anymore. Not after Tawny walked out with his heart, his savings, and his ability to trust in her rolly suitcase.

Ignoring his insistence that he was fine being single, and insisting that it was time to get back out there, Joie spent the past few months playing matchmaker. So far she'd set him up with three socialites, a lawyer, and a librarian with a penchant for silk ties who he'd rather forget. All of them nice enough, pretty, smart, interested. Yet not a single one inspired anything other than lukewarm feelings.

Whatever gene it was that helped McGraw men pick the right one must have skipped Cal, because his picker was so far off center, he somehow managed to mistake trouble in a miniskirt for forever.

"I guess Glory called Judge Holden to see if there was any way to work this out, and since Gunther refused to sign the arrest report, the judge agreed to an informal meeting in his chambers tomorrow. He wants both parties present to get to the bottom of the assault charges," Brett said.

"Well, that's good for Glory. Holden will take one look at her and drop the charges."

"I hope so but Glory's up for some big position at the hospital that she's worked her ass off for, which will mean nothing if this gets out of hand. And we both know that Jackson loves to play hardball with her, which is why I'm calling." Cal got that squirrelly feeling in his gut. The same kind of sick knotting that happened right before Payton asked him about feminine products. "You know I wouldn't ask you if there was anyone else, and I know that she isn't your favorite person, but Glory's my best friend and she needs someone on her side. Hattie's taking Jelly Lou to a doctor's appointment and there is no way I can make it back in time."

"I don't want to get involved. Jackson's my friend and this is already complicated," Cal said. Not only were the Duncans huge financial backers of the Sugar Medical Center, but they were also a huge part of the reason McGraw Construction won the bid to build the new pediatric ward.

"He's mine, too, which means that we both know how jaded he can be when it comes to Glory. Christ, Cal, he kept her in cuffs all night. Not to mention, you and I both know that the charges are complete BS."

"I'm not a lawyer, Brett, and I wasn't there at the time of the arrest." Although he'd been there afterward, when she'd cried in his arms, soft and vulnerable, and like an idiot he'd kissed her. And she kissed him back and—*holy hell*—what a kiss. Two seconds of touching her was enough to turn Cal from sensible single dad to the kind of guy he'd been when he met his wife. Which was the only excuse he could come up with for his embarrassing as shit display yesterday at the hospital. "I posted her bail, made sure she got home safe, what more do you want me to do?"

Brett paused and then hit him with the one thing Cal couldn't ignore. "I want you to be a good guy. The same guy who always stands up for what's right, but I forgot we're talking about Glory here, so never mind. I'll just tell Joie that we'll need to head back tonight. We can take the babymoon later."

"No, wait," Cal said, digging his fingers into his temples. He was a good guy—always had been. Just his luck, *that* was branded into his DNA.

He stood and walked to the window, relieved to find there wasn't a single rain cloud in sight. "I'm on it."

Chapter 6

⟋

"Assault is a serious charge that carries serious consequents, Miss Mann," Judge Holden said from behind the bench.

"Yes, sir." Glory took in a deep, calming breath. It didn't help. She was going to be sick.

No matter how many times she told herself she'd be okay, the scenery said differently. She had walked through the doors of Sugar County Municipal Courthouse a whole fifteen minutes early to find Judge Holden already situated behind the bench and not a single seat in the house empty.

Okay, so there had been one empty seat. Situated at the front of the courthouse, behind the defense table with a big RESERVED FOR GLORY GLORIA MANN sign taped to it—just in case there was a sole left in town who was confused as to exactly who was on trial today.

She eyed Jackson, who sat smugly on the other side of the room. But instead of giving in to the intimidation, she smiled. Big and bright. "I understand the severity, which is why I have decided not to press charges against the sheriff or the department."

"Come again?" Holden said, taking off his glasses and leaning forward.

"What?" Jackson bellowed, coming to a stand. "You want to press charges against me?"

Glory kept her eyes on the judge. "I decided to let the matter of Sheriff Duncan keeping me cuffed in a cold cell all night go, since I did dent his cruiser. And his pride."

She heard someone chuckle from behind her. Glory turned and her stomach gave a little flutter. Because her chuckling someone was a giant sexy sight for sore eyes, sitting right behind her in work boots, a snug McGraw Constructions T-shirt, and that protective attitude that made her nervous parts warm a little. Yup, Cal McGraw had strolled into that courtroom sipping on a latte and still managing to look big, badass, and as though he was there for her. He'd strolled up to the table and set down a steaming latte for the defendant, flashing one of his trademarked smiles and releasing those heart-melting dimples her way.

Sure, he hadn't said a word on her behalf. Even took a seat on the prosecution's first row. But that one simple gesture and Glory suddenly hadn't felt as alone.

"It was within my rights as an officer of the law to restrain a suspect who I felt held a risk to my men," Jackson defended.

Glory rolled her eyes and Cal winked. Apparently Judge Holden's BS meter was blowing a gasket, too, because he leveled Jackson with a single look.

"You had to be there. It was a dangerous situation," Jackson defended.

"She was on a tractor, Sheriff. In"—the judge glanced down at the report and back over his glasses at the sheriff—

"pajama bottoms and rubber galoshes. What kind of risk did she pose?"

"She hit me with a cow pie."

"You sure you want to admit to that, son? Here in front of your peers and voters?" A few hushed laughs sounded and Jackson's ears went red. "As far as I am concerned, this whole case is a big waste of my time."

"Noted, sir," Jackson mumbled.

It didn't matter that Jackson was packing or that the judge was dressed to swing a nine iron, not a gavel. One question from the Honorable Eugene Holden in that carry-and-conceal tone was enough to silence the excited murmurs filling the courtroom—and make Jackson take his seat.

Glory smiled. Until the judge turned the weight of his gaze on her. "Now, since you called this meeting, I assume you have information about the stolen tractor that isn't in this report. I'd love to hear it so we can drop all of this nonsense and I can get on to my next appointment."

Which, based on the cleats peeking out under the bench and his golf bag resting against the back wall, was at the Sugar Country Club. Not that Glory pointed that out.

Holden was tough on crime, unwavering when it came to justice, and he was the only judge in the South still on record in support of public lynching as a form of capital punishment. And anything that kept him from his tee time was considered a criminal act.

"I'm sorry, sir," she said.

Cal shifted in his seat, cleared his throat a few times, and sent her enough silent gestures to make up the Sugar High Play Book. Glory sent him a hard look in return.

"Sorry that you're holding information pertinent to the stealing of the mayor's tractor? Or sorry that you called this meeting and yet you aren't going to make this any easier?"

"Sorry, that I can neither confirm nor deny how the tractor ended up in my garage. And thank you for agreeing to meet with us." She looked at the crowd. "Informally."

The honorable judge made a dignified raspberry sound and then looked at Cal. "How about you, son?"

And there went the silent signals again. Cal's eyes met Glory's and she sent him a few gestures of her own. For Jelly Lou, driving her tractor in the Sugar Pull this year meant so much more than a race. It was the end of an era for her grandmother, her last stroll in public with her Ned. And the last shot she'd probably get to do this. So it meant everything to Glory that she got that chance.

Jelly Lou had stood by her through so much, sacrificed her relationship with her son to make sure Glory had a home growing up, loved her like she was her own—even though she wasn't. So there wasn't much Glory wouldn't do for her grandmother—and Cal had to know that, so she gave him one final signal that she hoped he understood.

Please, she mouthed feeling a rush of warm fuzzies when he nodded. She'd kissed Cal only forty-eight hours ago and now there he was, just a few feet away, offering her his support.

"Nothing to add," Cal mumbled, irritation tightening the corners of his lips. "I just posted bail, your honor. As a favor to my brother."

"Uh-huh," Holden mumbled, not believing a word.

Glory, on the other hand, believed every word he'd said. Knew that Cal bailed her out because Brett asked him to, and understood that was why he had shown up there today. So then why, instead of feeling relieved that he didn't rat out the grannies, did his words cause every one of those warm fuzzies to fade into confusion?

Holden took off his glasses and rested them on the desktop and then leaned in—way in so everyone knew just how serious he was. "I've been dealing with your grandmothers' antics and feuding for most of my career. I bet if I added up all the time they spent in my courtroom hollering and pointing fingers, it would account for a good third of my docketed time."

Glory would bet it was more, but wisely kept silent.

"What I should do is toss all three of you out of my court so I can get to my tee-time." If only Glory could be so lucky. "Unfortunately, there is still the matter of a damaged patrol car. And since no one has anything else to add and replacing the bumper, crumpled hood, and leaking coolant system is going to cost the good taxpaying people of this county a pretty penny, it looks as though I'm not going to make that tee-time after all."

And just like that, Glory felt her heart fall to the floor. Any hope she'd had that Holden would let her go with a stern warning vanished when he held up a statement from Kiss My Glass Tow and Tires.

"Because we still have the issue of twenty-three hundred dollars to resolve."

"Twenty-three hundred dollars?"

"And a seven-hundred-dollar fine."

Okay, time to panic. Glory didn't have that kind of money. Nursing school had maxed out her credit cards, and she'd cut back her hours at the bar because of how intense summer classes had been. It would take months of waiting tables and tending bar to make enough tips to pay for that.

"Is there a way I can set up a payment plan?" Glory asked because if he said no then she was completely screwed.

"The system doesn't work that way," he explained and Glory felt the sting of tears. "Which is why I'm sentencing you to two hundred hours community service."

He rapped the gavel—even though this was an *un*official sentencing.

"Community service? Does that go on one's record?"

"Not if you meet the required time by the end of the year."

Glory released a sigh of relief. Between organizing Senior Night at the Fabric Farm and her hours volunteering at the medical center, she could accrue two hundred hours by the end of the year, no problem. More important, her record wouldn't be tarnished. "I think that is fair, your honor."

"Well, I am so glad that you are in agreement." He looked at Jackson. "Sheriff?"

"I think that is fair, your honor," Jackson mumbled.

"I'm glad you both agree," he said, not glad at all. "I was starting to think this was some kind of history repeating itself with a new generation and I'd just as well throw you all in jail for contempt of court. But the paperwork"—he waved a hand—"I'd never get on the green today."

"This isn't history repeating itself," Glory promised, sending Jackson what she hoped was a friendly look. He did not look back—friendly or otherwise.

"You have no idea how pleased I am to hear you say that," Holden said with a smile that had Glory shifting in her seat. "Since you will be serving all of those two hundred hours as the new harvest commissioner."

Shocked gasps filled the room. And Glory did a little gasping of her own. Just hearing her name in reference to the harvest commissioner made her stomach get all tight.

"I can't."

"Excuse me?"

"I mean, that doesn't work for me. Being harvest commissioner doesn't work for me."

Glory didn't have time to take on something as comprehensive as the Harvest Fest. If she intended to finish the

Community Outreach Program proposal in time to present to the hospital board, on top of studying for her finals—which she did because not passing her classes was not an option—then Glory would need every spare second to prepare. Not to mention, the harvest commissioner crowned Miss Peach, and the thought of walking into that ballroom alone brought back way too many emotions she'd worked hard to overcome.

"Yes, well, you'll need to make it work since our former commissioner is currently fishing in the Gulf at the request of her treating nurse." Holden skewered Glory with a glare and she sank farther into her chair. "To make matters worse. Yes, if you can believe it, they do get worse. The only two willing candidates I have are Kitty Duncan and Hattie McGraw, both of whom have been calling my office, my home, my cell, my wife, the country club. Each accusing the other of unsavory practices, which doesn't work for *me*, Miss Mann. So unless you have the funds to pay off the damages today then you will step in as acting harvest commissioner until you have fulfilled your two hundred hours of service or the current commissioner returns to reclaim her seat, whichever happens first."

Glory hadn't even accepted the position and already she felt her heart slamming against her rib cage and the walls around her closing in.

Peg was right. This is what dying feels like.

It was hard enough to overcome your past and move forward, especially when people kept reminding you where you'd been. And in a town with two blinking lights, two restaurants, and two specialties—growing peaches and harvesting prattle—reinventing oneself was difficult. Especially if you were at the heart of the biggest scandal in Sugar's history. Which was why Glory kept her head down, went to school, and did her best to avoid attention—and the Miss Peach Pageant.

There was no position more high-profile than the harvest commissioner—not to mention important to the town. If she screwed this up, and Ms. Kitty would see to it that she would, then all her years of hard work would have been for nothing, and the hospital board might deem her an unfit candidate for the position. So returning to the scene of the crime was not an option. Preferably never, but most certainly not until *after* the board read her proposal.

Judge Holden looked at his watch and stood. "Then there is nothing left to say other than congratulations, Miss Mann."

"Wait." She stood, too, praying to the luck fairies to sway him. Although he didn't look very swayable. "This position means a lot to a lot of people, I'm just not one of them. I don't know a thing about how to run a pageant or a tractor pull and well..." Desperate, Glory admitted the one thing that was sure to change the judge's mind, "I don't even like peaches, your honor."

She heard Cal laugh at her admission, but the rest of the courthouse was silent. Nope, the people of Sugar responded as though she'd admitted she didn't bleed Atlanta Falcons red—which she didn't. Glory might don the red jersey when she tended bar on game nights, but that was just for tips. She hated football. Almost as much as she hated peaches.

"They give me hives," she added right as the courthouse doors blew open and the sudden rustling of fabric on wood benches filled the room as everyone turned—and sucked in an excited breath. Glory, however, nearly passed out.

There in the doorway, dressed in a Jackie O–inspired shift dress, white gloves, and a hat big enough to grace the Kentucky Derby, was Ms. Kitty Duncan with a briefcase in one hand and her bloodhound, The General, leashed to the other.

The sheer level of awe wafting off the audience was enough to make Glory roll her eyes. But the confident gleam in the older woman's eyes made her nervous. Very nervous.

"A peach hater in power. We can't have that, now can we?" Ms. Kitty asked, her pearls clacking together with every step as she strode down the aisle, eyes locked and loaded on the judge as though silently dismissing everyone else. "Which is why, with Peg on leave until fishing season ends, I am more than willing to step up and take charge. I already secured us a new Sugar Pull location and have compiled a list of changes that are long overdue, including rezoning of committee responsibilities, updating Sugar Pull entry qualifications, and I'd like to get some opinions of the menu and design theme I had drawn up for Cotillion."

"Last I checked, this was still my courtroom and my meeting, Kitty," Judge Holden barked. "Not a damn town hall discussion."

Ms. Kitty didn't stop moving until she hit the bench and handed over her new manifesto. One which, Glory was sure, would send Hattie over the edge. Not to mention, somehow exclude Jelly Lou from racing. "Then maybe you should have answered your phone and saved us all some time."

"Didn't need to," Holden said, not even sparing the folder a glance. "I have already appointed a new commissioner." His eyes went to the defense. "I suggest you stock up on Benadryl, Miss Glory, because I see a lot of peaches in your future. Your first meeting as presiding chair will be a week from Wednesday."

"Over my dead my body will a woman of her reputation head up an event so treasured by this town and these people," Kitty said, her hand rising dramatically to include the packed room. "Last time she was allowed to be a part of the pageant, a judge was disqualified, my son was chased out of town, and for the first time in pageant history, there was no crowning ceremony. No Miss Peach."

Someone from the back of the room gave a hearty, "Amen."

"This pageant is about inspiring young woman, instilling in them a sense of inner grace and strength—"

"By telling them they need some tool in a tux to feel validated," Glory heard Cal mumble from his pew. Unfortunately so did Kitty.

"A true Southern belle can't present *herself*, now can she?" Kitty skewered him with a look that would make most men cry.

Not Cal—he leaned back, calm and completely in control. "I don't know, my daughter's been walking just fine on her own since she turned one."

"To be escorted by one's peer is tradition," Kitty argued. "And we need to maintain our traditions, Mr. McGraw." Ignoring him completely, she turned back to the bench and flapped a glossy presentation folder in Judge Holden's direction, "If you read my new guidelines for the Harvest Fest, you'll see my first order of business is to move the Sugar Pull to my property; that way the tractors can be on display for Cotillion."

For Glory, Miss Peach had been so far out of her class and social standing, her decision to enter had been a shock to the community. Not only did she lack the daddy for the daddy-daughter dance at Cotillion, she also lacked the upbringing. Walking into Ms. Kitty's historical plantation home with its dual staircases, circular domed ballroom, and museum-quality décor would be intimidating for any girl. For a girl like Glory, it was like walking into her own personal hell. And that was before she'd been caught with Damon.

"We need someone of strong morals and even stronger

spirit," Kitty went on and Glory was surprised to discover
how a simple reference to her character could still cause her
to burn with shame. How she felt the overwhelming urge to
slip inside the protective bubble of the man sitting a few feet
away. "They need roots, your honor, deep in the community,
that can be traced back generations."

"Excellent point," Holden said, as though he'd just had
a life-altering epiphany. "Which is why I have decided to
place Cal McGraw as co-chair, since he seems to have such
strong opinions on the matter."

"With all due respect, sir," Cal said, jumping to his feet,
because it was obvious he didn't want his life altered. Not
like this. "Hell, no. I am here in a supportive capacity only,
not on trial."

"You sure about that, son?" Holden asked, standing and
picking up his golf bag. "Because we can always take a field
trip out to the parking lot and have you explain to everyone
here about how that tractor-sized dent ended up on the back
of your truck."

Cal had already missed his meeting with the inspector by
the time he walked out of town hall and into the suffocating
morning heat. Summer in Georgia was like living in a sauna;
the weight in the air clung to his skin and shrink-wrapped
his shirt to his body as he made his way toward his car and
tried to shake off what happened back there. At least make
sense of whatever was going on between him and Glory. A
harder task than he imagined.

Boots clicked on the sidewalk behind him. Afraid that it
was Glory rushing out to wrap her arms around him in a giant thank-you hug, which would make him feel all noble and
protective, he picked up the pace until he reached his truck.

He was sticking his key in the lock when an irritated—

and definitely not female voice—asked, "What the hell was that?"

And then Jackson was standing beside him, one broad shoulder propped up against the cab of Cal's truck. He'd put his deputy's hat back on—but his deputy's code of ethics, Cal wasn't so sure.

"I don't know, you tell me," Cal returned. "Aggravated assault of an officer? That's a dick move and you know it."

Jackson blew out a breath. "I was just messing with her. I would have dropped the charges but she jumped the gun and called the judge."

"Since when do you use the badge to screw with people?"

"About the same time you started screwing with trouble," Jackson said, crossing his arms. The innuendo in his tone pissed Cal off. "And showing up with coffee for the defense. Blindsiding me in there was a dick move."

"You made a bad call. Brett went all protective, asked me to stand in for him, and I got suckered into wasting my morning in a courtroom where I was punished for something I had nothing to do with. End of story." The coffee he'd thought of all on his own.

"So that's it?"

Jackson had a way of looking through all the BS and sniffing out the truth; it was what made him the perfect sheriff. So Cal worked hard to school his expression, keeping it carefully blank.

"Yup. That's it."

He knew working alongside the tantalizing and tempting Glory for the next four weeks and keeping his dick in check was going to be hard. Keeping an emotional distance was imperative, though—even when she was wearing a flowy sundress with cute cowgirl boots, which stirred in him something a whole hell of a lot more than mere lust.

Especially then. Because all it would take was one look from her and he'd be toast. Those big mossy eyes would look up at him like they had in the courtroom and he'd start feeling like some kind of hero. And his hero card was tapped out—keeping his daughter's world spinning in the right direction was a full-time job.

Jackson must have been satisfied with Cal's level of sincerity because he clapped him on the shoulder. "Good to hear because trouble seems to follow that woman wherever she goes. And I'd hate to see your family get swept up in her tornado of destruction."

Although he appreciated his friend's concern, he had to acknowledge that Jackson was a bit jaded on the topic of troublesome women. Like Cal, the sheriff had married a woman who was sexy, high maintenance, and always looking for an adventure. And like Tawny, Jackson's ex-wife found her adventure in some other guy's bed. But most of his issues were rooted in what happened back in high school.

"Tornado of destruction." Cal laughed. "Your dad's the mayor. You're the sheriff and Kitty is still running this town by way of intimidation. I don't think your family suffered all that much."

"She ruined Damon's life, man. He hasn't been back since that summer."

"Damon was a grown-ass man who should have known better than to mess with a student."

And Cal was a grown-ass man who knew better than to mess with trouble in a pair of cowgirl boots.

Chapter 7

❧

Several hours later, Glory sat at the back of the Fabric Farm, measuring tape in hand, staring at the magazine cutout Payton placed on her sewing table and hoping to God the girl was joking. Out of the thousands of dresses to choose from, Payton had picked the most revealing option available. It was backless, cleavage-central, and stopped way too high to even be considered mid-thigh.

"Is that what you need me to measure you for?" Glory asked, wondering how, out of all the women at Quilting Night, Payton happened to come to her sewing station for help.

"Yup. It's just like my mom's. Look." Payton pulled out an aged photo from her backpack and held it up. It was of a very young, very beautiful former Mrs. McGraw wearing a pink sash, tiara, and yes, a very similar dress. "This was when she was crowned Miss Georgia State back in college. My dad was her escort. It was their first date."

Which explained so much, Glory thought, feeling less and less confident about her offer to help.

"My mom said she'd order me this one." Back to the magazine photo, only now Payton was clutching it to her chest, her smile so bright it broke Glory's heart. "But she can't come up this weekend."

"That must be hard," Glory said softly. She didn't know a lot about Payton and Tawny's situation, but she'd heard enough through Brett to understand that it wasn't the ideal mommy-daughter relationship—and that often Payton came in a devastating second after Tawny's new family.

"No biggie." Payton shrugged, but her eyes said it was beyond a biggie. "Except the website says this dress takes three weeks for delivery so she needs to order it now, only she doesn't know what size to order." And didn't that say so much. "I need it soon so that my escort can get a matching bow tie for the Miss Peach Pageant."

"I didn't know you were entering the pageant," Glory said causally, wondering if Cal had any clue of her intentions.

"Yup." Payton smiled. "Were you ever a Miss Peach? Is that why they made you the new harvest commissioner?"

"No, not really my thing."

Although that hadn't always been the case. As a girl, Glory had big dreams about being crowned Miss Peach and having her daddy show up. He'd present her to the town at Cotillion and tell everyone who would listen how proud he was of his girl. Then Glory would remember that she wasn't his girl, and that her daddy didn't have a name or a face, and her days of dreaming about crowns and Cotillions were over.

Well, they had been until about six hours ago. And Glory had a feeling this time around Miss Peach would end with the same disappointing results.

"Really? Mom and I have been waiting for me to be old enough for like forever," Payton said, accentuating every syllable of the last word. She opened up her backpack and pulled out a Miss Peach application, complete with a ré-sumé, head shot, and essay. "I got my head shots done a few weeks ago when I went to visit my mom in Savannah. She even helped me with the application, but I wrote the essay all on my own. Last week. It's attached to the back."

Glory looked over the application, smiling at the hearts dotting the *i*'s, and flipped to the essay and…it was all coming together now. Payton's essay was titled, FROM MISS GEORGIA STATE TO MISS PEACH: A FAMILY CONNECTED THROUGH PAGEANTS, and the look on her face was one that Glory knew well.

She flipped back to the application, noticing that one of the guardian signatures was blank. "Your dad didn't sign this."

Payton paused before answering. "Is that a problem?"

Hell yes, it was a problem. First, there was no way she could accept Payton's application behind Cal's back. Sugar was a small town, he was bound to find out, and when he did, he would hate her. And she wouldn't blame him one bit. Second, and most important, he'd kissed her, and even though she'd said it was just a kiss, Glory didn't take kisses lightly, especially not kisses like that, so *Yes, Payton, this is a problem of epic proportions.*

"My mom signed it," Payton explained ever so inno-cently. "And it says at the bottom that I only needed *a* guardian's signature, not both. Just one, see? And I got one."

Glory read the fine print, and just her luck, it did say that.

"Payton, I can't accept this without your dad's signature on it. I need to know that he's okay with you being in the Miss Peach Pageant." It was clear today that Cal was def-initely not the type of father who supported pageants, let alone some guy escorting his daughter around town in a low-

cut dress. He also didn't seem open to the idea of Payton
going on a date—ever.

"But he won't sign it," Payton said quietly. "He'll freak
out like he always does and say this is all about some boy."

"Is this about some boy?"

"No."

Glory raised a brow and Payton smiled, flipping her hair
off her shoulder in a move that was all teenage confidence
and big britches. "I think an upperclassman might offer to be
my escort."

"You mean Brand Riggs?" Glory ventured, and if saucer-
sized eyes and mouth forming the perfect O of shock weren't
confirmation, then Payton's behavior over the past few
months would have been. Especially since all-American, all-
state, and let's-take-it-all-the-way varsity quarterback Brand
Riggs seemed to always be hanging around the Fabric Farm
whenever Payton joined her grandma for Quilting Night.
And if that weren't obvious enough, Payton always needed
to get something from the car at the exact moment Riggs
pulled up.

"Now you see why I have to go," Payton pleaded, then
her eyes went. "Plus, my mom promised to help me with
my makeup and the talent portion and show me how to walk
when I'm presented. Every girl in her family did this. It's my
destiny."

Glory wasn't so sure about the destiny part, but it was obvious that this pageant meant more to Payton than a cute boy
and a crown.

"Didn't you ever want something so bad that you'd do
anything to get it?" Payton asked, and Glory thought back
to being a teen, and wanting to feel special and valued and,
okay yes, wanting it so bad that she was willing to lie and
sneak around to get it.

And look where that got her.

"Have you tried talking to your dad about how much this means to you?"

Payton shot her a look that was all *duh* and disbelief. "Have you been in a room with my dad?" No, but she'd been in his truck, and what she'd learned about him, she'd liked. A lot. But she didn't think that was what Payton meant, so she remained quiet. "He doesn't talk, he dictates."

"He's also the co-chair of the Harvest Council so he's going to see your application."

"I know." Payton blew out a dramatic breath. "Which is why I was hoping you could hold on to it."

"No way." Glory held out the application but Payton pushed it back in her hand.

"Just until my mom comes out to pick me up. She promised she'd talk to him, make everything okay. The cutoff date for applications is next Friday and she won't be out until Saturday, and if I wait until she comes... there isn't time and I won't be able to enter, which is why I came with my grandma tonight so I could give you my application. My mom was supposed to talk to him this weekend, explain how much this means to us, but..."

She was a no-show. Glory got it. More than she wanted to admit.

"Fine," Glory said, and the minute the word left her mouth, she felt awful. A big part of her job as a nurse was discreetness, but this felt different. It felt like a lie and she didn't like lies. As far as she was concerned, omitted truths were just as harmful, but she also understood why Payton wanted this so badly.

To a fourteen-year-old girl whose parent had left for greener pastures—and another shiny new family—the pageant was a way of reconnecting with her mom, giving them common ground, and giving Payton something that Tawny could take interest in. Something that her new family couldn't provide. Another Miss in the family.

"Just until next Friday."

"Ohmygod! Are you serious?" Payton launched herself at Glory, giving her a hug that went a long way toward easing the guilt. "Thank you so much."

"Don't thank me yet." Glory pulled back, getting eye to eye with Payton, wanting to be sure that they were clear on things. "I'm not going to hide it from your dad. I will simply put it in with the stack of others, but if you and your mom don't talk to him by next weekend, then I will point yours out. Understood?"

The teen nodded excitedly.

"I want to be clear, though," Glory added, hating that she felt like she was betraying Cal somehow. "Your dad is amazing and he loves you and I still think that you should come clean and tell him how important this is to you." Payton opened her mouth to argue and Glory held up a hand. "So I am only agreeing to this because there is a time issue, not because I think your dad shouldn't know or have a say. So, if Cal isn't okay with it, you forfeit your spot. Period. No begging, no arguing, no pitting your parents against each other."

Payton busied herself checking her cuticles. A telltale sign that that was *exactly* what she was planning on doing if things didn't go her way.

"So, if he says no, it is the official ruling of this committee and there will be no Miss Peach for you this year. Deal?" Glory stuck out her hand.

"Deal," Payton relented. "Who are you going with?"

"No one."

"What?" she said horrified. "You can't walk in there stag. It just isn't done."

Didn't she know it? Glory had thought of that the second she'd walked out of that courtroom and realized just what being a co-chair would entail. Then she remembered how Cal showed up for her, and wondered what it would feel like to walk into that Cotillion on his arm. To show up to the biggest event of the year with Sugar's most respected bachelor, and for once feel like she belonged, like she was starting out on top instead of defending her right to be there.

Then she thought about how he'd disappeared before Glory could even utter a simple thanks, pushing through the crowd as though there was a family emergency. And who knew, with his grandma maybe there was. But somehow it felt as though he was running from her.

She looked down at her tape measure and finally thought about how she was going to measure his daughter for a dress that was more hoochie than high-class and said, "Nothing's wrong with going stag."

"Uh-huh," Payton said, so not convinced.

"Can I give you a piece of advice?"

"I guess," Payton said skeptically, as though advice from someone pathetic enough to go stag wasn't a good idea. And it probably wasn't. But Glory was pretty sure the girl would agree to the Ten Commandments if it meant Glory keeping her secret for a while. "The kind of guy you bring home to your dad should be someone who is sweet and respectful. A guy he would be comfortable giving his permission to take you out. A guy who"—and here went the part that Glory had wished someone had told her—"will respect you and treasure you and treat you like you matter. Because you do."

And that guy was not Brand Riggs. A guy who was notorious for his aggressive offense and fast hands—on and off the field.

"Thanks," Payton whispered and gave Glory another

hug—and it felt great. She pulled back and wiped her eyes. "Do you think you can help me with my measurements?"

"Sure," Glory said, a rush of warmth filling her chest at their little moment. "And if you ask me, the blue dress on the other page would look amazing on you. It is sophisticated, understatedly elegant, very Miss Peach. Plus it matches your eyes."

"It does, huh?" Payton picked up the magazine and studied the more age-appropriate floor-length gown, which said sweet, respectable, 100 percent Daddy-approved, then said, "Maybe next year. This year I want to make a statement."

It made a statement all right, one that was going to give Cal a coronary. That dress wasn't interested in courting sweet or respectable; it was all about finding trouble—with the school's most famous player.

"What in God's name were you thinking?"

Glory closed her car door and did her best to ignore the welcoming committee. In the barn, dressed in peach coveralls and the most bedazzled ball caps known to man, were Jelly Lou and her Pit Crew Mafia: MeMaw, Dottie, Hattie, and Etta Jayne. Bills pulled low over their eyes, grease marring their faces like war paint, they stood around the Pitter, tools in hand looking like an official NASCAR team—except with orthopedic shoes. Bright white ones.

"You'll have to be more specific," Glory said, thinking over her hellish day.

"Asking me and Hattie to take your grandma to her therapy so we'd both miss your hearing," Etta Jayne said, shooting Glory "the eye."

Glory looked over at her grandmother, who was looking back awfully disappointed.

Glory didn't do well with disappointing people, especially people she loved. Which was why she failed to mention the special hearing with Judge Holden today. Yes, Jelly Lou did have a physical therapy session which she couldn't miss, but Glory didn't want any of the Pit Crew Mafia speaking up and costing Jelly Lou the Sugar Pull—or Glory her shot at landing that new position at the hospital.

And okay, lying was hard enough, but doing it in front of the few people who looked at Glory as if she mattered was not going to happen.

So she pulled an extra shift at the hospital, avoided checking in on Jelly Lou until she had gone to bed last night, hoping that she could talk to the judge, work something out in private, and pray her grandma never found out.

Only she had. That much was clear.

"I'm sorry, Grandma."

"No, dear, I am," Jelly Lou said with heartfelt understanding, rolling her chair closer. "I can't believe they have you planning the pageant."

"It's just a pageant."

Glory resisted the urge to check if her pants were on fire for that lie.

"We both know that it's not just a pageant." And it wasn't, but it had really been a long time ago and Glory had moved on. She was ready for the town to move on. "I'm going to tell the judge the truth. There is no way he can expect you to oversee it."

"No, Grams. Please don't. I am fine." Glory must not have looked fine because all five ladies looked at her with so much pity Glory wanted to cry. But since that would only get Jelly Lou disqualified, she threw back her shoulders and said, "I promise, I'm over it. It was years ago; no one probably even remembers."

The grannies all exchanged concerned looks.

"I am the new commissioner and I am not going to let Ms. Kitty or anyone else scare me off." Not again. "I didn't tell you about the hearing because I wanted to handle it myself."

"Great to hear it." Etta Jayne was so convinced that she went from sympathetic to shotgun-serious. "But your little stunt gave that Kitty Duncan all the headway she needed to hijack the Harvest Council. Already got a manifesto floating around town and is pretending like Jesus is on her side."

"Which doesn't matter since I'm the new harvest commissioner." She thought of how stressed and shocked Cal had looked and groaned. "Well, co-commissioner."

Poor guy had come to offer support and she'd sucked him right into her never-ceasing drama. Then, six hours later, she accepted his daughter's application and agreed to hide it from him.

"That's why I gathered the girls," Jelly Lou said, placing a reassuring hand on Glory's arm, then giving it two of her little *we got this* squeezes, which never ended well for anyone involved.

"Oh no," Glory whispered, a knot forming behind her right eye as she flopped back against the hood of her car. "The last time you all 'gathered,' I was arrested for grand theft auto. The time before that, my boyfriend Leon was found hog-tied to the town's flagpole. Naked."

"Because we found him with his flagpole at full mast, waving in the breeze at that co-ed from Georgia Tech," Hattie said, and sadly, it was true. Glory's final attempt at finding true love had been with a guy who suffered from penile ADHD.

"Saved you years of hurt and a few diseases," Dottie said with a smile. "You should be thanking us."

"Should I also thank you for the time you used my picture

on Match.com and I ended up with a bar full of single men calling me Etta Jayne?"

"I was scoping them out, seeing which ones had potential to handle a woman like myself," Etta Jayne defended.

"Here's how we see it," Hattie said. "Ms. Kitty got to plead her case in a court of law. Now it's our turn. That woman is a cheat, she's using illegal tractor parts, and we have proof."

Glory took a deep breath and held out her hand. She'd had enough experience with the blue-haired brigade to know that they weren't going to let this go until they felt they were heard. And that they'd won. "Let me see your *proof*."

Etta Jayne smacked her hand away and looked around suspiciously. When she was satisfied that no one was spying, she gave a nod. Hattie reached into the front pocket on her jumpsuit and pulled out a Ziploc.

One look and Glory sighed. "Your proof is moldy hay?"

"Hay from the Duncans' barn and that isn't mold on there."

"Please don't tell me that you broke back into Ms. Kitty's barn while I was sitting in jail?"

"Okay, we won't tell you then," Hattie said, unfazed. "Plus, we didn't know you were in the pokey until later. Now smell this."

Before Glory could refuse, Hattie opened the bag and stuck it under Glory's nose. Pungent enough to singe her nostrils, Glory grimaced and pulled back. "What is that?"

"*That* is the smell of a cheat," Etta Jayne said, victory lacing every syllable. "Green E15 fuel."

Glory rubbed her temples. Day one into her new role as commissioner and already she needed a fishing trip. "Your big evidence is that Kitty uses green gas in her tractor?"

"It wasn't in her tractor yet; otherwise you would have

had quite a ride the other night. But she's got to be hiding Green E15 somewhere on her property."

"So?"

"So?" Hattie said. "She's got 98 octane fuel which is specially engineered stuff that is hard to get your hands on, unless you own a NASCAR team or work for one. Last month, my youngest grandson, Jace, said he saw Ms. Kitty in Atlanta, taking in a NASCAR race. From the owners' booth!"

"Now what would a prissy pearl like her be doing at a NASCAR race?" Etta Jayne hissed, her hands shaking.

"Buying Green E15?" Glory guessed.

"Buying Green E15 is right!" Hattie clapped her hands. "Which means she's got to have some kind of illegal parts under her hood."

Jelly Lou placed her hand on Glory's. "And as the new commissioner, dear, it's your job to expose her for being in direction violation of Sugar Pull Bylaw 22B, which clearly states she's stacking the cards, and therefore should be disqualified."

"There are Sugar Pull Bylaws?"

"Asks the new commissioner," Etta muttered, disappearing into the barn, only to return holding a leather-bound book.

One look and Glory knew that she was screwed. It was the size of Atlanta's phone book, looked more intimidating that any human anatomy text Glory had ever owned, and based on the spine cracked from extensive use and the overwhelming mothball scent, predated Etta Jayne. Quite possibly the town of Sugar itself.

Etta Jayne flipped to the middle, a dog-eared page that had a rainbow of faded pencil and highlighter marks. Her eyes settled on a pink block at the top of the page and read,

"All tractors are to remain true to the tradition and intent of the race. Any parts outside factory specifications post-1939 need to be made in the spirit of fairness and equality." She looked up. "Meaning rich folks can't pimp out their tractor just for the sake of making it faster, because then the regular folks wouldn't stand a chance."

Glory looked at Jelly Lou. "You added a harness to yours."

"That's a safety upgrade," Jelly Lou said sweetly.

"Completely legal." Etta Jayne flipped to another section, a yellow one. "Like the Seatbelts Addendum of '66 or, here"—more flipping—"if a company suddenly ceases making a particular part and finding a replacement part or used parts becomes impossible, then the participant may bring their replacement technology to the commissioner for consideration."

Etta Jayne went through the entire process and Glory found herself drifting off. Bylaws were as boring as football.

"Then, after careful evaluation, a consensus may form, which may lead to a new technology being adopted by the Harvest Council and incorporated into the bylaws."

Glory looked at the bag of hay. "And Green E15 isn't bylaw approved."

"Green fuel isn't even street approved. Which means Kitty's breaking the rules again." Etta Jayne snapped the book shut and handed it over to Glory. "And you, Miss Commissioner, need to disqualify her. Before the Harvest Council meeting."

Chapter 8

⌒

Cal was screwed.

He looked at his in-box filled with more than three dozen messages, all concerning the Harvest Fest, and scowled. How had this happened? Again? His life had gone from chaos to bat-shit crazy in the single slam of a gavel.

He'd agreed to do Brett a favor. A simple show up and give your support kind of deal that should have ended with Cal looking like the good guy. Nothing to it. Instead he was sentenced to do four weeks hard time sharing a social cell with the only woman in town who managed to turn him inside out.

A soft, warm, *sexy* woman who, even if he wasn't determined to keep his sex life outside the Sugar County limits, was drama personified. Way too much drama seemed to follow Glory for him even to consider dropping by to make sure she was doing all right.

The instant he'd entered that courtroom, saw the crowd of people, he knew he was walking into a shitstorm. Even told himself to turn around, get back in his truck, and go to work. He had an inspector to meet, a foundation to finish, and trouble in a sexy sundress to avoid. But Glory had looked back at him, saw the extra coffee in his hand, her big green eyes widened with surprise and then relief—relief that she wasn't in this mess alone—and he had taken his damn seat in the front row.

Maybe it was because he felt bad for her. Or maybe it was because of that soft yellow sundress she wore, the one that floated around her knees and made her look younger than he remembered. Lost even. As though it was her against the world. Which it was. So he'd stayed and now he was screwed.

The doorbell rang. Cal snapped his laptop shut and made his way to the front door. He opened it and nearly toppled over his lawn boy.

Dressed in varsity red and wearing a SUGAR SHEEP FOOTBALL cap with the school's mascot peeking out from between the two *e*'s, Mason looked ready to hurl.

"You okay, son?" Cal said apologetically while gripping the kid's bony shoulders and righting him. "Didn't see you there."

Mason just nodded, took off his cap to wipe his forehead, put it back on, and nodded again.

"Ah, hell." Cal patted his pocket, looking for his wallet. "I forgot to pay you again, didn't I?" He knew how hard the kid worked and how most of his money went to help out his mom.

"Yes, well...no, sir." The kid quickly pulled off his ball cap and cupped the bill. "I mean, yes sir, you owe me for two weeks, but I'm not here on business."

Cal had to bite back a smile. He liked this kid. Always on time, a hard worker, respectful. A real standup guy. And it looked like he was ambling for a raise. One that he more than deserved.

Cal folded his arms and leaned casually against the doorjamb, giving Mason time to state his price. "All right. What are you here for then?"

"Well, sir, I'm here for Payton."

"No," Cal said and, smile gone, slammed the door. Only to reopen it, right as Mason was getting ready to knock again. "And you're fired. Worst lawn boy I ever had."

Cal went to slam the door again but Mason wedged his foot between the door and the jamb. Cal raised a challenging brow.

Mason swallowed, wiped his hands on his pants. "Sorry to hear that, sir. But like I said, I'm not here to talk about work. I came because I'm Payton's Cleats and Pleats Pep-Luck chaperone."

The kid lifted his foot to show off his spanking new cleats, as though that would make Cal say, "Why the hell not, kid. Take my fourteen-year-old for a joy ride on that big bench seat in your truck."

"Is that right?"

"Yes, sir. And I'm starting by driving her to the school." He looked over his shoulder at the POS rusted pickup in the drive. "I've got flowers in the car that might wilt, so if you could just tell her that I'm—"

The kid went silent. Eyes dilated, lips subtly twitching, breathing nonexistent. Cal knew the look. He'd given it a time or two. In fact, he'd given it just the other day in Judge Holden's courtroom.

"Oh hey, Mason," Payton sang sweetly from behind Cal.

"Hey, um." The kid swallowed, his ears going pink. "Morning, Payton."

Cal turned and saw exactly why Mason was practically

choking on his tongue. His daughter stood at the top of the stairs wearing white tennis shoes, a tight red skirt with a crap-ton of slits and a barely there matching red top that had TEAM BAAAAAD plastered across the chest. Her hair was slicked up in some complicated do that even with the pristine red bow said piece-of-tail instead of ponytail.

"What the hell is that?"

Payton, hands out to the sides, gave a twirl. "My uniform."

"What happened to the sweats?"

"That's my practice uniform. This is game day uniform."

"Last year it was..." Cal's hands made billowing gestures around his chest. "Baggy and had sleeves and covered"— more billowing—"you."

Payton laughed and gracefully bounded down the stairs, ponytail and polyester shirt swishing back and forth. Cal heard Mason sigh.

"Daddy, last year I wore a sweater because I was on JV. Now I'm on varsity." She leaned up and kissed Cal on the cheek, and he felt a bead of panic rise up and take hold. He could tell by her animated tone, the confident way she spoke, that his little girl was going to drop some mature, responsible reason that somehow made fabric scraps acceptable fashion. "The cheer constitution says that I have to wear it." And there it was. That ridiculous list of rules some twenty-something coach typed up on her little laptop and passed off as law.

"You look great," Mason said.

"Thanks, Mase." She smiled serenely and swished side to side, drawing her skirt up higher and *Mase's* eyes down lower.

"Yeah, well *my* constitution gives me the right to bear arms." He glared at Mason, who took a step back, then at

Payton. "And to point them at any guy who decides to look twice at you *or* your uniform. Understand? So either throw on a pair of those leggings you just *had* to buy last week or you'll spend the pep rally sitting right next to your dad. Got it?"

"God, you're impossible!" And there went the stomping, and the dramatic sighing, and the slamming of the doors.

Cal exhaled and turned around to find Mason, foot still wedged between the door, hat in hand. "Didn't I fire you?"

"Yes, sir." He didn't move.

"Then why are you still here?"

Mason swallowed and exhaled a big breath before puffing out his chest and opening his mouth to—*sweet Jesus*, the kid was going to run through his entire spiel again.

Cal held up a hand. "Pep-Luck chaperone. Got it."

Mason smiled.

Cal looked at the determined, but respectful, gleam in the kid's eye and almost smiled himself—almost. He had to admire him. No doubt, the kid had balls.

Which was exactly why he wasn't letting Mason anywhere near Payton.

"Tell me something, Mason. You got kids? A daughter I don't know about?"

"God, sir, no," Mason sputtered.

"Then as far as I can tell, you don't have the qualifications to be a chaperone. Now move the foot or Sugar High will need to find a new kicker."

The kid moved and Cal shut the door, leaning back against it and closing his eyes. When had his life become so damn complicated? It felt like just last week he was crawling around on all fours in a saddle and veil playing princess ponies with Payton. Now she had suitors with truck beds and a smile like her mama.

* * *

"What kind of woman do you think I am?" Ms. Kitty asked from the other side of the coffee table as she set down her teacup with a clatter. "Questioning what parts a woman has under her hood. And in her own home no less."

The exact reason Glory had been hesitant about confronting Ms. Kitty at the Duncan Plantation. Accusing the woman who had made it the town's agenda to ruin Glory's life was bad enough. Having to do it on Kitty's home court made her palms sweat.

But Ms. Kitty argued that since it was Glory who had called the meeting, it should happen at Glory's inconvenience, not hers. Etta Jayne had argued that she was just trying to buy time to cover up the crime and if Glory didn't take action, she would—and was then spotted at the Frank Brothers' Taxidermy, Ammo, and Fine Jewelry, purchasing a pair of night-vision goggles and a stun gun. Judge Holden argued that any more arguing would result in additional community service for the co-commissioners.

Which was how Glory wound up sitting on a formal wingback chair in her work uniform, facing down not one, not two, but three generations of Miss Peaches, who were in the middle of the annual Miss Peach Tea. An army of cashmere sweaters and matching pumps took up every available toile-covered settee in the grand salon, looking onto their leader for direction.

It was as though every Miss Peach was in attendance, pearls swinging, tittering with excitement. Well, every Miss Peach except Etta Jayne, who seated herself right next to Glory—stating her alliance.

Glory was tittering, too, but not with excitement—with nerves. She couldn't imagine spending any more of her two hundred hours of community service in a place that reminded her repeatedly that she didn't belong. Everything was cream or gold. And regardless if it was cream or gold, it was polished. So polished that all Glory could think about was her cowgirl boots. Red and well-worn, they were discolored from years of slinging beer and bound to scuff something.

And they matched the rest of her work uniform. Which was itty bitty, Falcon inspired, and so short that the toile cushion stuck to the backs of Glory's legs. She wanted to be in something delicate and classy, something that made her feel pretty, but she didn't have time for pretty. After leaving here, she'd have to rush to make it to work in time for the opening shift.

The result: Glory had never felt so out of place in all her life—and that was saying a lot.

"An unnamed source has approached me to express a concern about the possible use of unsanctioned fuel, which if accurate would put that tractor and its owner in direct violation of Bylaw 22B, maintaining a fair and equal standard," Glory said, proud of how official she sounded. She was exhausted and now knew more about tractor engines than most mechanics, but reading the entire Sugar Pull Handbook, all 287 bylaws and 92 addendums, was worth it for this one moment. "It would also violate Bylaw 136, use of a highly controlled flammable substance to gain an advantage."

"She means that Green E15 you've got in your barn," Etta Jayne said.

There were a few gasps, followed by some heart patting, and Glory concentrated on not rolling her eyes. So much for trying *not* to draw attention to her "confidential" source.

"Which could result in the possible violation 18B," Glory continued. "Unintentional combustion or smoldering of the hosting orchard without prior consent."

"Prior consent, huh?" Cal mused from the wingback chair beside her.

She'd never been so aware of a man before. His scent, the way he crossed his legs—ankle over knee, bringing his thigh mere inches from her hand—even the way he sounded when he breathed. From the moment she'd pulled into Kitty's drive and saw him leaning against his truck in his contract-for-hire gear, waiting for her, Glory had felt that tug. The one that started in her chest and traveled south of the border.

Cal McGraw was impossible to ignore. A sentiment that seemed to be universal for women everywhere. He'd said three words the entire meeting, and even holding a dainty cup, he'd instantly grabbed the attention of every female in the room.

"What if it is an intentional combustion or smoldering?" he said, and the female gallery listened intently as though he'd just asked for the meaning of life.

"Then that would be a 19A infraction," Glory said primly, eyes on Kitty. "And would result in a lifetime expulsion."

"Are you accusing me of illegal practices and making threats in front of my guests, Miss Glory?" Ms. Kitty lifted her tea and took a measured sip as though she wasn't the one on trial.

"She's doing her job, Ms. Kitty," a stunning blonde said as she crossed the room. Willowy, cultured, and probably the most elegant Miss Peach in the history of the pageant, Charlotte Holden was a Southern belle in every sense of the word. She was also the current regent of the Sugar Peaches—so any pageant decisions made would need her approval. "Making sure that everyone is following the rules."

Ms. Kitty smiled serenely as Charlotte took a seat on the other side of Glory. "Well, then I will chalk her behavior up to ignorance, rather than an intentional attack on my character. And I didn't know you were coming. Your mother said you were at the hospital this morning."

"I am the current regent of the Sugar Peaches and a four-time Miss Peach." Charlotte matched that smile, only it had a bigger impact on the room. "There was no way I'd miss the fun. Now, why don't you explain your side then we can get to the luncheon."

"My pleasure." Ms. Kitty slid an official-looking paper across the table. Glory leaned forward to pick it up, the heavy scent of magnolia blossoms and Aqua Net thickening the closer she got to the Peach Gallery. Wrinkling her nose, she snatched the invoice, leaned back as far as she could, and read through it—twice. Then looked up and met the older woman's eyes. They were smug. "Any upgrade to a tractor or its engine approved by the harvest commissioner is legal. And as you can see, the new fuel pump and lines on the Prowler needed replacing, and since the manufacturer doesn't make my model anymore, Peg approved a new install, with modifications to keep it sanctioned, of course."

"Let me see that," Etta Jayne said, snagging the form. She perched her reading glasses, which hung on a camouflaged lanyard, on her nose. "Peg would never approve racing parts."

"She didn't. I had a new John Deere pump installed. Read the form."

Etta Jayne did. Then frowned and glared over her half-rims. "John Deere doesn't make parts that work with Green E15."

"Exactly." Kitty narrowed her eyes. "So before you start pointing fingers and stealing tractors, you need to check your facts. And the facts state that you were wrong. Not that any of us are surprised." Before anyone could argue, Kitty looked at Glory and added, "Now, if you have any other concerns, I suggest you address them to the former harvest commissioner."

Etta Jayne scooted so far to the end of her chair that Glory was certain she was going to fall off. "She's in the Gulf and you know it!"

"Not my fault." A room full of eyes settled on Glory and she felt her face heat.

Of course, the one person who could confirm or deny the authenticity of this install was fishing in the middle of the ocean—at her request.

"But since I don't want to waste any more of the committee's time on this nonsense, why don't you talk to my mechanic, Lavender Spencer. I believe her shop, Kiss My Glass Tow and Tires, is still a committee-approved mechanic."

And there went any chance the ladies had for winning this argument. Spencer could rebuild anything with an engine, never took shit from anyone, and was honest to a fault. Meaning she couldn't be bribed and wouldn't hesitate to lay out Ms. Kitty if she started throwing her power around.

Glory knew it. Kitty knew it. And the whole room knew it. If Spencer did the install, then it was up to regulation. No question.

"Or you can lift up your hood and end the speculation once and for all," Etta Jayne said. Glory was pretty sure Etta Jayne would have launched herself at Kitty if Cal hadn't placed his hand on her chubby knee, restraining her in her seat.

"So you can see what makes a winning machine? Steal my secrets?" Kitty snapped back. "What's under my hood is my business and the founding council agreed, which is why if you want a look, then you'll have to bring me a signed order from the council saying you have the right to look. Until then, stay out of my bay."

"Well, then Glory will give the order right now, won't you, Glory?" Etta Jayne said smugly.

"On what grounds?" Kitty asked. "Moldy hay? Harvest commissioner or not, she needs real evidence to get the whole council's approval. Anything else would look like an abuse of power for her family's gain."

"Hold on, there are two commissioners here, and no one's abusing anyone's anything," Cal said, setting his teacup on the side table, and Glory felt herself actually take in a breath. "As the new co-chairs, we're finding our way through this and we want to make sure everything goes smoothly. And that includes people being heard, following up on concerns, and upholding the rulebook. Right, Glory?"

She looked at him and nodded. She didn't know what else to do. It was such a silly thing, but Glory hadn't had a man stand up for her in such a long time that it felt strange. And nice. And a tad bit scary.

"Handbook," she corrected and smiled up at him.

"Handbook." He smiled back and addressed the room. "So why don't we table this discussion until next Wednesday's Harvest meeting? It will give Glory and I a chance to follow up with Spencer."

"I think that's a wonderful idea," Charlotte said. "Don't you, Kitty?"

"Wonderful," Ms. Kitty deadpanned and stood. The sounds of twenty pairs of heels hitting the floor as the majority of the room rose echoed off the marble tiles. "The former Miss Peaches and I are already behind on our schedule. We have taken the liberty to come up with some ideas for the theme and décor to share with the council on Wednesday. So if there are no other objections, then I assume you can show yourselves out."

Glory did have objections. The first being that Ms. Kitty

was hijacking the pageant. Her pageant. Not that Glory had
wanted the position of commissioner but now that she had it,
she didn't want Kitty taking over.

Second, there was no way in hell the pageant would be
held there. She couldn't imagine some poor girl who wasn't
a part of the "in" crowd feeling comfortable entering that
place. But as she looked around the room and found everyone looking back, her stomach bottomed out. Kitty knew
once the Peaches were reminded of just how regal her family's three story, twenty-seven-room plantation home was,
complete with a grand ballroom, which had hosted everyone
from celebrities to presidents over the years, getting them to
agree to another venue would be impossible.

Glory had been played. This entire meeting was an intentional violation of 22B. Hosting the pageant, inviting
the former Miss Peaches, inviting Glory over at a time
so that she'd have to go straight to work afterward—and
would show up in her uniform—hadn't maintained fair and
equal standards. Nope, Ms. Kitty in her perfect house, with
her perfect reputation, and her perfectly laid out plans only
highlighted all of Glory's imperfections.

But when Glory went to open her mouth, Charlotte gently touched her hand and whispered, "Not now, Glory.
Wait until you're calling the meeting, then you can call the
shots."

Glory nodded and with a wink Charlotte stood and followed the other Miss Peaches as they headed toward the
ballroom, talking in excited voices about what color lace
should billow from the chandeliers. Glory went to stand, but
found her legs wouldn't hold her. She was tired of always
being on the losing side.

"Unintentional smoldering?" Cal asked quietly. He stood
and his arm brushed her, just barely, but enough so the hard

muscle against her warm skin created some serious sparks. "Did you memorize the entire handbook?"

"No." She looked up at him and, *call the fire department*, smoldering didn't even begin to describe the look he gave her. He was smiling, dimples flashing for her alone, and then those intense blue eyes locked on hers and for a brief moment everything seemed to disappear and Glory didn't feel like the loser. Didn't even feel out of place. With him looking at her like that, she actually felt like she belonged. "Just the parts that were useful."

"And sanctioned combustion and smoldering laws peaked your interest?"

"Anything that evens the playing field with Ms. Kitty peaks my interest." Glory remembered the full room and felt her confidence sink. "Not that it mattered. There is no way anyone will take me seriously with her in charge."

"According to a district court justice, they have to take you seriously," he said with a smile.

"Tell that to Kitty. I mean the woman amassed a cashmere army of experts. How can I compete with that?"

"First of all, you don't have to compete. Ever," he said and her stomach tingled. "You just be you. People want options, so give them some. And if they still won't listen, then amass your own army of experts. "

There was so much confidence in his voice that even though she didn't know any experts in the pageant world, she didn't feel so hopeless.

Cal offered her his hand and she took it. A warm zing started in her fingers and spread out across her entire body as he helped her up—and right into his chest. His big, strong, yummy male chest.

"I need an army then," she admitted. "Because we can't have the pageant here."

"And why's that?" he asked quietly, still holding her hand.

She looked around at the domed ceilings, the art on the walls, the crystal chandeliers, and her chest started pinching again. It was all too much. Suffocating for a girl from the sticks. Too many chairs to choose from, too many rules to remember, too many memories to fight all at once. "Too many bedrooms."

"You have a thing against bedrooms, boots?"

She looked down at her cowgirl boots and then gave him the one reason he'd side with. "You know what a group of high school boys would do with access to a few dozen teenaged girls and twenty-seven bedrooms?"

His eyes dropped to her mouth and she felt her lips throb. Then a warm tingle started in her belly and slid lower so she had to fight the urge not to squirm in her boots. "You're right, bad idea."

What the hell was he doing? Nothing good, that was for sure.

Cal dropped her hand and took a step back. It was safer than touching her while talking about bedrooms and what he'd like to do in them—with her. Which was a lot.

He'd come here to do his job, make sure the issues were resolved without bloodshed, then report back to Judge Holden. Not that he was thinking about his job or Holden now. Nope, that honor went to Glory. Not sexy nurse Glory or soft sundress-wearing Glory, but beer-slinging, red-lipped saloon Glory in her inspiring top and fantasy-inducing boots that, if they were to make it to one of those twenty-seven bedrooms, he'd beg her to keep on.

She was all soft curves with heart-stopping beauty, her exotic eyes locked on his mouth as though she was remembering their kiss, too—as though she might be open to leaving the boots on if he asked. That was to say nothing for the way her ass looked in that skirt. *Jesus*, it started below her navel and had just enough denim to cover her cheeks, exposing a pair of legs that left him with a hard-on, twenty-seven bedrooms, and three different Glorys to choose from.

The damndest thing, though? Cal wasn't sure which one he'd choose. He couldn't keep his eyes—or his hands—off the Glory in front of him now. But it was the vulnerable Glory, the one who'd sat in his truck in a pair of torn galoshes and flannel bottoms that drew him in, spoke to his true inner nature, the side that wanted nothing more than to pull her in and protect her. And somehow that Glory was the one looking up at him from beneath all the makeup and sweet curves.

"Why did you come, Cal?"

He could have lied. Should have made up some story about doing Brett a favor. But this decision had been all his. At breakfast Hattie started yapping about illegal fuel and Glory throwing the book at Kitty and he figured she'd need some backup. The next thing he knew, he was here and not at work overseeing the biggest project in his company's history. "Like I said inside, there are two chairmen. You and I are in this together."

"When I saw you standing there..." She shook her head and swallowed. "Not a lot of men would risk a room full of pageant queens talking color palettes and tasting menus to rescue me."

There it was. The reminder that he needed. Because Glory was looking for "that Cal," the one who did the right thing. And the right thing didn't include thinking about her ass in that skirt. Especially because that ass and its owner were co-chairing a committee with him.

"I just spent a weekend surrounded by a giggly cheerleading team and their moms," he said, ushering her toward the front door. He needed to walk her to her car, erase any fantasy he had about finding out what was beneath that skirt, since the two of them together would lead to nothing but trouble, and send her on her way. "Color palettes are a breeze compared to boy and makeup talk."

"Oh, that's right. The Pep-Luck was Saturday. How did it go?" Her legs struggled to keep in step with his longer ones, so he slowed his pace.

"It went."

"That bad?"

"She made me drop her off at the front of the school, then go find parking so I'd have to meet her inside." Actually she had ignored him the entire ride.

"Ouch." Glory slid him an amused look and he wanted to ask what was so damn funny. Nothing about Saturday had been amusing.

"You drove her?" she asked as he opened the front door.

"Yeah."

"Wasn't she paired up with Mason Simms?"

The bright August sun radiated off the circular drive, immediately causing sweat to bead on his skin. He could almost feel the humidity clogging his lungs, making it hard to breathe. Or maybe it was the sound of the prick's name.

Nope, it was the way Glory looked in that skirt when she walked. The swish swish of her hips as she headed to the driver's door of her car sent that skirt of hers on a trip due north and left him to wonder what color panties she had on—because it was clear she wasn't wearing much else under there.

"Oh no," she said. "I know that look."

"What look?" Was he *that* transparent?

"This one." She scrunched her face and glared. It should

have been scary as hell to be hit with that look, but on her it only managed to look adorable. "Brett gets it sometimes when he's being stubborn. Which means you didn't let her go with her football chaperone."

Oh, *that* look. "Hell, no I didn't. She's fourteen. She doesn't need some boy sniffing around. What she needed was to go to the Pep-Luck with her dad."

"Are you listening to what you are saying?" When he didn't answer, she reached in her purse, fished out her keys, and then looked him right in the eye and laughed. She laughed. At him. "You had the perfect scenario, Cal. A respectful kid wanted to take your daughter to the *school* for pancakes during the light of day at a school-sponsored event. With *you* chaperoning."

When put like that, it sounded almost innocent. But Cal knew better. He'd been a respectful kid once upon a time. Being respectful was a key factor to getting laid when you were a teen. Just ask Brett.

Cal grabbed her keys, thrust them into her lock, twisted, yanked, and wrenched open her door. He handed her back the keys. "The kid's lucky I didn't show him into last year."

"He mowed my grandma's lawn last week just to buy Payton some flowers. He's a good kid."

"He's a boy. They lose their ability to be good after they discover boobs."

"You do hear yourself, right?" She dropped one hand to her waist, that shirt of hers riding up high enough for him to make out a little flower tattooed on her right hipbone, proving his point.

"Yup."

The other hand went to her hip, and Cal had a hard time not looking at her tanned midriff. But he didn't want to get distracted. He'd had his share of women since his divorce. Even dated a few of them. But never once had he talked about his daughter. Either it wasn't the kind of date that required personal information, or the woman hadn't been interested. But Glory not only looked interested in Payton's life, she looked like she genuinely cared. And she also looked at him like she thought he'd made a mistake.

He leaned back against the side of her car and crossed his arms. "What would you have done?"

"Me?"

"Yeah, you seem to have an opinion on this. Are you saying that if your daughter shows up dressed for a night waiting tables at Hooters, starts arguing about how not all boys are trying to get in her kick pants, and then some kid shows up at the door ready to take her away in some…sex wagon, you'd let her go?"

"Yes." She smiled up at him as though she thought he was cute. He scowled. "You raised a great daughter, Cal. Payton is smart and sensitive and has a good head on her shoulders. Let her practice those skills you worked so hard to teach her. And to be clear, Mason drives a pickup, too rusty and small to be considered a wagon, sex or otherwise."

"I drive a pickup." He looked at her lips. "And look what happened with us."

She laughed, but when she spoke, her voice was serious. "The Pep-Luck is a big deal and a huge honor for a sophomore. Mason understood that, even made sure he picked Payton up because she's the only girl on varsity who doesn't have a license and he didn't want her to be embarrassed."

"By what? Me?" He felt his face crease into a frown. "Are you saying my daughter is embarrassed to be seen with me?"

Glory rested her hand gently on his chest and damn it if he didn't feel it everywhere. "I'm saying that your protective personality is charming. But to a fourteen-year-old, it might come off as . . . smothering. And maybe a tad embarrassing."

Payton was embarrassed by him? When had that happened?

"So you think I'm charming, huh?"

"Did you hear anything else I said?"

"Nah, I just focused on the important parts."

She smiled, and man oh man, he was in trouble. Serious trouble. For the first time since becoming a single dad, Cal was tempted to break his own rule. Because what was the point of looking for fun outside Sugar, when the fun he wanted was not only well within the city limits, but standing right in front of him.

Chapter 9

⟨ornament⟩

After yesterday's encounter with Ms. Kitty, followed by a lengthy discussion with the Pit Crew Mafia over the validity of Kitty's invoice, Glory knew the only way she was going to get a moment's peace was to follow up with the one person who could put this argument to rest.

With less than an hour before class started, Glory parked her car in front of Kiss My Glass Tow and Tires, grabbed Ms. Kitty's invoice, and hurried over to the tow truck idling a half a block down Maple Street. The early morning heat was already sweltering and carried a sweetness from the nearby peach orchards.

"You're up and about early," Glory said as she approached.

Spencer came out from behind the truck wearing a GREASE YOUR OWN MONKEY tank, stained work pants with enough metal tools hanging off her belt to ensure electrocution in a lightning storm, and combat boots. Both mechanic and ensemble were covered in what had to be two days of grease.

Spencer caught Glory's eye and gave a brisk nod in greeting, then leaned through the unrolled window and pushed a lever on the dash. When she reemerged from the cab, she was smiling. Odd since Spencer rarely showed her teeth before lunchtime—unless it was for intimidation.

"Haven't been to bed yet," Spencer hollered over the sound of hydraulics as the wheel lift of her tow truck slowly lowered to the asphalt. "Been up all night, watching and waiting for it to hit six fifty so I could tow this bad boy."

She patted the hood of the black truck, which was parked directly behind hers. It was ridiculously high with big mud tires, even bigger flaps, and a gun rack on the roof. It also had a sheriff's hat sitting on the dash.

"You're towing Jackson's truck?"

"I'm towing a truck that has been parked at an expired meter for over twenty-four hours," Spencer said, showing more teeth than lips. Definitely a victorious smile. "Illegal is illegal, doesn't matter whose stupidly overdone truck it is."

It was a lie and they both knew it.

"So this has nothing to do with him confiscating your gun last month?"

"He was showing the Gun and Garden Club the new handguns the sheriff's department purchased." Spencer secured the wheel lift to the driver's side front tire and walked around to secure the other. "I had a bigger barrel in elementary school than that thing he was flashing so I whipped out mine to do a little comparison and he tagged me for open carry."

"You drew a loaded gun out and pointed it at the sheriff in town hall."

"Which is where the Garden and Gun Club meets. It was pistol envy, so he had to wave his badge around." She tugged on the metal chains that wrapped around the tires and stood.

"Just because JD carries a badge doesn't mean he gets to walk around like he's a god."

"You don't need to convince me," Glory said and held out the invoice, noticing that her arms were already glistening in the morning heat.

Spencer let out a low whistle. "Wow, not even a week in and Kitty's already got you jumping through her hoops."

"I'm not jumping through anyone's hoops."

"Ah-huh," Spencer mumbled, unconvinced as she looked from the still rising sun to Glory, and raised a brow. Fine so it was early, and she had a lot on her plate, but she was there to do her job, not Kitty's bidding.

"Can you tell me if this invoice is real?"

Dusting off her hands, which made not an ounce of difference, Spencer took the paper. She flicked it open and took her sweet time reading it. "You should've called. It would have saved you the drive into town."

"So Kitty was telling the truth," Glory asked, careful not to brush up against Spencer's truck. "You did the install?"

"Yup. Ordered the parts and installed them a couple of months back. Peg came out to the shop and signed off on everything. It's not the standard pump for that kind of tractor, but it abides by the guidelines."

"You mean that I was arrested and sentenced to two hundred hours of community hell for nothing?" Glory slumped back against the door of the tow truck, no longer concerned with her sundress.

"You got to hit JD with a cow pie."

"Well, there was that. Then again, I also got stuck planning a pageant for a bunch of entitled debutantes whose Cotillion, according to the former Miss Peaches and Kitty, will be held at Duncan Plantation."

Spencer yanked the chain and, satisfied with her handiwork, walked toward the front of her truck and leaned a hip against the fender. "Tell Ms. Kitty and the Peaches to kiss your ass and then have the pageant wherever you want. You're the commissioner."

"Co-commissioner." And Kitty made a good point the other day in court. "Kitty's offering to host it for free at Duncan Plantation, so it would cut way down on the budget and that means more scholarship money."

The only part of the pageant that interested Glory. She wasn't excited about the fanfare or even the Cotillion—although it had been a long time since she'd had an excuse to dress up—but she loved the idea of helping some really deserving girls go to college. And after thumbing through the stack of applications that had already come into the Harvest Commission's office, Glory was surprised to find that, while many of the girls were expected subjects—debutantes and "it" girls wanting a crown—there were a small handful of entries from girls who were interested in the community involvement aspect as well as the scholarship.

"Ten grand," Spencer said with a low whistle. And that was just for Miss Peach. There were other, smaller but still impressive, scholarships for the top five runner-ups. "Do you know what I could have done with that kind of money after high school?"

Glory had a pretty good idea. Ten thousand dollars would have paid for her nursing school. She wouldn't have had to juggle working full time while taking classes and trying to study. It would have changed her life.

"All I'm saying is that you have the chance to do something cool and plan an event where kids like we used to be feel comfortable coming. *And* stick it to a Duncan at the same time."

Glory laughed at the idea of Spencer in heels and a tiara

and then immediately sobered when Spencer started toying with a really sharp-looking tool on her belt. "Um, I didn't know you were into pageants."

"I'm not. But I'm also not into creating unfair advantages that only help the already advantaged." Spencer opened the door and hopped in the cab of her truck. She rested her forearm on the window frame and leaned out. "So you can either let the Duncans walk all over you again or grow a pair. Your choice."

Spencer hit the lever on the dash of her truck. A loud beeping filled an empty Maple Street, scattering a family of morning birds from a nearby giant oak, then the front of Jackson's truck slowly lifted off the ground.

The engine revved a few times and Spencer pulled out onto the street, flashing the lights and laying on the horn as she passed the Sheriff's Department.

For the first time since Glory had been caught driving the stolen tractor, she felt nervous. Kitty was on the up-and-up, everyone was playing by the rules, and now it was up to Glory to pull off a great Harvest Fest.

Up until now, everything had seemed simple enough— sift out the cheaters, level the field, and plan a fancy dance where teen girls got to play dress-up. But suddenly everything became real and Glory realized that there were a lot of girls counting on her to get this right.

Girls who, like Glory, might not have a champion in their corner.

Glory walked back to her car and, grabbing her cell out of the center console, scrolled through her contacts. Before she lost the courage, she hit Send. Her pulse pounded through her chest and the possible outcome of what she was about to do made her hands sweat. Taking on Kitty Duncan was insanity. Then again, insanity had never felt so good.

If Glory could make this right, it was as if she could make everything else in her world right.

"Please tell me you aren't calling from jail," Charlotte said by way of greeting.

"No." Then because she wasn't entirely confident of what the future would hold, she added, "Not today. But I am calling to ask you a favor. It's about the pageant."

"Will it set Ms. Kitty on fire?"

"Yes, which is why I'll understand if you pass."

"Honey, when she started talking doily sizes and using the town flag as a color scheme, I started looking into other places. So what did you have in mind?"

Glory smiled because Charlotte was resourceful, sneaky when needed, and probably the savviest Miss Peach in the history of the pageant. If anyone could outsmart Kitty at her own game, it was Charlotte.

"You free for lunch?"

It was twelve thirty sharp when Glory pulled into the Gravy Train. As she parked in front of the old ranch house turned eatery, she couldn't help but smile. The more she thought about what Spencer had said, the more excited she had become.

Grabbing her idea journal and the applications off the passenger seat—all the applications but one, which was still tucked in the bottom of her purse and added the weight of the world—Glory walked toward Sugar's only smokehouse BBQ.

Jessie James lay in the doorway, his eyes closed, dead to the world. JJ, the restaurant's resident welcome dog, spent his days holding down the doormat and his nights sniffing out doggie bags. But the applications in Glory's hand rustled when she reached for the door, like a paper to-go bag and

JJ leapt into action, hitting the "how can you say no to this face" position and aiming those big wet puppy eyes her way. Then he tilted his head for effect.

She put the applications out for him to sniff. "Sorry, buddy, going in, not coming out."

JJ snorted his disappointment, then plopped back down, this time blocking her path completely. With a pat to the head, Glory stepped over the big guy and opened the door. She was greeted with the smell of warm cornbread, barbeque sauce, and lemongrass.

Specializing in Asian-infused Southern eats, the Gravy Train didn't just serve the best ribs in town, it served up an eating experience that was as unique as its menu.

Peanut hulls covered the dark saloon-style floors and a dinner bell marked the kitchen door. The ceiling was a grid of exposed wooden beams with Chinese lanterns hanging at every intersection, and customers sat at picnic tables covered with red-and-white-checked cloth.

Above the mid-lunch crowd, Glory spotted Charlotte already seated at a booth near the back. She was dressed in a sleek blue dress with even sleeker heels, and when she caught Glory's eye, she waved her over.

"You're early," Glory said, taking a seat.

"I just got here." Charlotte pushed her menu to the side of the table. "And since I have to be back at the hospital in thirty minutes, I called in our order. A slab of the Baijiu ribs, emerald pulled pork sliders, daikon slaw, and a round of Thai teas to celebrate. I hope you don't mind."

That was enough food for a family of four, but Glory didn't complain. "I start my rounds in an hour, so good call. But what are we celebrating?"

"Besides *not* having to explain away a ridiculous assault charge to the board? Glo, you are orchestrating the biggest teen event in the county," Charlotte said. "It can only help you establish credibility."

Glory hadn't thought of that. Up until that moment she had considered the Harvest Fest as one more thing in a long list of responsibilities she had to push through.

"Did we miss lunch?" Joie McGraw, blond hair pulled up in a ponytail, hands resting on her swollen belly, half waddled half walked to the table. She was the only woman on the planet who could make a pair of capris and sunny maternity top look couture.

"What are you doing here?" Glory asked, patting the bench. "I thought you and Brett were taking a babymoon."

"We did. The Napa Valley was wonderful and romantic and Brett was so sweet. Then on day two it was like the smell of the rotting grapes was everywhere, even in the hotel room and..." Joie broke off with a grimace and then sat.

"If she throws up and ruins lunch, she picks up the tab," Spencer warned, plopping down next to Charlotte. "I don't care if it is hormones."

Joie pointed to her baby bump. "One day this will be you and I will remind you of this moment. And you will cry. Like a baby. And I will film it and put it up on Facebook so everyone can see just what hormones are capable of."

"They make you mean, that's for sure," Spencer said.

Joie ignored her. "So co-commissioner, huh? Cal ripped Brett a new one over that."

Glory grimaced. "I felt so bad that he got stuck helping me run the Harvest Fest."

Although a secret part of her was excited at the idea of spending time with Cal—and not just her girly parts.

"Don't." Joie laughed. "I actually think it will be good for him. He's been griping nonstop about that pageant all summer. Maybe being forced to work on it will show him that

Miss Peach isn't some male-created ruse to get girls to parade around in bikinis."

"Do you know if Payton is going out for Miss Peach?" Glory asked casually, not wanting to break her word, but wanting out of this situation completely. She had no idea what she'd been thinking to accept the application in the first place.

"She is obsessed with entering," Joie said with a smile. "Although I'm pretty sure Cal's got a different opinion on the situation and I don't think any amount of eye batting and charm will sway him this time."

"Who knows? Maybe it would be good for her." Cal saying yes would be amazing for Glory—and her ever-increasing guilt level.

"I think it would be good for *him*," Joie said, resting her hand on her belly. "Cal needs to loosen up. He is so busy trying to make up for Tawny leaving that he's holding too tight to Payton."

"I think it's kind of sweet," Glory admitted. What she would have done to have a parent who cared that much about her. "A bit over the top, but sweet all the same."

"He is sweet. And sometimes I think lonely. He's put everything he had into raising Payton, and now that she is growing up, I think he needs to get back out there." Joie leaned in and lowered her voice conspiratorially. "Which is why I am so excited about this Cotillion. It is black tie, romantic, and the perfect place to meet someone. Someone special."

She waggled a brow in Glory's direction and Glory felt her face heat. She was pretty sure Joie didn't know about her ridiculous crush, or that she was secretly hoping that after their kiss Cal would ask her to be his "someone special" for Cotillion.

A warm bead of excitement started in her tummy at the idea that maybe he'd been thinking the same thing. That maybe he'd talked to Joie about it, which would explain the mischievous spark in her friend's eyes.

"I didn't know that Cal dated all that much," Glory said, careful to come off casual in case she was reading way too much into this. She didn't think Cal had been a monk since his wife walked out, but as far as she knew, he hadn't dated anyone seriously either. Although he'd kissed her.

"Which is why I need your help. I want to find Cal the perfect woman." And just like that, the bead turned into a hot brand poking her in the chest. "She has to be smart, and sweet, and of course, cute. Oh, and a great mom for Payton."

Glory's smile hurt from the weight of keeping it in place as Joie outlined her plan to land Cal the perfect wife. She could tell by the way Joie was talking that Glory wasn't even in the running to make the ballot, let alone a qualified applicant for a place in Cal's world. And for the life of her, Glory couldn't figure out why.

Joie was one of her closest friends and yet she didn't stop to think that maybe Glory would be a good fit for Cal. Even worse, Joie knew Cal, knew what he was looking for, and what he needed. Apparently it wasn't her.

"Hope you're hungry." Skeeter, the owner and head chef, moseyed up to the table. The man was going on four thousand, moved with the speed of a slug, and had more teeth than hair. He also had five platters, four plates, two baskets, and a round of drinks balanced on one tray. Fancy trick for a guy with only eight fingers.

Food hit the table but Glory's appetite was gone. Her breakfast of a parfait and black coffee, which she'd inhaled at the crack of dawn, had worn off in the middle of her Adolescent Psychology class, but suddenly her stomach was too upset to eat.

"This looks delicious," Joie said, eyeing the ribs with intent.

"Thanks, Ms. Joie. I saved a piece of my peach crumble with ice cream for you."

Joie might be a new to Sugar, but Yankee or not, she had already won over most of the town. Including Skeeter.

"Can't wait." Joie paused, put her hand on her belly, and with her eyes closed, transported to some weird in-utero plane. Her eyes snapped open and she frowned. "Better skip the ice cream. But bring extra pie."

"Yes, ma'am." With a sheepish smile, Skeeter took off.

"So why are you all here again?" Glory asked as plates filled and forks stabbed, wishing she could just disappear. Except she'd called Charlotte to get a better understanding of how the pageant side of the festival works, and to brainstorm ideas for how to make this year's Cotillion something that the girls of Sugar would remember—all the girls of Sugar.

"Because rumor has it you grew a pair," Spencer said around bits of pulled pork and bun.

"You said you wanted to light up Ms. Kitty." Charlotte lowered her voice. "So I called in backup."

Glory felt everything inside her still. She had never had girl backup. Oh, she'd had Brett and the blue-haired brigade, but this felt different. This felt all warm and mushy and what having girlfriends was like. Maybe Jelly Lou had been right and all she had to do was open up—push down the fear of being rejected and reach out.

She had, and it worked, and suddenly she wanted to cry. Not the kind of tears that burned through, but the ones that warmed from the inside out and reminded her that every day was a fresh start at finding happiness.

"I don't know what to say," Glory admitted.

"How about you start with how I get to help you stick it to a Duncan," Spencer said, not a hint of humor lacing her words. "That's why I came. And the ribs."

"I don't want to stick it to the Duncans," Glory said and then, because she wasn't big on lying, added, "Much. I want to make this year's pageant accessible for all the eligible girls, and the Sugar Pull fair."

"And I think the best place to start is to find a new location," Charlotte said. "One that offers everything that the Duncan Plantation has, only better. Which is why"—she flashed her dazzling smile Joie's way—"I was thinking the Fairchild House would be a perfect solution. It's a historical building, has plenty of property for the Sugar Pull, and the stage Cal built for your grand opening last year would be perfect for the Presenting Ceremony."

"And there is the dance floor," Spencer added.

Last year, Joie had moved to Sugar to turn her great-aunt's dilapidated boardinghouse into a five-star culinary retreat and rejuvenation destination, making Fairchild House one of the top-rated and most popular boutique hotels in the South. And not only did it have everything they needed to host and feed a few hundred people, but it didn't belong to Ms. Kitty. Which made it perfect.

"As long as the inn isn't already booked that weekend, the place is yours," Joie said while double fisting two ribs. "I'll donate the location, tables, and chairs. And twinkle lights. I have lots of twinkle lights."

"Are you sure?" Glory asked, blown away with gratitude. "We can pay you."

Charlotte cleared her throat and made a slicing motion with her hand.

Right, every dollar spent on a location was one less dollar

toward some girl's education. And what was the point of making the pageant accessible to girls who could really benefit if there were no benefits to be had? She didn't want to plan a glorified prom.

"I mean, not a lot, but surely something to offset your costs."

Joie waved a rib at the offer. "You can pay me back by helping me paint the nursery. Brett is set on a golf theme and Pixie here wants fairies."

Charlotte clasped her hands in delight. "You're having a girl?"

Joie stopped mid-bite, set her rib down, and leveled the whole table with a look. "Does it matter? Fairies are unisex these days, which is what you will tell Brett when you all show up to our painting party. In fairy wings."

"Told you," Spencer said. "Mean."

"We will be there with wings on," Charlotte, always the peacemaker, said. "I'll look into party rental costs and see if the company the hospital uses for our Annual Gala can cut us a deal."

"I can call around about caterers," Joie offered.

All eyes went to Spencer, who was licking BBQ sauce off her fingers. "What?"

"If we're going to take on Kitty, we need to make sure we have all the bases covered," Charlotte explained.

"Fine, I'll come and look intimidating," Spencer offered. "As the official Sugar Pull mechanic, she won't want to piss me off."

"Why? Because then you'll tow her damn truck," Jackson said, storming up to the table with two days' worth of stubble, enough dust to cause acute asthma, and an expression that said he was short on humor and a ride home.

"Afternoon, Sheriff," Charlotte chimed in.

Jackson gave a self-conscious nod, as though just realizing there were other people at the table. "Ladies, pardon the language...and the smell." He went back to glaring at Spencer. "Where the hel—heck is my truck?"

"Was that *your* truck, JD?" Spencer sat back and stuck a toothpick between her teeth. "The one that was parked at an expired meter for over twenty-four hours?"

"You know damn...darn well it was. And I was out on department business, leading a search and rescue in the mountains behind Magnolia Falls. A couple of backwoods boys got drunk and started shooting at the fish, pissed off a bear who chased them halfway to Alabama, then pissed themselves when they realized they were halfway up a cliff. It took ten hours to get to them and another six for the rope team extract. They rode home in my car."

"Sounds like a rough night." Spencer crinkled her nose. "Smells even worse."

"Which is why if you don't tell me where my truck is in the next thirty seconds, I'm going to walk my smelly ass across the street and let myself into your apartment. Then I will sleep for the rest of the week in your bed so you can experience firsthand just how bad it was."

"If you're looking for an invite to my bed, all you had to do was ask, Sheriff," Spencer said, and Jackson's ears went pink.

"Where's my truck, *Lavender*?"

Spencer blinked and, *no way*, the tough, don't-screw-with-me mechanic was blushing. At the sheriff. Which must have ticked Spencer off because she threw her napkin at him. "Impound yard, *JD*."

"Impound?" He laughed. "You're slacking. I'll have it out in ten minutes. Tops." He looked at the table and nodded, "Ladies," then grabbed Spencer's sandwich right off her plate and headed out the door, a colony of dust bunnies stuck to his ass.

"How long do you think it will take for him to figure out his truck is impounded in Magnolia Falls?" Charlotte asked.

A loud shout came from outside, followed by a blue streak that had the restaurant going silent. Jessie James starting howling.

"It's been fun, ladies." Spencer stood and dropped a twenty on the table. "See you at the next meeting?"

Chapter 10

⁓

Thursday night, Cal wanted nothing more than to throw back a few cold ones with his crew. The foundation had been poured, stripped, and they'd finally started damp proofing the sublevels. He was beat, needed a shower, and some time to unwind.

What he didn't need was a night at his sister-in-law's. But Joie had called earlier to let him know they were back from the babymoon and that she wanted him to come over, without Hattie or Payton, supposedly for a nice dinner to catch up.

He was pretty sure it was a setup.

Lately, everything with Brett and Joie seemed to be a setup. At least the women Joie picked were nice, sweet, and easy to ignore.

Cal had been betting on the fact that she'd be too busy being pregnant to meddle. Unfortunately, his sister-in-law had made it her life's mission to see Cal happy, settled, and loved—three things that he did not need a wife to accomplish. He had a great family, great friends, and his company had doubled in size over the past year. So happiness level— check. His life was as settled as it could be for a single dad— uh, check and check. And his daughter owned his heart.

What more could a guy want?

Okay, he could think of one thing he wanted.

Glory. Sparring with her had been exciting, challenging, a complete turn-on. Being with her, talking about his life, had felt like more than a connection. It had felt intimate, like intellectual foreplay that was as surprising as it was refreshing. And in spite of the overwhelming odds that he and Glory together would be a complete disaster, he still wanted her. Bad. Even though logic told him that nothing about them worked or even made sense.

But Cal was a man, so sex always managed to overrule logic. And sex with Glory would be hot and intense and like free-falling through a freaking category five tornado. Too bad the aftermath would be much of the same, which was why he was pulling into his brother's drive and not the Saddle Rack with his crew.

He turned onto the gravel road leading to Brett and Joie's new place when his phone chirped. He looked at the screen and swore before answering. "Hey, Tawny."

"You didn't return my call." Tawny's voice filled the cab of his truck.

Cal had promised himself that, for Payton's sake, he'd be civil with his ex-wife—some days were harder than others. Between Tawny bailing on the Pep-Luck, Payton giving him the silent treatment, and him swinging hammers in triple digits all week, today was one of those days.

"Didn't know you called," he drawled. Tawny hated his drawl, said it made him sound small town.

"Four times. On the fifth try, your grandmother answered

and I told her to have you call me." Which explained why
he never got it. Hattie was never a big fan of Tawny's. After
the way she screwed Cal over in the divorce, then failed to
show up at nearly every milestone Payton had reached along
the way, Hattie had thrown down redneck style and declared
Tawny dead to her.

To make sure that his ex got the message, as well as the
rest of the town, Hattie placed an ad in the *Sugar Gazette*—
the obituary section.

"Did she tell you to try my cell?"

"No, she didn't speak but I could hear her judgment
through the phone." Tawny let out a few judgmental huffs of
her own. "The woman is crazy and disrespectful and it kills
me that Payton might pick up on her treatment of me. A girl
should never see her mother being disrespected."

"I'll talk to Hattie." Although he knew it would accomplish jack shit.

"Good, because how are we supposed to co-parent if I
can't even leave you a message?"

"Call my cell," he repeated, resisting the urge to point
out that in order to co-parent, both parties had to show up.
"What's up?"

"It's about this weekend."

"You aren't canceling again, are you? Payton is really
looking forward to spending time with you."

"Of course I'm not," she spat.

Thank God, he thought as he drove his truck around the
gravel circle and threw it into Park.

"You act like I'm a bad parent, Cal." He was so not going
there. "Between work and Randal's promotion, things are
just busy around here."

Cal rolled his eyes. Tawny's work consisted of looking
good and hosting parties so Randy looked good. And

Randy's promotion meant that he got to make more guilty rich men look less guilty.

"In fact, he just landed a new account with a big oil company based out of Houston and I have to get him to the airport, which is why I'm calling."

And here it came, the reason she was going to give for breaking her daughter's heart. Cal leaned his head back and stared at the ceiling wondering what he'd been thinking the night they met.

Tawny was gorgeous and sexy and exciting—and had a selfish stick shoved so far up her ass he had no idea why it took him so long to see it.

"I was hoping you could bring Payton to Atlanta tomorrow."

"Payton has practice after school, which she can't miss." Missing school events, extracurricular or not, without both parents agreeing broke their custody agreement. Tawny knew that. "And I have three different crews coming out to the medical center site tomorrow."

"I was going to treat her to a girls retreat in Atlanta, spend the weekend getting manicures and shopping."

All things that Payton would love, and he felt shitty saying no, but he'd been here, done this song and dance with Tawny before, and it never worked out in his favor. There wasn't much he wouldn't do if it meant Payton getting to spend time with her mom, but tomorrow was a big day for the project and he had to be on-site. Period.

"There is no way I can get away. So you'll need to come get her as planned and I will pick her up Sunday as planned."

"Well, I can't come get her, Cal," she said in that same tone that used to make him feel like the biggest disappointment in the history of mankind. Now it just pissed him off. "For God's sake, it's just a couple hours out of your day."

"Four. Four hours round trip. Which, like I said, I don't have."

"Well, then you can tell Payton we'll have to reschedule. I'm sure she'll understand." The phone went dead.

"Always a pleasure," he said to the silence, tired of seeing his baby girl get the short end of every Tawny-inspired situation. Tired of watching his ex manipulate the situation so he wound up looking like the bad guy. Cal was just damn tired.

Releasing a breath, he turned off the truck and climbed out. Even though the sun was setting, and their place sat on the edge of Sugar Lake, the evening air was still heavy with heat and reminders of being home again.

Of what it felt like to love hard and lose big.

Cal made his way up the wide front steps, trying to keep his emotions at bay. Even though his parents had been gone a long time, and Brett's new farmhouse with a kid-ready porch and clapboard siding had erased every physical reminder of the fire that had shattered their family, being there was still hard. Being there after his blowout with Tawny was suffocating.

Up until recently, Cal would drive an hour around the lake if it meant avoiding his parents' old property. Looking at the charred remains of his childhood had been a painful reminder of just how much he'd lost, how that one night had changed everything. He'd gone from a carefree college student with a bright future, loving parents, and a life of his own to head of the house with two brothers to raise and no chance of leaving Sugar, all in one summer storm.

"Hey." Cal tapped on the screen door before letting himself inside.

"We're around back," Joie hollered.

He walked through the front room, admiring the distressed pinewood floors and dramatically framed archways.

His crew had done a top-notch job on the build, and Joie had designed the kind of house that his mom would have been at home in. The kind of house he'd dreamt of building for his own family.

Following female laughter through the kitchen, which looked like *Iron Chef* tied the knot with *Paula Dean*, he opened the French doors and found the one woman he'd been set on avoiding.

"Evening," he said and four sets of female eyes looked up at him. Three of them were twinkling with welcome, and one looked as shocked to see him as he was to see her.

Sundress Glory sat at the head of the table. Her hair hung in soft waves over her shoulders, her lips were lightly glossed, and her dress was a pale pink with tiny buttons and even tinier straps. She looked so beautiful and delicate, and out of nowhere, Cal felt a sharp tug in his chest that made breathing impossible.

Convincing himself that there was nothing but heat between them while watching her sling beers was one thing. Convincing himself of that while she sat there all soft and sweet and down-home girl-next-door was another.

"Cal." Joie pushed off the chair and came around the table for a hug, her belly making contact before her arms fully wrapped around his middle. "You made it."

"You said six, right?" He looked at his watch. "It's six."

"I figured you'd find some excuse to get out of coming." She grabbed a pitcher of sweet tea and poured him a glass. "Have a seat, we're just finishing up. You know all the girls, right?"

He forced his eyes off Glory to acknowledge the rest of the table—a hard task when she was looking every bit the sweet Georgia peach right then.

At the opposite side of the table, sitting by Joie's now

empty chair, was a willowy blonde who looked familiar. She was a real mom type, short layered hair, big brown eyes, sweater set, cute enough, and blushing up at him like—

Oh, hell no. There was no way his luck could be this bad. He looked at Joie and she was vibrating with excitement.

"You already know Charlotte and Glory." Joie ticked them off so fast he didn't even have time to do anything but nod. "And this. *This* is Anna. She's new in town, has a girl Payton's age on the cheer team, and is my new event planner at the inn."

"Hey, Cal," Anna said, standing and offering up her hand. "It's good to see you again." Cal must have worn a blank expression because she added, "I was working the juice booth at the Pep-Luck."

"Oh yeah," he lied, taking her hand.

"Joie has told me all about you." He just bet she had. "It's nice to meet another single parent with a teenager in town."

"Which is why I invited her tonight." Joie winked—not sly at all.

"So, what are you all doing here?" He asked the question to no one in particular but his eyes found themselves right back on Glory—who was too busy flipping through a stack of papers to acknowledge him.

"You mean besides scaring off all the fish," his brother drawled coming up the back porch with a fishing pole in one hand and an empty fish bucket in the other.

"Again," Joie said, looking at his empty bucket and giving him a little peck on the cheek. "You haven't caught anything in weeks."

Brett shrugged like it was no big deal that he'd come home empty handed. "A bad season is all."

"Is that what you're telling yourself?" Cal asked because it had been one of the best fishing seasons in over a decade.

"Hey, bro," Brett said, setting down the bucket to salute Cal, with his finger. "Good to see you, too."

Brett McGraw was imposing, worked out enough to intimidate most men, and one of the most competitive SOBs in the country. He was the only guy Cal knew who could lose it over a friendly game of Uno. And yet the guy grinned like an idiot when he leaned down to kiss his tiny wife while holding a white ball of fluff dressed in doggie-camo gear—and no fish. "Looks like we aren't having fish for dinner."

"That's all right. We'll figure something out." Joie kissed him back until Brett picked her up with one arm for an annoyingly long kiss that had everyone looking away.

Cal took the opportunity to look at Glory. Really look at her. Warm eyes, soft smile, hardly any makeup at all. The woman was stunning. She was also fidgeting with her skirt and looking everywhere but at him.

"Go wash up and then come back out," Joie said to Brett.

Brett walked right past him, checked him hard with his shoulder, and whispered, "Have fun."

His little dog Boo tapped the deck behind him as man and purse-dog made their way into the house.

Cal picked up a few diagrams of a hotel ballroom. It had little round tables penciled in and a gazebo drawn on the back lawn. "What's this?"

"An alternate option to having the pageant and Cotillion at the Duncan Plantation," Glory said. "But it's really expensive and would blow most of the budget." She looked nervous. And damn if he wasn't right there with her. Which was ridiculous. Cal didn't do nervous with women. Hadn't ever since Tawny. "We were hoping to have it at Fairchild House."

"But I had already booked a wedding and two culinary

tours that weekend," Anna said apologetically. "It's an All Things Peach tour coming in for the Harvest Fest."

"So we're looking into other options," Glory said. "I was going to e-mail you about this later, but you're here now."

"That I am." He looked at Glory and then back to the table. "And it looks like you found your army."

"Our army," she clarified. "Charlotte, being a former Miss Peach and the current regent of the Sugar Peaches, has agreed to step in as our expert on all things pageant."

"I volunteered to oversee food selection and the menu," Joie said. "I'm working with the executive chef now to see what kind of pricing we can get. And Anna so generously offered her talent to plan the logistics of the day. She is just amazing at event planning and reimagining spaces. Talented, organized, and knows teen girls. She is the perfect person to give this pageant a face-lift." Joie poured Cal a second glass of sweet tea and placed it by the seat right next to Anna. "Show Cal your ideas to update the Presenting Ceremony."

Cal would rather sit next to the dog. Or be shot. Anything to get out of sitting next to Anna and her "ideas," which was nothing more than crafty woman-speak for "setup." And Cal didn't like to be set up, on dates or otherwise. Nope, he didn't do dates, didn't do serious, and he most certainly didn't do mothers of his daughter's teammates.

But Anna looked at him with shy expectation, Joie preened over her handiwork, Glory was back to ignoring him, and Cal had no choice. Either admit he'd kissed his brother's best friend or sit down next to a cheer mom.

Anna suddenly looked so uncertain that he almost just blurted it out. But he didn't because Joie was watching him closely and she could read him almost as good as Brett, so Cal took his seat and looked over Anna's idea. Not that he heard a word she was saying—he was too busy being aware of Glory, and fighting with the urge to move, explain, do something other than sit there staring.

It was obvious to everyone what was going on and Glory was a smart woman. *Jesus*, this was why he didn't date locals.

Not that they were dating, he reminded himself. They'd shared a kiss. An incredibly hot kiss that—*whoa*, just thinking about her lips had him shifting in his chair, which was a bad move since she stopped flipping and looked up. Her on one side of the table watching him on the other, with who he assumed was his dinner companion for the evening.

"This all looks great," he said, his gaze solidly on Glory. Joie's was still on him and Cal could tell it wasn't a good conclusion his sister-in-law was coming to.

The correct one, but not a good one.

"You should check out the applications that have come in." Glory held up the stack as proof, then dropped them on the table—right next to her—while flashing him a hopeful smile. "We have over twenty Sugar Pull entries but only a quarter of that for Miss Peach."

"It looks like you've done a great job handling the pageant, so why don't I head up the Sugar Pull and get everything there in order. Divide and conquer."

Glory opened her mouth as though she was about to tell him that was the stupidest idea ever, then closed it, picking up the stack of applications. Maybe she was nervous about Kitty or being in charge of the pageant or the fact that they had a sexy little secret. Hell, he didn't know, but for some reason he cared.

"Okay," she finally said, sounding disappointed, and damn if that didn't have *him* fidgeting. "I guess there's a lot to go over before next week's Harvest Council meeting, so splitting up the workload would be smart."

"Agreed."

"Good. I'll e-mail you the rest of the information, so we are on the same page." Purse in hand, applications clutched to her chest, Glory stood. So did Cal, so fast he nearly knocked over his chair. "I have to get going but thanks, everyone, for all the help."

"You aren't staying?"

"No, I have a test to study for," she said. "And you have dinner."

He looked over at his date, who blinked up at him with hopeful expectation, and an unsettling mix of helplessness and disappointment collided in his chest, making it hard to breathe. Because Cal realized he wasn't upset about Joie setting him up on a blind date. He was upset that Glory wasn't his blind date.

And wasn't that all kinds of ridiculous.

The guy who kept it casual, striving for surface, was actually upset because he wasn't going to get the chance to talk with Glory about his day, his chat with Tawny, and how the hell he was supposed to tell his kiddo that her mom was going to be a no-show. About how that was going to break his heart.

Even worse, Cal was upset because Glory was the one to, once again, remove herself from an uncomfortable situation, leaving to make it easier on everyone else, when all he had to do was ask her to stay.

Chapter 11

If last night had been awkward, today was a disaster. Glory spent the majority of her morning in urgent care, fielding patients who all suffered from different ailments, but were seeking the same outcome—a "Gone Fishing" prescription. With a good-patient sticker and a friendly smile, they were sent on their way. All except Frank, who was twenty years Glory's senior and co-owner of Frank Brothers' Taxidermy, Ammo, and Fine Jewelry. His request was for a different kind of therapy—one that apparently needed to be said directly to her breasts, so he'd been escorted out by security—no good-patient sticker for him.

By lunch it became clear that there was an epidemic of head lice going around the playground, which resulted in three students taking scissors to their hair, one student taking scissors to someone else's hair, and Cole Andrews, wanting to save Chewbacca from the embarrassment of being shaved, stuck him in his cave—and was waiting in Exam Room 11. Which was why when Dr. Holden paged Glory, she happily handed off her charts to another nurse, and made her way to Charlotte's office.

At first, Glory thought she was being summoned to talk about pageant stuff or, worse, her abrupt exit last night. But when she got to Charlotte's office, the door was open and the good doctor sat at her desk looking over Glory's proposal.

Determined to do something productive, mainly not spend her whole night picking apart what had happened at Joie's—or more accurately what had not happened—Glory had spent most of her evening, and part of the morning, working on her proposal. She'd never written a proposal of this magnitude before. There were so many moving parts, which would all be scrutinized by professionals, so she'd sent it off to Charlotte to see if she was on the right track.

Based on the traffic jam of notes in the margin, Glory was pretty sure she'd not only derailed, but managed to obliterate the track.

She tapped on the door. "Is this a good time?"

Charlotte looked up and smiled. Good news, bad news, end of the world, she was a true steel magnolia. "Have a seat."

She gestured to the chair facing her desk and Glory checked the hallway, looking for a frantic mom with a lice-infected second grader. No such luck. She took a seat.

"I got your proposal this morning, and although it has all the elements I asked for, it's obvious you've never written something like this."

"Is it that bad?"

Charlotte took a moment to look at her office door then leaned in and lowered her voice. "I did some checking into our competition and there are two candidates who have me worried."

That didn't sound good.

"They both have stellar résumés, spent years in hospital management, and have advanced degrees. But their ideas are nothing special and too big-city to really work in our small town. We need something that makes us really stand apart from the pack, really highlight the benefit for the patient *and* the volunteer."

Glory thought back to her conversation with Spencer about the scholarship and how with the right girl it could change her life. Then remembered how Dr. Blair had given her direction, an environment where she felt useful and successful, and he gave her the confidence to find her own personal reason to push forward. "I think I might have a few ideas."

"Good." Charlotte took out a glossy-covered proposal and slid it across the tabletop. It was sleek, professional, and nothing like what Glory had created. "This is a proposal from a few years back. The program doesn't relate and I've blacked out any confidential information, but I want you to see how they structured it and use it as a template for yours. First impressions mean everything with the board; they are easily impressed by flash," she said, rolling her eyes, then flipped to an extensive spreadsheet with graphs and charts. "You'll need an accurate operations budget and a twenty-four-month Gantt chart, but don't forget to make it personal; make them picture all the teens and pediatric patients who will be better off because of you and your program."

Glory willed herself not to panic. "When do you need this by?"

Charlotte picked up her phone and scrolled to her calendar. "The proposals are due on the thirty-first. If you can get it to me by the twenty-seventh, that will give us time to adjust it if needed."

The homework in her book bag wasn't going to do itself,

and between the Harvest Fest, earning a living, and rounds at the hospital, the only time Glory wasn't pushing close to crazy was the five hours a night she slept—four on weekends. But this project meant everything to her—apparently more than sleeping because she said, "You bet."

She had no idea what a Gantt chart was or even how to balance her own checkbook, but there was no one submitting who had a more personal mission than Glory. And unlike charts and spreadsheets, passion wasn't something that could be googled.

"Now." Charlotte leaned in, steepling her fingers under her chin. "You want to talk about what's going on with you and Cal?"

Oh boy.

"Nothing is going on." At least not anymore.

"Honey, last night Cal looked like he'd been caught with his pants down." She put her hand to her chest, then fanned herself. "There was this smoldering heat that singed the table, and then you hightailed it out of there."

"He had a date and I didn't want to interrupt and . . . what? We're planning the Harvest Fest, that's all." When Charlotte's cucumber cool glare was too much to handle, Glory sighed. "Fine, I might have had a teensy crush on him, and was considering asking him to Cotillion, but it's obvious that Joie has someone else in mind, so no biggie."

She refused to roll her eyes even though she sounded exactly like Payton right then.

"It's a shame." Charlotte shook her head, her blond layers swinging with effortless style. "Passing up a chance with a McGraw is like telling Jesus you'll take a tour of heaven later."

"Then why don't *you* ask him to Cotillion?"

"Me and McGraw men don't mix so well, romantically

speaking," her friend said, her voice laced with an uneasy mixture of disappointment and sadness. "It brings on a case of heartburn that never goes away."

Glory stilled. This was bad. Really bad. There was no way Charlotte could be referring to Brett—she knew every Sugar conquest he'd ever had—and the good doctor wasn't on that list. And Jace was too backwoods and bad-boy for a Sugar Peach, which only left one McGraw. "I don't remember you mentioning that you had a romantic history with a McGraw."

"I didn't." Without another word, Charlotte stood and with an elegant smile walked out into the hallway, giving Glory one more reason to steer clear of Cal.

Three hours later, and well after Glory's shift ended, she found herself in the break room watching an animated professor with bushy brows on YouTube give a tutorial about how to create a Gantt chart using Excel in three easy steps.

"Three easy steps, my ass." She was still on step one: Enter project tasks. She typed in "finish proposal" and then drew a blank.

"Three easy steps, huh?"

Glory looked up to find Cal's big, badass body in the doorway. His hair was slightly tousled as though he'd just come in from outside and he had a small notebook in hand. His expression, however, was all business, just like the blue button-up and fancy dark jeans he had on.

Okay, so he was a little windblown and his shirt was untucked, but he looked hot. Seriously hot.

"Can you repeat what those exact steps are? You know, in case there is a test on your ass later? I want to be prepared." He waltzed into the room, all charm, muscles, and easy swagger, and Glory knew, without a doubt, exactly what steps and tasks would fall on the GET CAL MCGRAW NAKED Gantt chart. No tutorial needed.

"Unless"—he stopped short of the table and looked at the stacks of paper and scribbled notes—"I'm interrupting something important."

"Important? Yes. Interrupting?" She shook her head at the sad truth. "You could come back in the morning and I'd be sitting right here looking exactly like this. Just more bags under my eyes." Speaking of appearances. "You going to church or did someone die?"

He looked down and smiled as though he was just remembering what he wore. "I had a meeting with the hospital's board."

"How did it go?"

"They wanted an updated timeline for the new wing and to make sure we hit the major milestones as promised. We are on target, which they already knew, so it ended early." He straightened and pushed off the wall. "Then I figured since I was inside the hospital and not covered in concrete and sweat, I'd come see you. One of the nurses said you'd clocked out but I saw your car in the parking lot. So I waited."

"But I saw Charlotte and Mr. Holden leave over an hour ago."

He shrugged. "About an hour in, I figured I'd come find you."

While she appreciated the way his button-up hugged his broad chest and matched his baby blues, she was more interested in the fact that Cal had waited by her car for over an hour. Because an hour, in dress shoes, was a long time for a guy to wait... unless he thought she was worth the wait. And that made her heart skip. "Why?"

His easy swagger faded into confusion, as though he

wasn't sure himself. Then he held up a coffee cup and a to-go box, both with the Gravy Train logo on them, and Glory's stomach grumbled, a reminder that it was well past dinnertime. "Lemon bar, a latte, and an apology. Last night was—"

Awful. Embarrassing. A wake-up call. "Awkward?"

"Okay, we can go with that," he said, setting the offering on the table. The mingled scents of strong coffee and sweet vanilla filled the room.

"Not just a latte." She took the cup and inhaled. "A hazelnut vanilla latte."

"Not that it's an excuse, but I wasn't in the best mood when I got to Joie's last night to start with. Tawny called on the way to cancel her weekend with Payton," he admitted and Glory's heart went out to him.

"How did Payton take it?"

Cal reached for his hat, only to find it was missing, so he ran a hand through his hair, making it stand up on end. "Not good."

That was the understatement of the year. She'd seen how excited Payton had been, *knew* how much she was counting on her mom to talk to Cal about the pageant. No Tawny meant Payton would have to come clean with her dad all by herself or withdraw.

Poor kid.

Even poorer Cal. Glory remembered the look on Jelly Lou's face every time she had to explain why Billy wasn't going to be able to make it to her birthday, or Christmas, or Father's Day. He was wearing it right now.

"I'm sorry."

"Yeah, me, too." He sounded tired, the kind that went soul deep. "About Tawny and about last night. When I walked out on that patio, I didn't know what to say or if

I should even say anything. Joie asked me to dinner so I walked in expecting dinner."

"And you found me and your date at the same table."

"I didn't know she was my date."

"I know," Glory admitted. "I was being a jerk. Joie said she was going to find you a date for Cotillion; I just didn't know I'd be there to see it. So I left."

"I'm not taking Anna to Cotillion."

"You're not?" That was a surprise. Anna was sweet, cute, a great mother, and according to Joie, Cal's perfect match.

"No," he said and Glory's heart, already thumping fast against her chest, sped up until all she could hear was the blood rushing in her ears and Cal's weighted silence. "I already have a date."

Glory held hard to that smile, determined not to show how much those five words stung. "Who are you taking?"

"Payton."

"Payton." She laughed, relief making her chest relax. Holding on to Payton's application and not telling Cal had been eating at her. She was happy that Payton had come clean. "I bet she's ecstatic. She'll make a great Miss Peach contestant."

"Contestant?" Cal frowned. "She's not entering. I'm just taking her."

And there they were, back to awkward.

"She's been talking nonstop about the pageant and with Tawny canceling…" He lifted one shoulder and let it drop. "I figured a fun night of getting all dressed up would take her mind off things. I'm going as a chaperone; I might as well take her as my date. Don't say anything, though, I want to surprise her."

Oh, Payton was going to be surprised all right. Almost as surprised as Cal would be when he learned his daughter ordered a dress that covered less than Glory's bar uniform and had a date with a teen boy and his sex wagon. Glory considered telling him, just putting it all out there so everyone would be on the same page—and Glory wouldn't have to carry around the guilt that application brought—but she'd given Payton until the end of the weekend. And the last thing that girl needed was another woman going back on her word.

"Joie will be disappointed." Oddly enough, so was Glory. Not that she thought Cal would ask her, especially not after last night, but there had been a tiny seed of hope that had grown over the past few days.

"Joie has it in her head that she's a matchmaker, but what she fails to understand is that I don't want to be matched, which is why I hardly ever date. I've discreetly seen a few women over the years but nothing serious. Very few have been from Sugar and never anyone who knows Payton."

He shifted in his chair and suddenly Glory realized that he wasn't talking about matchmaking or dating or even Anna—he was talking about them.

Not that she should be surprised. Cal had been up front with her about where he stood on dating and she tried to respect where he was coming from. Had to. Cal was an amazing man who had managed to do what so many others had failed at—put his daughter first.

"For what it's worth, I think you're a great dad."

"Thank you. Sometimes I feel like I'm screwing up at every turn." He held out his hand. "Still friends?"

"Is that what we are, Cal, friends?" A hard thing to be when he'd spent most of the past few years avoiding her and the past few days kissing her.

"I'd like to think so."

"Me, too." Glory could count her friends on one hand,

so it should have been an exciting offer. Instead it left her feeling deflated. Plastering a smile on her face, she took his offering, and the second their skin made contact, they both froze because no friend-zone she'd ever heard of created sizzle like that.

Cal pointed his chin to her makeshift workspace. "Can you put this on hold for a few hours?"

"Depends on what for." She made a big show of studying the sample proposal. "This is pretty exciting stuff."

The only thing exciting her right now was that Cal still hadn't released her hand. Maybe that was because her brain had pretty much checked out an hour ago. But the idea of analyzing charts and spreadsheets was far less important than analyzing Cal and his whole "friend" speech.

He glanced over the documents and his lips twitched. "I can see that. But I think I can do you one better."

"Better than tasks and timelines?"

"Sweetheart, tasks and timelines don't even hold a candle to what I have planned." He looked down at her scrubs, bright blue with tap-dancing ducks, and smiled. "You wouldn't happen to have a change of clothes on you? Something that requires heels?"

Glory looked at their still linked hands and softly asked, "Since when do heels and holding hands equate to friends?"

"Since there's a third person in the equation who happens to have access to a ballroom?"

She looked up and was at a complete loss for words. Or maybe this was what genuine excitement felt like. "Oh my God! You found us a place to host the pageant?"

"I found us *the* place for the pageant." He smiled and it was so charming that she couldn't help but smile back.

"Does a dress and boots work?"

* * *

Cal sat on the back deck of the Falcon's Nest, the only cloth napkins and champagne brunch kind of place in the whole county, and realized that, for a guy who was so adamant about not dating, this was the closest he'd come to a real date in years.

Their knees kept accidentally sharing space under the intimate table for two as the sun gave way to an inky sky behind the town. And he was in a button-up. A goddamned button-up while Glory sat so close, the skirt of her sundress brushed back and forth across his leg with the breeze.

And her dress—*holy shit*, that dress—was silky, light blue with little white polka dots, and every time she breathed, it was like the dress was flirting with him.

Then there was the little belt that was about a half an inch thin and fastened right under her breasts, which made no sense at all because belts were made to go around the waist, but he wasn't complaining. It accentuated her curves and inspired a hundred different situations where a belt like that would come in handy.

Like secured to the headboard of his bed. Or hers.

"Would you like to see a wine list? We have one of the largest cellars in the area," the manager, Chuck, explained while offering Glory a wine list and a smile that was all male appreciation.

Glory waved off the wine list. "I was thinking of an alcohol-free menu. Maybe an offering of drinks that are fancy and sophisticated without the added temptation for teens to sneak a sip when the adults aren't looking."

Right. Because they weren't on a date. They were here to check out the Sugar Country Club to see if it would be the perfect match for the pageant, not check out if they would be the perfect match in bed.

He looked at her belt and groaned. It wasn't often that Cal

allowed himself to play the what-if game, especially when it came to women, but he was seriously beginning to wonder *what* they would be doing right now *if* he'd just kept his mouth shut about the whole dating embargo. Not sitting here talking to fucking Chuck, who diligently catered to Glory's every whim the second she said they were here to tour the grounds—as friends—that was for sure.

"Plus, I am not sure we can afford an open bar. We are working on a tight budget and we haven't even discussed the rental cost for the back lot or the restaurant and ballroom. I mean, a bunch of tractors racing through the driving range will destroy it. Are the owners aware of that?"

"They are. The driving range I showed you is scheduled to be ripped out this spring to make way for the new clubhouse and indoor racquet ball courts, so that isn't a problem." Chuck made a big show of waving his hand as though he'd personally secured the range.

Glory smiled.

Cal rolled his eyes.

"As for the Falcon's Nest and grand ballroom, I placed a price list in the booklet I gave you. Why don't I give you a chance to look it over and see if it works with what you were thinking, while I go and see what the bartender can come up with for a fun but still sophisticated kid-appropriate drink list," Chuck said—to Glory's chest. "Can I get you anything from the menu to sample before I go?"

She studied the menu for a long and thoughtful moment, gently nibbling on that pinup girl mouth and—be still, his heart—ordered the chicken buffalo dip and sliders. Not the pan-seared abalone or the lobster bisque, like most women he knew. Nope, Glory sat at the only five-star restaurant this side of Atlanta and ordered a Shirley Temple and the most inexpensive items on the menu.

"Be right back." Chuck gathered up the menus, leaning way over to place Glory's napkin in her lap, cleverly peeking at Glory's belt, and then disappeared.

"Out of everything on the menu, you ordered the chicken buffalo dip?" Cal asked.

"If they had wings, I'd have ordered those," she said, primly draping a napkin across her lap, only to crack a smile. "Somehow ahi tuna tartar doesn't scream teen-approved. I think that the sliders and buffalo dip will be a big hit, though. What do you think?"

"Judge Holden was right to put you in charge," he said genuinely. "Moving the pageant to a neutral place is a great idea and I think once word spreads about the new look of Miss Peach, it will open the door to girls who normally wouldn't enter."

"That's what I'm hoping," she said, leaning in until she was so close he could smell her shampoo, until her hand was within holding distance. Until all he had to do was move his fingers just an inch and they'd tangle with hers. "Have you had a chance to look at the e-mail I sent you this morning?"

"Not yet," he said and, well, shit, that was the wrong answer. Glory leaned back, hands in her lap, way out of holding distance, and looked out at the fading orange in the sky. "But since I haven't had a chance to see your e-mail, and we finally have a moment to talk." *Without Chuck staring at your breasts.* "Why don't you give me the highlights?"

"It was just an outline about last night's meeting, a list of volunteers and applicants, which there aren't many . . . of either," she said, her eyes imploring him to what—he didn't have a clue. "That's all."

But that wasn't all. Her expression said there was so much more.

Cal was fluent in she-speak. A master of subtext. He could decipher, down to the exact meaning, what each sigh, roll of the eyes, or huff translated into. Could even gauge within a point-one accuracy rate, where a specific gesture ranked on the doomed-for-meltdown scale.

Except with Glory. For whatever reason, with her, he couldn't gauge a damn thing. It was as frustrating as it was intriguing.

"Anything important about the list?"

"Yes, which is why you should read it." Questions were getting him nowhere, so he pulled a play from his single-dad handbook and let her fill the silence. And damn if it actually worked this time. "I guess what got to me was that the majority of the applicants were just who'd you expect."

"Debutantes?"

She nodded. "Which is great. But I was hoping to get more girls this year, a different kind of contestant, but I think that so much emphasis has been placed on the crown and family lineage over the years that people forgot that Miss Peach is about honoring high-achieving girls and opening up doors to new opportunities outside of Sugar. *All* kids of girls."

And suddenly it clicked. Cal had spent so much time focused on how pissed he was that *he* got sucked into co-commissioning, that he never stopped to think just how uncomfortable this must be for Glory. Ms. Kitty, the pageant, all of it would feel like one painful walk down memory lane.

"With the application deadline being over," she eyed him expectantly, "I was thinking of asking the council to consider extending the deadline for another week or so, to give us time to announce the changes and give more girls, including ones who were too nervous before, time to sign up."

"Then that's what we'll recommend," he said, confident that was what she needed to hear. That he was on her side and she wouldn't have to face down the Sugar Peaches and Ms. Kitty alone.

Her body visibly relaxed and, *bingo*, there it was. A smile—real and bright and just for him. If he'd known that was all it took, a reminder that he had her back, then he would have said it the second he showed up at the hospital. Because, hot damn, it was an incredible smile. Warm and genuine and so damn contagious. Smiling Glory was by far the sexiest thing he'd ever seen—and compared to the competition, that was saying a lot.

Cal slid the Sugar Country Club pamphlet across the table. "Now, are you going to open the price list or just keep pretending that it doesn't exist?"

"I was hoping to enjoy the buffalo dip before the dream is shattered and I have to admit that we can't afford this place, and we are stuck having the pageant at Duncan Plantation."

With a sigh, she picked up the pamphlet and flicked it open and started on line one.

If it were him, he'd skip to the bottom, see the total cost, then backtrack and look at each itemized cost to see where he could trim. Not Glory. Nope, the woman took her sweet-ass time, looking ever so adorable as she carefully read each itemized cost and expense.

Cal sat back and took a sip of water.

He knew the moment she reached the grand total. Two wide green eyes met his over the top of the brochure. "They're giving us the venue for free."

"Are they?" he asked but already knew the answer. They were giving them the Falcon's Nest, grand ballroom, and driving range free of charge. Something he'd negotiated before bringing Glory here.

"This has Brett written all over it," Glory said, a little flustered, and damn if that didn't hurt a little.

When you were a three-time Masters Champion like Brett, getting stuff for free was as easy as showing up. So he could see how she'd make that jump. But Cal didn't trade on his brother's name—ever. He'd made this happen on his own. Why, he wasn't sure, but he'd done it all the same. Not that he was about to tell her that.

She set the pamphlet down. "We can't have the pageant here."

Whoa. Not what he wanted to hear. He'd busted his ass and offered a ridiculous discount to get the owner to agree. "Why not?"

"Brett's my friend, and in the end, this will cost him a whole lot more than the ten grand they're donating," she explained, shaking her head. "They probably made him promise to MC their annual Golf Ballers Gala or build the new clubhouse." *Right barter, wrong brother.* "I wouldn't feel comfortable using him like that."

He didn't see that coming. Strange how that kept happening around her.

Sure, Glory had a loyal quality about her that Cal had always admired. Soft and sure and so unwavering it was humbling. But the way she cared for her grandmother, for her friends, for the community? Yeah, that reached him on a level that surprised the shit out of him.

"Brett isn't building the new clubhouse," he finally admitted, a ridiculous amount of embarrassment filling his body. "I am. Well, McGraw Construction is."

"I don't know what to say," Glory whispered as Cal walked her around to the passenger side of his truck. A gentle evening breeze cooled her skin and cleared her head. Too bad her body was still all hot and ready to go, and her heart—well, she didn't want to go there.

Enjoying a romantic dinner for two at sunset with the sexiest friend on the planet could do that to a girl.

"Not that you've changed your mind, I hope," Cal said, unlocking her door. "We've already signed on the dotted line and just think about how hard poor Chuck worked on that teen-approved menu for you. I don't know if his delicate man feeling could handle that kind of rejection."

"He'd recover." Not that she cared. Guys like Chuck came into her bar nightly. Cocky, handsome, and looking for a fun, no-strings night, and for whatever reason they were always interested in Glory. But she wasn't interested in no-strings or the Chucks of the world.

Nope, in true Glory fashion, she was interested in a guy who wanted to be her friend. "I'm more worried that I'll never be able to repay you for making this happen."

"Like I said earlier, I had already signed on to do the build," Cal said, sounding so exasperated that Glory smiled. "I was running by some details with the owner this morning, I happened to mention the Harvest Fest, and he was gracious enough to offer his help. It was simple."

Glory knew that there was more to it than that, but kept silent. What Cal had done was beyond sweet, beyond doing his part, and it went way beyond what a casual friend would do. And they both knew it.

"What are you smiling about?" he huffed.

"Nothing," she said, smiling even bigger. "Absolutely nothing." *Except that you're getting all pissy about helping me.* "Just wanted to say thank you for a fun night. And for securing us the venue. Even though, like you said, it was no big deal."

"Uh-huh," he said, taking a step toward her, and with

nowhere left to move, Glory found herself backed up against the side of his truck. He studied her mouth and then his eyes met hers and held. "You're still smiling."

"Okay." She bit her lower lip to keep it from curving up.

"Not helping," he said, the low gravel in his voice kicking her pulse into overdrive and her resolve to the curb. But then his eyes became intense and heated and, as usual, they gave away nothing of why he'd helped her or why he was so determined to keep it a secret.

Then again, Glory had a secret of her own. One that involved his daughter and an inappropriate dress. The new deadline gave Payton a second chance to come clean before submitting her application, but if Cal discovered Glory knew about it before him, she didn't think he'd give her even a second to explain—let alone a second chance.

"I thought we weren't doing this," she said but he smelled so amazing all she could think about was how she wanted to do this, how her body seemed to be swaying closer.

"We're not." But he was suddenly right there, all hard lines of hammer-swinging muscle wrapped in a double dose of yummy man, sandwiching her between the side of his truck and his delicious body. He braced his palms on the passenger window, caging her in until she had to tilt her head back to look up into his eyes.

"Right, because we're friends."

"Friends," he repeated and she expected he would back up, he didn't. "There are all kinds of friends."

"Yeah, well, I don't go on dates with my friends."

"Neither do I."

"Then why are you looking at me like you're about to end this friendly nondate with a not-so-friendly kiss."

When he looked like he was about to do just that and she was afraid she wouldn't push him away, she said, "You don't date locally, remember? You're more of a dine-out kind of guy."

He frowned, as though he wasn't sure if he liked the sound of that, but didn't speak up to correct her. And Glory began to wonder if Cal had the right idea earlier, putting on the breaks before someone got hurt. Namely her.

Abort now, while you can, her brain screamed because he was the kind of man she could easily fall for and then spend her life trying to prove she deserved. Cal McGraw was the kind of man she wasn't sure she could live up to even on her best day, let alone when he wasn't open to exploring more than a friends-with-benefits arrangement.

"You don't do serious," she said quietly, reaching behind her to open the passenger door. "And I promised myself that I'd never be someone's secret again."

Chapter 12

"Five minutes, Payton, and then I turn off the hot water," Cal said, giving a warning rap to the door.

It was Monday morning, he was still in yesterday's stubble and boxers, and he had a meeting with the planning department in one hour. Payton had barricaded herself inside the bathroom over forty minutes ago, after a teary meltdown about how her life was officially over. He wanted to ask, since her life was already over, if he could use the shower first, but knew that it would be a waste of time.

"I still have to use my face scrub."

"Five minutes," he said, ignoring her dramatic plea about the great pimple of Pompeii, and headed straight for the kitchen—and the smell of bacon frying on the griddle. He needed a hearty breakfast and a cup of caffeine if he was going to make it through this morning.

Hattie stood at the stove, flipping a fresh batch of flapjacks. She wore a bright yellow track suit with matching visor and an apron tied around her waist. She also had enough bacon stacked on the platter to feed a family of five.

God bless her.

"Morning." He kissed her on the cheek and snatched a strip of bacon.

"Don't you 'morning' me." Hattie snatched it back and swatted his hand away. "I heard you're going to announce at the meeting today that Kitty Duncan and the Prowler are cleared to race."

"Where did you hear that?" Not that he had to ask. This was Sugar after all, and gossip traveled faster here than news of a gold strike in Alaska.

"Same place I heard you're dating Jelly Lou's girl."

Cal gave up on the bacon and went for the coffee, filling his mug to the brim. "Yes, Kitty is cleared to race, and no, Glory and I aren't dating."

"You sure about that, son?"

At this point he wasn't sure about anything—except he'd gone in for the kiss and she'd shut him down. "We are co-commissioners for the Harvest Fest, that's all."

She raised a brow. "Last time a man took me to the Falcon's Nest, he expected me to put out."

Cal choked on his coffee. "I hope that was with Grandpa."

"Falcon's Nest wasn't around when your grandpa was alive. And we all know what a man thinks when they take a lady there."

Breakfast over and appetite gone, Cal tried not to gag at the idea of his grandmother having sex, and failed. He knew that Hattie dated from time to time, but always told himself that dating in her world meant dance cards and bingo. Not fancy dinners and night caps.

"We were scouting out a new location for the pageant and

Sugar Pull, which we found, and you're welcome." He gave her a stern look to end the discussion. "Nothing more to report."

Hattie leveled him with an even sterner look that made him shift a little in his boots. When he refused to comment further, she pulled her phone out of her apron pocket. A few thumb swipes to the screen later, she held up a Facebook photo of Cal and Glory at the Falcon's Nest, looking mighty cozy and 100 percent date-like at their secluded table for two with the sunset as a backdrop.

"Christ," Cal said, noticing there were more comments than there were people in town. "Who the hell posted this?"

"Mable from the market. She was celebrating her fiftieth wedding anniversary when she saw, what she reported as"— Hattie read from the screen—"'a steamy, secret tryst between the town's wild child and Sugar's sexiest bachelor. It says here at the bottom that you're only the sexiest by default. Brett would have won but he's married and Southern women don't publically admit to coveting another woman's husband—even if she is a Yankee."

To say that Joie and Hattie hadn't started on the best of terms would be the biggest understatement in the history of women. But over the past year, they'd worked out their differences, mainly that Hattie was a busybody and Joie was a Yankee. Neither could change a thing about that, but they'd come to accept their differences.

"Is that true?"

"That I'm the default McGraw?" It was. Cal had held his own with women before Tawny. But Brett had the female population locked down by middle school and that was one area he didn't mind letting his kid brother dominate.

Hattie wacked her thigh with the spatula. "That you were having a secret date with Glo."

"It wasn't a secret." Hell, it wasn't even discreet. "And it wasn't a date." Although the picture said differently. He could call it whatever he wanted, but one look at that snapshot and—his chest tightened and heart gave a hard, frustrated bump.

God, this was bad.

Glory was leaning in, her eyes twinkling with excitement—she had been telling him about her proposal for the new pediatric ward, and even though Glory in a miniskirt or sundress got him going, the image of her in scrubs working with kids melted something deep inside him that had no business melting.

Then there was his smile. It was as big and stupid as a smile could get—and Cal wondered when was the last time he'd smiled and laughed like that with a woman.

Sophomore year of college. He'd met this wild and sexy Savannah socialite at a party, bought her a drink, and asked her to dance. A two-step around the room was enough to seal his fate and Cal had fallen hard. He thought she'd felt the same, until a year later his parents died, and Tawny, not wanting to do the long-distance thing, broke it off.

Four months later, she'd shown up in Sugar, panicked and pregnant, and Cal, not wanting to miss out on a second chance with the love of his life, proposed. They were married and parents by the end of the year. Tawny had checked out emotionally by Payton's third birthday, physically by her fifth, and two long and painful years later she'd packed up and moved back to Savannah.

Cal never figured out what he'd done to lose her or why he hadn't been enough to make her happy. He'd watched his parents together, witnessed the incredible love they shared, really believed he'd had that with Tawny. But he'd been wrong. So incredibly wrong.

Cal had given Tawny everything—his heart, his name, every ounce of his love—and she'd walked. Not just on him, but on Payton. That was a mistake he wouldn't make again.

It was his job, his role as a parent, to model for Payton what a healthy relationship was, but when it came to women, Cal had learned he couldn't trust his judgment, which was why going in that deep with a woman wasn't an option.

"Yup, we're just friends." And he meant it.

But that picture. *Christ.*

Payton burst into the room, backpack slung over her shoulder, cell phone attached to her fingers as she texted at supersonic speeds. She wore cowgirl boots, painted-on jeans, and a skimpy top that didn't even qualify as clothing. Her hair was styled so that she was a good three inches closer to God and her lips were shimmery.

Her phone chirped. She swiped, read, and squealed in a way that had Cal wanting to peek over her shoulder. It was the kind of noise teen girls made when conversing with or about a boy. Either way, he wasn't having it.

"Is that Kendal?" he asked, referring to Payton's BFF since the second grade.

"Nope. Mom," Payton said, her heart right there in her eyes for everyone to see. Problem was, the only one who didn't seem to notice was his ex-wife. "Coach e-mailed us that the newspaper is sending out a photographer to the game to take a picture of the team. The *cheer* team. For the front page! Can you imagine?"

He could and he was damn proud of her. He wasn't thrilled about her cheering for seniors, but she'd worked hard to earn her place on the team.

"I called Mom and she freaked, and then she called Bless Her Hair and made us appointments. She's going to get a mani and I am going to get bangs and a blowout. She said she'd drive me to the game, since all the girls' moms meet in the locker room to do hair and makeup." Payton grabbed a strip of bacon and took a bite. "Oh, and she wants to have dinner after, the three of us. To talk."

"Sounds great."

Cal hoped he sounded genuine. He didn't know how he felt about Payton wearing makeup or not driving her to her first game. But what had every one of his warning bells going off was that Tawny wanted to talk. Knowing his ex, it was something that would make his life more difficult. But Payton was excited and happy—two things he hadn't seen from her since the Pep-Luck from hell—so he needed to man up and go with it.

Thirty minutes, and a ten-point explanation on how all teen girls wear makeup, later, Cal dropped Payton off at school and stopped by the Gravy Train for his morning latte and a few minutes' peace. He stepped out of the restaurant, to-go breakfast in hand, and found an empty park bench across the street. He leaned back, pulled out one of his breakfast eggrolls—he was starved so he'd ordered two—and took a big bite, washing it down with a sip of latte while savoring the blessed quiet.

It was as close to peace as he'd come in weeks.

"You going to eat all of that?" Brett asked, taking a seat next to Cal, the crinkling paper bag cutting through his quiet.

Brett was in khaki shorts and a polo, and his face was way too sweaty for the time of morning, which meant he'd just come from the driving range.

"You going to warn me when your wife tries to set me up next time?"

Brett grinned. "Yeah."

"Great." Cal stuffed the rest of the eggroll in his mouth,

licking the hoisin sauce off his fingers. "Then next time I'll get you one."

"Most guys would have been thanking me," Brett said. "What's wrong with spending some time with a sweet and seriously hot woman?"

"Nothing." Unless that time was shared with a sweet and seriously hot nurse with whom he'd talked himself right into friend territory.

Brett was quiet for a moment. "Nothing, huh? I mean, it's been a long time since Tawny left and if you've forgotten how to—"

"I haven't forgotten anything." Except how much he hated talking about this kind of shit with his brother.

"Whoa." Brett laughed and put his hands up. "I was going to say date, but then I guess you've got that handled, too, right?"

Cal slid his brother a glance and blew out a breath. "Shit, you saw Facebook."

"The whole town saw Facebook, including Joie. So I don't think you have to worry about any blind dates from her for a while."

"It wasn't a date." *Jesus*, how many times would he have to say it? "So before you go warning me off, telling me it's a bad idea, we're just friends."

"Why would I do that? Glory's great. Sweet, funny, real," Brett said with so much confidence Cal had to check himself. "But if you say you're just friends, then you're just friends."

"You believe me?" Cal asked, not sure why Brett's belief in him rubbed him the wrong way. Why him not pointing out what everyone else already knew—that he and Glory were a train wreck waiting to happen—didn't make him feel any better.

Maybe it was because his brother was investing his blind trust in a guy who was playing it off as harmless flirting while secretly hoping that their co-chairing time together would lead to, well, time *together*.

Naked and panting.

Brett stared at him a little too long. "You're the most stand-up guy I know and right about now Glory could use a friend like you."

And didn't that make him a million different kinds of bastard.

Cal felt a red-hot rush of guilt because Brett was right. Sure, he wanted Glory, but he was also starting to like her. A lot. And just because that was all he was capable of offering didn't mean she didn't deserve more.

"Just remember that when it comes to her and this town, people talk. Between her grandma's health, that job at the hospital, and this BS about being commissioner, she already has a lot on her plate, so try to make sure that your friendship makes her life easier right now, not harder."

Cal wanted to ask how the hell he was supposed to accomplish that, since nothing between him and Glory was easy, but Brett was already walking down Maple Street—with Cal's breakfast eggroll in hand.

Glory made it a point to arrive early to the Harvest Council meeting. She wanted the firing squad to come to her, not the other way around, plus the town hall had air-conditioning, high-speed Wi-Fi, and free coffee—three things that her apartment did not. And after a long, restless night thinking about her annoyingly sexy co-commissioner, she needed caffeine and a concrete understanding of Excel if she was to make any kind of progress on her proposal.

That had been the hope, at least.

"Stupid piece of shit," Glory mumbled, hitting Cancel on the "circular reference error."

An hour and three different YouTube tutorials later, Glory was looking at the same error warning, but she had composed a task list that spanned sixteen items long, which seemed like plenty. Except the sample proposal Charlotte gave her listed over a hundred carefully laid out steps, all with dependent timelines and a color-coded key to specify which department within the hospital it depended on—legal, corporate, human resources, administration, or medical staff—and what the estimated turnaround time was for each of the respective departments.

Glory didn't have a clue as to how long it would take legal to create a Liability Waiver for the volunteers or if the hospital already had one she could modify. And if they did have an existing one she could use, would she have to modify it or would they? Which led to another three questions and, ultimately, another three steps.

Her *other* list, however, was going swimmingly. The one she'd started last night appropriately titled PROJECT GRANNY PANTIES: ACM—as in Avoiding Cal McGraw, or rather, abstaining from, she corrected, because *that* was hard work, especially when his lips were a millimeter from hers the other night.

She flipped the page on her legal pad and, wow, look at that, fifty-seven clear reasons to keep her distance from Cal. The most recent being that she didn't want to keep her distance from Cal.

"Still winning friends and influencing people, I see."

The low, gravelly voice had her adding, DANGER TO HEALTH: CREATES IRREGULAR AND ANNOYING HEARTBEATS WHEN NEAR.

Glory made a big deal of flipping the page back and scribbling FINISH TASK LIST to the bottom of her *other* task list and then hit Save on her spreadsheet before she looked up, even though she hadn't added anything useful since the last press of the button.

She took him in—all six foot two of chiseled muscle and messy male. "Busy day at the office?"

Cal looked down and shrugged, as though he'd had worse. His work boots were splattered in concrete, his jeans weren't much better, and his T-shirt clung to his body, defining every one of his ridges. He looked a little sweaty, a little dirty, and a whole lot like the guy in her dream last night—only in her dream he had on a tool belt and nothing else.

He strode over with all the grace and strength of a man who walked across steel beams while balancing two-by-fours for a living and took the seat next to her, setting a red tin lunchbox on the table. He glanced at her legal pad and smiled. "How's the project coming along?"

"Great," she said in her confident authority tone that worked on just about everyone she'd ever met. Except, of course, Cal, who reached over and touched the keypad.

Her laptop sprang to life and a dancing paperclip wearing bright yellow shoes and matching scarf appeared on her screen. Cal's finger hovered over the Play button.

"Don't."

But he did and the paperclip pulled out a cane and top hat, while belting out a catchy little show tune about how with perseverance and proper planning, and a bunch of other *P* words that Glory hadn't managed to master yet, the *can't* would disappear right out of her *Gantt*.

Cal shot her an amused look, only on him, amused came off as sexy. Hell, anything came off as sexy on Cal McGraw. All it took was those intense blue eyes to fall her way, combined with the slight tilting of those lips, and it was as though the temperature in the room had shot up fifteen degrees.

"According to Professor Paperclip, all I need to do is enter all of these steps into a spreadsheet," she said primly.

"Professor Paperclip, huh?" Cal opened his lunchbox and pulled out a sandwich, setting it on a folded napkin. Something spicy and hearty filled the air. Next came a bag of BBQ potato chips—her absolute favorite—followed by a chocolate chip cookie and ice-cold can of diet cola. Glory eyed the condensation dripping down the can and felt her mouth water.

Cradling half the sandwich between his big hands, he brought it to his mouth and was about to take a bite when her stomach, picking up on what she'd bet her best boots was meatloaf, growled.

His gaze meet hers over the crust of the bread, and she saw his eyes crinkle and knew that he was smiling—at her. He took a bite and made a huge deal over moaning and savoring the sandwich—the big jerk.

"You want half?" he mumbled, pushing the napkin toward her.

She waved it off. "I have an energy bar." Which would taste as good as the napkin his sandwich lay on. Actually, the napkin would taste better since little bits of grease and hot mustard had dripped down the side of the bread.

"Take a bite. Just one," he said with so much authority that she reached out to grab it before even realizing her hand was moving.

She paused. "Did Payton make it?"

"No, it came from the Gravy Train so you're safe."

Unable to turn down Skeeter's meatloaf, Glory picked it up, gave it a quick smell, and took a big bite. *Sweet baby*

Jesus, it was the perfect balance of spice, tang, and mouth-watering grease that was like a party in her mouth.

"Oh my God, this is so good," she said around bits of bun. "So much better than my energy bar."

"Glad to hear it. Here." He cracked the cola open with a sizzle and slid it her way. "Wash it down with this."

"I don't want to take your drink." But she so did and he knew it because he smiled—and man, what a smile. It supported number seventeen on PROJECT GRANNY PANTIES: ABLE TO SPIKE CORE BODY TEMPERATURE WITH A SINGLE QUIRK.

"I have another." He pulled out another cola, equally cold but no *Diet* on the front, along with a second bag of chips and—be still, her heart—a second chocolate chip cookie.

Either he had the appetite of a horse or this was a pre-planned, quiet lunch for two—and she wasn't really sure what that meant or how she felt about it. "Why are you really here, Cal?"

"I had a meeting with the planning department down the hall earlier and heard you having it out with your poor laptop there. Since you were still here, and still screaming up a storm, when I headed out for lunch, I called the Gravy Train and changed my order from one to two and staged an intervention." His gaze met hers. "Skeeter said the mo shu meatloaf sandwich was your favorite." He took a gulp of soda. "Funny thing about that, boots, is it's mine, too."

That he took the time to find out what her favorite dish was caught her completely off guard. That his ridiculous nickname made her feel all girly and breathless did not bode well for PROJECT GRANNY PANTIES.

"I meant what I said last night." *Last night* being the key components of that statement. In the light of day, with him looking like sex with a tool belt, she wasn't so sure.

She wanted to be more, so much more it scared her. So did he; she could see it in the way he watched her. Too bad their ideas of *more* didn't match up.

"So did I." He smiled but it wasn't full of charming or nefarious intent; it was soft and warm. "Now tell me, what seems to be the problem?"

"I think Excel and I are breaking up," she admitted, popping a chip in her mouth. "He doesn't listen, constantly points out my shortcomings, and refuses to give me what I need."

"That's a pretty big problem." Cal's grin widened until Glory was certain her core body temperature was well in the danger zone. "You're in luck since your needs are a constant concern of mine." Just when Glory's heartbeat was becoming totally erratic, Cal gave a sly grin and whispered, "We're co-chairs after all. Best to help each other however we can."

His gaze slid down her body, then made a lazy trail back to settle on her eyes once more, Glory was ready to toss her sense, and her PROJECT GRANNY PANTIES list, out the door.

"I also happen to be an Excel ninja with a black belt in Gantt charts." Cal laced his fingers and cracked his knuckles over his head. "Now, do you already have a spreadsheet?"

And there it was, the ice water of reality Cal seemed to throw right after he made her entire body buzz with heat.

With a deep breath, she worked to refocus on the matter at hand: her proposal. Not Cal. Tell that to her "granny panties," which were now a bit damp.

Cal used the trackpad to move the cursor down to the spreadsheet tab, which had taken her all morning to create, and Glory smacked his hand away. "Yes, I have a spreadsheet. I'm not an idiot."

"Spreadsheet formatted, got it."

"Well, kind of. It keeps giving me a circular error, which

isn't a big deal since I can't figure out what the steps are to put them in order yet," she said in a rush because she hated admitting she wasn't competent in something. It was almost as bad as admitting she was wrong.

Cal took her legal pad and tore off the front sheet, exposing her secret list below. All he had to do was glance down and he'd see every embarrassing detail of her crush.

"That's for school." She reached for the list but he held it over his head. "Give it back."

He looked up and read, " 'Project Granny Panties: ACM'? What class would that be?"

She leveled him with a look, one that displayed just how serious she was as she lied her granny panties right off. "It's for my geriatric theory class."

"So 'buns of steel' would refer to?"

"The importance of glute strength in the aging." She leapt out of her chair, snatched the pad back, zipped it up in her backpack, and stuffed it under her chair to be safe.

"Ah-huh." He wasn't looking at her anymore. He was busy taking her proposal task list, which she'd spend the better part of a day on, and tearing it into little strips.

"What are you doing?"

He didn't answer, just continued to make paper ribbons out of her hard work. Then with confidence, and a surprising amount of grace for a man with hands his size, he fanned out the strips and organized them into an efficient line. Minus a few gaps, which appeared to be intentionally placed, it created a perfect timeline. "How did you do that?"

"I have to do this all the time for projects." He was leaning back now, proud of his handiwork. "Think of it like building a house."

"Which would be a brilliant suggestion," she deadpanned. "If I had ever built a house."

"Well, lucky you that you know someone who has. And he's good. Better than good."

"Lucky me."

"That's the attitude." He reached into his Marry Poppins lunchbox and pulled out a stack of three-by-five cards and took her pen. "Pretend we're decorating a room. Your room." He snapped his fingers. "Your *bed*room."

"How did we go from charts to discussing my bedroom?"

His dimples flashed and he said, "Sweetheart, any conversation with you always ends up with me thinking about your bedroom."

"Do you spend a lot of time thinking about your friends' bedrooms?"

"Nope, just yours." He clicked the pen. "What would your dream room look like?" She eyed him skeptically. "Well, I can tell you what my dream bedroom of yours would look like, but this is your dream, not mine."

She decided to play along. "I would want it to feel relaxing, like the day spa at Joie's inn. So green walls." He scribbled down something on a flash card and then looked at her to go on. "Dark furniture with orange and white accents, and a comfy bed with a big wooden slatted headboard—"

"I imagined a big headboard, too, but mine would have bedposts to attach—"

"Curtains." She tapped the next flash card and he got back to writing. "Sheer gauzy curtains, lots of plants, and maybe some pretty artwork to hang over the bed...are you writing this down?"

"Sorry, you said *bed* again. If I didn't know any better, I'd say you were trying to seduce me." He went back to his cards. "Vegetation and artwork, got it." He scribbled down a few thoughts of his own and then made quick work of fanning them out. "I like to start at the end and work backward. So the last card is?"

"Hang artwork over four-poster bed," she read.

He smiled. "I took some artistic license since I am the professional here."

Didn't she know it.

"We can't hang the artwork until the bed is centered and the rest of the furniture is arranged, right?"

She nodded; this was actually making since. "And I couldn't arrange the furniture until it is delivered, which means I need to add a task to go shopping and buy new furniture and the artwork."

"Right. And green paint. You have to tape, primer, and paint the walls so they can dry before the *four*-poster bed is delivered and placed against the wall." He sat back, hands laced behind his head, his big, long legs stretched out, looking awfully smug.

"And here I wasted all that time with Professor Paperclip."

"Boots, when showing your spreadsheet to a man, make sure he's got more in his tool belt than a cane and top hat. You want a guy who comes equipped to get the job done."

Glory has seen Cal's tool belt, and she had no doubt that he not only came properly equipped, but knew how to use each and every tool in his belt to get the job done.

"So what is the end goal?"

"What?" Glory's eyes flew to his face, and she realized that she'd been trying to get a glimpse of his equipment. Cal knew, too, because he smiled.

"Of your project? Where do you want it to lead?"

"Right." Glory cleared her throat. This was the easy part. Glory knew exactly what kind of program she wanted to run, the kind of kids she wanted to reach out to, and the opportunities she could facilitate.

"I want to create a volunteer program that connects high school kids looking for a place to make a difference with children who need a champion in their corner. Which, I know, sounds like every other candy-striper program. But I want this to be a kind of internship, where students can earn school credits toward their senior project and an hourly wage that will accrue over their time at the hospital and can be applied toward their college fees."

Mr. Excel ninja didn't so much as bat an eye, didn't interrupt or point out that it was too big of a project for her to take on. He just leaned in and gave her all of his attention. And being on the receiving end of that kind of intensity, and what she thought looked a lot like respect, made her heart do this funny little flutter in her chest.

"I want to start with seniors, but over the next few years open it up to sophomores so that they can work their way up into positions with more responsibility. Also, it would help with turnover so patients who are here for longer stays will have a buddy to go through the entire process with."

When he still didn't say a word, just kept staring at her, she felt a rush of insecurity come back. She knew that convincing the board to hire teenagers was going to be tough; getting them insured as employees was going to be even harder. But giving kids the chance to experience a life outside Sugar, a life that might not be possible without additional funding like the one her program could provide, was the heart of her mission.

"You know, give them something stable in the middle of all the craziness."

To everyone, her mission statement would come off like a way to help and inspire local teens. But the kids she was hoping to help were kids like her. This proposal was her life in a series of charts and spreadsheets, right there for anyone to see if they knew what to look for. And Cal was looking and suddenly she was terrified of what he'd see.

"Well? What do you think?"

"That the hospital would be lucky to have you," he said with a quiet smile, and her heart gave a soft bump. "And that Brett's right. You, Glory Mann, are amazing."

Then a not so soft bump. And because Cal was looking at her as though she were amazing, she began to *feel* amazing...more than amazing. He made her feel adored.

Then his smile faded, and so did hers, because she was aware of just how close they sat, and how badly she wanted him to lean over and kiss her. Cal's eyes seemed to say he was on board.

"Is that why you came?" she asked, hating how much his answer mattered. "Because Brett asked you to?"

"I came because I wanted to be a good friend." Cal looked at her lips and released a breath before sitting back. "Which is what I'm going to do."

Chapter 13

The Falcon's Nest won't work, because the location has already been decided," Ms. Kitty said, marching toward the easel at the front of the room with every intention of placing her presentation right over Glory's. "The pageant, its Cotillion, and the Sugar Pull will be held at the Duncan Plantation."

"Actually, the Duncan Plantation is *one* option on the table," Glory said, positioning herself between the easel and the older woman. When Kitty just stood there, poster board in hand, Glory pointed to the other side of the room. "Which you can set on that easel. Over there. And if you'd like to present *your* option to the room, you'll need to consult with Spencer, our new, uh, operations specialist, so she can put you on the agenda."

"Agenda?"

Spencer held up a clipboard from the back of the room, and Kitty's face puckered as though she'd just sucked on a lemon.

"This is a trick. You knew your idea would be shot down

so you're abusing your power to get your own way, to the detriment of this community and all of those young girls."

"I think the girls will benefit from a new, more neutral location," Glory said confidently.

"Harder to cheat when you're not drawing the racing lines, isn't it, Kitty?" Etta Jayne said, and the rest of the Pitt Crew Mafia applauded. They took up the entire front row, their matching TIME TO CLEAN OUT THE LITTERBOX T-shirts proudly on display.

"Neutral location?" Kitty scoffed as though no one else in the room was concerned with the reigning Sugar Pull champ using the official racing track as her practice grounds. "I have been a respected member of this committee for over fifty years, so you and your grandmother's little stunt won't work. We will not be kowtowed."

Cal wasn't so sure. Not a single strand of pearls clacked in Kitty's support. In fact, it didn't appear as though Kitty was going to get her usual grandstand from the Sugar Peaches. It could have been the way Charlotte had taken a strategic seat next to Glory when she'd waltzed through the doors, or because Spencer was shooting daggers at anyone who looked ready to stand in opposition of Glory, while sharpening her pocket knife. But Cal had a feeling that everyone was waiting to see who would come out on top before aligning themselves—and so far it was Glory, one, Kitty, zip.

"Actually, I am just following the bylaws," Glory countered, and Cal grinned.

Kitty had come here with an agenda, and she wasn't ashamed to bulldoze right over Glory to do it. But Glory wasn't backing down.

"Since when do I have to be put on an agenda to speak on behalf of the Sugar Peaches?"

"Since it's time to scoop out the poop," Hattie said and a loud *whoop* sounded from the front row.

Glory silenced them with a single look. It was impressive. "Since the current regent of the Sugar Peaches is here to speak on their behalf."

Charlotte stood and smoothed down her skirt, and it was as though the entire room held its breath, waiting to see how the reigning queen would weigh in.

"When Glory called me last week, asking for my input on the pageant, I knew that she had the best interest of the community and the Sugar Peaches in mind. I was so impressed with her willingness to listen and learn about our traditions, and her desire to introduce a new group of girls to the pageant, I immediately signed on."

"Just the rumor of a location change has doubled the entries for the pageant," Etta Jayne pointed out.

"Doubled," Jelly Lou repeated loud enough for the room to hear, her cheeks two full circles of pride. "Did you hear that, Kitty? My girl doubled the entries in her first week in office."

Glory toed the floor with the tip of her boots at the praise, something she seemed to do when she was flustered.

Which was why, in his best co-chair voice, he tore his eyes off the tan skin peeking out of those sexy boots and explained, "In order to give every girl who is interested the opportunity to go out for Miss Peach and the scholarship, we decided to extend the deadline until next Wednesday."

Kitty looked at Cal, and for the first time in his life, the woman looked nervous. "But double the girls means double the people and I've already ordered the doilies."

"Well, you may need to unorder them because according to the book here"—Cal held up the Harvest Fest Bylaws— "any and all decisions about the Harvest Fest, including lo-

cation and decorations for the events, have to be presented
to the council by the chair."

"Or co-chair, as it may be, and then approved by a majority vote," Glory said and smiled. Cal smiled back. How
could he not? She was looking at him like he'd just made her
day—and he wanted to make her day.

"You have my vote," Charlotte said. "Not only do I move
that we relocate the Harvest Fest to the Sugar Country Club
and extend the deadline for the Miss Peach applications, but
I would be honored to head up the Harvest Decoration Committee."

"We already have a Harvest Decoration Committee. I
have the list right here," Kitty said, flapping a sheet of paper
wildly. "And you're on it!"

"Well, if we're all sharing our lists, I got one, too," Jelly
Lou said in her best Sunday school voice, angelic smile in
place. "Your name's on the top of it, Kitty."

"And it ain't no decorating committee list," Etta Jayne
added.

Charlotte ignored this. "Actually, I'm withdrawing my position from your committee and offering to head up Glory's."

Any hope Kitty had of winning by reputation just flew out
the window. Kitty's power came from money and position,
Charlotte's came from money, position, *and* a good dose of
hard-earned respect.

"It is because of my family's generosity that there is even
a scholarship," Kitty said, clutching her poster board to her
chest and facing the room. "If the group decides to go in
another direction, I might just have to pull my support this
year."

The room fell silent—except for Glory, who sucked in a
panicked breath beside Cal. Because by *support*, every person in that room knew she was talking about money.

The Duncans' endowment went a long way toward making the Miss Peach Pageant so successful. In fact, her donation accounted for over half the total budget and scholarship allotment. If she bailed, the pageant could be canceled.

"We don't want that," Glory said gently. "You and your family have done so much for this community so of course we want your input, but we also want to give girls who would never have considered entering the pageant a chance to compete."

"Last time we pulled in a different demographic of contestant, well, I'm sure you don't want to go there." Only Kitty had gone there—and it was a direct hit.

Not much got past Glory's tough girl exterior—at least that was the vibe she gave off.

Over the years, Cal had witnessed her stare down a group of jack-ass jocks, not to mention break up some of the nastiest bar fights he'd ever seen, never once showing an ounce of fear. But one backhanded comment from Kitty, and just like in the courtroom the other day, Glory's whole body seemed to sink in on itself. Her smile became strained and her eyes went big, like a deer in the headlights, as she looked around the room to find her grandmother, to make sure that the comment hadn't upset her. And damn if that didn't bring out every protective instinct Cal had.

"Which is why we'd understand if you decided to pull your support," he said, standing.

"But then you'd have no scholarship program. Are you willing to deny those girls a chance to go to college?" Kitty threatened and it was a good enough reason to back down. Only he couldn't, because Brett was right; he was a good guy. And right now he needed to be Glory's good guy.

"Since the girls you are referring to will go to college regardless of the scholarship, I don't think they're worried,"

Cal argued but Glory was opening her mouth, ready to back down so that the scholarship wouldn't be lost. He wasn't going to let that happen. "As for the other girls, they will be fine since McGraw Construction is willing to match dollar for dollar whatever is lost, should you decide to pull your support."

"What?" Glory said, her big green eyes going even bigger. "You don't have to do that."

"I know," he said. "But I want to help. The Harvest Fest benefits the whole town; I think it's time that the rest of the businesses pitch in. However, my offer only applies if the application deadline is extended to include Sugar High students who didn't feel comfortable applying before."

"You can count on the Saddle Rack to help out," Etta Jayne offered and three other local business owners pledged their support.

It was as though all of the air was sucked out of the room, and people were weighing in what was happening. Then Charlotte said, "Now who would like to sign up on my decoration committee?" and an explosion of hands went up.

Ms. Kitty had lost the battle and it was going to be around town before the meeting let out. But that wasn't what had Cal smiling. Nope, that honor went to Glory and the genuine surprise on her face.

The room was a flurry of activity, so no one noticed when she walked up to him, stopping inches from his boots and toeing at the floor again.

"Thank you," she said quietly, having a hard time looking him in the eye. "For lunch and for helping me with my proposal and for, well, everything. I don't even know what to say, except thanks."

"That getting easier?" he asked.

"Admitting that you're a good guy? Nah, I always knew

it." She looked up and let loose a big smile and, *yup*, he'd made her day all right.

And the damn thing was, he was suddenly interested in what she'd look like if he made her world.

Cal was doing his best not to think about Glory, but even shoveling gravel in the hot-ass Georgia heat wasn't helping.

He had spent all day yesterday digging the trench around the perimeter of the foundation for the drain tile, and hours that morning laying the pipe, and he was damn tired. So tired that thinking should be impossible. But that look she'd given him was going to kill him.

Literally.

He was so busy trying not to think about that look or what it meant, he didn't pay attention to the loud beeping of the dump truck until it was too late. The bed lifted right as he looked up, covering the worksite with two tons of sand and, because he was standing downwind, covering him with two tons' worth of sand dust.

Coughing and smacking the gray powder off his jeans, he felt his phone vibrate in his pocket. He looked at the screen and answered.

"Hey, Brett," he shouted into the mouthpiece. "What's going on?"

"We've got a problem."

"I must have heard you wrong." Cal walked toward his truck, putting distance between himself and the noise of the site. "I thought you said *we* have a problem, which couldn't be right, since I am officially retired in the helping your ass out department."

"You might want to rethink that statement since I am currently sitting outside your bathroom door, trying to bribe Payton into coming out." Brett let out a sigh that was utterly defeated and Cal felt his head begin to ache. "I've tried everything, man. Ice cream, crying it out with her favorite uncle, that stupid dance movie she loves. I even offered to buy her a pony."

"A pony?" The last thing he needed was one more life to be responsible for.

"Don't worry, she opened the door, screamed she wasn't a baby, and slammed it shut."

Cal pinched the bridge of his nose and released a breath, a small cloud of dust expelling. "Let me guess, Tawny isn't there."

"Nope. I guess she is stuck in traffic or running late." More like she didn't leave on time. "Payton called, asking for Joie. I told her Joie wasn't home; she said her life was over and hung up. When I got here, she was already barricaded in the bathroom, and unless you're willing to let me put a sweet-sixteen convertible on the table, I suggest you get home. And bring your tools. At this point we might have to pick the lock."

"Ah, shit." Cal took in the three trucks lined up and waiting for his signal to deliver the supplies, the two crews working hard to get the pipes laid and covered in time for the drain tile inspection on Monday, and his foreman who was waving him over—for what he assumed was another unforeseen setback.

Walking off the site now meant that there was a good chance they wouldn't be ready for inspection come Monday. Which could set them back. Big time.

But Payton was his number one. Always.

"I'll be there in ten minutes," Cal said, heading over to talk to the foreman. An ear-piercing scream came through the phone, followed by several "Ohmygods!" and hysterical sobbing. "Make that five."

And just when Cal thought his day couldn't get any worse, Brett added, "And Cal, be ready. There's a dress."

He stopped, everything inside him telling him not to ask. "What kind of dress?"

"The shop delivered it about ten minutes ago. It's blue and poofy and pageanty," Brett said, and the asshole had the nerve to chuckle. "It doesn't have any sleeves. I guess she expects to hold it up with her... you know."

Yeah, Cal knew. Just like he knew he'd been played. Only this time Tawny had pulled Payton into the game.

"A dress, Tawny," Cal barked into his bluetooth as he pulled out onto the highway. "What the fuck? We talked about this and decided she was too young."

"No, Cal." Her voice filled the cab of his truck and grated like biting on tinfoil. "You decided she was too young. I started in pageants when I was three and loved it."

She was also pregnant and married by twenty—and not in that order. Cal loved his life as a single dad, wouldn't change it for the world, but he wanted more for Payton. He wanted her to understand how intelligent and talented she was, and that, sure she was pretty, but she had so much more to offer the world than her looks.

"Since we both need to be in agreement, and I'm not, the pageant isn't happening."

"For God's sake, she's entering a pageant, not applying at Hooters." Cal had been to a few pageants, knew what they wore, and didn't see much of a difference. "She is so excited about this, Cal. We have been talking about it and planning all summer."

"Funny, since I'm her dad and this is the first I'm hearing about it." Although if he were being honest, Payton had brought it up in passing several times. But not a word about it from his ex. "You should have been talking to me, Tawny. Not going behind my back to get a dress so I have to either say yes or be the bad guy who wrecks Payton's world."

"Then don't wreck her world," she said as though she knew he was going to cave. And normally he would, but not this time. Not with her canceling two weeks in a row and then showing up late to the most important night of his daughter's sophomore year. "This means a lot to her. To both of us and she was afraid you wouldn't understand that."

All he understood was that once again his ex had manipulated the situation. And sure, he might not understand the finer points of makeup or what was so important about a pageant that Payton would feel the need to lie to him, but he made sure that he was always there for her. He showed up, took an interest, and listened because that's what good parents did for their kids.

"*Tonight* meant a lot to her, Tawny." More than a dress, Cal thought, pulling onto the gravel road to his house. "She was looking forward to spending time with you, showing her mom off to her friends, and now she is crying in the bathroom. What could be more important than you showing up for that? And don't give me the traffic bull you told Payton."

Silence filled the cab of his truck, every second pressing farther down on his shoulders. Tawny only got silent when she was about to drop a bomb, and the last time he'd felt this kind of weighted silence was when she told him she was filing for divorce.

"I'm not coming from home. I'm coming from the airport and my plane from Houston was delayed so I landed two hours late." She exhaled—hard. Which had his heart thumping against his rib cage. "Randal wasn't interviewing a perspective client; he was interviewing for lead council and he got the job."

Cal parked his car by the front porch and rested his head against the steering wheel. Payton was going to be crushed by the news. She barely saw her mom as it was and they only lived a few hours away. Four states between them was going to take their relationship from strained to more of a rotating-holidays one, and she deserved more.

"How long does Randal have to make his decision?"

"It's an incredible opportunity for us," she said, completely oblivious to the fact that she'd just turned Payton's world upside down. "Why would he wait?"

"I don't know, maybe to talk to your daughter, see how she felt about her mother living in a different state." What had he ever seen in her? "Did you even stop to consider how hard this might be on her?"

"Of course I did," she snapped. "Which is why Randal and I want to ask her to come with us. I was going to bring it up at dinner tonight."

"Jesus, Tawny." Cal's heart stopped—right there in his chest. "What about talking to me about this first?"

"I'm talking to you now, aren't I?"

"Only because I called." She went quiet, a clear sign that she had planned on railroading him tonight at dinner. His ears went hot, a clear sign that he was about to lose it. "You know what, the dress, your stupid games, none of it matters because it's not going to work, Tawny. Payton lives here. In Sugar. Her family, her friends, her life, everything is here."

He wanted to point out that he was there, too, and Payton *was* his life.

"I'm her family, too, and she only lives in Sugar because that's where you chose to live." He didn't choose but whatever, the second Payton came along, he settled in for the long haul to give his daughter roots and stability. "She has no idea what else is out there."

"And you're going to show her that? You can't even handle being a parent every other weekend, and you want me to believe you can handle it full time?"

"It's not about what you want anymore, it's about what Payton wants." Easy to say when armed with a pageant dress and a designer house on the Gulf. "She is fourteen now, old enough to choose. And I'm not saying she'll choose to come with me, but I hope she does."

Cal's phone buzzed. It was Brett. "I gotta go, we'll talk about this later."

"Tell Payton I'll be there in time for the start of the game."

Cal disconnected without a good-bye and clicked over. "I just pulled up."

"Thank God," Brett said, his voice clipped with the same panic Cal felt coursing through every cell of his body. "I convinced Payton to open the door, but I gotta warn you, I don't think even a pink convertible will be enough to fix this."

Back in the Saddle Night at the Saddle Rack was always held on the fourth Friday of the month—and it was always packed. The only two-step social in three counties that recognized senior discounted cocktails, it was a Sunday boots mandatory, dentures optional kind of crowd where Hank Williams ruled the jukebox, Bengay was applied in advance, and bathtub gin and mint juleps were the drinks of choice.

The theme changed weekly, the crowd was always the same, and since tonight was Bootleggin' Days—and the staff had to dress accordingly—Glory was wearing a silver beaded drop-waist dress, vintage cowgirl boots, and had a flask strapped to her inner thigh.

"Hey, Miss Glory," Skeeter hollered over the elevated cheers as the first notes of "Hey, Good Lookin'" filled the room. "Pretty crowded tonight."

Crowded? A good portion of the town's retired sector was already there and the Senior Shuttle was doing a steady pickup and drop-off every fifteen minutes. In fact, the next one was due to arrive anytime, and if it was as packed as the last, it would keep her too busy to obsess over confusing sexy single fathers.

"Sorry about the wait, we're a little understaffed tonight."

She was the only staff. The cocktail waitress and hush-puppy runner was a no-show. Not that Glory was surprised. Stella was twenty-two, twice-divorced, and had already missed two nights that week alone, citing "personal problems."

"What can I get you?" Glory asked, thankful Skeeter would say something from the tap and not a drink that would require a shaker, blender, two hands, or way too much time. Skeeter came in every week, parked his spare tire in the same stool at the bar, then watched everyone socialize while he nursed his Lone Star. "The usual?"

He did a little shuffle in his chair, cleared his throat, and even smoothed all seven hairs on his head over to the side. "How about something a little more educated?"

"Educated?"

"Yeah, cultured, like one of them martinis." Glory blinked, long and slow. "But I don't like green things in my drink. Do I have to have the green things in it?"

"I could do a lemon instead of olives."

"Then yeah, one of them." Skeeter leaned in and lowered his voice. "And a mint julep."

"Mint julep?" Glory raised a brow but poured the vermouth and gin in a clean shaker. "Those are some pretty fancy drinks." The official drink of choice by Sugar Peaches everywhere. "You trying to impress someone?"

Glory meant it as a joke. Everyone in town knew that Skeeter had a thing for Etta Jayne; not that he'd acted on it. When courting a woman who used to castrate bulls for a living, timing and delivery were important. Which was why Skeeter hadn't done more than tip his hat in Etta Jayne's direction since his wife passed away nearly twenty years ago. But he hesitated, for just a moment, his mouth going a little slack. Glory's mouth, on the other hand, fell open.

Now that she thought about it, Skeeter was dressed for church, even left his hat at home, and he looked a little sweaty and a whole lot nervous. Like he might just pass out.

Glory leaned in and lowered her voice. "Are you on a date, Skeeter?"

"No," he sputtered, not sounding all that convincing. "I'm here alone. But..." Skeeter glanced over his shoulder at the front door and pulled at the collar of his shirt. "I'm hoping to make an impression on someone. A real class act and nothing says high class like a julep. And sweets."

He set a pink and white metal tin on the bar. Inside were six handmade truffles, each in a red paper cup and tied with a pink bow. If there was one thing Etta Jayne wasn't, it was a pink kind of lady.

"That is very sweet of you," Glory said, a ridiculous smile forming when she thought about Cal showing up for her the other day. He'd helped take her proposal from amateur to front runner in one afternoon—and brought her a meatloaf sandwich with a cookie.

"Sweet?" Skeeter looked horrified. "Ah, hell, it is, isn't it?" He wiped the sweat off his brow with the cuff of his shirt. "You know what, just make it a Lone Star and skip the julep. Don't know what I was thinking. She's not here yet so I bet she won't even show."

Tension pinched between her shoulders as Glory looked down the length of the bar. It was already three people deep, nearly every table was full, and through the window she could see the next shuttle pulling up. Or maybe what was pricking her wrong was that Skeeter was going to give up—and Glory wanted someone to win in the game of love.

"But she might," Glory said. "And when she does, you'll need a drink in hand for your classy lady. Who knows, she might even let you take her for a spin around the dance floor."

"Or she might tell me where to shove it."

Etta Jayne was more a woman of action than words, so he should be more worried about where she'd stick it. "At least the wondering would be over and you wouldn't come in here week after week, sitting and watching and wondering."

Something Glory knew all too well. She's been sitting and watching Cal for years, and now that she knew what he tasted like, she had to admit that all of her wondering didn't even come close to the reality.

Cal McGraw was about as perfect as a man could get—and instead of ignoring her, he wanted to be her friend. She wasn't sure which was worse.

"When did I start paying my employees to stand around and flap their gums?" Etta Jayne asked, making her way through the crowd and sliding behind the bar.

"I thought it was your night off and you were coming here with the girls," Glory asked, emptying Skeeter's drink from the shaker to a martini glass, sliding a lemon on the rim, and going to work on the mint julep.

"And I thought you were handling business. Mable Facebooked that she'd been waiting so long to get her drink she'd died of old age and if someone could notify her son in Tampa to come retrieve the body." She held up her phone as proof. "Plus, Jelly Lou wanted me to tell you that you have to sit Road Kill this weekend."

"This weekend?" The last time she'd been left to sit Road Kill, the grannies had been kicked out of Atlantic City for counting cards and Road Kill had eaten a hole in every single pair of Glory's underwear. "I thought you ladies had choir practice tomorrow morning."

"Plans change."

"Please don't tell me your plans have anything to do with Ms. Kitty and the Prowler." Because that was all Glory needed right now, some Green E15 added to the fire.

"Then I won't tell you." She looked at Skeeter, who was looking back like a man in love, and her hands dug into her pudgy hips. "You had too much to drink already, Skeeter? Or you having a stroke?"

"No, ma'am, just not used to seeing your knees bare is all," Skeeter said, reaching up to tip his hat—only to realize he wasn't wearing one.

Etta Jayne stopped, her face going red as a Falcons' jersey, then sputtered. Skeeter, looking confused and a little bit terrified, did some sputtering of his own.

With a sigh, Glory stepped in. "You're right, Skeeter. Etta Jayne is looking pretty tonight."

Etta Jayne was in a knee-length dress. Mourning black with a matching organza church hat. Her boots were ankle high and steel toed, and her expression was dialed to "Can I get a witness," but she was showing leg and wearing lipstick.

"And you're looking like you're one shuttle arrival from going under." The older woman tied a beer-stained apron around her round middle and looked at the drink in front of Skeeter. "You want an umbrella with that, Skeeter?"

The poor guy swallowed hard but silently shook his head.

"Would hate to think you'd gone soft." She grabbed the shaker from Glory's hand, took a sniff, and narrowed her eyes. "Or that you'd be courting some society pearl."

"Not me, Etta Jayne," Skeeter said and, leaving his drink on the bar, got up and left in a flurry.

"Mint julep," Etta Jayne muttered as she poured the drink into a mason jar, added a mint sprig, and slid it down the bar to Mable.

"I was afraid I was going to die of dehydration," Mable said, patting a bony hand to her chest.

"You'll suffocate from running your lips long before that," Etta Jayne hollered back.

Grabbing a rack of mason jars, and all the ingredients in her pudgy hands, she looked at Glory. "Give me a dozen gin and tonics using that bathtub gin we found at Letty's place, and a dozen of those juleps everyone seems to be so big on. Unless it comes in a bottle or out of a tap, this is all we're serving tonight."

"You didn't have to scare off Skeeter like that," Glory chided. "You know that drink was for you."

"Are you offering me dating tips?" Etta Jayne laughed, and Glory zipped it. She hadn't gone on a date since the un-regulated raising of Leon's flagpole. "That's what I thought. Now, I got an hour before the girls and I head out, and Stella's not coming till nine, so go get me some limes."

Glory kissed her boss on the cheek and whispered, "Don't be snappy just because a man got you flustered," then made her way to the other end of the bar.

"Poor Skeeter," Glory mumbled, pulling out a handful of limes.

"I don't know, at least he's one step closer," Charlotte said, sitting primly on a barstool in an adorable yellow and white polka-dotted dress with a white belt and matching clutch. "How about you, Glory? You going to take your own advice or just dish it out?"

"I have no idea what you're talking about." Gaze on the cutting board, knife moving at the speed of light, Glory efficiently wedged the limes—and avoided eye contact. Because she knew. And Charlotte knew that she knew.

There was a full beat of silence but Glory stood firm. Charlotte wasn't one to let things go and her teeth were sunk so far into this conversation, Glory could feel the pricking at her neck. "So then you don't want to talk about you and Cal?"

Glory looked around to make sure no one had overheard, then leaned in to whisper, "There is no me and Cal."

"Ah-huh. As a former McGraw addict, I know the symptoms when I see them. And you've got an acute case."

Oh my God, there were symptoms? Of course there were; Glory had a list three pages long detailing just how severe her affliction was. "Wait, former addict? So you and Cal?"

This was more awkward than watching the man you kissed go on a blind date with the perfect catch.

"Lord no," she said her hand on her chest. "Although that would make things so much simpler. Unfortunately, the town's golden boy is far too cultured for my liking, it seems." Cal? Cultured? The man swung hammers for a living. "Plus my mother would approve."

The only McGraw who didn't come with the Sugar stamp of mother approval was the youngest and most notorious McGraw. Jace's talent for causing trouble was almost as legendary as Glory's.

Just ask Judge Holden. During high school, Jace was a regular in his courtroom.

"You and Jace—"

"Aren't up for discussion."

"Well, neither are Cal and I." Glory looked at her friend with feigned disinterest, then realized she was too tired to pretend any longer. "I thought there might be more but he made it clear that he isn't looking for anything more than friends."

"The last time a man was adamant about being friends, I ended up naked in the backseat of his '68 Camaro." And the smile Charlotte gave at the memory was neither proper nor prim, and in no way former Miss Peach appropriate.

"Yes, well, naked friends might be on the table for him but not me. I want more."

"Well, then smile," she said. "Because Cal just burst through the door looking delicious, determined, and like a man on a mission. And honey, my bet is you're the target."

Chapter 14

I need you," Cal said when he reached the bar and, *whoa*, those three words packed a punch.

"Well, isn't that the declaration every woman dreams of hearing," Charlotte said, sending Glory a not-so-sly waggle of the brow.

"Are you busy?" Cal asked.

Glory laughed. Was he kidding? There wasn't a spare inch in the joint.

Only Cal didn't laugh. Didn't look at anyone but her. His clothes were filthy, his face was smudged with what appeared to be chalk, and his eyes were grim. Something was wrong.

"Charlotte." She took off her apron and tossed it at her friend. "Can you handle the bar for…" She looked at Cal, wondering just how long he needed her and hating herself for hoping he'd say, "Forever."

"Ten minutes tops," he said, finally looking around. "I didn't even realize it was so busy."

"Honey, take as long as you need," Charlotte said with a mischievous smile. "Every minute I stand behind that bar, mixing sin in a glass, I come one step closer to horrifying my mother." She was already tying the apron around her Sunday dress and pouring gin in a shaker when Cal took Glory's hand and pulled her through the crowded bar.

"What's going on?" she asked once they were outside, sprinting across the parking lot toward his truck. Not that she was opposed to being whisked away by a sexy bachelor who needed her, but she had a feeling by the frantic pace he was keeping that this had nothing to do with stealing a few kisses in his truck.

"You'll see," he said then stopped at the driver's side of the truck and reached for the handle.

"Am I driving?"

"No." He turned to face her, and if she thought he looked filthy inside, in the sunlight the man looked as though he'd been in a mountain when it exploded. He had bits of gravel in his hair, his face looked like he'd been mining sandstone, and his clothes were hidden under a thick layer of dirt. "And whatever you do, don't let her know how bad it is. She'll only cry more and I can't handle another forty minutes of tears."

Before she could ask him what he was talking about, he opened the door and shoved her inside the cab of his truck. The passenger seat was empty and at first glance so was the rest of the cab. The only clue that she wasn't alone was the little wet sniffles that came in a succession of threes.

Glory leaned over the backseat and found the source of the sniffles—and Cal's panicked state.

Payton sat on the floorboard in her cheerleading uniform, enough makeup to pass for a pole dancer, and a new set of bangs that looked as though they'd been cut with a weed whacker. She also looked like she'd rather die than face the world—and Glory felt for her.

Every girl, at one time or another, attempted to give themselves a new style. It rarely, if ever, turned out good.

Doing her best to play it cool, Glory asked, "Kitchen scissors or a hair trimmer?"

"Quilting sheers," Payton said, her voice catching. "Dad said it's not that bad, but I think he's lying."

Glory wasn't a parent, and she wasn't sure how Cal wanted her to handle this, but she knew that teens could smell BS a mile away, so she went with honesty. "He's lying. It is pretty bad."

"I knew it." And the little hitch in her voice became the beginnings of a sob.

"But," Glory said, digging through Cal's glove box, "nothing we can't fix."

"Before the game?" There was so much hope in Payton's voice, it pulled at Glory.

"You bet," she said with a reassuring smile, relieved Payton seemed to be pulling her tears in check. "Now"—she located a pack of wet wipes and passed them over the seat— "take off the makeup while I go grab my bag from the bar. I think a more all-American girl-next-door glow will work better with the uniform."

"I was trying to get the attention off my hair."

"Mission accomplished." Glory looked at the smoky eye shadow and then to the Alfalfa bangs and reconsidered changing her statement. "I'll be right back with my stuff. Oh, and Payton, I'm also bringing back your application."

Payton froze, wide-eyed and panicked. "You can't."

"It wasn't mine to accept to begin with."

And there went the waterworks again. At this rate, Payton would cry off all her makeup. "Dad already saw the dress.

I can tell he's super mad but waiting to talk to me about it because of, well." She pointed to her hair. "I need more time so he can cool down."

"You have until Monday. And it has to have his signature on it or it will be rejected."

"What if he won't sign it?" She sniffed.

"What if he does?" At that, Payton blew out a *like that will happen* raspberry. So Glory got firm, channeling that velvet-stick tone Jelly Lou had perfected when Glory had been a teen. "You want him to treat you like a responsible teen? Act like one. Don't sneak and go behind his back or pit your parents against each other to get your way." The teen finally had the decency to look busted. "Explain to him why this is so important to you and have enough faith in him to respect his decision. Now wipe, I'll be back in a minute."

It took three minutes to locate her bag and a pair of scissors, explain to Etta Jayne what was going on, and get back outside. Cal was pacing the lot looking like an expectant father.

"I'm sorry I busted in on you at work," Cal said, meeting her in the middle of the parking lot. "I was so wrapped up in Payton I didn't even realize how packed it was. Did I get you in trouble?"

"Nah." She laughed. "Etta Jayne reminded me of the time I got my hair frosted. I wanted blond highlights but Jelly Lou got confused and told the hair dresser I wanted it frosted, like hers." Cal looked at her as though she was speaking Latin. "It turned my hair gray and we didn't have the money to fix it so I went to school for a whole month with white streaks in it. Everyone called me Bride of Frankenstein for the rest of eighth grade. Compared to that, fixing bangs is nothing."

Cal released a long, slow breath that had his shoulders

sinking an inch. "It's just been a hard day. Tawny's late and we got into a huge argument and then I came home to find Payton rounding DEFCON-2 and heading straight toward nuclear meltdown, and I didn't know how to fix it."

Hearing the strain in his voice shook her. But it was the distress in his expression over not being able to fix Payton's world with a single hug that did her in. Reconfirmed for her what an amazing father Cal was, because he wouldn't give up on Payton. He would do whatever it took to keep her safe—make her happy. And that, more than anything, reached Glory on a deeper level.

"It's just hair and makeup. Nothing that water and a bit of styling product can't fix," she said gently because he looked so upset. Regret clogged her throat, making it difficult to swallow, because—the application in her bag suddenly felt like it weighed a million pounds. Guilt could do that to a person.

"But that's just it. I don't understand makeup or hair or why all the things that used to make her smile don't work anymore." He ran a hand down his face. "Jesus, I'm trying but no matter what I do or how hard I listen, I just don't seem to get it."

Moved by the amazing man in front of her who was facing the reality that he had a teen daughter in his life, Glory reached out to cup his face but then remembered that Payton was within sight and settled for brushing the backs of his knuckles with her fingers. "You understand what's important, Cal. And in the end, that's all that matters."

After Payton's game and the most uncomfortable family dinner of his life, Cal found himself back at the Saddle Rack, sitting next to Glory's car staring at the blackened sky and waiting. For what, he didn't have a clue.

But talking about the possibility of his baby girl partic-ipating in the Miss Peach Pageant, something he promised to think about, made him angry. Because if Tawny hadn't thrown giving Texas a trial run into the mix, something Payton promised Tawny she'd think about—God, that damn near broke his heart—he wouldn't have had to pre-tend that the pageant was going to happen in the first place. So when he loaded up his daughter's duffel bag and kissed her good-bye, he'd called Brett to meet up for a drink. One strong enough to make him forget that his perfectly un-planned life, which he loved so much it hurt, was rapidly turning to shit.

Only instead of going inside and drinking it out with his brother, he'd left Brett hanging and spent the past hour sit-ting on his tailgate in the back parking lot, waiting for Glory to get off work and say...what?

That with a little water and styling product she could fix his mess.

That she could fix him.

Jesus, what was he doing here? He'd come to thank Glory, not dump more of his problems on a woman who al-ready had a truck full of her own. And sure, Tawny had done one on him tonight and he wasn't his usual self, but if he were a smart man, he would stick a note under Glory's wind-shield wiper, pack it up, and go home. Alone.

Except that's what he'd be, totally and completely and pa-thetically alone. Payton was with her mom, Hattie had gone to Atlanta for a girls' weekend with her Bible group, and Brett had moved out and into his new blissful life. And Cal? He was exactly where he'd been the day Tawny walked out.

Which was the only reason he could come up with for why, twenty minutes later, he was still sitting on his tailgate watching the stars when trouble walked out the back door, riffling through her purse for keys. And maybe, just maybe, he was there because being with Glory was like seeing the plans to a new build for the first time—exciting, invigorating, a fresh shot at being a part of something amazing.

Her hair was pulled up in a flirty ponytail with little pieces hanging loose, framing her incredible face. Her lips were still tinted a bright red, and her top had tiny little straps and one of those built-in bra thingies that were made to mess with a man's mind and—*look at that*—she had on cowgirl boots.

Saloon Glory was done with her shift and looking a little messy and a whole lot tempting, and suddenly, he knew just why he'd come.

She looked up, spotted him, and stopped. Then let loose a killer smile that had him smiling back. "What are you doing out here?"

"Waiting for you," he said, not feeling like a pussy. At all. "What are you doing off so early?"

Her boots echoed off the pavement, not letting up until she was standing close enough to touch. Close enough to smell—which was freaking incredible. "I only worked a half shift so that I could study for my final exam. It's on Monday."

"Well, then I won't keep you, I just wanted to say thanks for helping Payton out tonight."

"How did it go? Did she make it in time for the photo?"

"We pulled up right as the photographer was organizing the team. She looked great and everyone was talking about her new bangs," he said.

Glory smiled and set her bag on the end of the tailgate, the motion causing one of those little straps to slip off her bare shoulder. She asked something else about the game, maybe the final score, only he was too busy trying not to look at the more than inspiring view of her breasts the fallen strap provided. Breasts he'd had spent the past two weeks convincing himself couldn't be as perfect as he'd imagined.

They weren't. They were even better. World-class, in fact. Not that he could see all of them, but he wanted to.

"I thought we weren't doing this?" she said with a low chuckle, letting him know he was caught. He raised his gaze and—*oh yeah*—she flashed him one hell of a wicked smile. And his brain checked out. Just like that. One smile and he was toast.

"We're not," he said quietly, reaching out to fix her strap, only to cup her hips instead, drawing her toward him and parting his legs to make room. Not because he needed to touch her, okay, he needed to touch her, but that seemed a whole hell of a lot safer than slipping a finger through that strap and testing just how far it could slide.

"You sure?" She shimmied forward a little until their bodies brushed. Hers soft and warm, making his hard and ready and he wasn't sure about a damn thing.

"Yes, I came here to thank you," he said but her gaze had slid to his mouth, which was fine with him since his hands slid right over her spectacular ass to trace the hem of her skirt. He felt her tremble beneath his touch so of course he did it again.

"Is that the only reason you came here?"

"No." At that, her hand went to his shoulders, brushing back and forth, barely skimming the fabric of his shirt while that bombshell body of hers fit snugly against his. "I came here to talk."

"What about?" She tilted her head, sending the ends of her ponytail over her shoulder to brush against his arm, and causing all kinds of stupid shit to happen to his pants. Which worked for him because he didn't want to talk anymore. Didn't want to think. Didn't want to pretend they were just friends or ponder the million or so reasons why kissing her would be a bad idea.

He just wanted—

"This."

And damn if her lips didn't meet him halfway.

This, Glory decided, was the best conversation she'd had in weeks, years even.

Cal's mouth should be registered as a weapon of serious mass destruction, since it had the power to obliterate every sane thought on contact, and take her from tired bartender in desperate need of a bath to crazed woman bordering on orgasmic levels with one simple brush.

He nipped at her lower lip, starting off slow, then moved straight into confident demand. His fingers, they were confident, too—teasing the edge of her skirt, tracing down her bare thighs only to explore higher, stroke farther, on the return. Making her hotter—and a little crazier every trip he took. His thumbs crested the bottom of her bare cheeks and someone moaned. Okay, she moaned. It was needy and desperate and—

Oh my God, she was in a parking lot with her tongue down Cal's throat and his hands up her skirt. Where anybody would pass by and see.

As if reading her mind, Cal pulled back enough that they could both suck in a much needed breath of air. Not that it helped; it was hot and thick and weighed heavily in her lungs. And his hands were still firmly planted on her butt, making delicious little circles.

"What was that?" she asked against his mouth.

"You kissing me and me trying to figure out what it is about the women in my life tempting hyperthermia with their clothing choices?"

"I believe you kissed me. Again."

"You attacked me."

"I did not." She looked down and found her hands bunched in his shirt, gripping on for dear life. It took everything she had to let go. She'd dreamed of kissing him like that for a long time. Maybe forever, even.

"This is my uniform and I didn't know I qualified as a woman in your life."

"I'm not sure what we are, but I sure as hell don't obsess about random women and what they're wearing under their uniform." His fingers were on the move again, rubbing back and forth across the soft skin right below her ass. "Lace or silk, Boots?"

She smacked his hands away. Not that it helped. "A little of both."

That earned her a little half smile, which always managed to make her knees quiver. "Are we talking black, pink, red?" He looked at her boots. "Please say they're red."

Thinking back to Jelly Lou's big talk, about how a man's never going to buy the tractor if they can test drive it all day long, Glory grabbed his wrists, pried them out from under her skirt, and stepped back. "That ranks as date five kind of information."

His face puckered in confusion. "Date five? Don't you mean date three?"

"Nope. Five. Four if they're really special." And he was special but they obviously still wanted different things. Only moments ago, Glory had thought she could do this, have a fling with the guy she'd had a crush on since she was a teenager. But sadly, she couldn't. Not with Cal.

Disappointed, she grabbed her purse and headed toward her car, not surprised when Cal followed. Even less surprised when he leaned against her door, blocking her escape.

With a sigh she looked up, amused at the confusion on his face. Poor guy had no clue what had just happened.

"Look, men get stuck on the third date being the portal to automatic sex, so I make them go the extra mile, to make sure they're interested in more. Because *I'm* interested in more." And for the first time in a long time, she actually believed that she deserved more. She deserved what her grandparents had, and she wasn't going to settle for less this time.

"But you are interested in sex?"

"Yes."

"With me?"

She crossed her arms. "Despite all logic, yes."

His smile was back. Hers was not. She was too nervous to smile because she was about to grow a pair.

Waiting to experience what everyone else seemed to come by naturally hadn't panned out for her so well in the past, so she was done waiting. She'd never know "what if" unless she took a chance. And the chance to be with Cal was greater than the fear of rejection.

"But I want more."

His gaze went wary. "You need to define *more* for me, because I'm not a long-term bet. At least not right now."

So he'd pointed out. Several times. Yet here he was looking at her like she was the only thing keeping him grounded.

"I'm not asking for a ring or to wear your jacket or anything, just a chance to see if there is more here than simple chemistry."

His face went soft and he brushed a piece of hair behind her ear. "There's more, Boots, but I need to think about Payton. She comes first."

"I get that." She respected it even. His daughter was going through a difficult time, and the last thing she needed was another woman in her dad's life making things even more complicated. "I worry about Payton, too." A lot more as of late. "And I would never do anything that would hurt or confuse her."

"I know," he said, seemingly surprised by his own statement.

"Good, then if you'd like to see where I fall between friend and woman in your life, I'm free Monday night. No pressure, and if you don't show, I won't bring it up again. Promise."

She went up on her toes and kissed him good night on the cheek, which he accepted without complaint, damn him. But when she reached for the door, instead of backing up, he moved even closer, taking her hand in his bigger one, turning it over and studying it for a moment before delivering a sweet kiss to her palm.

His gaze went to hers, quiet and reflective. "Don't go anywhere. Give me a minute."

She watched his fine ass disappear around her car, tapped her foot as he rummaged through his truck, and almost gave up and drove home before she went back on her word, when a minute later he returned—jacket in hand.

His big body taking up all of her personal space until there was nothing but him, he slipped the jacket over her shoulders and then drew the ends around her, zipping it up tight.

It was too hot for a jacket, but it smelled good. Fresh sawdust and rugged man good. And felt like a promise. Not a forever kind of promise, but one that had her resolve, and her heart, melting.

"What's this?" she asked, snuggling deeper into the Calcocoon.

"My jacket." He held out his arm like the gentleman that

he was. "Now, Boots, I know it's too late for dinner, but how about a little dessert? And I promise to have you back in time to study for your exam."

She would pull an all-nighter if it meant going on a real date with Cal McGraw.

She laced her arm though his. "I think the Creamery is still open."

"Vanilla?"

"What's wrong with vanilla?" Cal asked, opening the shop door and following Glory out into the evening. A bell jingled behind them and he couldn't help but notice that, even though his jacket dwarfed her tiny frame, Miss Glory had a jingle all her own when she walked—a sexy sway of the hips that had her bottom moving and her boots clacking with every step.

"There were over a hundred flavors and you went with vanilla," she said on low laugh, as though she were accusing him of wearing tighty whities. Then she took a lick of her double-scoop Firecracker Surprise in a confetti-dipped cone. "Old people order vanilla."

"Why change when I know what's best?" he explained, then wondered why he even bothered when she snorted. So he liked vanilla, so what? It went with every kind of pie and cake, didn't give him heartburn, and never left him disappointed.

"Ah-huh," she said dryly, in that female tone he was more than familiar with.

"I've had enough surprises tonight," he admitted.

Even though it was dark on Maple Street, as most of the storefronts had already turned off their welcome signs, Cal could still make out the genuine concern in her eyes as she looked up at him. "I can't see Payton moving."

"Neither could I." Until he'd seen Payton's face light up at dinner. "But a house with no rules, no expectations, and no limitations is pretty tempting for a teenager." That it housed the one person Payton would do anything to be close with made it a slam-dunk. "Did I mention it's on the beach?"

"Although the beach does sound pretty tempting, it doesn't have you," she said quietly, taking his hand. Hers was cool from holding her ice cream, but managed to pack one hell of a hot jolt.

"You mean it doesn't have the guy who is always telling her no?" He slid her a glance. "And by the way, saying no as a parent is so much worse than hearing it as a teen."

"Ah-huh."

He stopped and turned Glory around to face him. "*Ah-huh* is woman-speak for 'Are you really that clueless?' And I'd like to think that when it comes to my daughter, I'm not. So please, enlighten me."

She studied him for a long moment, most likely gauging his seriousness. He was dead serious. If he was missing something that could help him with Payton, he needed to know.

"Fine. Don't say no all the time."

Right, because it was *that* easy. Between hormones, boys, and the arrival of boobs, the only way to make sure Payton stayed safe was limits. And limits meant having to say no. Something Tawny would never understand.

"If I did that, I'd have an out-of-control teen."

Glory coyly licked her cone, not believing him at all. Yeah, so he'd told her about the two-hour bathroom sit-in.

"Okay, a *more* out-of-control teen."

"Payton is not out of control," she said dryly. "She's just figuring out how to go from a daddy's little girl to a young lady, which is normal, trust me."

Strangely he did. He'd bet Glory saw a lot of things at the hospital, things that he would do anything to keep Payton from experiencing. "So you think I should let her move to Houston?"

"I think you should start small." She was swinging their hands, and he had to admit it was kind of adorable. Irritating, but adorable. "Find ways you can feel comfortable saying yes, so she can figure things out in a safe environment."

"Like?"

"Like…" She dragged out the word as she tugged him along the sidewalk. Not that she had to do much tugging; he was pretty sure that he'd follow her just about anywhere. "Instead of a hard, no-dating-until-you're-sixteen rule, maybe you drop her off at the movies with her friends for a safe, casual co-ed Friday night."

"There are no dating rules for Payton, since Payton can't date until college." Glory snorted. "I'm serious. Do you know what teenage boys think about ninety percent of the time? Sex. So group date or not, that kid is going to be thinking about sex ninety percent of the time he's out with my daughter."

"What will he think about the other ten percent?"

"How to *have* sex with my daughter."

She slid him a sideways look. "And what do guys your age think about?"

"I already told you, lace," he admitted with a grin, tucking her against him and slipping his arm around her. "Ten percent of the time I'm wondering what color you're wearing; the other ninety percent I'm plotting how I can get it off you as fast as possible."

"What percent are you thinking about now?"

"I'm still hoping for red."

Her hand did some slipping of its own, around his waist

and into his back pocket. "And even though you wonder, I also know that in the end you're a gentleman and will respect my boundaries, which is why I said yes to dessert."

Which meant he wasn't going to get to see her panties tonight. And surprisingly, he was okay with that. It had been a long time since he'd felt this kind of connection with someone, had this much fun just eating ice cream and talking. "How can you be sure I'm a gentleman?"

Because around Glory he sure as hell didn't feel like a gentleman. He felt like a man possessed, willing to do whatever it took to strip her naked and make her smile.

Jesus? Make her smile? Not make her scream or pant and yell out his name? He wanted to make her smile.

"I know because I've been around enough jerks to pick out who the good ones are. Payton needs experience with boys, friends, hobbies, life, if she is going to figure out who she is and what she wants."

He let out a breath. "So you're saying I should loosen up."

"I'm saying that if you don't give her space to grow, she'll either find a way to do it without you knowing, or even worse, she'll never be able to stand on her own two feet."

Without another word, she rested her head against his side and slowly strolled with him down Maple Street, their bodies brushing with every step as they ate their ice cream in silence.

Unlike the other women in his life, Glory didn't push her opinion, didn't give him a million and one examples or stories to prove her point, didn't even ask redundant questions that were the equivalent of "I told you so." She just walked next to him, her hand cupping his ass through his pocket, letting him have the time he needed to process.

They strolled down the cobblestone sidewalk, along the gas lamp–lined street, licking their ice cream and making their way back toward the Saddle Rack. Well, Glory was making headway on her cone; Cal hadn't touched his. He was too busy thinking about Payton, thinking about what Glory had said.

"What if I let her go and she doesn't come back?" he asked quietly as they reached the bar's back parking lot.

No matter how much time he took or how many different ways he looked at the situation, Glory was right. He knew it. It was just that he didn't do letting go so well, never had. He'd been forced to let go of his parents, then his brothers, one by one, and finally Tawny. Every time he lost someone, they took with them a little part of his soul, a part of himself that he didn't know how to get back, leaving a space he didn't know how to fill. So he ignored those spaces, put everything he had into loving his daughter, and he didn't know if he could let her go. But deep down, he was more terrified that if he didn't, he might lose her. For good.

Glory stopped and reached up to cup his cheek with her free hand. "No matter how fun living with her mom sounds or how many times you tell her no, Payton will always come back home because you're here. Stubborn, overprotective, embarrassing, it doesn't matter. You are her whole world, Cal, and she loves you and knows that you love her. Unconditionally."

He swallowed hard, wondering how she knew exactly what he needed to hear. Then he realized that *that* was Glory, in a nutshell. After all of the amount of crap slung her way over the years, most people would have packed it in and moved on. Not Glory. She'd stayed here and stuck it out when starting over, anywhere else, would have been a hell of a lot easier.

"Is that why you never left? Because of your grandma?"

She looked at her boots and shrugged. "She's not really

my grandma," she said so quietly he thought he'd misunderstood. "I was only six when my mom blew that secret. She took off and my dad didn't want anything to do with me. He said to put me in foster care but Jelly Lou wouldn't hear of it."

"You were hers," he said, and she lifted her gaze to his, looking surprised by his statement, which told him more than he needed to know about Billy Mann. It also explained a lot about the woman standing in front of him.

"Billy made her choose, and Jelly Lou said that since I was a little girl and he was a grown man, she didn't see much of a choice to be made. He took a job in Tuscaloosa a few weeks later and never came back." She didn't need to mention her mom; the whole town watched as that drama unfolded.

People still talked about Julie-Marie Mann cutting out of town with someone else's husband and leaving her daughter alone on the steps of town hall with nothing more than an ice-cream cone.

"Sugar is her whole world and she's mine," Glory said, and he could hear the conviction in her voice, love so unwavering and yet so simple, it leveled him. "So as long as she wants to stay here, it's home."

He placed a finger under her chin and tipped her face to his. "You're a good granddaughter."

"I try," she said on a low, self-conscious laugh, then looked at his ice cream. "You haven't even touched your cone? Told you vanilla was boring."

He hadn't dated much over the years, but he was pretty sure that making a woman cry on the first date ranked right up there with asking her the color of her panties, so he let the change in topic go. "Nothing is wrong with vanilla."

"Only because you've never tried Firecracker Surprise."

She took a lick and moaned. It was a sexy moan that had him scooting closer. "It's the perfect combo of sweet and spicy. Here, try it."

Cal prided himself on his ability to follow directions. So he leaned in until their mouths were a breath apart and whispered, "If you insist."

Then he kissed her, tugging at her lower lip with his teeth, then taking a taste of her entire mouth. It was everything she'd promised and more. Sweet, spicy, and so damn surprising it could tempt even the most honorable gentleman. And he was tempted all right, but come hell or high water, he was going to be a gentleman tonight. Even if it killed him.

Which it might.

She pulled back enough to look up at him, her face flushed and her eyes blazing. "Surprised?"

"Not sure yet." He licked his lips. "It was sweet and spicy, but I was expecting more fire."

"Oh." Smiling with wicked intent, she took another lick of her cone, this time leaving plenty of ice cream on her plump lower lip, which of course, he just had to nibble off before lowering his head even farther to take a nip of her neck.

He could feel her pulse beneath his mouth, so he sucked gently on the spot, loving it when she released a little whimper. Then her cone hit the ground, her fingers wove themselves through his hair, and it was game on.

Her hands were everywhere, as though she'd been fantasizing about touching him as much as he had her. And he'd fantasized all right. He hadn't had a decent night's sleep since he saw her in those ducky galoshes.

"So, what do you think?" she asked, gripping his head and planting one hell of a kiss on him.

That he'd found his new favorite flavor.

"Definitely felt the heat that time," he murmured against her mouth. "But there is still something to be said about vanilla."

And there was something to be said about this woman. Glory was sexy and feminine and so damn beautiful it hurt to look at her. But it was this new side, the vulnerable one she kept hidden from the world, that reached out and pulled him in. All the way in.

"Nothing about the two of you looks very *vanilla*, if you ask me," Brett said from behind.

"No one asked you," Cal mumbled, not interested in prying himself away from Glory or her sexy mouth.

"Brett," Glory said, stepping back and smoothing down her hair, although it didn't help. Not one bit. Her ponytail was coming undone; little wisps of hair blew in the wind and clung to her lips. She looked thoroughly kissed. "What are you doing here?"

"Oh, just out for a stroll," he said and smiled. Cal wanted to punch him. "You guys?"

"The same," she said while unzipping Cal's jacket. "Cal was just walking me to my car, and look, we're here. All together."

She handed Cal his jacket all businesslike and looked as if she was going to bolt, only he saw her take a calming breath and force her body to stay put. Long enough to say, "Thank you. For everything. I had a great time." Then she gave him a sweet smile, and before he could tell her that he didn't want her to go, that he didn't want their date to end, she was dashing toward her car.

Her door slammed shut, the engine started with a crank, and she tore out of the parking lot like her ass was on fire.

"So you want to explain to me how I ended up fending off arthritic advances for the past two hours while you were

out here sticking your tongue down my best friend's throat?"
Brett asked, raising his arm and giving a prissy little wiggle
of the fingers at her taillights.

"You want to tell me why I have a dozen catfish in my
garage freezer when Joie thinks fishing season is over?"

Brett stuffed his hands in his pockets and rocked back on
his heels.

"That's what I thought."

"Good catching up." Brett clapped Cal on the back and
headed toward the front parking lot, adding an oh-so-funny
"Better eat up, bro, you're dripping vanilla."

Cal looked down at his cone—which he was somehow
still holding—and tossed it in the trash. He told himself it
was because he wasn't hungry, not because he wasn't sure
he was a vanilla kind of guy anymore.

Chapter 15

✑

An hour later, ceiling fan set to hurricane, Glory was sprawled out on the couch in her favorite shortie pajamas with her textbook. She'd picked up Road Kill, showered, organized her class notes, and made a comprehensive flash card glossary of terms for Monday's final—her fingertips had the ink stains to prove it.

With Road Kill sitting next to her, his little armadillo hooves determined to turn her couch cushion into a cozy den, she began transferring the chapters she'd outlined earlier in the week to her master study guide. Anything to take her mind off the fact that she'd made out with Cal in public.

Twice.

Thank God Brett had interrupted when he had. She didn't want to think about what they'd be doing right know if he hadn't. Her tummy, along with other, more interesting, parts, quivered at the possibilities.

When it came to kissing, the man was a miracle worker. And his hands were sheer magic. Two skillfully clever tools with orgasm-inducing powers that had her picking up her cell and finding his number, ready to ask him just what kind of benefits came with being his friend.

"It's happened," she said to Road Kill. "My sex drought has officially made me crazy."

Road Kill gave a disapproving grunt, then went back to his burrowing.

She put down the phone and closed her eyes. "You're right, I need to stay strong."

After Leon, she had promised herself that she wouldn't have sex with someone who she couldn't see forever with. Which meant that she hadn't had a man-made orgasm in over two years.

She was overdue, the only explanation she could come up with for her silly five-date fib. It didn't take five dates to get her naked; it took a serious commitment. But she was tempted to bend the rules. Why? Because, Glory Gloria Mann, the town's perceived wild child, was man-starved and the only person who could feed her craving wasn't applying for a long-term position.

Which meant that first thing tomorrow, she was going to explain to Cal just how serious she was about that five-date rule. Jacket or not, she wasn't going to give in that easy.

Road Kill stopped mid-dig, his ears rotating like two little satellites until they zeroed in on the front door. His tail twitched and he let out a grunt-pant combo that didn't sound the least bit intimidating. A knock sounded at the door, and with an ear-piercing screech, he leapt off the couch and hustled his little armored butt down the hall and into the bedroom, his claws scuffing her hardwood floors.

Glory walked to the door and peeked out the peephole, doing some panting of her own when she recognized Cal's sexy blue eyes peeking back.

She knew the minute he realized she was on the other side of the door because he smiled and took a step back, as though waiting for her to just open up her door and welcome him inside.

"I know that you know it's me, Boots, so open up."

Oh, she knew it was him all right. Her nipples told her that the second he'd knocked. Plus she could smell the testosterone through the door, and his soap, which from the looks of it he'd showered, too. Although, she thought bitterly, he'd put on a fresh pair of jeans and an untucked gray button-up, not a pair of shorts with dancing pigs on them and a tank that said RESIDENT BED HOG across the chest.

"Or I can go get my tools from the truck—your call."

And since the thought of Cal with tools made her hot, she opened the door—wide enough to see his face.

"What do you want?" she asked, more than aware that she hadn't put her bra back on after her shower.

"Our date wasn't over."

Time to be firm. "I had a fun time, I'd love to do it again, but like I already told you, panties are a strict date five topic."

"You said date four if they're special."

She had said that, *damn it*.

He pushed the door open a tad and his eyes dropped to her pajamas. He grinned. "And, Boots, those shorts don't leave much room for imagination." He pushed the door open wider and leaned in. "Or panties."

He was right. She was commando under there. Not that she'd confirm his suspicions or even had time to. Before she knew what was happening, Cal took her hand in his and led her down the stairs toward his truck—and the already opened passenger door.

She stopped at the bottom step. "I'm not wearing shoes and I'm in my pajamas."

"Which answers the question of what you sleep in. Although, I have to admit, I took you for more of an in-the-buff girl." She felt her cheeks heat but played it cool. "Ah, good to know."

Okay, maybe not so cool.

Cal slipped his jacket over her shoulders, then turned around to offer her his back. "Pajama issue solved. Now climb on."

Knowing that he wasn't going to let her be until she did as he asked, at least that was the lie she told herself, she wrapped her arms around his neck and legs around his middle—which only managed to smash her front deliciously against his broad, muscular back.

He walked her over to his truck, sat her on the seat, and shut her door, not saying a word until he was in the driver's seat with his door shut.

He didn't start the engine, didn't explain what he was doing, just turned to her and smiled. "I had a great time tonight, which after my day seemed impossible. But you made it fun, made it easy to talk about Payton, and just...easy. With you, tonight, it all seemed so easy, so thank you."

And wasn't that the most romantic thing anyone had ever said to her. "I had a great time, too."

"Good." His smile was back and he got out of the truck, walked around, and opened her door.

Glory rolled her eyes, but inside she was melting. "What are you doing?"

"Walking my date to her doorstep." He looked at her bare feet and waggled a brow. "Or carrying."

"That's okay, I can walk." But one hand was already around her back, the other firmly planted on her butt, and he was scooping her out of the truck, not putting her down until he was up the stairs and at her door.

Hands shoved in his pockets, he leaned against the rail. She opened her mouth to speak when he said, "Hang on." He reached out and closed her front door. "There. Now, you were saying."

"Just, thank you," she whispered and neither of them moved, neither of them spoke. It was as though time hung, and in that one moment nothing else mattered. Only the two of them and this insane connection.

His eyes dropped and he cleared his throat. That's when she realized he was waiting for his jacket.

"Oh, right. Sorry." She started to take it off when he gripped the collar and tugged her to him.

"I don't care about the jacket, I'll get it next time."

Her knees wobbled at the idea that he wanted a next time.

Oh my God, Charlotte was right, she had it bad. Glory was a certified McGraw addict; she had every last symptom, even down to wanting their next time to be now.

Cal must have been suffering from the same affliction, because he tilted his head and delivered a gentle kiss that seemed to last for hours. Languid and soft and with deliberate control, the man kissed her as if there was nowhere else he'd rather be. This wasn't a race or a sprint to the bed; to him, kissing was his way of connecting, sharing.

By the time they came up for air, Glory's bones had turned to mush and her entire world had shifted because Cal wasn't just special, he was perfect.

Then he did the one thing that could have made her fall, had her opening herself up to all the what-ifs and going all in. Cal gave her one last kiss on the cheek and made his way down the stairs, giving her what she wanted, time to prove he was serious, that she was worth waiting for, worth fighting for.

Only every step he took caused her chest to coil tighter and tighter until it hurt to breathe.

One date. A hundred. It didn't matter. This was Cal. He was one of the good ones. He'd come all this way, in the middle of the night, to escort her to the door, and there she was, watching him walk away, wondering if she'd get another chance.

The least she could do was invite him inside and offer him a cold beverage.

He was rounding the truck when her feet finally got the message from her brain, and she took off down the steps, not stopping until she was standing in front of him. "Don't go."

Well hell, it wasn't as though Cal wanted to go home to an empty house and even emptier bed, but he was trying to do the right thing here. Not that she was making it easy.

Glory was looking at him like he was a triple scoop of Firecracker ice cream and she wanted to lick him from head to toe, so his brain was having a hard time figuring out if this was some kind of cruel test—which he hoped to God it wasn't—or if he'd just become the luckiest SOB ever to walk the earth.

The still night air hung thick, nothing between them but moonlight, a few fireflies, and then she met his gaze and thinking became imperative. Beneath the storm of need was a hint of something raw that had him pausing.

It was no secret that Glory's life had been a revolving door of disappointment, and he refused to be another guy who let her down. Blowing this wasn't an option—too bad neither was walking away.

"Are you sure?" he asked, giving her a chance to back out and strong in his conviction that if she did, he wouldn't cry. Much.

But to his relief she fisted her hands in his hair, dragged his face to hers, and—*hallelujah*, his prayers were answered—planted one on him.

Cal, a grand master of nonverbal communication, took her tongue in his mouth as an affirmative, her hands smoothing down his chest and, *bingo*, right over the front of his pants as a giant green light that she was sure.

Even better, that it was on.

Always a team player, he did his part, molding her hips with his hands, backing her up, and caging her between his body and the grill of his truck, making sure she felt his green light, front and center.

The heat radiating off his engine was almost as intense as the big freaking hot ball of fire that raged between them. Part pent-up tension and part bone-deep lust made for a whole hell of a lot of chemistry.

And since he was more than convinced that she was sure, he scooped her up, he couldn't help it, and sat her amazing ass right there, on the hood of his truck.

Pressing himself between her legs, he trailed little kisses down her throat to the creamy cleavage he'd been dreaming about. She smelled good. Insanely good. Like turned-on woman and red hots.

She felt even better. Soft and curvy and—*holy shit*, her hands were on the move again, plucking one button at a time until his shirt was open and her talented fingers were exploring every inch she'd uncovered...and more.

He knew he should carry her inside, make love to her in that soft bed of hers, but he wanted a few more moments under the stars. With her hands on him just like this.

She must have felt the same because she pulled back enough to look down at him and, without a word, lifted her arms in invitation.

Cal RSVPed to that party in no time flat, easing his thumbs under the hem of her tank top and slowly pushing it up. The higher he tugged, the harder he became, until his thumbs brushed the undersides of her breasts, and he stopped.

"Is this one of the hundred and forty minutes of your day when you're thinking about what color my lace is?" she asked, her eyes dilated and a little dazed. "Because I promise you, one more inch and you'll know."

"But then the anticipation of wondering will be over."

"It will, won't it?" She laughed, and before he could blink, she pulled it up and over her head, tossing it on his windshield, and Cal's breath lodged itself in his throat. Because no amount of wondering or fantasizing could have prepared him for what was beneath.

Tiny waist, flat stomach, incredible breasts right there for his viewing pleasure. Glory was perfectly naked under that top. It was a no-lace-required kind of look that officially blew his mind.

"Are you still wondering?" she whispered when he just kept staring.

"Just savoring, give me a minute."

He wanted to savor her all night. He started by letting his eyes roam over her, then his hands, exploring every single inch of silky skin.

He got to her waist and ran his palms over the band of her Bed Hog shorts and around to cup her ass. She was either completely commando under there or wearing a G-string. Both scenarios had him reeling.

"It's a matching set," she said, and he wanted to weep with joy.

"I had a feeling."

She leaned back on her hands, giving him a view that he'd remember until the day he died. "Isn't the real thing better than wondering?"

"You tell me." He jerked her forward, until her ass

teetered on the edge of the hood and those perfect tens were eye level, and then he pulled her into his mouth, teasing, nibbling, and gently biting her nipple.

Her breath caught so he did it again.

"So much better." She let loose this sexy little moan, her head falling back, giving him a full-access pass to explore, which he took.

His mouth moved down her breasts, along her rib cage, until he placed an openmouthed kiss on the inside of her right thigh, then the left, and then because she seemed to like that so much, he pressed her legs open even farther and placed one right in the middle of her cotton shorts.

"But not as much heat as I'd hoped," she challenged.

Challenge accepted. She wanted heat; he'd give her heat.

"You might want to hold on to something," he said right before he gave her so much heat, her body melted on the hood of his truck. He used his tongue, his teeth, teasing and nipping until her breathing was coming out in short gasps and her body was so primed it was humming.

Pressing her legs as far apart as he could, he pulled the shorts to the side and slid one finger in, meeting sweet moisture. Her whole body tensed, so he slid in another, loving how she fisted her hands in his hair and held him there, as if he didn't already know what she wanted.

He knew all right, and he was going to give it to her.

Slowly, he started pumping and her hips pressed forward to deepen the friction. The way she closed around his fingers when he sank even deeper was enough to drive a man insane.

"Hot enough?" he rasped.

"Hotter," she screamed out as he curled his fingers, hitting the jackpot. He did it again and again until the heat rose past surface-of-the-sun and rounded un-fucking-believable.

He had her shuddering in one swipe and with a last well-placed nibble to her swollen, wet flesh, she exploded and, lucky guy that he was, melted into him, sliding down his body until her feet were on the bumper and his hands were under her ass, doing some sliding of their own.

"Lift up," he said, those shorts of hers sliding right down her legs, joining her top on the windshield. His shirt quickly followed, and while she was vibrating with aftershocks, he unzipped and was covered, wrapping her legs around his waist and sliding home in one desperate stroke.

She gasped. He didn't move. Just stood there, holding on tightly and welcoming the feeling of finally being inside her, being with her. Glory was doing the same thing and he wondered if she felt as thrown by how irrevocably right this felt.

She shifted her hips ever so slowly, tightening her arms around his neck until there wasn't even air between them and they started moving together. Slowly at first, then he braced her up against the grill so his hand could participate, stroking every inch he could reach, stretching for some of the more important spots.

She started to tighten around him, a good thing since he was about ready to lose it, and did this little swivel action with her hips. Breathing turned nonexistent, his chest felt too big for his skin, and he wanted to run and stay right there forever, all at the same time.

She lifted up and clenched before sliding all the way back down his length and—

He buried his face deeper into her neck. "Christ, you feel so good."

She did it again, only this time she lifted her head to meet his gaze straight on, looking at him as though he was one of the good ones and—bam—things got serious. Real fast.

Cal gripped her hips and rose up, moving faster and deeper. He wanted to make this last, wanted to blow away every "what-if" she'd had about them, but then she clenched again and her head fell back, thrusting those magnificent breasts out while sexy little moans escaped her mouth, which officially drove him right over the fucking line.

The pressure built, hotter and higher, and he fought to keep himself in check, but her thighs tightened around his waist until he thought he'd pass out and then, *thank you, Jesus*, he felt her start to shake and she pushed down as he came up. The sweetest sound he'd ever heard was his name on Glory's lips.

Which worked for him since he was mumbling her name as he finally gave in to the heat. Everything went black and he dropped his head to her shoulder, pressed his face to her throat, and took her in, while Glory collapsed against him, both breathing hard.

"I was going to ask if you wanted to come in for a cold beverage," she said after a long moment.

"Mighty neighborly of you," he chuckled and, when he was able to look up without dropping her, pressed a dozen or so gentle kisses to her throat, making his way up to her mouth, and once he got there, it was slow and languid and oh so perfect.

Which scared the shit out of him.

It was almost noon when Glory finally stirred. Well, opened her eyes was more like it. Hard to stir with two-hundred-plus pounds of solid man wrapped around her.

Cal's face was pillowed between her breasts, his leg was draped over her thighs, and his hand cupped her butt like he owned it—after last night and twice already this morning, he totally did.

She was pretty sure he owned her heart, too. Not that he needed to know that. She'd just gotten him open to the idea of exploring the possibility of more; she didn't need to burden him with any kind of declaration. Glory wasn't that dumb.

She was also far too sated to declare. Multiple orgasms could do that to a girl. They could also leave her grinning like an idiot because, unlike the rest of Glory's life, which had been one big game of wait and watch and wonder, last night had been the first real step toward creating the kind of future she deserved.

Instead of waiting for her life to start, for love to find her, or for the big "what-if" to finally reveal itself, Glory had gone after what she wanted—and he was currently twisted around her like a big, naked, manly pretzel. A pretzel whose hands were on the move.

"You can't be serious," she said and he shifted, his statement of just how serious he was pressing hard against her thigh. "We have been in bed for ten hours and I think we've slept a total of two."

"We didn't make it through all of your panties yet," he mumbled sleepily, gently biting her shoulder. "And I am still waiting for the red pair."

"I don't have a red pair." She had black, blue, teal, pink, yellow, polka dots, stripped, a lime green pair, which currently hung from her bedpost, and orange ones with little NO HUNTING signs on them. But no red.

As he already knew.

Last night, after they'd stumbled inside, he tossed her on the bed and proceeded to riffle through her drawer, pulling out, inspecting, and making her model each and every pair she owned. Sometimes in conjunction with his jacket, sometimes without, but he always insisted on taking them off himself.

With his teeth.

Without warning, Cal rolled on top of Glory, pinning her hands above her head. "I still think you're holding out on me, Boots."

"You're joking, right? You tore through my entire collection."

"There are three things a Southern man never jokes about. Bacon, morning sex, and—"

"Let me guess, football?"

"I was going to say panty collections." Then his face went serious. "And, Boots, no one in the South jokes about football. No one."

She rolled her eyes and shoved at him; the big jerk didn't budge. "I'm not holding out. Now, get off, I need to study."

"For what?" His gaze slid over her breasts and she shivered. "Human anatomy? Because I am an expert on the female form."

Yes, yes, he was. Too bad her final was on Pediatric Health Theory. "Nope, and I need to study. So this"—she looked at his most impressive erection pressing into her stomach—"will have to wait."

He studied her long and hard until she wanted to say forget hitting the books and hit *it*—again. With him.

"Does your final cover the power of panties or"—he shifted again—"the lack thereof?"

Didn't she wish. "Sorry."

He frowned, then delivered a hot smack to the mouth and rolled off her, walking his naked backside out of her room, not even bothering to put on his pants.

"Where are you going?" she asked, straining to see him mosey into the kitchen.

"Since panties and morning sex are off the menu and the Falcons don't play until tomorrow, I'm going to fry up some bacon. And maybe make you some flapjacks."

"Do you even know how to make flapjacks?"

He peeked his head back in and waggled a brow. "I am a flapjack master."

"I thought you were the panty master."

He winked. "That, too."

Chapter 16

Early Monday morning, Cal gently tapped on Payton's door. She didn't answer, which wasn't a shocker since she hadn't said much on the trip home, had said even less during dinner last night—about the pageant or the possibility of her moving to Texas. She'd cleared her plate, asked to be excused, and gone to bed.

But this morning, he'd awoken to find a slice of astonishingly good rise-and-shine cake, a Miss Peach application on his desk, complete with the required essay, and a note asking him to read before making a decision.

So he had. Twice. And damn if it hadn't broken his heart.

How had he missed the fact that the pageant was his daughter's way of connecting with Tawny? That it was a heartfelt attempt to gain her mother's attention and approval?

Easy. He'd been so focused on Payton being right in front of him that he forgot to see her, actually *see* what she was going through. And damn it if that didn't seem to be a recurring problem with the women in his life.

He raised his knuckle and tapped again; he knew she was awake, could hear her texting through the wall.

A moment later the door creaked open and his daughter's solemn face peeked through the crack. Her eyes were puffy and her skin blotchy, and if there was one thing he hated more than seeing Payton cry, it was knowing he was the cause.

"Can I come in?" he asked, praying she said yes but willing to leave it be for a while if she said no.

And in true teen fashion, Payton did neither, just walked over to her bed and left the door ajar.

Deciding to take that as an invitation, Cal followed, not giving her a chance to renege. Also, big point to Dad, not commenting on the length of her shorts—nonexistent—or how the new top Tawny bought her showed her bra straps.

Didn't even mention the strapless blue dress that hung on her closet door. Maybe it was because they were all signs, signs he'd been determined to ignore, that somewhere between playing dress-up and pajama parties, his little girl had grown up.

She didn't speak, wouldn't even look at him. Just plopped down on her bed, pulled her knees to her chest, and hugged the stuffed toad he'd bought her for her tenth birthday, and suddenly Cal's chest ached, because he got it. Her growing up was just as hard for her as it was for him, maybe even harder.

"I tried your breakfast cake. It was really great."

"Mom and I made some yesterday for breakfast. She'd put a cube of butter instead of a cup of butter when she e-mailed me the recipe." That would explain the brick-like texture. "It was going to be my Miss Peach talent."

"Speaking of Miss Peach, I read your application and I thought a lot about what you and your mom said."

He wanted to talk about whether she'd thought about moving like she'd promised, and what she'd decided, but he knew that he had to bridge this gap first.

"It doesn't matter anymore," she said with a fragile smile, and a bad feeling started low in Cal's gut. "Mom texted me." She held up her cell. "I guess they got the house she wanted, so she has to get their old one ready to go on the market. She can't make it to the pageant."

He felt frustration and helplessness and a giant heaping of anger swell up and strangle him—which made him want to strangle Tawny. She got Payton all excited, excited enough to go behind his back, and now she was bailing and leaving behind a heartbroken daughter and a mess for him to clean up. Payton deserved better than that. And so did he.

"I'm sorry to hear that, baby." He sat down next to her and leaned back against the headboard, resting his hand on her knee. "You put a lot of time and heart into that essay."

She plucked distractedly at the fur around Hopper's foot, and when she looked back up, her face was a one-two punch to the gut: heartache and apology.

"I thought it would be fun, you know. Mom always talks about being Miss Georgia State and how cool it was." Cal didn't have the heart to tell her that it was only cool because Tawny had emotionally peaked at nineteen. "And then when I went there this summer, she took me to get head shots and try on dresses and I know I should have told you before, but I wanted to talk to you about entering the pageant with Mom here because…"

She paused and Cal could tell she was debating between telling the whole truth and the dad-friendly truth. He decided to help her out. "Because you thought the two of you could corner me into saying yes?"

She nodded and her eyes went glassy. "I'm sorry, Daddy.

I just wanted to do it so bad and I knew that you'd say no, so I went behind your back."

Unable to help himself, he pulled her to him, relieved when she didn't resist and instead melted into his side, laying her head on his shoulder like she used to. "I don't like being lied to or manipulated. Family doesn't work that way."

"I know," she whispered on a sniffle.

"But I'm also sorry I made you feel like you couldn't come to me and talk about it." She tilted her face up, all wide-eyed with surprise—like *he'd* never apologized before. "That's not very family-like either."

And if he wanted to keep his family together, he had some growing up to do, too.

"I love you so much it makes me crazy because I want to keep you safe, make sure you're happy, and that sometimes means saying no, even when I know you want me to say yes."

"I know," she said, trying to sound all put out and one hundred percent teenager, but coming off more wounded than anything. And that was when Cal decided to make good on his promise to keep her safe *and* happy, because right now she was about as miserable as a girl could get.

He pulled her application out of his back pocket and handed it to her. She looked down at the scrawl on the bottom and with a gasp, shot up, elbowing him in the ribs in the process. "You signed it."

He did. And it had taken everything he had to do it, but in the end he realized that Payton was an amazing kid and she deserved his support—even if she did go about getting it the wrong way.

"I'm sorry your mom can't come, I know how much you were looking forward to spending time with her. But if you still want to do Miss Peach, I'd love to help. I don't know a lot about pageants or rise-and-shine cake, but I'm sure that between the two of us, we can figure it out. Like always."

Payton looked at his signature again, then squealed and launched herself at him. He tightened his arms and breathed her in, noting that under all of the fancy shampoo and watermelon lip gloss, she smelled exactly the same—like home.

"Thankyouthankyouthankyou."

"Just promise me something, kiddo." He took her face in his hands to make sure she understood how serious he was, so she could see how much he loved her, and what an amazing young woman he thought she was. "Make sure that you do this for you. Not to make your mom happy or me crazy or impress some boy who won't matter in two years." He tried hard not to stress the last part. "Do it for you, your way."

"I promise," she said on a little stutter, another tear escaping down her cheek. And even though watching her cry ripped out his heart, the hug she gave him went a long way to making everything all right. "You have no idea how much this means."

Even though the idea of her in that dress gave him heartburn, he knew signing the application was the right thing to do. If they were going to make it through the next few years, they were going to have to start trusting each other. And that meant he was going to have to start seeing Payton for the beautiful young lady she was becoming—and treating her accordingly.

Oh, there were still going to be rules, and he was still going to have to put his foot down at times, but he was willing to have an open discussion about how they could both give a little.

"Wait." Payton pulled back, once again weary. "You've seen the dress, right?"

"Yes." He was trying to block it from his memory.

"And you do know that there will be dancing? With boys? And me? Me and boys dancing to slow music."

Cal ran a hand over her face. It was a fact he'd been wrestling with all weekend. "Yes, I was once a teenage boy and remember Cotillion well." Almost too well. "Which is why we will be setting some guidelines."

Her body slumped and she gave him a *here we go* look of exasperation.

"But first why don't you tell me what's important to you about being in the pageant and we'll see how we can make that happen while keeping me sane."

Glory awoke to two beady eyes starting her down. When she feigned sleep, Road Kill shuffled closer, sticking his wet nose against hers and letting her know the gig was up.

"Five more minutes," she mumbled sleepily and rolled over when he made it clear that he wasn't going anywhere until she fed him.

She had stayed up most of the weekend studying for her final; the rest had been spent mooning over her date with Cal. The date that started Friday night and lasted well into Saturday afternoon when she finally had to put on something other than panties and drag herself to work. And now she had to drag herself to class if she was going to make it to her final in time.

A low rustling, followed by irritated gnawing, came from beneath the bed.

"No, Road Kill!" She leaned over the bed and lifted the bed skirt, catching Road Kill red clawed, his little teeth wrapped around the waistband of her favorite neon green panties, his front claw holding them by the crotch. "One bite and you'll end up as someone's shoes."

Road Kill stopped to consider this, then with a deep grunt

reared his head back, ripping her panties right down the center. Then dropped them and waddled to the kitchen—where Glory assumed he was waiting for his breakfast.

With a sigh, she rolled out of bed and padded after him, nearly tripping over the anthill of panties in the middle of the room. There was a gnawed corncob sticking out from beneath it.

She looked at Road Kill, hands on her hips in the most intimidating pose she owned. He looked at his bowl and then pushed it closer. And so her day began.

It was well past lunch by the time Glory pulled into the hospital's parking lot to start her shift. She had taken and aced her final—thank you very much—picked up the last batch of pageant applications from town hall, and printed out her proposal for Charlotte to look over. All she had left to do was arrange for the bleachers at the high school to be delivered to the Country Club, deliver the finalized list of Miss Peach entries to the *Sugar Gazette*, and get through her shift. Then she could go home and sleep until tomorrow.

She parked her car in the usual spot and watched in sweet surprise as Cal pushed off the wall and came toward her car, taking slow, easy strides that rejuvenated every inch of her body with sudden alertness and bone-tingling interest.

She opened her door right as he stepped off the curb and into her space. Not that she was complaining. He looked good. And he smelled even better. Like summer air, sawdust, and...fresh-cut flowers?

"For you," he said, pulling a bouquet of dahlias out from behind his back—red, of course. It was a simple but elegant bunch, tied together at the stems with a silky red ribbon that crisscrossed its way all the up to the base of the bouquet.

"Thank you," she whispered, taking a heavenly whiff of

the arrangement and promising herself she wouldn't cry. She had never received flowers from a man before. That they were from Cal made them even more special. "What are these for?"

"For acing your final."

She blinked. "How do you know I aced it? Professor Clark hasn't even posted the grades yet." Although he had agreed to grade Glory's final while she waited after class, since so much was riding on her score.

"There was never a doubt in my mind that you wouldn't." He said it so confidently, so matter of fact, as though his belief in her was unwavering, that Glory had to focus on the flower petals before she embarrassed herself.

"I picked up the last batch of applications on my way here. We have a total of twenty-six entries and more than half of them are girls who have never entered a pageant before," she admitted, feeling awfully giddy for a girl who'd had only two hours of sleep. From the flowers or the realization she was making a difference, she wasn't sure.

"Actually, I have one last name to add to the list." Cal pulled an application out of his back pocket and handed it over. "If it's not too late."

"No, of course not." Glory looked down at the familiar hearted *i*'s and smiled. "You're letting Payton enter?"

He shrugged. "We set some ground rules, ones she could live with and I could feel secure in the fact that I wouldn't have to stalk her and her date all night."

Glory laughed; she couldn't help it. He looked so adorably miserable. "Are you saying that she is going with a boy who isn't you?"

Cal let out a long, tired breath. "Yeah, Mason Simms came to see me during his lunch break. He wanted to speak man to man, he said, then asked my permission to escort

Payton to Cotillion. He made some valid points, promised to treat her like a lady, and understands that if he lays a hand on her, he'll have to explain to his future wife why he can't have kids. "

She scooted closer and cupped his cheek, noticing he was already sporting a five o'clock shadow and it was barely one. "That must have been hard for you, letting go and giving Payton space."

"I don't like space." And to prove it, he slid his hands around her waist and pulled her flush against him. "And I don't like letting go."

Glory didn't think he was talking about Payton anymore. Then his expression turned serious and a little seed of hope budded deep down in her chest.

"Go with me to Cotillion, Boots."

"As your friend, your co-chair, or as your date?" She needed to be certain of what he was really asking. Because assuming had gotten her in trouble in the past, and she didn't want to go down that road again.

"As the woman I want to have on my arm when I walk into that room. The woman I want to spend the evening dancing and flirting with and wondering what color she has on under her dress." And if that didn't have her heart exposing its tender underbelly, then his next remark did. "You can even wear your boots."

Six words and she was a goner. Falling so incredibly hard, she felt the impact on her body, felt the air whoosh out of her lungs, felt everything change, become brighter, warmer...better.

"They'll be red," she whispered, rising up on her tiptoes and pressing a gentle kiss to his lips.

He lifted a brow. "The boots or the panties?"

"Both."

He kissed her hard, and when he pulled back, they were both panting. "Is that a yes, please say it's a yes?"

"Yes."

"Thank God." He kissed her again and then lifted his head. With one last searing look, which had her toes curling, he was gone.

Glory slumped against her car and blew out a ragged breath. It wasn't the flowers or the pageant that had her giddy; it was the man himself. Cal made her feel special and happy and like she had a place. And for a girl like her, that was a potent combination.

Thursday night, Glory got off work late, which meant that she didn't have time to change out of her scrubs before rushing over to the Country Club. Tonight was the final run-through for the pageant, and even though Joie and Anna were responsible for orchestrating the event, Glory wanted to be on-site in case anything went wrong.

In the end, it was her freedom on the line.

She arrived and was relieved to discover that all of the girls had shown up prepared and they were in the middle of running the talent segment, which due to the number of entries, was to be held Saturday morning in the grand ballroom before the Sugar Pull.

Currently, Mrs. Ferguson's grand-niece was center stage dressed like a St. Polly's Girl and clogging to a techno remix of "Georgia on My Mind" while ringing cowbells. Glory grabbed her clipboard and slipped backstage to check on the props, and make sure that the fire extinguisher was on hand for Jenni Lynn's flaming hula hoop rendition of "Honky Tonk Badonkadonk."

"Miss Glory," Payton whispered from behind the curtain.

"Where's your costume?" Glory asked, a little panicked.

Because instead of the pink and white gingham chef's costume with a spatula, Payton was sporting a pair of cleats, a softball jersey, and wielding a well-worn glove. "You're on in two acts."

"I know, that's what I wanted to talk to you about." Payton looked at the other girls all dressed in glitter and glam and took a breath. "I want to change my talent."

"Now?" Payton was scheduled to do a cooking demonstration, making a batch of her mother's rise-and-shine cake and then presenting it to the judges. A lot of difficulty went into securing the equipment she needed. "The oven should be here any minute."

"But I'm not a cook. I suck at cooking," she said desperately, and Glory wisely remained silent. "I don't play an instrument or juggle or mime, and I have no idea how I'm going to walk in the heels my mom bought me, but I hold the league records for the fastest underhand pitch. It's faster than most college girls. And it's my talent."

Glory was torn between hugging Payton and strangling her. The rules clearly stated that once their talent was submitted, it was final. Not only would she have to bend the rules; she would have to find a way to make throwing a ball a talent that the judges could easily weigh and score.

"Before you say no, I already called Sheriff Jackson and asked him if we could use his radar gun to track the time. And here." She handed over a professional-looking handout on the history of softball, complete with some of the fastest pitches on record. "My dad and I put it together this morning."

"I have to clear this with the Sugar Peaches; it's up to them if they will accept a talent change this late in the week." She looked at her clipboard and then at the time. "But for today, why don't you do your pitch, and if the Sugar Peaches reject your request, we will figure it out then."

"Thank you," Payton said, giving her a hug, and Glory felt awkward. Not about the hug, but about the fact that she was dating the girl's father and didn't know what to say. "And thank you for telling me to come clean. My dad only kind of flipped out."

"He loves you very much and deserves your honesty." And Payton deserved Glory's honesty, but she wasn't sure how to do that without stepping over Cal's clearly drawn line.

"Yeah, he's pretty cool." The music stopped and the cowbells gave their final ring. "Thanks for keeping my secret, though, and for extending the application date so I could enter."

Glory really hadn't extended the deadline for Payton; it had just worked out that way. Glory opened her moth to explain, but Payton said, "I better go warm up my arm," and then was gone.

Glory tried not to get in the middle of Cal and Payton, but somehow she had. Then again she'd also tried to keep her panties on, and look how that had ended up.

Cal stood on the edge of the driving range, hammering a brace into the bleachers that had been delivered for the Sugar Pull, when Jackson walked up, tool belt and a frosty six-pack in hand. The sheriff had been calling him all week, and Cal was pretty sure what he wanted to talk about so he'd ignored him.

Jackson set the beer on the bottom bleacher and pulled out his phone. Two seconds later Cal's rang. Without looking, he sent it to voice mail and went back to hammering. The sun was setting and he'd promised Glory that the bleachers would be finished so that the decoration committee could work their magic first thing tomorrow morning.

"You don't return my calls, you don't text," Jackson said dryly. "And here I thought what we had was special."

"Maybe I'm just not that into you." Cal picked up his discarded shirt off the grass and wiped the sweat from his face. The early evening temperatures still hung in the mideighties, but the humidity made it feel much higher.

"Yeah, well, I need to talk to you."

"If it's about taking Glory to Cotillion, I don't want to talk about it," Cal said, not sure why he was being a dick, except that he didn't feel like explaining him and Glory to anyone until he knew exactly what him and Glory actually meant.

Jackson went still. "You're taking Glory to Cotillion?"

"You got a problem with that?"

"Would it matter if I did?" Jackson asked quietly.

Cal thought about this for a moment, surprised that, no, it didn't matter what anyone thought. Glory was funny, smart, real, and hot as hell, and he didn't know where they'd lead, but he was open to exploring just how hot things could get.

Jackson picked up a beer and popped the top, handing it to Cal. The condensation on the side of the bottle was too tempting to resist. "Just because our first time around we picked wrong doesn't mean that all relationships are a heartache waiting to happen."

"You've been watching *Dr. Phil* again?" Cal asked before raising the bottle to his lips and taking a long pull.

"Nah, too busy watching my friend be happy for the first time since his wife took off." Jackson opened another beer and then saluted.

"What about Damon?"

Jackson's eyes laughed at him over the bottom of his bottle. "Didn't know you were interested in my brother. I could get you his number."

"You know what I mean. He won't be too excited about me dating Glory. But you being okay with it might ruffle a few Duncan feathers."

"You were right, Damon made his own drama," Jackson said. "It just took me a long time to realize it, and losing one of my best friends over his mistake doesn't sit well with me."

"That means a lot." And it gave him the courage he needed to talk to Payton about his date when he got home.

"I'm not all that excited about the particular lady who managed to finally light you up," Jackson admitted. "But then who am I to judge? I married the sexiest peach in town and she left me for another woman."

Cal choked on his beer. "I thought Sadie left you for a rodeo guy?"

"So did I." Jackson laughed. "Turns out Alex is a five-foot-three barrel racer from Tuscaloosa, whose tits are even bigger than Sadie's. And if you ever tell a soul, I will deny it then show everyone that picture of you pissed drunk and crying over Tawny's wedding announcement. Now"—Jackson picked up a steel brace—"you want to stand here all night talking about your feelings or get this knocked out so we can catch the end of the Falcons' game?"

Chapter 17

Flanked by her head of security and the current Miss Peach, Glory took the stage, aware that a few thousands sets of eyes were on her. The midafternoon sun reflected off the shiny podium, cooking her shoulders and face. At least her sundress was lightweight and cool, giving off a playful but elegant flair. Her orange cowgirl boots, however, screamed confident and kick ass.

She desperately needed a little kick ass in her day.

The Sugar Pull turnout was more than anyone had anticipated, spectators overflowing the stands and lining the track, making this the largest—and most lucrative—turnout in recent Harvest Fest history. Not a soul in the county was about to miss the big showdown between the Pitter and the Prowler, which was scheduled to start as soon as the current Miss Peach, Magnolia Rose, gave the go-ahead so Spencer could fire the gun. A stipulation for her agreeing to be the on-site mechanic.

Glory tapped the mic, a bead of perspiration dripping between her cleavage. "The times have been calculated and we have our two finalists."

The stadium went silent with anticipation. Glory looked at Spencer. Dressed in head to toe black with steel-toed combat boots, and SECURITY plastered across her chest—just in case someone missed the Taser and riot baton strapped to her hip, she stood poised, gun ready to fire.

Glory stepped back and Magnolia Rose approached the mic, giving the crowd a dignified wave. "If the Peach Prowler and the Pitter could please make their way to the starting line, we can get our race on."

The crowd went wild, jumping to their feet and hollering as the two final tractors revved their engines, creeping forward until their front tires were at the line.

"Hang on," Frank, the owner of the Frank Brothers' Taxidermy, Ammo, and Fine Jewelry, said, weaving his way toward the podium, his generous spare tire slowing him down a little, and making him wheeze. "We've got a problem."

Glory sighed. They'd managed to make it through the talent portion of the pageant without any hysterics or fire scares, twenty Sugar Pull qualifier races without bloodshed, and now, *now* that Kitty and Jelly Lou were within spitting distance of each other, with only three minutes left in the event, they were having a problem.

"What kind of problem?" Cal asked firmly from behind, stepping forward and placing one hand over the open mic and the other at Glory's back in a show of support.

Glory smiled up at him, a shiver racing through her when he smiled back—right there in front of the whole town.

"It seems we got ourselves a tie for second," Frank said from beneath the shadow of his fishing hat, the tip of his nose already peeling from the day's rays.

Limited by track width, only two tractors could race safely at the same time. So the Sugar Pull held a series of qualifiers throughout the day to whittle down the competitors. The fastest time in each race went on to compete in the next round, and so on until it was narrowed down to the top six tractors. Then the two tractors with the best combined overall times went head to head in the title run. A tie was within the realm of possibilities, but had never happened.

Until now.

"Let me guess, our two favorite grannies," Glory ventured, looking at Jelly Lou sitting atop the Pitter in her racing jumpsuit with NED'S PEACHES bedazzled on the front. She was shooting Ms. Kitty the eye, and Ms. Kitty, who was standing next to the Peach Prowler, piloted by a former NASCAR champion, was shooting her the finger.

Never fond of kitties, Road Kill peeked his head out from his copilot basket attached to the back of the tractor and bared his teeth.

Frank took off his hat, his white hair plastered to his head. "Actually, Kitty's in first by a whopping six seconds." Which seemed nearly impossible since first and second place usually fell within a hundredths of a second difference. "Jelly Lou and Skeeter are tied for second."

"Are you sure?" Glory asked because, although this was the race everyone had come out to see, it was the situation the judges had been trying to prevent. With Jackson, Cal, and the mayor all sitting on the judges panel, Jelly Lou and Kitty going head to head couldn't end pretty for anyone. Placing an innocent man in the middle of it was downright negligent.

"Retallied the times three different ways, still got the same results," Frank said. "We got ourselves a three-tractor race."

Cal smiled, as though this were good news. "Well, then I guess we'd better call Skeeter to the line so we can get this race on."

Glory nodded and Magnolia Rose leaned into the mic. "Ladies and gentleman, we have a last-minute addition to the lineup. For the first time in Sugar County history, we have a third qualified tractor. If the Rust Bucket could please head to the loading zone so they can load the trailer."

A gasp of shock ignited through the crowd, since everyone knew Skeeter hadn't raced a day in his life. As far as Glory knew, he hadn't even owned a tractor until last week when he won the Rust Bucket off Mr. Ferguson in a game of high-stakes bunko. They'd all assumed his streak today was beginner's luck.

"I'm already loaded and ready to go," Skeeter hollered over the roar of the engines. With all three fingers on his right hand, he pulled himself up in his seat. "Was just waiting for you yahoos to figure out you made a mistake and call my name so I can win me my Peach."

Hand clutching her sash, the reigning Miss Peach looked at Glory with utter horror. "He doesn't get to win me, right?"

"You just have to ride in the winner's tractor for the victory lap," Cal assured her.

It took two minutes to get Skeeter in place, another seven for Jelly Lou and Kitty to stop arguing on whether or not one had an inch more advantage over the other, and finally Spencer lifted the gun and the shot rang out.

Engines gave their final rev that vibrated the ground and grandstands and Road Kill hunched low in his basket as the line of tractors jerked forward. The Prowler shot into the lead at such a velocity that several crates slid off the back of the trailer and crashed to the ground, sending peaches spilling across the track.

Jelly Lou dropped it into second and picked up speed, laying on the horn as she came up on the Prowler's tail, blasting Mr. NASCAR with a rendition of "Dixie" that was loud enough to make his ears bleed. But it wasn't nearly enough; there was no way she could close the gap the Prowler's blast-out-of-the-gates had created.

Glory's heart sank farther when they passed the midway marker. The Rust Bucket and the Pitter were fighting for second, both falling a disappointing three whole seconds behind the lead tractor. There was such a difference in position they could call the race right then, and Ms. Kitty was going to come out the winner.

Cal moved in a little closer, leaning down to whisper, "Win or lose, Jelly Lou still got to race her final lap with Ned."

Glory felt the backs of her eyes burn because Cal was right—this wasn't about getting there first; it was about Jelly Lou going on a journey with the man she loved. Having her one last stroll in public with her soul mate. That he'd listened to her story and paid attention to how important it was to her touched her deeply.

"Thank you for that," she whispered, looking up into his eyes and feeling a rush of emotion. It was as though they were racing toward something, too, something wonderful and real and special, and for the first time in her life, Glory believed she could come out on top.

A loud bang cut through the air and the crowd gasped. By the time Glory turned, everyone was on their feet, waiting to see how this would all play out.

"Ho-ly shit," Spencer said loud enough for the mic to transmit it to the crowd. "Kitty's choking up a hair ball."

Because there on the track, five feet from the finish line, with smoke piling out of the hood, was the Peach Prowler and one very pissed off NASCAR champion. The tractor sputtered and jerked, fighting for its last few feet and losing.

Skeeter gunned it, black smoke exploding out of his exhaust pipe as the Rust Bucket pulled ahead of the competition in time to cross the finish line a fraction of a second before the Pitter.

No one breathed. No one said a word. They all silently watched the Prowler sputter to a stop a few inches shy of finish. Astonishment thick in the air, it took a moment to absorb what had just happened.

Jelly Lou flew by the finish line in second place and came to a stop, turning around to find Glory in the crowd. Their eyes met and Glory smiled because her grandma was hugging Road Kill and looking like she'd just seen her Ned again.

Mr. NASCAR hopped off the tractor and pried open the hood. It took a few seconds for the steam to clear, and when it did, the crowd fell silent. Because in one lift of the hood, Mr. NASCAR exposed a mighty fancy—and highly illegal—engine and Ms. Kitty as a cheat.

The crowd stared at Ms. Kitty in shocked horror, and Ms. Kitty looked a million years old. Devastation was so engrained in her expression it was hard to watch. She stood alone at the edge of the bleachers—face drawn, both hands pulled in toward her chest, her head slowly shifting back and forth as though the movement alone would undo what had just transpired.

Kitty Duncan's decisions had finally caught up with her and no amount of money or spin-control could make this go away; that was obvious by the way not one Sugar Peach came to her side in a show of support.

Strangely, instead of feeling vindicated, all Glory felt was genuine sorrow—and a strange sense of kinship. Ms. Kitty hadn't just lost the Sugar Pull; she'd just lost her place in the community. Even worse, it had been obliterated in front of the entire town.

And Glory knew exactly what that felt like.

"Where's my Peach?" Skeeter hollered, oblivious to what was happening in the stands. He hopped up on the hood of his tractor and took off his trucker's hat, scanning the crowd. "I want some sugar from my Peach."

"You said I only had to ride with him," Magnolia Rose cried, and before Glory could calm her down, Skeeter shocked everyone by pointing at Etta Jayne, who stood in the pit area in an equally bedazzled jumpsuit. Only hers was smudged with grease and said, GEORGIA'S FINEST.

"You got two minutes to get yourself up here so I can take you for a ride," Skeeter hollered.

"You old fool, the rules say you have to take her." Etta Jayne pointed to Magnolia Rose with a meaty finger.

Miss Peach blanched.

"They say nothing of the kind," Skeeter countered. "I know 'cuz I spent the last two weeks poring over every by-law in that manual you tote around, and nowhere in there does it say the winner has to take the current Miss Peach on their tractor. It just says Miss Peach, and the one I want happens to be a Ms., not a Miss."

Skeeter hopped down and hooked his thumbs in his belt loops. "Now you going to climb up on my tractor and let me take your for a spin, or am I going to have to put you there myself? Either way this ride is happening."

Etta Jayne opened her mouth, closed it, and opened it again, but nothing came out. She looked just like the Prowler, sputtering and steaming with no hope of winning.

"That's what I thought." Skeeter gave a little bow and offered his hand like a gentleman. "Now, hop on up and be ready, 'cause when this ride is over, I'm going to get some of that sugar I've been waiting twenty years to experience. And I'm going to experience it here, in front of God and witnesses, to make sure you don't mistake my intentions."

"And what intentions are those?" Etta Jayne spat, but even from a distance Glory could see the older woman blushing.

"That I'm staking my claim, and it's you, Etta Jayne. So be ready for the ride of your life, 'cuz I'm going to make you mine before this night is out."

And with that, Skeeter hopped up on the one-time champion, the Rust Bucket, and with one arm on the wheel and the other around his Ms. Peach, he took the woman he loved on a victory lap around the stadium.

It was nearly seven, Cotillion was about to begin, and instead of standing under the twinkle lights of the Miss Peach arbor with her super-hot date, Glory found herself staring up at Duncan Plantation. It looked the same as it had back in high school, like one of those fancy homes they showcased in *Architectural Digest*'s "Southern Splendor" segments.

Taking a deep breath, she lifted her hand to knock, but felt her inner strength deflate like a popped balloon. Ten minutes ago she had been bubbling with confidence and forgiveness, ready to be the bigger person and put this mess behind her, so she could move on and claim her fresh start. Only to remember that a million years ago, her seventeen-year-old self had stood in this same spot and told herself the same exact thing.

You're not seventeen anymore.

She also wasn't naive enough to think that one night of mingling with high society would change her life. She finally understood that if she wanted a new and improved life here in Sugar, she had to stop waiting for permission and just go for it.

Shoulders back, she rapped boldly on the door. Glory hadn't even dropped her hand when it swung open.

Ms. Kitty stood there, backlit by a massive chandelier and dressed in a silky, sapphire blue, floor-length robe with feathers lining the collar, matching kitten heels—also accented with feathers—and pearls.

"I figured you'd given up and scampered away by now," Ms. Kitty said, once again in lemon-sucking mode. Glory seemed to have that effect on her. "But you leave me no choice; I'll just have to call the sheriff."

Phone already in hand, her finger hovered with threat over what Glory assumed was the speed dial button for Jackson.

"No need, I'll be gone before you even hang up," she assured. "I just came to say I'm sorry about…a lot. I didn't understand until today what this festival meant to you and I apologize that I haven't always considered your feelings."

"Huh," the older woman said, crossing her arms and not making this any easier.

"I didn't want this position, but I know that you did." Glory reached in her handbag and pulled out an envelope.

"What's that, an official notice banning me from all future Harvest Fest events?"

That was what Charlotte and Etta Jayne had said she should do.

"No, it's the official list of the finalists for Miss Peach." Charlotte had tallied the scores and placed the winners inside the sealed envelope. Even Glory didn't know who had won. "This pageant is what it is partly because of your generosity and dedication. And we would be honored if you would agree to resume your position as host for the Presenting Ceremony."

"Well, pretty big britches you've got, speaking for the town as though God made you queen," Ms. Kitty said, her eyes glued to the envelope.

"Well, Judge Holden made me co-commissioner, and he's one step from God in this town, so I am allowed to speak on behalf of the council. And as my final act as co-commissioner of the Harvest Council, I am reinstating you as a council member and asking you to come to Cotillion."

"Final act?"

"Yes, Peg Brass is back from her trip and will be taking over as harvest commissioner, but I asked her if I could make one last ruling. She said as long as you are prohibited from ever running for office and banned from the Sugar Pull, I had her full support." Glory extended the envelope again.

Ms. Kitty took it and ran a shaky finger over its edge, then shook her head and offered it back. "Me going to that Cotillion would give everyone what they want, a chance to see how far the mighty have fallen."

Glory didn't think Kitty Duncan was all that mighty anymore. She didn't even think that the woman was happy. Kitty buried herself in committees and boards the same way Glory buried herself in school and work, as a way to belong.

"Locking yourself in here is a better option?" Glory asked. "You're the great Kitty Duncan. You only have to remind people of that."

Ms. Kitty didn't look like she had it left in her to do anything of the sort. "I think they know who I am and walking into the lion's den won't help any."

"Sometimes we do things out of desperation, things that feel right in the moment but aren't," Glory said quietly.

"But one bad decision"—or in Kitty's case a decade plus—
"doesn't have to define you."

And Glory truly believed that now.

"I hope you decide to come to Cotillion. If not, I'll be
here next year, knocking on your door, bugging you to
come," Glory teased.

"You won't have any power next year. You'll go back to
being a big nobody," Kitty said and then vanished—with the
list of finalists, Glory noted with a smile.

Chapter 18

The Falcon's Nest normally formal dining room was wrapped in twinkling lights and shimmery stringed balloons that littered the ceiling. Cocktail tables lined the back of the round room and a giant arbor covered in peach leaves and roses advertised just what tonight's event was, in case someone missed the giant Miss Peach banner hanging above the entry.

Cal checked his cell for the tenth time in five minutes, disappointed to see not a single missed call or text. Glory had texted about an hour ago explaining she had a last-minute errand to run and would meet him at the Country Club. He considered calling her but didn't want to come off needy.

Grabbing the little white box off the cocktail table he'd made his temporary home, he checked the entry hall to the Falcon's Nest one last time. He was supposed to be in the holding area, waiting to present Payton to society, but he needed to find his date first—make sure she was okay.

Make sure she didn't change her mind and show up with someone else—like *Chuck*.

Instead he found Ms. Kitty, draped in diamonds and entitlement, striding through the front doors with purpose.

"What are you doing here?" Cal asked.

"Being late for the Presenting Ceremony because that lady friend of yours drives like a slug."

"You're doing the presenting?" This was news to Cal.

"Well, when the co-commissioner comes up banging on my door, all but dragging me from my home, saying that Cotillion couldn't possibly go on without me, what am I supposed to say?" Kitty smoothed her hair down. "So for the good of the event, I decided to put my differences with the current council aside and be the bigger person. Now, if you'll get out of my way, I have a queen to crown."

Cal stepped aside moments before she would have whacked him with her purse. And speaking of his lady friend, Cal stood rooted in surprise as the front doors opened and in walked the most beautiful woman he'd ever seen. Her hair hung in soft waves, tumbling down her back, while little wisps curled forward, framing her face.

At first glance, the dress was simple and elegant. A shimmery peach fabric that started at her collarbone, hugging her body and covering enough leg to be classy but leaving enough bare to make his mouth go dry. And her shoes—hot damn, her shoes.

No cowgirl boots for this girl.

Tonight she wore sleek and sophisticated mile-high heels with a tiny strap crossing her red-tipped toes and another wrapping around the curve of her ankle. But as he stepped closer, things got interesting. The fabric shimmered in the light, giving the illusion of being sheer while showing nothing and making him wonder about everything—like what she had on underneath.

"They match my toes," she whispered, leaning in until he

could feel her lips graze the outer edge of his ear. The music inside the ballroom stopped and Ms. Kitty's voice boomed through the speaker, announcing the start of the Presenting Ceremony.

Glory peeked over his shoulder. "What are you doing out here?"

"Waiting for you."

"But the ceremony is about to start. This is Payton's big night. She can't walk herself through the presenting arbor."

"It's also your big night. And you shouldn't have to walk through the door alone. Now, if you will do me the honor." He took a corsage out of the white box he'd been carrying around for most of the night.

"Cal," she whispered, touching the petals but not taking it. "It's beautiful."

"Payton picked it out. She said that peonies are the flower of honor and that they stand for romance and happiness to come," he said, as if that wasn't the pussiest sentence in the history of mankind. If his crew ever heard about this, he'd never live it down.

Then Glory looked up at him and he stopped caring what his crew thought, because he was pretty sure that Glory was the most amazing person he'd ever met. And that he was one kiss away from falling completely. And he was surprisingly okay with that.

"Payton knows? About us?" She sounded horrified.

"I'm pretty sure the whole town knows about us. And those who don't are about to figure it out."

With that, he took Glory's hand and pushed open the doors to the ballroom. Everyone turned to look as he slipped the corsage over her wrist. Offering his arm, he escorted her into the center of the packed room, and together they faced the crowd of curious onlookers.

* * *

Cal might not have kissed Glory in front of God and town, but everyone there knew that she was his. It was in every touch, every look, and when he eased her in his arms to slowly move her around the dance floor, their bodies brushing with each step, she finally allowed herself to believe that she was his. And that what was between them had the potential to go the distance.

"Payton looked so grown up tonight," she said as Cal led her through a few turns, his hand never slipping past proper, but the small nuances in his hold and body language making a very wicked promise for what was to come. "And happy."

"Happy, yes." A deep scowl crossed his face. "But I don't want to talk about the other part," Cal grumbled.

"Do you also not want to talk about how your eyes went a little misty when she was presented?"

Making no comment, he swept her across the floor—and off her feet if she was being honest—spinning her until she was too breathless to speak. Too caught up in the moment to care about giving him a hard time.

"Jackson told me what you did for Kitty," he said, absently trailing a finger over the zipper on the back of her dress. "Not many people would have done that."

The exact reason Glory had gone over there in the first place. Kitty messed up, no question about that, but it didn't detract from what she'd done for the Harvest Fest over the years. She had been hosting the Presenting Ceremony since before Glory was born and was as much a part of the evening as the crown.

She might not be the right person to run the pageant, but so what, she deserved to be there.

"I know what it feels like to have no one in your corner. It sucks."

Cal's serious eyes studied her. "So you went over there to tell the woman who has made your life hell that *you* were in *her* corner?"

When put that way, it sounded silly. But looking at Ms. Kitty arguing with Darleen Vander over the balloons deflating was proof that, although bringing her here had been the right move, Glory had been wrong on several accounts. Like for one, she didn't need to fit in. She was happy standing out if it meant being herself. In fact, she didn't need to find her place; she had created one on her own and she was proud of it.

Finally, and this was the most important part, Glory didn't want what everyone else had. She wanted something special, something all her own. She wanted Cal.

And she was pretty sure he wanted her back.

Cal didn't miss a step—not easy considering he felt like his heart was going to explode out of his chest. Because standing there on the dance floor with Glory in his arms, looking up at him with those big mossy eyes, he realized he didn't want to be in her corner—he wanted to *be* her corner. Which shouldn't make sense, yet it did.

Between his job, his family, and his daughter, Cal would be crazy to add one more person to his list of responsibilities. Although looking at Glory right then didn't feel crazy; it felt right. The more he thought about it, spending time with Glory was what had kept him sane these past few weeks.

"Cal," Glory said and he realized that the song had ended and he was about to kiss her. Which wouldn't have been such a bad thing except that his daughter was standing right behind him—with the lawn boy.

"Sir," Mason began, running a hand across his forehead.

Cal liked that he made the kid sweat. "I wanted to say thank you for allowing me escort Payton tonight and I hope that I've shown her the kind of good time she deserves."

"You're welcome," Cal said with a pleasant smile, but it took some serious effort. "And she's still fourteen, so her good time ends at a few slow dances."

Payton went to argue, but Mason gently touched her arm and she zipped it. "Yes, sir. Of course. And even if she were eighteen, I wouldn't expect more than a few slow dances. Maybe some hand holding." The kid leaned in and whispered, "Girls have soft hands."

Cal rolled his eyes. "Why don't we save the hand holding until next year?"

"You bet." Mason smiled as though he'd just won the lottery. "I came to ask your permission to take Payton to have ice cream. I'll still have her home by her curfew."

Cal looked at his watch. "Which is in an hour and the deal was you drive her here, I drive her home."

"You're right. That was our deal," Mason said, taking a step back, but Payton nudged him forward. "But since it's tradition for the Miss Peach court to get ice cream in town after Cotillion and since Payton is part of the court, we were wondering if you'd consider renegotiating the deal."

Payton hadn't been crowned Miss Peach, but she been named third runner-up, which was a pretty big accomplishment for a sophomore. It not only made her an honorary Sugar Peach—Cal wasn't sure how he felt about *that*—but also increased her college fund by a thousand dollars.

And he was proud of her. She'd worked hard, been herself, and come out on top, so he wanted to give Payton the freedom to enjoy her success with her friends, but letting a boy drive her was a big step for him.

Cal looked over at Payton, who was a foot away in her

strapless blue dress, surrounded by the rest of the Peach Court and looking for all the world like this one moment would forever cement her future.

He looked at Glory, who was doing her best to stay neutral. "This is where I'm supposed to say yes, isn't it?"

"Not if it doesn't feel right," she said and he gave her a look that he hoped conveyed that none of this felt right. "Right. Okay, what if Mason drove her to the Creamery and you picked her up at ten thirty and drove her to Kendra's?"

Glory emphasized *you* since no one else needed to know that with Payton sleeping at Kendra's, Cal would be sleeping at Glory's.

"That's fair." Payton nodded vigorously, her blond up-do bobbing with every excited nod.

Cal looked at the ceiling and let out a big breath. This was it. One of those times Glory told him about where Payton could explore freedom in a safe, controlled environment.

"Actually, Mason." Cal clapped him on the shoulder—a little too hard, but he was trying. "Why don't you take Payton to Kendra's after the Creamery?"

"Ohmigod! Thank you, Daddy." Payton threw herself into his arms and sank into him. He took every second of appreciation she offered, then took one more when she tried to pull back, tightening his arms around her and reminding her of the rules.

"You made me proud tonight," he whispered at the end and her arms tightened even more.

"I made me proud tonight," she said so softly Cal felt his chest do one of those painful jabs that he'd become so familiar with as of late. Then with a final squeeze, he let go.

Damn, that was hard. His hands were sweating and stomach felt like he was riding shotgun in one of Jace's race cars doing well over a hundred with no seat belt.

"Just call me the second you get in," he added in case he hadn't said that before. Payton's face said that he had. Payton turned to leave and he grabbed her by the shoulder. "I mean it, Payton. If I don't hear from you by ten thirty, I will drive over to Kendra's myself and check on you."

Glory cleared her throat. Right. He let go. "And have fun."

"Promise." She kissed him on the cheek and reached for Mason's hand.

Mason froze, looked at Cal, and held his arm out. Payton glanced back at her dad, rolled her eyes, but took the proffered arm. And the two of them slowly made their way toward the exit. Cal watched in silence until he couldn't see his daughter anymore.

"You did good, Mr. McGraw," Glory assured him, placing her hand on his arm. "Mason is a respectful kid, and Payton doesn't want to lose her newfound freedom."

"I hope so."

Glory smiled. "How much trouble can they get into in an hour?"

"You say that like I can't come up with a dozen or more things we could do in an hour." He looked at her dress, her shoes, and then to the deck where they'd had dinner a few weeks ago. It was a first date, really, and they both knew it. He had just been too stubborn to admit it. "I already have one. It involves you, your headboard, and my tie."

"Would you like to come inside for a cold beverage?" Glory asked, standing by her front door, keys in hand, and looking up at Cal, who was a model of male perfection in his dark suit, missing tie, top two buttons already undone.

With a smile he closed the distance, his hands skimming

down her dress as he walked her back a few inches. The door was at her back, and he was pressed impressively against her front. "You say the sexiest things."

"Is that a yes?" she whispered, her hands doing some skimming of their own, up his glorious chest, around his broad shoulders, and into his hair.

"No to the cold beverage, but yes to the coming inside." He flashed her a wicked smile that had her pulse skyrocketing, her mouth going dry, and everything else going wet. Just like that, a single look, and she was vibrating with want. "Yes, to coming period."

Something that Glory could get on board with immediately. He leaned down and she knew he was going to kiss her. It would start soft and warm and take only a matter of seconds to explode into inferno and then she'd be plastered against the door, naked with her legs wrapped around him, and her dress would end up armadillo bedding. And she loved this dress.

Almost as much as she loved the feeling of him.

Inside her.

All she had to do was unlock the door. Glory fumbled with the keys, somehow managed to locate her house key while Cal's hands were roaming everywhere all at once.

"I need to know," he said against her throat as she found the key hole. "Thong, G-string, or those little cheeky ones that drive me fucking nuts?"

"I do love driving you fucking nuts," she confessed.

He swore roughly and captured her mouth with his. There was no sweet or warm; it was inferno from the word *go*.

A quick twist of the wrist and they were stumbling into her apartment. The kisses got deeper and hotter, and Glory's hands somehow found their way into the front of his pants, which seemed fine with Cal since he was back to swearing again. Then he was moaning and his eyes rolled all the way back in his head.

"Jesus, Glory," he moaned, stepping back out of her reach. "Not yet." He kicked the door shut and straightened, his eyes hungry as he undid the rest of his buttons. "Off. Now." He scanned her body. "All of it but the panties."

Glory wasn't big on taking orders, but she was big on Cal, so she reached behind her, grabbed the little zipper, and gave a slow, long tug all the way down to her lower back.

"I thought about getting you a boutonniere, but I figured this was more your style." A single roll of the shoulder had her dress sliding to the floor in one swoop. "It matches." She fingered the petal of her corsage.

Glory watched breathlessly as his gaze slid ever-so-slowly from her bra to her stomach. By the time he reached her red cheeky panties, she was trembling with need.

"Don't move." He shucked his shoes, tore his shirt off over his head, and went for his pants. She reached out to help. "I mean it, Glory." He pinned her with an authoritarian stare that had her shivering in the best way possible. "Not one inch."

Not a problem, since Glory couldn't remember how to breathe let alone move with him looking at her like she was his cold beverage and he was going to drink her down. Who knew taking orders from Cal would be a total turn-on? Then again, everything about Cal was a total turn-on.

Completely and magnificently naked, he stepped closer, running his hands down her back, molding her new undies to her butt and pressing so far into her space she could feel him hard against her stomach.

He smelled good, felt even better when he leaned down and placed a devastating kiss on her mouth. But Glory didn't move.

Cal's eyes opened and he tried it again but she held strong. Not amused, he pulled back. "What are you doing?"

"You said not to move." She smiled. "Not even an inch, you specified."

"You decide to listen to me now? When you're wearing this." He tugged the leg band of her panties and let them go with a gentle snap.

"You seemed pretty serious," she confessed.

"Oh, I was serious all right." He scooped her up in his arms and placed a kiss on the lace edge of her bra before walking her down the hallway. "And you're about to see just how serious I can get."

"Does that mean I can move now?" She lay limp in his arms.

With a challenging arch of the brow, he tossed her on the bed. And then a six-pack of condoms. "Try not to."

And before Glory could come back with some smart-ass remark, her butt met the edge of the mattress, her panties the floor, and Cal's mouth met swollen, sensitive skin.

She jerked, just a fraction of an inch, but he noticed and she felt him smile against her. "Was that you moving?"

"Nope."

He lifted his head and grinned, so she closed her eyes. "You sure?"

"Positive."

"Because it felt like..." He trailed off as his tongue trailed right up her center, lingering until she had to grit her teeth not to move. "There. Did you feel that?"

Oh, she felt it all right, racing through her body and short-circuiting her brain. And no matter how stubborn she was, she was no match for Cal and his masterful mouth.

"I'm not sure," she said. "Try it again and let's see."

Cal, never one to turn down a challenge, gave a smile that

had her body quivering—on the inside, since there was no way she'd lose this battle—and got down to business.

And, *Lord have mercy*, Glory understood firsthand why Cal was such a successful businessman. His mission statement must be *Try, try, and try again*, she thought, because he teased and kissed her as though he couldn't get enough, as though he was content to spend the rest of the night right there, in the Holy Land, driving her over the edge, again and again, until he got the job done.

Being kissed by Cal was a religious experience, one that had her panting and weeping and, yes, moving—in every direction all at the same time. It also had her begging him for release.

Which he did, immediately, putting his fingers into action, masterfully working her until she couldn't stand it. She couldn't hold back. Her orgasm took her by surprise, everything inside her coiling higher and higher, and then suddenly shattering.

Crying out, she arched up and then slowly melted back to the mattress, her body reduced to a big limp puddle of *Oh my*.

She was pretty sure she had her legs vised around Cal's head, most likely suffocating the poor man. But he had ordered her not to move, so she held her position, allowing wave after wave of pleasure to pour over her.

A long moment later, Glory was still struggling to open her eyes when Cal *tisked*. "I'm pretty sure you moved."

"You have no proof," she mumbled, still half-conscious. "It's my word against your—oh God," was all she could get out as Cal gripped her hips and drove into her in one long, fluid stroke, filling her entirely, only to pull back completely.

She whimpered.

"I'm flattered, really I am. But you can just call me Cal,"

he whispered and then drove back into her. "And, Boots, there was so much movement they felt it in Atlanta. Now you want to change your earlier statement?"

No, she did not, and she was about to tell him when she opened her eyes and something shifted between them. She felt it resonate in the way he looked at her, as though really looking at who she was deep down inside. Being at the center of his focus was like being lost and found all at the same time. She didn't know how else to explain it, other than a feeling of being treasured.

His.

Her heart skipped a beat. She felt like his. And she wanted desperately for him to be hers.

Suddenly, all she cared about was seeing this moment through, seeing where it led. Seeing if what he had in his eyes was what he also felt in his heart. Because it's what Glory felt.

"Move me, Cal," she whispered.

With an intensity that shook her to her core, Cal pressed a gentle kiss to her cheek, her jaw, the corners of her mouth. His palm moved over her breasts, up her throat, to gently cup her face. And he kissed her again, on the lips, languid and unrushed, as his other hand slipped lower, gripping her bottom and pulling her to him, until she felt so full, so complete.

Connected.

"Move me," she repeated.

And move her he did. She lost herself in every slow stroke, and even slower kisses, which moved her farther and farther away from the soul-deep loneliness that had become her life until it melted completely and all she could feel was him and their connection.

And love. She was pretty sure she felt love, too.

"Cal," she whispered, afraid she was going to cry.

"I've got you," he said and pulled her tighter, pulled her until she had no choice but to give in to him. She buried her face in the curve of his neck and they moved together, climbing toward something that was going to change everything.

Then he whispered her name, not Boots, not Glory, but Glo, the name her grandmother called her, and that combined with the weight of his body took her to a place that was impossible to hold back. Her body exploded and his name tore from her lips. Cal gave a final thrust and joined her.

Long moments later, he finally rose up on his arms, his body still shaking slightly, and looked down at her and smiled. "I'm pretty sure you moved. But if you give me a minute, we can try it again, just to be sure."

Glory laughed, which was a whole lot better than crying. "I am pretty sure that I moved. I have sheet burns on my back to prove it."

"Those would be rug burns, honey." Glory turned her head and found herself staring at the leg of her nightstand. When she looked back, Cal laughed. "Don't look at me. You're the one who wrestled me to the floor with those legs of yours."

She felt her face heat, as well as her other, happier parts.

"Not that I'm complaining. It was sexy as hell." He nipped her earlobe and whispered, "But since I am a gentleman, and I know how important it is for a lady to be right, how about I help with that not moving test you seem so set on winning."

"I think you helped me enough," she said, smacking his bare butt and shoving him off. He didn't budge, except to hold up her panties and send a wicked glance at her bedpost.

"What happened to your tie?"

"It's in the truck. I'm improvising." He ran the lace edging over her breasts and down her stomach. "What do you say?"

She was about to say, hell yes, only she'd be tying him up when a phone rang from the front room. It was hers. Cal didn't care; he was too busy tickling her, trying to distract her from answering.

The phone rang again. "It could be Jelly Lou. Sometimes she needs help at night."

With a defeated huff, he rolled off. She gave him a peck on the lips and stood, grabbing her robe off the end of her bed. He yanked it back, refusing to let go.

"Fine." She walked naked out to the front room, sure to swish her hips the entire way. She heard him groan, and she smiled until she saw the name flashing on her screen.

"Payton," she said. The only response were some loud sniffles. "Are you okay?"

Cal appeared in the doorway. Still naked and fully aroused. She put a finger to her lips, then picked up his shirt and threw it at him.

"Payton, are you there?"

Cal picked up on the situation right away, slipping his pants on and holding out his hand for the phone. Glory shook her head.

Cal gestured for the phone again.

"Glory, I messed up," she whispered in a tone that had Glory slipping into her dress and searching for her keys. "Can you come get me?"

"You bet, just tell me where you are."

"Only if you promise not to tell my dad."

Glory looked at Cal, chest puffed out, expresion as calm as the eye of a storm, Daddy-mode in full effect. "I don't think that's a possibility, honey. Now tell me where you are."

"Fine, but you have to make him promise he won't yell at me." Glory heard laughter—male laughter—in the background. "He's so going to yell at me."

"I promise, he won't yell at you," Glory said, sending Cal a stern look. His look was sterner and scarier—and he still had his hand out for the phone. Glory turned her back on him, only to hear the laughter turn to chanting and she could have sworn they were saying, "Chug, chug, chug."

Oh boy.

"I'll try, but you have to tell me where you are. Now."

"At the country club, by the eighteenth hole." The phone muffled and Payton yelled, "Brand, stop being stupid." Then she was back. "Hurry."

Chapter 19

Glory stared at Cal as he hopped out of the car, striding across the lawn like a man on a mission. To say he was on edge would be an understatement. All they knew was that Payton was not at Kendra's house; she was at the country club with a boy.

With let's-take-it-all-the-way varsity superstar, and every dad's nightmare, Brand Riggs.

Cal wore his slacks and button-up from earlier, both of which looked as though they'd been used to tie her to the bed, and enough pissed-off-dad face to turn what could be a growing experience into a dividing line.

The tone in Payton's voice told Glory that she didn't need a lecture right then. She needed her dad to tell her that everything would be okay. And in order for that to happen, Cal needed to take it down a few thousands notches.

"I know you're angry and disappointed," Glory said, hopping out of the truck, her dress, she noted, equally wrinkled.

He didn't slow down, just kept walking, tension rolling

off him. "*Angry* and *disappointed* aren't the words I'd use. She played me, plain and simple."

Glory stepped in front of him, placing a hand on his chest and not speaking until he looked down at her. When he did, she almost wet her pants. "Part of growing up is making mistakes, and Payton made a huge one tonight and I know it will be hard, but try to give her a chance to explain before you go nuclear," Glory said in her calmest voice, which had the opposite effect on Cal.

Or maybe it was the red and blue flashing lights that cut through the night sky, alerting them that this was more than two kids kissing behind the eighteenth hole.

She hoped to God they'd just been kissing.

"Oh, she'll get to explain, all right." Cal's tone held very little promise of an actual dialogue happening anytime soon. "She'll have a whole year of being locked in her room to tell me what the fuck she was thinking."

He moved. She did, too—blocking him again.

"And then the next time, she might not call at all," Glory reminded him gently, her heart aching for him. Cal had done the right thing, which she knew was hard for him, and it hadn't worked out, and she wanted to tell him that she understood his anger, his frustration, wanted to ask Payton why she'd abused his trust like that, too. But going in there locked and loaded wouldn't get him anywhere—except a fast track to weekend visitation.

"I'll try," he grumbled and then shooed her with his hand.

Cutting around her, he strode right past Deputy Gunther, through the entire Miss Peach court complete with tiaras, sashes, and escorts—who parted like the red sea—shoulder checking Brand Riggs hard enough that the kid stumbled backward, and past Jackson.

"Good, you're here." Jackson took off his hat and even

Glory felt sorry for him. He looked more stressed than Cal—and that was not a good sign. Neither were the plastic cups and empty bottles littering the course. "We need to talk."

"It'll have to wait," Cal said, not stopping until he was toe to toe with Payton.

She was shivering, her dress was a disaster, and it was obvious by the streaked makeup she'd been crying. She also looked pathetically young and so, so lost. And just when Glory thought Cal was going to snap, he slipped his jacket off and wrapped it around his daughter, pulling her in for hug that made Glory choke up.

He hadn't been angry, he'd been terrified, Glory realized, watching as he held Payton tighter and tighter, rocking her back and forth as though she were still seven. And Payton allowed him to, burrowing even closer into the safety of her dad's arms in a way that was so raw, so real, it drew Glory in. The moment was private, unconditional, and without waiver, and it made watching difficult.

He kissed the top of her head and then pulled back, his eyes studying every inch of her, and when he seemed satisfied that she was okay, said, "Want to explain to me why you're here and not at Kendra's? We had a deal."

"I know," Payton whispered.

"Then what happened?" Cal scanned the crowd. "And where is Mason?"

Payton looked at the grass and shrugged.

"That's it?" Cal voice was a little too controlled. "I trusted that prick to drive you to Kendra's. You called me—*from Kendra's*—to tell me you were safe. Then an hour later you call Glory, asking her to come and get you and I show up to what looks like a party. And all I get is a shrug?"

"I called Glory because I knew that I'd messed up and that you'd flip out," Payton said, sending Glory a betrayed look.

Glory, feeling every bit the busted teen, shrugged herself.

"Well, *I'm* here and you haven't even seen the beginning of me flipping out!"

Oh boy. There went any hope of a nice bonding moment. Cal's voice was low and furious; Payton's arms crossed with enough rebellious teen to have Glory rolling her eyes.

"Fine, you don't want to tell me what happened?" Cal turned to the group of teens a few feet away. Glory couldn't see his face, but it must have been terrifying because the whole group took a collective step back. "Mason Simms, either show yourself now or I swear to God I will hunt you down myself. Your choice, but I'd suggest you take option one."

"Ohmigod," Payton hissed, pulling Cal's arm. "He isn't here. He drove me to Kendra's like he promised and then Brand picked me up and brought me here. Okay?"

"No, it's not okay. You got in the car of a boy I don't know, who brought you to a party." He kicked a red plastic cup and it narrowly missed Brand. Glory snagged an empty bottle of Jack Daniels that was within kicking reach, in case the cup had flown wide of its intended target. "Without asking me. Nothing about that is okay."

"Like you would've said yes," Payton argued, her voice escalating.

When Cal spoke, it went up another bazillion decibels. "Because a fourteen-year-old at a party with seniors where there is drinking is a stupid idea. What the hell were you thinking?"

Silence exploded off both of them, so heavy with anger and disappointment Glory could hardly move.

"I don't know," Payton yelled. "That a really cute senior wanted to take me to a party and hang out with me. *Me.*" Payton pressed a palm to her chest, and Glory felt the pressure in her own. Tawny had done such a number on her over the years, and Payton was desperately trying to find her worth. "And I knew you'd take one look at him and say no. It wouldn't matter what I thought or how I felt; you would just tell me how it was going to be."

"So you decided to break every rule in one night to prove me wrong?"

Wrong thing to say, Glory thought. And Payton must have agreed because she dug her hands into her hips and gave Cal a look that singed his soul.

"That is so you! I have worked hard, all summer, to do the right thing and you never noticed. Not once. I was always home by curfew, missed out on parties that my whole team went to because you said no, that's it, just no with no other reason except you said so. I picked the right dress—"

"There was another dress?"

"Yes, and it was awesome. Just ask Mom." Glory didn't think the teen was helping herself any, but stayed quiet. It wasn't her place to step in. This was between father and daughter, Glory reminded herself, and she didn't have a lot of experience in that department. "But Glory told me that the blue one would match my eyes even though I knew she was just trying to get me to buy the longer dress because even she knew you'd freak."

Cal's eyes slid to Glory. They were tired and lost, and for a brief second she saw something soften there, something that reached out to her and begged her to have his back. So she took a step closer, showing him that he had this. But if not, she was there for him. He just had to say the word.

"I even picked the right escort so you'd feel comfortable saying yes," Payton said. "Just like Glory said."

Oh boy. Cal's gaze slid to Glory's once more, and she'd bet it was the same look he'd just given the teens because she took a step back. "You told her to pick a guy that I would say yes to?"

"Yes," Glory swallowed. "But I meant that she should date sweet guys, ones you'd approve of. Not use a sweet one as a cover."

Another torturous silence stretched out, only this time she was in the hot seat. "Wait? You helped her pick her dress? How long did you know she was going to enter?"

"I told her that if you didn't sign the application, she couldn't enter."

"How long, Glory?" He'd never called her anything but Boots and other nicknames, and hearing her given name from him for the first time wasn't exactly how she'd dreamed it would sound.

"The day we were appointed co-commissioners."

He gave a dismissive nod, one that her father had given her before. It was cold and devoid of any emotion and final in its delivery. It was his way of telling her she didn't matter anymore—at least not in this moment.

"Cal," Jackson said, and his tone set off every alarm in Glory's body. "I hate to interrupt, but there is more going on here than a simple trespassing violation." He turned a sympathetic gaze to Payton. "You want to tell them kiddo, or should I?"

She was back to shrugging.

"Apparently the pre-party started when someone hacked the alarm code to the Falcon's Nest and they raided the bar," Jackson began. "The rest of the kids are saying that Payton let them in."

"What?" Cal exploded. "You broke into someone's place of business and stole alcohol? Do you have any idea how much trouble you are in?"

"I didn't know that they were going to do that," Payton

cried. "Someone said they heard the ballroom was haunted and it would be cool to get in and see." *Someone* was undoubtedly Brand Riggs. "So I told them I knew the code, but I swear that I thought we were just going to walk around."

And kiss. Payton thought some really cute and cool boy was going to take her inside and give her her very first kiss. She probably thought it was going to be wonderful and romantic and change her life. Glory could only imagine how heartbroken she'd been to discover Brand had used her.

"So when they went to the bar, I called Glory."

"That was good, Payton, calling for help when it got out of hand," Glory said, cringing when Cal sent her a betrayed look

"Where did you get the code from?" he asked.

It was only the second time during this entire conversation that Payton looked Glory's way—and she knew the second she saw the girl's guilty eyes that this was not going to end well. For either of them.

"I saw Miss Glory punch it in the other day when she was locking up after a Miss Peach rehearsal. I'm sorry."

"Sorry doesn't cut it this time," Cal said. "You broke so many laws, I don't even know...that's it. I don't even know. What to say. What to do. I just don't know anything anymore."

He sounded as lost as Payton, who started crying. Cal didn't move to console her. Not an inch.

Glory wasn't her mom, and she doubted she was even her dad's girlfriend at this point, but she couldn't stand there and watch Payton cry. She moved a little closer and wrapped an arm around her slim shoulders, and the girl immediately crumbled into Glory's side.

"Hang on, don't go all end of the world," Jackson said gently. "We can work this out. In fact, the owners are willing to drop all the charges as long as the damages are paid for."

"Can't do that." Cal crossed his arms.

"You sure?" Jackson asked.

"Daddy?" Payton whispered.

"I want to fix this, baby, I do. But you made this mess by lying and you need to find a way to make it right. Me bailing you out will only encourage more of this." He gestured to the party.

What he didn't see was that this wasn't about Payton or some party. This was about the last fifteen years. Cal had been cleaning up people's messes from the day his parents died and left him two brothers to raise. Then his wife walked out, leaving behind a pile of guilt and sorrow—and mistrust. All of which placed a pretty hefty burden on Cal's shoulders.

"Cal," Jackson said quietly. "You do realize that I'll have to take Payton in. She'll have a record."

Glory could see him struggle between bailing Payton out or punishing her for lying. In the end, his anger won out. "She should have thought about that before she broke in and helped steal someone's property."

"I'll just call Mom," Payton said. "She'll come get me."

Direct hit. Cal's face went slack and Glory knew that his entire world had just drifted off course, but rather than changing his mind, he said, "That's your decision." He leaned down and kissed Payton's forehead, "Love you, kiddo," then walked back to his truck, letting Jackson know he'd meet him at the station.

"Don't leave without me," Glory said to Jackson. "If he won't come back, I'll go with you to the station so Payton doesn't have to ride by herself."

Jackson nodded and Glory took off toward the truck. She found Cal leaning against the cab, arms bracing his weight, head hung.

Glory didn't know what to do, how to fix this. She understood he felt betrayed by his daughter, but he'd let Payton down, too. She was intruding in a situation that didn't involve her, yet if she didn't, a lot more could be lost than a few hundred bucks in alcohol.

"You knew," was all he said. "You knew what I was going through with Tawny and Payton and you didn't say a god-damned word."

"When Payton came to me about Miss Peach, I didn't really know how against it you were," she said then cringed. "Okay, I knew you wouldn't like the idea of her entering, but I didn't think it was my place to get involved."

At that, he turned to face her, his gaze so cold it chilled her all the way through. "But you did."

It was the sad truth and now she was terrified that she'd hurt him. Which was the last thing she'd ever want to do. She had tried so hard to stay detached, to not care, but Cal and his daughter had pulled her in, and she was not only involved, but invested fully. This was it for her. This was her chance to have the kind of family and life she'd dreamed of.

"You took her application, coached her into how to win me over, got *me* to extend the deadline. Shit, Boots." The way he said her nickname, as though it hurt him deeply, made her throat burn. "You encouraged my own daughter to manipulate me to get her way and then took her side."

That was the opposite of what she'd set out to do, but Glory could understand how he saw it that way. She'd been trying to help and instead she'd hurt him. "I'm not proud of my decision. I should have told you and I am so sorry now that I didn't."

"Was it all some kind of game?" he asked quietly.

"No. Of course not." Her time with Cal had been more real than any relationship she'd ever had. "Payton wanted this so bad, I wanted to help her, and I thought that if you read her application, you'd see how much it meant to her."

"What about how much I meant to you?" he said quietly, the rawness in his voice telling her that he was questioning everything, stripping apart every moment they shared. And that, more than anything, created an ache so deep in her chest she was afraid to speak for fear that she would lose it all. "You tell me that you want more, that you want to see where this leads, and the whole fucking time you were lying to me. About my kid."

"I never lied. I just didn't tell you about the pageant." Even to her that reasoning sounded like a big pile of BS. "Everything else was real. You mean so much to me." He meant everything to her. "And I do want more." *Be brave, say it.* "I want it all. With you. I love you, Cal."

He closed his eyes and rested his head back against the truck. Not the reaction she'd been hoping for. "I told you, Payton comes first always."

"Never once have I asked for it to be any different," she said, looking up into his eyes and terrified by what she saw looking back. "But don't use her as an excuse to end this. She deserves more than that and so do we."

"I'm not using her as an excuse," he said. "And I deserve more than all of this." He flapped his hand to encompass the party, the cops, the situation, and most important, her. Which burned.

"This is life, Cal. Sometimes it gets messy, but don't give up because you're afraid to get dirty."

"I haven't ever given up a day in my life."

Glory let out a humorless laugh. Cal had given up on his own life the day his parents died, substituting his happiness and his needs for his family's, stubbornly protecting himself from more loss. Glory knew because she'd done the same thing when she found herself sitting on the steps of town hall and knew her life would never be the same. But he wasn't ready to face that truth yet.

"Good, because what we have is special and I think you know that. Just like I think that I'm not in this alone. You care about me, Cal. It might not be love yet, but you're on your way and I made a mistake not telling you, something that won't ever happen again. I love you," she repeated shakily, taking a step forward, grateful when he didn't jump in his truck and burn rubber out of there.

"You keep saying that." She was pretty sure by his tone that he wished she'd stop. "But if this is what your love feels like, I don't want it."

"That's not fair," she said, struggling to hold it together. Her heart felt as though it was cracking and it hurt so badly that breathing became impossible and anything other than searing pain nonexistent. "I know you're hurt and I know I messed up, we both have, but I know we can fix this. What we have is worth fixing."

"That's just it. I don't want one more relationship to fix."

"You mean you don't want me," she asked, putting her hand to her chest to make sure it was still intact, because she felt like it'd been run over by a tractor.

"I don't know what I want anymore..." He trailed off, but it was clear that he didn't want her. "I don't think my family could survive any more of your love."

Glory took a staggering step back, his words replaying over and over on a paralyzing loop. All she did was love completely and somehow her world always fell apart, shattered and scattering, leaving her alone to absorb the blame.

Suddenly it seemed like the ground was swallowing her whole while the sky was pressing her down, making her small and insignificant and so terrifyingly alone that she stopped breathing. Couldn't. Everyone she'd ever loved had left her, thrown her heart back in her face as though it wasn't enough. As though it were toxic.

And for one small, incredibly stupid moment tonight, Glory had convinced herself that, for Cal, she was enough. Her love was enough. That to him, she was special. Someone to be treasured. Someone to fight for.

But she wasn't. That much was clear. And she was tired of not being enough; tired of always being alone; tired of being the only one willing to fight.

Just so damn tired.

Chapter 20

⌒

The good people of Sugar waited until after Pastor Linden's Sunday sermon, which ironically dealt with the teachings of Sodom and Gomorrah, to spread the news about what was being called the Miss Im-Peach-ment Kerfuffle. Payton had been stripped of her title, the rest of the Miss Peach court was under review from the council, and Glory received a request from the hospital's board to appear before them first thing Monday morning.

If that wasn't enough to signal the second coming of Glory Gloria Mann, then the photo of her on Facebook holding an empty bottle of Jack—*thank you, Brand Riggs*—solidified her biggest fears.

It was over.

Not just her shot at the community outreach manager position, but with Cal. He hadn't called her once, and when he'd shown up to bail out Payton—at least he'd gotten it together where his daughter was concerned—he'd walked right past Glory as though she wasn't even there.

"This isn't as bad as you think," Charlotte said, handing Glory a cup of tea and curling up on the other end of the sofa.

After the board called, Glory gave herself exactly one hour to cry, then headed straight over to her friends, determined to somehow fix this.

"Then the board isn't calling me in to say they are rejecting my proposal?"

"Okay, it's what you think." Charlotte reached behind her for a snifter of brandy and poured a generous finger in Glory's tea. "But no matter what happens, you'll have a job at the hospital. I may not have as much influence with the board as I'd like, but I am still in charge of hiring for my department."

"You don't have to do that," Glory said, wiping her eyes.

"And lose the best nursing graduate to another hospital? No way." Charlotte nudged Glory's leg with her bare foot. "And I was talking about Cal."

Glory felt her chest expand and contract so fast she groaned. "Can we not say that name for a while? It gives me heartburn."

"Been there. And trust me, close proximity to the man only makes it worse," Charlotte said and Glory believed her. Standing next to Cal last night and having him look right through her had hurt worse than his words. "So you have two choices, fix it or move."

Glory wanted to laugh, because Charlotte said it as though fixing the paralyzing loneliness in her chest was as simple as deciding not to give up. But Glory was afraid one chuckle would lead to another endless night of tears. "Is there an option C?"

"Afraid not."

Well, damn. Heartbroken or not, Glory wasn't leaving

Sugar without Jelly Lou, and her grandma would never willingly leave.

Fixing things with Cal? Glory snorted, not going to happen. He'd made his decision more than clear.

"I kept a secret from him about Payton, he found out, and I wisely chose that moment to tell him I love him."

Charlotte grimaced. "Oh, honey, telling a McGraw you love them before they're ready to admit it is the quickest way to send them hightailing it out of your life." *She tells me this now.* "They're stubborn and fierce about love, whether it is giving it or losing it. Especially Cal. That man has spent most his life making sure everyone else is taken care of, I don't think he knows that he's allowed to be taken care of, too."

"I kind of figured that out." About the time she watched Cal's taillights disappearing into the night.

"A rookie mistake." Charlotte shrugged. "Nothing that can't be fixed."

"And how did you fix it?" Glory asked, wondering how Charlotte kept her relationship with Jace a secret. Sugar wasn't known for its discretion, and when the town's belle gets involved with the hell-raiser, lips are bound to flap.

"I moved home," she admitted and studied the pattern on her teacup. "And years later I still wonder if I made the right decision."

"Does it get easier?" Glory asked, praying to God that Charlotte said yes because she couldn't imagine living with this crushing pain every day. "With time?"

"No," Charlotte said quietly, and Glory could hear the sorrow still fresh in her friend's voice. "But for women like us, life goes on. So you need to decide if you go on alone or if you go on with the man you love."

"What if he doesn't love me back?" she whispered,

afraid if she said it too loud, it would be like admitting it was true.

"Oh, he loves you all right." Glory wasn't so sure about that. "Don't give me that look, he does, he just can't help it if he's slow on the uptake. He's a man." She paused and smiled. "A McGraw man at that."

A McGraw man who looked at her like she'd ruined his life by telling him she loved him.

"Can we not say *McGraw* either?" She took a sip and let it burn her throat. "Let's also add the word *man* to the list."

"You're an asshole," Jackson said, leaning back in his chair, taking way too much joy in Cal's current situation. It had been two days since the pageant and Payton still wasn't talking to him. She hadn't called her mom to come and take her away either—so there was still hope. "Even your fancy shirt and clean boots can't hide the truth."

Cal looked down at his button-up and dress boots and shrugged. "I have to meet with the inspector about some issue with the foundation. As for the asshole part, I'm agreeing to community service, aren't I?"

It had taken Cal a whole ten minutes to realize he'd overreacted and driven to the station to pick up Payton. Even less time to figure out he'd blown it with Glory. He'd known that the second he saw the anguish on her face.

"I was talking about Glory," Jackson said.

Yeah, he knew that, too. He'd been trying to forget it, with no such luck. He'd hurt her. Badly. She'd finally allowed herself to let someone in, and he'd abandoned her at the first sign of trouble.

"You going to call her? Tell her you're an asshole?" Jackson asked.

"Since when are you for Glory Mann?"

"Since she went out of her way to make my grandma happy," Jackson said bluntly. "And if you'd let her, I think she could make you pretty damn happy, too."

"If I *let* her," Cal asked in a tone that would have a smart man running. "What does that mean?"

Jackson was not a smart man. In fact, he was as stupid as they came, because he leaned forward, resting his elbows on his deck and bringing his face within smack-down reach. "That for the first time since Tawny, you had a shot at something good and you would rather piss that away than admit that you might actually need someone."

"With friends like you, what more do I need?" Cal said dryly.

"No wonder you chased off the only good woman you've had in years. And for the record, you're not my type." Jackson smiled. Cal didn't. Because he hadn't chased off Glory. He'd walked out on her. And Cal knew exactly how that felt.

Fuck.

Cal leaned back and rubbed his hand over his chest, trying to ease the raw ache that had been gnawing at him. It didn't help. Nothing he seemed to do helped. It just got worse, deeper, hollower. "Between Tawny, Hattie, and now Payton, I've reached my quota of scheming woman."

"Are you hearing yourself? No? Then let me be the first to tell you that you officially sound like a pussy." Jackson shook his head. "Payton and her friends are less annoying."

"She lied. About Payton. End of story." How many times did he need to repeat himself before people got it? Someone who claims they love you doesn't lie. Ever. Especially about something as important as family.

"What exactly did she lie about? Because from what you've told me, she took an application, which was her job as the co-commissioner, made your kid fess up to applying, which should have been your job as her dad, and fell in love with you even though you're an asshole."

"I didn't tell you she loved me," Cal said.

"Didn't have to. Only love could make you this crazy," Jackson said quietly and Cal realized he was talking about him being in love. Which was ridiculous. Sure he *liked* Glory. A lot. But love?

"With Payton thinking of moving and Tawny trying to win her over with trinkets, I don't have time to focus on a relationship."

Or love.

Cal didn't know where that came from. The last thought or the little flutter he felt thinking it. He told himself the other night he was done. That it was better this way, to walk away before they became too invested—even though he knew he was already gone.

"Plus I screwed up massively with Glory."

He knew what to say to hurt her, like she'd hurt him. And he'd used it. And he hated himself for that.

"All right. Then fix it. Isn't that what you do?" Jackson said without a trace of humor. He was dead serious. "You get all up in people's lives like a meddling old lady and make things work. Why is this different?"

"Because it is." Cal stood, shoving the chair back. So done with this conversation. Done with everything.

Jackson stood, too, came around the desk, and blocked his path. "Why, though? Brett and I have given you a million reasons to walk away, but you keep coming back like some disease."

"Because. Just because." Because she'd kept things from him. Because she made him believe she was different. Because he could handle Jackson or Brett leaving, but if Glory walked out, he wasn't sure he'd make it. Because he wasn't only her corner; she had somehow become his.

"Fuck." He sat down, or maybe it was his legs gave out. He wasn't sure, but suddenly the weight of what he'd had and then lost was too staggering to remain upright.

"Yeah, that's what I thought." Jackson clapped him on the back. "Now you might want to figure this out before she walks into that meeting with the hospital's board. According to Spencer, she is going to be passed over for that position because she is taking the fall for your kid."

A burst of fierce protectiveness rushed through his body and pounded against his rib cage over the thought of Glory taking on that board alone. At the same time a soft warmth, unlike anything he'd ever known, filled that empty place in his chest when he thought of how amazing and incredibly loyal she was to take the fall for Payton.

Not that he'd let that happen. "Since when do you and Spencer *talk*?"

"Since I stopped her for doing twenty-seven in a twenty-five." Jackson shrugged. "What can I say? I'm not ready to stop being an asshole."

Ten minutes later, Cal was sprinting down the hall of Sugar Medical Center when he saw an IN SESSION sign on the conference room door. He also saw Payton sitting quietly on a bench wearing a pretty sundress and a ponytail—no makeup.

"Daddy," Payton said, surprised, standing and smoothing down her skirt. "What are you doing here?"

Cal motioned for her to take a seat and eased down next to her. "I was about to ask you the same thing. You should be in school."

"I cut class to come to see Glory and say I'm sorry, but

she was already inside when I got here." She slid him a side-long glance, waiting for his reaction. When he had none, other than genuine pride that his baby was doing the right thing, standing up for a woman who deserved their loyalty, she narrowed her gaze. "Why are you here? Dragging me back to school?"

"No." He rested back against the bench. "I cut a meeting for work to come here and see Glory and say I'm sorry."

Payton laughed and Cal felt his chest tighten. It was the sweetest sound he'd heard all weekend—hell, all summer. Then her eyes filled and she covered her face.

"Come here." He pulled her to his side and she rested her head against his chest.

"I'm so sorry, Daddy. I didn't know everything would happen like that, and I didn't mean to get Glory in trouble. I just wanted Brand to like me."

"I know, baby." His kissed her head. "I've done a few stupid things to impress a woman." Like agree to build a new clubhouse for practically nothing. "And I'm sorry for letting you think you were going to get arrested and for losing your title. I know how hard you worked for Miss Peach."

She shrugged. "I don't care about that anymore. I mean it was totally embarrassing in first period, with everyone talking and staring, but all I could think about was how mad you'd been."

"I wasn't mad." She looked up, calling him on that lie. "I wasn't. Much. I was more scared than anything. Scared of you growing up, of losing this." He tightened his arms. "Scared of losing you, Payton."

"I'm not moving to Mom's," she said, looking him in the eye, and *Christ*, if he didn't cry a little.

"Are you sure?" he asked because she needed to know that his love didn't come with strings or ultimatums. "Because I'd miss you like hell, but we'd make it work if that's what you wanted."

"I want to visit her more, but I want to be here in Sugar. With you." Well, hell, if that didn't make his year. "And this spring I want to try out for the all-county softball team. They travel, and I want to go to overnight games alone with my team."

"Payton," he said thinly.

She held up a hand. "I already checked with Coach and it won't conflict with cheerleading. None of the other kids bring their parents unless they're a coach, and I don't want you to be my coach again. If I'm starting lineup, then I want to know it's because I'm good, not because you're my coach."

Had that been why she quit? "We'll talk about it."

She smiled. "Oh, I know how I want to spend my community service." She pulled out an application, homemade and written on binder paper, and handed it to him. He looked at where she was applying and felt something swell in his chest. Pride and a good dose of humble pie.

"I can support this," he said then frowned. "Wait, how did you get here?" Because he'd dropped her off at school over an hour ago.

"Mason drove me." She waved to the end of the hallway, where Mason was coming around the corner with two sodas from the vending machine. He saw Cal, stopped dead in his tracks, and looked for the nearest exit.

That's right buddy, you're caught.

Although, instead of running the other way, which most boys would have done, Mason threw his scrawny shoulders back and walked over with all the confidence of a knight on a horse—Cal knew the walk well, had used it a few times himself.

"I know what this looks like, sir," he began, his voice quivering only a tad. "But I was running late to school when I saw Payton walking down the highway and offered to give her a ride. She said she would only come here so I drove her." He straightened. "And I would do it again."

Cal straightened, too—all the way to his full six-two and puffed out his chest. To his surprise, Mason looked ready to piss himself, but he held his ground. Cal smacked him on the shoulder. "Good to hear, son."

Glory was right; the kid was one of the good ones. Glory had been right about a lot of things, he decided. The biggest one being that he did care about her a lot. In fact, he was pretty sure he loved her. The all in, head over heels, never going to stop kind of love that should scare the shit out of him.

Only, for the first time since his parents died, he wasn't scared to love. He wasn't scared of anything except losing the most incredible thing to happen to him since Payton.

He reached into his pocket and pulled out a twenty, handing it to Payton. "Why don't you take your friend across the street to the Gravy Train and buy him a coffee. Then I can follow you both back to the school and explain why you're late."

"Thank you, sir, but I've got money."

"Yes, but if you buy my daughter coffee, then it's a date," Cal explained slowly. "And although Payton is old enough to have male friends, she's not old enough for a boyfriend. Understand?"

"Yes, sir."

"Plus, I think my daughter has some apologizing to do," he said and Payton smiled.

"What are you doing?" Payton asked, standing.

"I've got some apologizing to do, too." Only his was go-

ing to take a whole hell of a lot more than a cup of coffee
and batting lashes to fix.

Cal pulled out his phone and put that family name, which
he'd been so ridiculous about upholding, to good use.

"You do understand what kind of position this puts us all in,"
the elder Dr. Holden said, setting down Glory's proposal, his
face etched with frustration.

"I do." Glory stood, her legs rebelling from what felt like
an endless weekend. She'd spent half of it blissfully falling
in love, and the other half sobbing her eyes out over a gallon
of Firecracker Surprise. Which was probably why her dress
was a little snug this morning and Road Kill kept trying to
smell her breath. "And I apologize for any inconvenience
this weekend's mess caused. But I know that my proposal is
the best one in that stack, just like I know it addresses everything that this town and this hospital needs."

"Which is what makes this decision so difficult," he said
and Glory didn't have a good feeling. That Charlotte wasn't
meeting her gaze made it even worse. "The decision to move
ahead and fund your proposal was a unanimous one. In fact,
we already reached out to the high school to see if accruing
school credit is a possibility."

Glory's heart jerked with utter astonishment. "That's fantastic."

She wanted to see this program work, wanted to have a
place for teens to feel useful and important. She wanted this
to work. Needed for it to work.

"However, after this past weekend, certain members of
the board are concerned with your ability to manage minors.
And if members are concerned, we're certain that parents
will be as well."

It was strange—no matter how tight her chest tensed, she

refused to let her heart sink. They wanted Glory out. Too bad this time she wasn't going down without a fight.

"I did nothing wrong," she defended. "All of the events that fell under my jurisdiction went well. Better than well, actually. Fantastic. This year's festival brought in more money than any other year in recent history, and the pageant doubled its normal entries."

"It did. But since the entire fate of the Miss Peach court is pending, and we have already decrowned one of the princesses, I fear that none of that will matter," Charlotte's father said. "All the parents will see is someone who doesn't have a great track record working with teens."

"I can't think of a better person to work with my teen, and I'm the parent of the decrowned princess in question," an extremely familiar, extremely sexy voice said from behind.

Glory turned in her chair and felt her heart catch, because there, under the wide arch of the conference room door, stood Cal looking as handsome and strong as ever.

Dressed in a dark jeans, a dress shirt, and unyielding confidence, he looked like a knight for hire. Only she didn't want him to save her, she reminded herself painfully; she wanted him to love her. And that wasn't a position he felt himself qualified for.

"In fact, I am here to submit an application on behalf of my daughter for Glory's program." Cal strode to the front of the boardroom and placed a piece of creased binder paper in front of the board. "I know the wait list will fill up quickly, and Payton wanted to make sure she got the opportunity to work under Miss Mann."

Glory felt her throat tighten, but she was too afraid to allow herself to hope that his appearance was anything other than Cal doing the right thing. She didn't want to believe that this could mean more, only to be crushed again.

"I'm sorry, Cal, but the board hasn't decided if Miss Mann will be heading up this project," Dr. Holden explained.

"Which would be a shame if you ask me, seeing as I have a list of names right here"—he held up a second sheet of paper, this one an old blueprint with names scribbled on it—"that includes every single kid who was at that after-party. All of whose parents are excited about them spending a little time under the sure guidance of Miss Mann as they work their way toward paying back the damages of their decision."

He turned and his gaze met Glory's, tired but unwavering with belief—in her. And maybe a little in *them*.

"Thank you," she whispered.

"No, thank you," he said, coming to stand in front of her. "These past few weeks with you have changed my family. Payton not only transformed into a responsible and wonderful young lady"—he turned back to the board—"breaking into the Falcon's Nest notwithstanding"—then back to Glory, this time taking her hands—"but I finally started listening. My whole family, hell, my whole world has been forever changed by you."

She wanted to ask him what that meant, because he'd changed her world, too, and she didn't want to live in it without him. But she was no longer content to stay safely on the outside of his.

Cal turned back to the board. "No one else is as qualified for this position as Glory. The reason why it speaks to the town's needs is because Glory speaks to the town's needs. She has a huge heart and takes the time to really listen, cares about what kids have to say and what they aren't saying, and she understands that sometimes the right call is the hard call. But she does it anyways. Which is why when my daughter found herself over her head, she reached out to Glory, because she knew Glory would be there for her—no matter what." Cal paused. "I wasn't proud that my daughter didn't feel like she could turn to me, but I was proud that she had someone in her life that she could turn to like Glory."

Dr. Holden stood. "Thank you for your insight. You've given us something to consider."

Twenty minutes, and a signed offer of employment later, Glory walked out of the conference room with a huge smile and a heavy heart. The smile was because every single board member had voted in support.

Of her.

Not her idea or a fancy Gantt chart or some PhD from Georgia Tech, but her. The board had the chance to pick from a list of top-notch medical professionals from around the state, and they chose Glory Gloria Mann. Something that had never happened to her before, and the sheer awesomeness of it was humbling.

The heavy heart, however, was due to the fact that she didn't know if Cal would choose her. Sure, he'd announced to the board that he thought she was a good woman. But did he think enough of her to make her his woman?

Promising herself that no matter how much it hurt, knowing how he felt would be easier than living with the regret of what if, Glory pulled out her phone as she turned the corner.

She dialed, the phone rang, and then it rang a split second later—only it wasn't her phone she heard.

Glory looked up and faltered, because the man in question was standing at the end of the hall by the exit, holding up the wall with his body. He fished his cell out of his pocket and, eyes locked on hers, asked, "Did you get it?"

She held up the offer letter and smiled.

"That's my girl," he said into the phone.

Her smile faded and she pressed the phone closer to her ear. "Am I, Cal? Am I your girl?"

"No," he said quietly. One word and everything inside her stilled. It was so painfully still, she wasn't sure if she was even there. She looked at her chest and it appeared the same, which made no sense, because all she felt was empty.

She was so stunned by the vastness swelling inside that she didn't realize he had hung up until he was in front of her, his hand wrapped around hers, hitting end on her cell and putting the phone in her purse. Then he cupped her face between his hands and lifted her gaze to his.

"You, Glory Mann, are my world," he said quietly. "You make me laugh, make me question what I know, and you don't take my crap. You force me to be a better dad, a better man, and to try new flavors even when I am convinced they can't be better than vanilla."

He leaned in and gave her a gentle brush of the lips, but the contact resonated through her entire body, releasing hope and so much love she started laughing.

"To think I wasted all those years on vanilla, when there was something as amazing as Firecracker Surprise." He pulled back and he was laughing, too. "You make me happy. So goddamned happy I don't want it to ever end."

He wrapped his arms around her, nudging her closer, and Glory realized that somewhere between making him happy and him never wanting it to end, she'd started crying.

"The only other time I've ever felt like this was the day Payton was born."

"What did it feel like?" she forced through the tears.

"Like I was holding the rest of my life in my arms." Yup, definitely crying. "I love you, Glory, and I will do whatever it takes to earn your love."

"You love me?" she asked shakily.

His mouth curved. "I think I fell in love with you the second I saw you in those ducky boots, kicking that fence at the sheriff's station."

"I've loved you since the day you saved me from that truck full of jocks and drove me home," she admitted, and if he was surprised, he didn't show it. "Did you know that outside of Brett and the grannies, you were the only person to ask if I was okay back then?"

That did surprise him. And made him angry.

"No, and I'm sorry. For what happened, and how you were treated, and for not doing more."

He wrapped himself all the way around her, safe and strong like a shield, burying his face in her neck, and Glory felt her body melt into his.

"I'm sorry for everything, Boots. And I don't know the best way to go about this with a teen daughter. But I know that I don't want to spend another night like last night and I don't want to spend another moment without you in my life. Without you in my family."

"But you love me?" She was still stuck on those three words he'd placed in the middle of his declaration. Three little words that Glory had spent her entire life chasing, yet always seemed just out of reach.

"Loving you is the easiest thing I've ever done," he said with so much confidence behind his words that it shook Glory to the core. "But loving you the way you deserve to be loved, Glory; that's going to take me a lifetime."

"Then the rest we can figure out. Together."

He captured her lips in a kiss that was gentle and possessive and so right, she didn't care that it had taken her this long to find love. Because when Cal went in, he went all in, and being loved like that was exactly the kind of life Glory had dreamed of.

Charlotte Holden thought she was happily divorced—until her sexy ex returns to Sugar, Georgia, with a bombshell: they're still legally married. He offers her a quick, quiet divorce if she gives him thirty days—and nights—of marriage. But she doesn't know that this time, Jace McGraw won't let her go without a fight...

Please see the next page
for a preview of

A Taste of Sugar.

Chapter 1

D r. Charlotte Holden took pride in her decorum and her ability to show grace under pressure. As a three-time Miss Peach and current medical director of Pediatrics at Sugar Medical Center, there wasn't much that made her sweat—her mama had raised her better than that.

Not that she was sweating. But a distinct, thin sheen of perspiration seemed to be forming on her skin every time her phone vibrated with another message, and that really burned her britches. But she was nearing the important part of her tour with a group of potential donors when someone texted her a code silver in Exam Room 22—which was never a good sign.

"Do you need to take that?" Tipton Neil, chairman of Mercy Alliance, asked when Charlotte looked at her phone again.

The last thing she needed right then was to bring attention to the fact that there was a code silver. Not with so much riding on the hefty endowment that was up for grabs.

She'd invested three years and her entire heart into getting the new pediatric ward funded and built. The Grow Center—an outpatient clinic that would provide kids with the therapy and tools they needed to thrive in the world after hospitalization—was the final step in her realizing that dream.

"Nothing that can't wait, I'm sure," her father answered for her. Something he did often and bugged her to no end. Whereas Charlotte was the heart of the center, Reginald Holden the Third was all about the bottom line.

And the bottom line was—Mr. Neil was their last shot.

She took one last look at her phone, then her father—who was sending her every visual cue possible—and texted instructions to hand it off to the other doctor on duty.

"All handled," she said, powering down her phone. "Now over here is the centerpiece of the new Fairchild Pediatric Center." It was the centerpiece of the entire medical center—a prime example of what made Sugar Medical so special. "Our Grow Center."

Tipton took in the massive play center, the brightly colored PT room, and the state-of-the-art equipment. "I was skeptical about what a small and rural community could offer, but your new facility and unique approach to medicine could rival the Mayo Clinic."

Well, if that didn't butter her biscuit.

"My Grow Center can stand up to any big-city facility. We might be small, Mr. Neil, but we are certainty not backwoods." She laughed.

Her father did not. Dressed in his three-piece suit, suspenders, bow tie, and constant disapproval he looked the quintessential Southern medical director. "What my daughter meant to say is that being a smaller, privately owned hospital has allowed us to stay both profitable and cutting edge."

Actually she'd meant exactly what she'd said. Being family-owned allowed them to customize treatments and programs that fit their patients' unique needs. It wasn't just a small-town hospital; it was the *town's* hospital. And as such, it should benefit all of the town's people, not just the insured ones. But she wisely kept that to herself.

"This is the exact kind of project Mercy Alliance was created to fund," Tipton said, and Charlotte struggled to contain her excitement. But it was difficult. Almost as difficult as not blurting out, "I told you so."

When she'd reached out to Mercy Alliance, it had been nothing more than a Hail Mary. No one, including her father, had considered it a realistic possibility. But Charlotte had. Even though their medical center had been labeled "too small" or "too ambitious" by every investor the board had approached, she knew that all it took was one person to see the potential of their idea.

So when a friend from medical school mentioned that Mercy Alliance was pulling their funding from a midsized hospital chain out West, Charlotte reached out immediately. And now she was about to see her dream become a reality for thousands of kids in the area.

Beating death and living life were two separate challenges, and Charlotte wanted to bridge the gap where insurance left off. Her vision was to create a pediatric rehabilitation clinic where no child was denied treatment based on the family's ability to pay. Which was where Mercy Alliance, and their generous endowment, came in.

"But the board feels that at a bigger facility, our funds would go further, help more people," Tipton added, and suddenly all that excitement felt like a big, suffocating knot in her chest.

Why she'd thought all she had to do was convince this

one man that her plan was good enough, she had no idea. But her dad's look said he'd expected this all along. In fact, his grim expression seemed to be doing the I-told-you-so dance, all over her morning. "Paging Dr. Holden to Room 22," a slightly harassed voice came over the hospital's intercom. "Paging Dr. Charlotte Holden. Code silver in Room 22. Dr. Holden to Room 22."

And just like that, the knot in her chest grew to cut off her entire air supply.

"Please tell me I misunderstood the page," Charlotte asked, taking the medical chart from Dr. Benjamin Clark.

"Wish I could," Ben said, hustling to keep pace with her. He was handsome in that intellectual way that usually got her. And he had gotten her, which made him her ex. They'd dated all through undergrad and then again last summer when he'd been hired on at the medical center. He was bright, a rising star in medicine, came from a good family— and was just like her. Which was why they quickly decided they were better suited as friends. "I also wish I could have handled it myself, but the situation requires a woman's touch."

"Chicken."

"Damn right. She took one look at my anatomy and went straight for the boys. I barricaded myself behind the exam table and paged you."

"You always were a little skittish when it came to aggressive women." Ben rolled his eyes but didn't argue. "Keep watch and make sure no one comes in."

The last thing she needed right then was to have another patient—or God forbid, Mr. Neil—walk by. Charlotte tapped on the door, waited the respectful amount of time, then entered.

And sighed.

Four years of medical school, another three in residency at one of the top hospitals in Georgia, and this was what her life had come to. She stared at her patient, who was on all fours licking the soap dispenser, and allowed herself a quick roll of the eyes before plastering on her most Southerly smile and entering the room—sure to close the door behind her.

"Mrs. Ferguson," Charlotte greeted, then looked at her patient, who had moved from the soap dispenser to nuzzling the hospital gown on the exam table. "Woolamena."

June Ferguson stood and smoothed down her dress. It was denim with cowhide trim, and speckled in fertilizer—which was appropriate since she was co-owner of Ferguson Family's Feed Line and Fertilizer Farm.

The *code silver* in question dropped the gown and bleated a loud *"Baa-ah"* before huddling under the exam table—which was appropriate since Woolamena was a sheep. Not just any sheep, but the reigning Sheep Scurry champion of Sugar County, who was expected to defend her title at the Founder's Day Fair in a few weeks.

"I know what you're going to say, but it was an emergency," June explained.

"Then you know I'm going to remind you I am a doctor. Not a therapist or a life coach or a veterinarian. And this is a hospital. For humans." They'd had this conversation last spring when one of her prized heifers went into early labor and she tried to convince Charlotte to act as the midwife.

In fact, livestock in the hospital had become such a problem they'd even created a code and a room for such an occasion—Silver being the Lone Ranger's horse. The 22 was because Noah filled his arc two by two. Not that the big-city donors would understand that. Which was why Charlotte needed to clear that room stat, before the welcoming tour made their way in this direction.

"Your card says family practitioner." June produced a card from her purse as proof and waved it around. "And seeing as Woolamena here is family, I brought her to you." The older woman leaned in to whisper, "I think she needs some of those little blue pills you are all pushing these days."

Charlotte choked. "You want me to prescribe your sheep Viagra?"

"Woolamena. She has a name. And what school did you say you went to again?"

"A very good one."

"Ah-huh." The older woman didn't look so convinced. "I was talking about pills for people who are thinking of *buying the farm*." The woman mouthed the last few words as though the sheep, excuse her, *Woolamena* could understand.

"You think, uh, Woolamena is a risk to herself?"

"I think that Diablo led her on and now she's got a broken h-e-a-r-t."

"And Diablo is another sheep?"

"No, he is the stud we brought in for the heifers. Paid a farmer from Magnolia Falls a good price to bring him down, but instead of knocking up my cows, he came on to Woolamena, wooed the girl, then left her good and dry. Didn't he, baby."

At that, Woolamena's ears went back and she wedged herself as far beneath the table as she could get, clearly not open to discussing Diablo—or his leaving. June, however, was just getting started.

"After he went home, she started acting a little off, moping around Diablo's old pen, refusing to eat, tearing her wool out." Which explained the big bald patch on her rump. "Then, last week, I found her standing in the middle of the highway, staring down one of them big Red Bull trucks headed toward Mable's Market. At first I thought she was admiring the sexy bull, but I think she was tempting the devil himself, because today she wandered down to the lake and waded in, and she wasn't taking a bath neither. The water was already up to her brisket and closing in on her muzzle when my farmhand pulled her out and I said enough was enough and loaded her in the truck and came here."

When June placed a hand to her mouth and gave a few heartfelt sniffs, Charlotte handed her a box of tissues and pulled out her stethoscope. This was in part because any woman who'd delivered nineteen calves in one evening had more pluck than Charlotte, but also because she was a sucker for broken hearts.

Having suffered from one herself several years back, which she'd barely recovered from, Charlotte understood the delicate nature of loss. She also understood the power of ice cream.

Charlotte poked her head out of the door. "Ben, could you bring me one of those ice cream bars from the vending machine? One without the chocolate shell?"

With a nod, Ben was gone. Too bad dating him had been like dating herself. He was one of the good ones, and between decorating her new house, the stress of the grand opening, and her mother's endless matchmaking—since being single at thirty was a sin in the South—Charlotte could sure use a good man in her life. Not to mention an orgasm.

She could definitely use one of those.

Ben returned and something about the way he looked at her had every warning flag rising to full mast. They'd been friends too long for her not to notice the way he shifted in his loafers. A sign that he had bad news. "Oh, no. They know about the sheep."

Baa-ah came through the door.

He looked down the hall and back at her. "No, I just saw your father load Mr. Neil into his car." *Damn it!* "Reggie was wearing his cameo jacket."

Double damn it!

The only time Reginald Holden the Third wore cameo was when he was going hunting. Which meant he'd hijacked Charlotte's meeting. Not that she should be surprised. Her father's answer to any professional situation was to bond over a good boar hunt, then get down to business.

He might have appointed Charlotte as head of Pediatrics, but he still believed that the best boardroom in town belonged to the Sugar County Hunting Lodge—a members' only club that hadn't approved a single female applicant since Ada Bradly "accidentally" shot her husband in the backside. She claimed that she saw a figure in the distance, recognized it as the one that had rattled many windows of the ladies on her block, mistook him for the worst kind of dog, and took action.

Mr. Bradly lived, Ada was sentenced to community service, and anyone lacking a Y chromosome knew not to apply. So if Charlotte wanted to finish her meeting with Mr. Neil, she'd have to wait until after the weekend.

If her dad's "backwoods" business tactics hadn't screwed up the deal by then.

"At least they didn't see the sheep," Ben said, knowing exactly where her thoughts were going, and held out not one, but two ice cream bars. "Between your patient load, the meetings with the donors, and now your dad, I figured you hadn't had time for lunch and could use some ice cream right about now."

She eyed the bar, then looked at Ben. Really looked at him, and wondered if maybe it could work, then caught sight of his designer shoes, Sunday best attire beneath the white doctor's coat, and shivered—not in a good way.

They matched. Even down to the brand of stethoscope. "Nope."

He laughed knowingly. "Would make it easier, though."

It sure would. Unfortunately, her heart had long ago given up on easy and her other parts only seemed to be interested in courting hard—hard bodies with bad boy smiles and tattoos, she feared.

"Thanks for this." She took both bars—it was well past lunchtime after all—ushered Ms. Ferguson out of the room and into Ben's care, and closed the door.

Alone with the sheep, Charlotte sat on the floor at the edge of the exam table. "Now come on out."

When the sheep just looked at her, watching her carefully, Charlotte scooted closer and held out the ice cream. "We can talk about it or just plain eat it out, you choose, but moping around and pulling your hair out over a man is just not dignified. And a Southern woman with six titles needs to maintain her dignity at all times."

She let out *Baa-ah* of protest, but the ice cream was too much temptation to ignore. Eyes firmly on Charlotte, Woolamena slowly made her way out from under the table and took a tentative sniff. Then a nibble, and as though the sheep could recognize another lonely soul, she curled up against Charlotte's side and the two women ate their ice cream in silence.

It was a rare day in Sugar when Babette Holden graced the morning before the sun, especially when there was no one to bring her coffee in bed. But when Charlotte's mother had her mind set, not even the threat of puffy eyes, or lack of a front door key, could sidetrack her.

Babette stood at the counter in a cream pants suit and enough pearls to accessorize the entire Miss Peach court, staring down Charlotte's coffeemaker as though waiting for it to make her a cappuccino—irritated that she'd had to wait. "I hit the red button and nothing happened."

"You have to put water in it first." And since Charlotte knew *that* wouldn't happen in her lifetime, she moved into the kitchen, filled up the pot, and hit the red button.

"I prefer mine nonfat. Double shot, please."

"It comes in black, with cream or sugar. That's it."

Her mouth tightened. "If you had chosen to stay at home, where all good single Southern women belong, Mavis could have whipped us up a lovely peppermint latte, and delivered it to you in bed."

"Along with my clothes, which you'd pick out and have neatly pressed and laid at the foot of my bed, while you sat next to them staring me awake."

That was the main reason Charlotte had purchased her own home last month. She'd taken one look at the stately antebellum house with its pristine white stone structure, original leaded windows, and ornate wrought-iron enclosed balconies overlooking Sugar Lake and had fallen in love. That it was on the opposite side of the lake from her mother's only made it that much more appealing.

The lake house was the exact kind of home she imagined raising a family in. Not that she had a family or even a potential husband, but she still had hope. And for now, that was enough.

"You make it sound as though I smothered you," Babette said dramatically and Charlotte wisely chose not to comment. Then her mother carefully inspected Charlotte's outfit, a yellow pencil skirt, flirty pink heels with a matching skinny belt synching her white cap-sleeved top, and sighed.

"Yes, well, you really should invest in an iron, dear. And more pastels. They do glorious things for your complexion."

It was said as though Charlotte needed all the help she could get. And maybe she did.

Charlotte had spent a good portion of the weekend fine-tuning what she was going to say to Mr. Neil. The other part, when she wasn't pulling long shifts at the hospital and should have been sleeping, had been spent staring at the ceiling and waiting for the sun to come up, thinking about things she had no business thinking about.

Sitting there with Woolamena the other day had been like sitting with herself four years ago. And even though the pain had dulled and her heart had healed, the emptiness still remained, and Charlotte was tired of feeling empty. Tired of playing life safe.

Tired of watching everyone else around her move on, find happiness, while she stayed in the same place.

In fact, she was tired of being tired. So this morning, instead of staring at the ceiling, she'd gotten impatient and decided to fix her life. She was a master fixer; it was what made her such a good doctor. Only instead of fixing her patients, she was going to start with herself and act like the woman she wanted to be, not the woman she had become.

Last year, she'd set out to find living arrangements that didn't include sharing a zoning line with her parents and prove to the hospital board—and her father—that she was ready to head up the Grow Center. She accomplished the first, and was almost there with the second. Now she was determined to get the rest of her life in order. And that included really living again. Taking chances.

So she'd riffled through the endless supply of cardigans and pastels, past the tea-length and cashmere forest, to locate the one outfit hiding in the back. It was sleek, sophisticated, and said grown-up sexy instead of Sunday tea. And was something she'd been waiting until she gathered the courage to wear.

Not that she had the courage now, but she was willing to fake it for a while. Which was why she'd slipped on her naughtiest pair of panties, mile-high heels, and left the top button of her blouse undone, then marched downstairs—to find her mother in the kitchen.

Babette clapped her hands. "You know what you need?"

A new lock? A good night's sleep? Once again, Charlotte's mind circled back to that orgasm and suddenly she felt like unbuttoning her blouse two more buttons, but resisted. She had a full workload, with the average patient being in diapers or with dentures, and her "need list" was about four thousand pages long.

Yet based on the way her mother was smiling, Charlotte didn't think her mother's idea would even make her extended list. "I need to leave for work."

Babette's face puckered, as well as a face could pucker when the forehead didn't move. "It's Sunday. Who works on Sunday?"

"Sickness doesn't recognize the Sabbath." Apparently neither did her father since he'd decided to take a "personal day," choosing to finish up his hunting trip with Mr. Neil rather than work the urgent care unit like he was scheduled, leaving a huge gap in patient load coverage. And since the hospital was perpetually short-staffed on the weekends, especially in urgent care, it was up to Charlotte to pick up the slack.

"Well, it should."

Amen to that. "I'm covering a shift."

"That's sweet of you."

Not professional, not ambitious, but *sweet*. As though all

of the sacrifice and hard work Charlotte had put into her career was merely a way to pass time until she found herself a proper Southern man and set up a proper Southern home.

"I heard you had lunch with Benjamin."

And there's the reason for her visit, Charlotte thought while pouring coffee into a mug. She slid it across the countertop toward her mother, who looked offended, then shook her head.

"I had lunch with a patient," Charlotte said. And then not to give her mother false hope, clarified, "A female patient. Ben and I are just friends."

A car horn honked out front. Babette didn't move and Charlotte got a nagging feeling in her stomach that her mother was up to no good. She walked to the window and looked out to find a silver Lexus idling in the drive. Ben smiled through the windshield and waved.

"Mother, why is Ben here?"

"Maybe he wanted to ask you to lunch."

"It's seven a.m. on Sunday."

"Love does crazy things to a person." Babette glided to the window and gave a regal wave, a wave that could only come from Miss Peach 1977 since the pearl bracelets she wore flashed in the rising sun, yet didn't make a single sound.

Ben waved back and then opened his car door to walk over to Charlotte's to—look at her tires?

"Why are my tires flat?"

"A handsome man is out fixing your tires at this god-awful hour, and you are worried about how they got flat. Honestly, dear, you wonder why you're single."

Charlotte had never wondered about that. She knew exactly why she was single. Love hurt too much.

"My, he is handsome, isn't he?" Babette fanned herself as

Ben fished his phone out of his pocket—most likely to call the local tow truck. "He will bless his wife with such beautiful children."

"I'll be sure to tell his girlfriend that," Charlotte said.

Babette deflated at the news, which was good. Because when her mom sank her teeth into something, she was like a pit bull—a pit bull with a diamond-studded collar. And although a good Southern woman needed a good Southern gentleman, no lady poaches on marked territory—regardless of how blue his family's blood ran. So rather than clarifying that Ben's girlfriend was Scarlett Johansson, she let her mother come to her own conclusion.

"Well, it seems as though you have managed to scare off another one." Babette picked up her clutch and strode toward the front door. "What a waste of a morning. And to think I set my alarm for this." Since it was undignified to holler, Babette paused under the threshold. "Don't forget dinner tonight. Your father invited some big-city doctor over. Lionel is a Yankee, mid-forties, a bit on the pudgy side, but single."

"He is also the new podiatrist on staff at the hospital." But if her dad was bringing a guest to dinner, it meant he'd be at dinner, too, with his new hunting buddy. And although Charlotte wanted to secure the endowment, doing it while her mother passed around her baby photos was not how she envisioned her pitch going. "And has a habit of staring at ladies' shoes."

Babette eyed Charlotte's shoes, then her skirt. "Yes, well, we'll work with what we have since we can't afford to be choosy, now can we?" And then she was gone.

"Love you, too, Mom. We should do this more often," Charlotte said to the empty kitchen.

Chapter 2

⌐

The sun was setting and Charlotte was still trying to figure a way out of going to dinner at her mother's. Although she knew Mr. Neil was indeed on the guest list, if she wanted to be seen as a professional, she needed to present her case at the clinic. Not down the hall from her childhood bedroom.

And after ten hours on her feet—she was seriously rethinking the heels—a surprising case of chicken pox, and a conversation with Danny Mathews about how eating glue was a bad idea, all she wanted to do was go home, draw a hot bath, and eat ice cream while watching highbrow reality television, and be in bed before nine.

But that's what Charlotte did. Boring, ordinary, responsible Charlotte. There was an ache that suddenly raced through her chest, and for a moment, she thought perhaps she was on the brink of a minor attack. Placing a hand over her heart, she realized that no, it was still beating, the same sluggish beat it had for the past four years. It was the realization that nothing had made Charlotte hot, bothered, or even a little giddy in all that time. And that needed to stop.

Between eating ice cream with a depressed sheep, which was now in better spirits than Charlotte, and being set up on a blind date with a balding middle-aged man while her mother mapped out all the reasons she was still single, she'd hit her limit.

What she needed was a fresh dose of life. A sense of this new and improved Charlotte. And tonight, that's what she'd chase. Set on living a life outside of pastels—and other people's expectations—she grabbed her purse, undid the next two buttons, and strutted her way down Maple Street to Kiss My Glass Tow and Tires.

With the busy week looming ahead, she needed her car back, almost as much as she needed a drink. A strong one. And who better to help Charlotte celebrate breaking the mold than the town's own tough girl turned mechanic. Lavender Spencer was a ballbuster who took life by the horns and kneed it in the nuts when it pissed her off— something Charlotte needed to embrace if she had any hope of checking things off her list.

The back bay of the garage was still open and the lights were on. A big engine sat on a workstation; there were spare parts strewn across the floor like a puzzle that was yet to be put back together. Some kind of redneck rap was coming from the radio sitting in the back of the garage near a rusted-out shell of a muscle car that was missing all the windows and the passenger door.

Charlotte stepped over an open toolbox and around the engine, careful not to get grease on her shoes, stopping at the front of the car.

"You know what I'm in the mood for?" she addressed the only part of her friend that was visible, a grease-stained ball cap peeking out from beneath the underbelly. "A drink, maybe some dancing, and definitely horrifying my mom. You interested?"

"Depends," a low masculine voice said from beneath the car. "Is that a panties optional kind of offer?"

It wasn't the voice that had her heart racing. Nope, it was the bulging bicep with a familiar tribal tattoo spanning its length, which snaked out from beneath the car, that had her pulse bordering on dangerous levels.

Recognition hit hard and she went completely still.

Jace McGraw.

The dolly slid all the way out, stopping at her feet, and right next to her heart, which had plummeted to her toes when she saw those dark blue eyes zero in on her. Eyes she'd done her best over the years to forget. They locked on her face and held for a long, weighted second, then slid down to her undone buttons, over her hips, pausing at the hem of her skirt.

The dolly inched closer and his lips curled up wickedly on one side, releasing that lethal dimple. "Actually, I'm partial to the ones you have on."

She jerked back and pressed her hands to her skirt to avoid giving him more of a show. Because the only thing he was going to get from her was a piece of her mind. And maybe the finger. She'd never given someone the finger before, but for Jace she'd make an exception.

"What are you doing here?" she demanded.

"Working," he said, pulling himself up to his full height, surprisingly agile for a man his size.

Because, *Lord have mercy*, at six-foot-four, Jace was all rippling muscle and testosterone. And tattoos, lots of tattoos. Only two were visible, but she knew what lay beneath that low-slung button fly and fitted ARMY STRONG tee. The memory alone was enough to make her thighs quiver.

He was built like a tank, with buzzed hair and a killer smile, and had the confidence of a guy who could handle anything that came his way. A fact that had her good parts fluttering.

And wasn't that just wonderful. Her good parts decided that now was the perfect time to come out of retirement. If she'd hadn't known him, she would have welcomed the flutters, even allowed herself an extra minute to appreciate all that fine male yumminess.

But she did know him, and all of those warm tingles disappeared, replaced by tension. And a little panic. And a whole lot of something that she didn't want to acknowledge.

"You can't work here," she said, angry that he hadn't called to warn her he was coming home. He at least owed her that.

"Can and do." He grabbed a rag off the hood of the car and wiped off his hand, then stuck it out. "Jace McGraw, Sugar's newest resident mechanic."

She swatted his hand away. "Since when?" Because Jace didn't do home visits. And he didn't stick around one place long enough to be a resident of anywhere.

"Since yesterday." He cupped the bill of his hat and pulled it lower on his head. "Let me guess, you're here as the official Sugar welcoming committee. Where's my pie?"

"What pie?"

"Pie? Something in a covered dish? You know, all those neighborly things people are supposed to do when someone comes to town." He looked at her empty hands, and then without a word his eyes dropped to her skirt and there went the other dimple—and her good parts. "Unless, there's something I can do for you, *Charlie*?"

The way he said her name in that low, husky timbre, almost whispering it while flattening the vowels, reminded her of a different time, a time when she naively thought he'd meant it. But she wasn't that wide-eyed woman anymore. She knew what he was offering, and what he wasn't capable of giving.

After all, once upon a time she'd been married to him. Yup, Charlotte Holden had fallen in love with and married the town's biggest hothead and bad boy. Not that anybody except the two of them knew, since it had ended as fast and it had begun. But those three weeks as Ms. Jace McGraw had been the most amazing of her life—and what had followed had nearly broken her.

"Yes," she said. "You need to leave." Because wasn't that what he did best?

The briefest frown flashed across his face, and he grabbed some kind of wrench doohickey and busied himself with tinkering under the hood. "Wish I could, but it seems like my services are needed in Sugar for a bit."

Charlotte didn't know what hurt more—that he wanted to leave as much as she wanted him gone, which was ridiculous since him being here, during the most important time in her career, was a disaster waiting to happen—or that after all the time she'd prayed that he'd come back to Sugar, he finally had. Only it wasn't for her.

"That doesn't work for me," she said.

"Well, this isn't about you. Now is it." He wasn't even looking at her but tightening some bolt inside the engine. Which was a good thing since she was pretty sure her eyes went glassy at his comment, because at one time he'd made her believe that everything he did was for her. Including walking away from her. "Can you hand me that wrench over there?"

Was he kidding? "No, it's all greasy and I don't want to get dirty."

He looked at her over his shoulder and cracked a small smile. "Too bad, I always preferred you a little dirty."

She felt herself flush because she knew he wasn't just talking about rumpling her up.

"Well, I've changed. And I need to go. So if you could just point me in the direction of my keys."

He ran a hand down his face. "About that. Seems someone chewed off your valve stems. So it wasn't as easy as patching a hole."

"Chewed them off?" Was her mother really that desperate to marry her off?

"See here." Jace walked over to her car and squatted down. She did her best not to notice the way his jeans cupped his backside—tried and failed. He filled out a pair of Levi's like nobody's business. "Teeth marks. Looks like you got yourself a raccoon or possum problem."

Seemed she had lots of pest problems these days. "So can you just throw some new tires on it and I can be gone?"

"You don't need new tires; what you need are new valve stems." And wasn't that just like a man, telling her what she needed. "Which for your sporty, two-door tiara on wheels is a special order. Imagine that."

"So what you're telling me is that I'm stuck here. With you. And my car won't be ready until—"

"Best-case scenario. End of the week."

She let out a completely undignified huff and resisted the urge to stomp her feet. She'd begged the universe for a way out of dinner, and apparently whoever was in charge of granting wishes had chosen today to listen.

She looked at her phone, considered calling Ben, and then realized she could handle only one man from her past at a time. Plus, he was on a date with the new nurse from radiology, which meant Charlotte was stranded. Something must have shown on her face because Jace set the tool down and stepped closer—so close he was all up in her personal space, which did crazy things to her emotional space.

"I can take you home." He looked at her buttons and back into her eyes. "Or I can take you across the street to the Saddle Rack and buy you a drink."

Then he did something he hadn't done in over four years—he cupped his palms around her hips and drew her to him—and damn it if she didn't shuffle closer.

"Why would I let you buy me a drink?" she asked quietly, although her brain kicked off a hundred and one reasons on its own. The first being that was how their relationship had begun in the first place.

Charlotte had been a stressed-out resident in Atlanta, lonely and so homesick it hurt, when she'd walked into a bar and saw a friendly face. Jace had bought her a drink, and another, and before she knew it, he had sweet-talked her into his bed, then down to the justice of the peace.

"Because I think you could use a shot of something strong right now," he said. "And we need to talk."

"You lost the right to tell me what I need a long time ago. As for that talk you want, you're about four years too late."

"Not according to the great state of Georgia," he said and her stomach dropped. "Since legally we're still married."

Fall in Love with Forever Romance

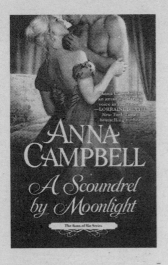

A SCOUNDREL BY MOONLIGHT
by Anna Campbell

Justice. That's all Nell Trim wants—for the countless young women the Marquess of Leath has ruined with his wildly seductive ways. But can she can resist the scoundrel's temptations herself? Check out this fourth sensual historical romance in the Sons of Sin Regency series from bestselling author Anna Campbell!

SINFULLY YOURS
by Cara Elliott

Secret passions are wont to lead a lady into trouble... The second rebellious Sloane sister gets her chance at true love in the next Hellions of High Street Regency romance from bestselling author Cara Elliott.

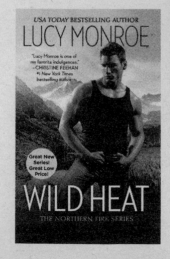

Fall in Love with Forever Romance

SUGAR ON TOP
by Marina Adair

It's about to get even sweeter in Sugar! When scandal forces Glory Mann to co-chair the Miss Sugar Peach Pageant with sexy single dad Cal MacGraw, sparks fly. Fans of Carly Phillips, Rachel Gibson, and Jill Shalvis will love the latest in the Sugar, Georgia series!

A MATCH MADE ON MAIN STREET
by Olivia Miles

When Anna Madison's high-end restaurant is damaged by a fire, there's only one place she can cook: her sexy ex's diner kitchen. But can they both handle the heat? The second book of the Briar Creek series is "sure to warm any reader's heart" (*RT Book Reviews* on *Mistletoe on Main Street*).

Fall in Love with Forever Romance

OWN THE WIND
by Kristen Ashley

Only $5.00 for a limited time! Tabitha Allen is everything Shy Cage has ever wanted, but everything he thinks he can't have. When Tabby indicates she wants more—*much* more—than friendship, he feels like the luckiest man alive. But even lucky men can crash and burn...The first book in the Chaos series from *New York Times* bestselling author Kristen Ashley!

FIRE INSIDE
by Kristen Ashley

Only $5.00 for a limited time! When Lanie Heron propositions Hop Kincaid, all she wants is one wild night with the hot-as-hell biker. She gets more than she bargained for, and it's up to Hop to convince Lanie that he's the best thing that's ever happened to her...Fans of Lori Foster and Julie Ann Walker will love this book!

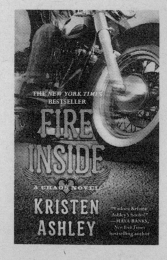